If the Dead Rise Not

If the Dead Rise Not

A BERNIE GUNTHER NOVEL

Philip Kerr

A MARIAN WOOD BOOK

Published by G. P. Putnam's Sons
a member of Penguin Group (USA) Inc.

New York

A MARIAN WOOD BOOK
Published by G. P. Putnam's Sons
Publishers Since 1838
a member of the Penguin Group
Penguin Group (USA) Inc., 375 Hudson Street, New York, New York 10014, USA •
Penguin Group (Canada), 90 Eglinton Avenue East, Suite 700, Toronto,
Ontario M4P 2Y3, Canada (a division of Pearson Penguin Canada Inc.) • Penguin Books Ltd,
80 Strand, London WC2R 0RL, England • Penguin Ireland, 25 St Stephen's Green,
Dublin 2, Ireland (a division of Penguin Books Ltd) • Penguin Group (Australia),
250 Camberwell Road, Camberwell, Victoria 3124, Australia (a division of
Pearson Australia Group Pty Ltd) • Penguin Books India Pvt Ltd, 11 Community Centre,
Panchsheel Park, New Delhi–110 017, India • Penguin Group (NZ), 67 Apollo Drive,
Rosedale, North Shore 0632, New Zealand (a division of Pearson New Zealand Ltd) •
Penguin Books (South Africa) (Pty) Ltd, 24 Sturdee Avenue,
Rosebank, Johannesburg 2196, South Africa

Penguin Books Ltd, Registered Offices: 80 Strand, London WC2R 0RL, England

Originally published in the United Kingdom by Quercus in 2009
First U.S. edition copyright © 2010 by Philip Kerr

Library of Congress Cataloging-in-Publication Data

Kerr, Philip.
If the dead rise not: a Bernie Gunther novel / Philip Kerr.
p.   cm.
ISBN 978-0-399-15615-1
1. Gunther, Bernhard (Fictitious character)—Fiction.   2. Private investigators—Germany—
Fiction.   3. Nazis—Fiction.   4. Germany—History—1933–1945—Fiction.
5. Berlin (Germany)—Fiction.   6. Havana (Cuba)—Fiction.   I. Title.
PR6061.E784I4   2010   200936134
823'.914—dc22

Printed in the United States of America
1   3   5   7   9   10   8   6   4   2

BOOK DESIGN BY AMANDA DEWEY

This is a work of fiction. Names, characters, places, and incidents either are the product of the author's imagination or are used fictitiously, and any resemblance to actual persons, living or dead, businesses, companies, events, or locales is entirely coincidental.

While the author has made every effort to provide accurate telephone numbers and Internet addresses at the time of publication, neither the publisher nor the author assumes any responsibility for errors, or for changes that occur after publication. Further, the publisher does not have any control over and does not assume any responsibility for author or third-party websites or their content.

That I have fought with beasts at Ephesus after the manner of men, what advantageth it me, if the dead rise not again? Let us eat and drink, for tomorrow we shall die.

—FROM THE 1559 BOOK OF COMMON PRAYER

For Caradoc King

PART ONE

Berlin, 1934

1

IT WAS THE SORT OF SOUND you hear in the distance and mistake for something else: a dirty steam barge puffing along the River Spree; the shunting of a slow locomotive underneath the great glass roof of the Anhalter Station; the hot, impatient breath of some enormous dragon, as if one of the stone dinosaurs in Berlin's zoo had come to life and was now lumbering up Wilhelmstrasse. It hardly seemed like something musical until you guessed it was a military brass band, but even then it was too mechanical to resemble man-made music. Suddenly the air was filled with the clash of cymbals and the tinkling of frame glockenspiels, and at last I saw it—a detachment of soldiers marching as if intent on making work for the road menders. Just looking at these men made my feet hurt. They came clock-stepping along the street, their Mauser carbines shouldered on the left, their muscular right arms swinging with a pendulum-like exactitude between elbow and eagle-embossed belt buckle, their gray steel-helmeted heads held high and their thoughts, assuming they had any, occupied with nonsense about one folk, one leader, one empire—*with Germany*!

People stopped to stare and to salute the traffic jam of Nazi flags and banners the soldiers were carrying—an entire haberdasher's store of red and black and white curtain material. Others came running, full of patriotic enthusiasm to do the same. Children were hoisted onto broad shoulders or slipped through a policeman's legs so as not to miss anything. Only the man standing next to me seemed less than enthusiastic.

"You mark my words," he said. "That crazy idiot Hitler means to have another war with England and France. As if we didn't lose enough men the last time. All this marching up and down makes me sick. It might have been God who invented the devil, but it was Austria that gave us the Leader."

The man uttering these words had a face like the Golem of Prague and a barrel-shaped body that belonged on a beer cart. He wore a short leather coat and a cap with a peak that grew straight out of his forehead. He had ears like an Indian elephant, a mustache like a toilet brush, and more chins than the Shanghai telephone directory. Even before he flicked the end of his cigarette at the brass band and hit the bass drum, a gap had opened around this ill-advised commentator, as if he were carrying a deadly disease. And no one wanted to be around when the Gestapo showed up with its own idea of a cure.

I turned away and walked quickly down Hedemann Strasse. It was a warm day, almost the end of September, when a word like "summer" made me think of something precious that was soon to be forgotten. Like freedom and justice. "Germany awake" was the slogan on everyone's lips, only it appeared to me that we were clock-stepping in our sleep toward some terrible but as yet unknown disaster. This didn't mean I was ever going to be foolish enough to say so in public, and certainly not when strangers were listening. I had principles, sure, but I also had all my own teeth.

"Hey you," said a voice behind me. "Stop a minute. I want to talk to you."

I kept on walking, and it was not until Saarland Strasse—formerly Königgrätzer Strasse, until the Nazis decided we all needed to be reminded about the Treaty of Versailles and the injustice of the League of Nations—that the owner of the voice caught up with me.

"Didn't you hear me?" he said. Taking hold of my shoulder, he pushed me up against an advertising column and showed me a bronze warrant disc on the palm of his hand. From this it was hard to tell if he was local or state criminal police, but from what I knew about Hermann

Goering's new Prussian police, only the lower ranks carried bronze beer tokens. No one else was on the pavement, and the advertising column shielded us from the view of anyone on the road. Not that there was much real advertising pasted on it. These days, advertising was just a sign telling a Jew to keep off the grass.

"No, I didn't," I said.

"The man who spoke treasonably about the Leader. You must have heard what he said. You were standing right next to him."

"I don't remember hearing anything treasonable about the Leader," I said. "I was listening to the band."

"So why did you suddenly walk away?"

"I remembered that I had an appointment."

The cop's cheeks flushed a little. It wasn't a pleasant face. He had dark, shadowy eyes; a rigid, sneering mouth; and a rather salient jaw. It was a face that had nothing to fear from death since it already looked like a skull. If Goebbels had a taller, more rabidly Nazi brother, then this man might have been him.

"I don't believe you," the cop said, and, snapping his fingers impatiently, added, "Identification card, please."

The "please" was nice, but I still hardly wanted to let him see my identification. Section eight of page two detailed my profession by training and in fact. And since I was no longer a policeman but a hotel employee, it was as good as telling him I wasn't a Nazi. Worse than that. A man who had been obliged to leave the Berlin detective force because of his allegiance to the old Weimar Republic might be just the type to ignore someone speaking treason about the Leader. If treason was what that was. But I knew the cop would probably arrest me just to spoil my day, and arrest would very likely mean two weeks in a concentration camp.

He snapped his fingers again and glanced away, almost bored. "Come on, come on, I haven't got all day."

For a moment, I just bit my lip, irritated at being pushed around yet again, not just by this cadaver-faced cop but by the whole Nazi state. I'd been forced out of my job as a senior detective with KRIPO—a job I had loved—and been made to feel like a pariah because of my adherence to the old Weimar Republic. The Republic's faults had been many, it was true, but at least it had been democratic. And since its collapse, Berlin, the city of my birth, was hardly recognizable. Previously it had been the most liberal place in the world. Now it felt like a military parade ground. Dictatorships always look good until someone starts giving you dictation.

"Are you deaf! Let's see that damned card!" The cop snapped his fingers again.

My irritation turned to anger. I reached inside my jacket for the card with my left hand, turning my body just far enough around to disguise my right hand becoming a fist. And when I buried it in his gut, my whole body was behind it.

I hit him too hard. Much too hard. The blow took all the air out of him and then some. You hit a man in the gut like that, he stays hit for a good long while. I held the cop's unconscious body against me for a moment and then waltzed him through the revolving door of the Kaiser Hotel. My anger was already turning to something resembling panic.

"I think this man has suffered some kind of a seizure," I told the frowning doorman, and dumped the cop's body into a leather armchair. "Where are the house phones? I'll call an ambulance."

The doorman pointed around the corner of the front desk.

I loosened the cop's tie for effect and behaved as if I were headed for the telephones. But as soon as I was around the corner, I walked through a service door and down some stairs before exiting the hotel through the kitchens. Emerging into an alley that gave onto Saarland Strasse, I walked quickly into Anhalter Station. For a moment I considered boarding a train. Then I saw the subway tunnel connecting the station with the Excelsior, which was Berlin's second-best hotel. No one would ever think to look for me in there. Not so close to an obvious means of escape. Besides, there was an excellent bar in the Excelsior. There's nothing like knocking out a policeman to give you a thirst.

2

———

I WENT STRAIGHT INTO THE BAR, ordered a large schnapps, and hurried it down like it was the middle of January.

The Excelsior was full of cops, but the only one I recognized was the house detective, Rolf Kuhnast. Before the purge of 1933, Kuhnast had been with the Potsdam political police and might reasonably have expected to join the Gestapo except for two things: One was that it had been Kuhnast who had led the team detailed to arrest SA leader Count Helldorf in April 1932, following Hindenburg's orders to forestall a possible Nazi coup. The other was that Helldorf was now the police president of Potsdam.

"Hey," I said.

"Bernie Gunther. What brings the Adlon Hotel's house detective into the Excelsior?" he asked.

"I always forget that this is a hotel. I came in to buy a train ticket."

"You're a funny guy, Bernie. Always were."

"I'd be laughing myself but for all these cops. What's going on here? I know the Excelsior's the Gestapo's favorite watering hole, but usually they don't make it quite so obvious. There are guys with foreheads in here who look like they just walked out of the Neander Valley. On their knuckles."

"We got ourselves a VIP," explained Kuhnast. "Someone from the American Olympic Committee is staying here."

"I thought the Kaiserhof was the official Olympic hotel."

"It is. But this was a last-minute thing, and the Kaiserhof couldn't put him up."

"Then I guess the Adlon must have been full as well."

"Take a flick at me," said Kuhnast. "Be my guest. Those oxtails from the Gestapo have been flicking my ears all day. So some shit-smart fellow from the great Adlon Hotel coming around to straighten my tie for me is all I need."

"I'm not taking a flick at you, Rolf. Honest. Here, why don't you let me buy you a drink?"

"I'm surprised that you can afford it, Bernie."

"I don't mind getting it free. A house bull's not doing his job unless he's got something on the barman. Drop by the Adlon sometime and I'll show you how philanthropic our hotel barman can be when he's been caught with his hand in the till."

"Otto? I don't believe it."

"You don't have to, Rolf. But Frau Adlon will, and she's not as understanding as me." I ordered another. "Come on, have a drink. After what just happened to me, I need something to tighten my bowels."

"What happened?"

"Never you mind. Let's just say that beer won't fix it."

I tossed the schnapps after the other one.

Kuhnast shook his head. "I'd like to, Bernie. But Herr Elschner won't like it if I'm not around to stop these Nazi bastards from stealing the ashtrays."

These apparently indiscreet words were guided by an awareness of my own republican-minded past. But he still felt the need for caution. So he walked me out of the bar, through the entrance hall, and into the Palm Court. It was easier to speak freely when no one could hear what we were saying above the Excelsior's orchestra. These days the weather's the only really safe thing to talk about in Germany.

"So, the Gestapo are here to protect some Ami?" I shook my head. "I thought Hitler didn't like Amis."

"This particular Ami is taking a tour of Berlin to decide if we're fit to host the Olympic Games in two years' time."

"There are two thousand workers to the west of Charlottenburg who are under the strong impression we're already hosting them."

"It seems there's a lot of Amis that want to boycott the Olympiad on the grounds of our government's anti-Semitism. The Ami is here on a fact-finding mission to see for himself if Germany discriminates against Jews."

"For a blindingly obvious fact-finding mission like that, I'm surprised he bothered checking into a hotel."

Rolf Kuhnast grinned back. "From what I've heard, it's a mere formality. Right now he's up in one of our function rooms getting a list of facts put together for him by the Ministry of Propaganda."

"Oh, those kinds of facts. Well, sure, we wouldn't want anyone getting the wrong idea about Hitler's Germany, now, would we? I mean, it's not that we have anything against the Jews. But, hey, there's a new chosen people in town."

It was hard to see why an American might be prepared to ignore the new regime's anti-Jewish measures. Especially when there were so many egregious examples of it all over the city. Only a blind man could have failed to notice the grossly offensive cartoons on the front pages of the more rabidly Nazi newspapers, the David stars painted on the windows of Jewish-owned stores, and the German Only signs in the public parks—to say nothing of the real fear that was in the eyes of every Jew in the Fatherland.

"Brundage—that's the Ami's name—"

"He sounds German."

"He doesn't even speak German," said Kuhnast. "So as long as he doesn't actually meet any English-speaking Jews, things should work out just fine."

I glanced around the Palm Court.

"Is there any danger that he could do that?"

"I'd be surprised if there's a Jew within a hundred meters of this place, given who's coming here to meet him."

"Not the Leader."

"No, his dark shadow."

"The Deputy Leader's coming to the Excelsior? I hope you cleaned the toilets."

Suddenly the orchestra stopped what it was playing and struck up with the German national anthem, and hotel guests jumped to their feet to point their right arm toward the entrance hall. And I had no choice but to join in.

Surrounded by storm troopers and Gestapo, Rudolf Hess marched into the hotel wearing the uniform of an SA man. His face was as square as a doormat but somehow less welcoming. He was medium in height; slim with dark, wavy hair; a Transylvanian brow; werewolf eyes; and a razor-thin mouth. Returning our patriotic salutes perfunctorily, he then bounded up the stairs of the hotel two at a time. With his eager air he reminded me of an Alsatian dog let off the leash by his Austrian master to lick the hand of the man from the American Olympic Committee.

As it happened, there was a hand I had to go and lick myself. A hand that belonged to a man in the Gestapo.

3

A S ONE OF THE HOUSE DETECTIVES at the Adlon, I was expected to keep thugs and murderers out of the hotel. But that could be difficult when the thugs and murderers were Nazi Party officials. Some of them, such as Wilhelm Frick, the minister of the interior, had even served a prison sentence. The ministry was on Unter den Linden, right around the corner from the Adlon; and Frick, a real Bavarian square head with a wart on his face and a girlfriend who happened to be the wife of some prominent Nazi architect, was in and out of the hotel a lot. Probably the girl, too.

Equally difficult for a hotel detective was the high turnover of staff, with honest, hardworking personnel who happened to be Jewish making way for people who turned out to be much less honest and hardworking but who were at least apparently more German.

Mostly I kept my nose out of these matters, but when the Adlon's female house detective decided to leave Berlin for good, I felt obliged to try and help her.

Frieda Bamberger was more than an old friend. From time to time we were lovers of convenience, which is a nice way of saying that we liked going to bed with each other, but that this was as far as it went, since she had a semi-detached husband who lived in Hamburg. Frieda was a former Olympic fencer, but she was also a Jew, and for this reason she had been expelled from the Berlin Fencing Club in November 1933. A similar fate had befallen nearly every Jew in Germany who was a member of a gymnasium or sporting association. To be a Jew in the summer of 1934 was like some cautionary tale by the Brothers Grimm in which two abandoned children find themselves lost in a forest full of hungry wolves.

It wasn't that Frieda believed the situation in Hamburg would be any better than in Berlin, but she hoped the discrimination she now suffered might be easier to bear with the help of her Gentile husband.

"Look here," I told her. "I know someone in the Jewish Department of the Gestapo. A cop I used to know at the Alex. I recommended him for a promotion once, so he owes me a favor. I'll go and speak to him and see what's to be done."

"You can't change what I am, Bernie," she said.

"Maybe not. But I might be able to change what someone else says you are."

At that time I was living on Schlesische Strasse, in the east of the city. And on the day of my appointment with the Gestapo I'd caught the U-Bahn west to Hallesches Tor and walked north up Wilhelmstrasse. Which was how I'd run into that spot of trouble with the policeman in front of the Kaiser Hotel. From the temporary sanctuary of the Excelsior it was only a few steps to Gestapo House at Prinz-Albrecht-Strasse 8—a building that looked less like the headquarters of the new Germany's secret state police and more like an elegant, Wilhelmine hotel, an effect enhanced by the proximity of the old Hotel Prinz Albrecht, which now accommodated the administrative leadership of the SS. There were few people who walked up Prinz-Albrecht-Strasse unless they really had to. Especially when they had just assaulted a policeman. Perhaps for that reason I figured it was the last place anyone would think of looking for me.

With its marble balustrades, high vaulted ceilings, and a stair as wide as a railway track, Gestapo House was more like a museum than a building owned by the secret police; or perhaps like a monastery—just as long as the order of monks was one that wore black and enjoyed hurting people in order to make them confess their sins. I entered the building and approached a uniformed and not unattractive girl on the front desk, who walked me up a stair and around a corner to Department II.

Catching sight of my old acquaintance, I smiled and waved simultaneously, and a couple of women from the nearby typing pool fixed me with a look of amused surprise, as if my smile and my wave were ridiculously out of place. And of course they were. The Gestapo hadn't existed for more than eighteen months, but it already enjoyed a fearsome reputation, and this was why I was nervous and why I was smiling and waving at Otto Schuchardt in the first place. He didn't wave back. He didn't smile, either. Schuchardt had never been the life and soul of the party exactly, but I was pretty sure I'd heard him laugh when we were both cops at the Alex. Then again, maybe he'd only been laughing because I was his superior, and as we now shook hands I was already telling myself I'd made a mistake and that the tough young cop I remembered was now made of the same stuff as the balustrades and the staircase outside the department door. It was like shaking hands with a deep-frozen undertaker.

Schuchardt was handsome, if you consider men with white-blond hair and pale blue eyes handsome. As a blond-haired, blue-eyed man myself, I thought he looked like a much-improved, more efficient Nazi version of me: a man-god instead of a poor Fritz with a Jewish girlfriend.

Then again, I never much wanted to be a god or even to enter heaven, not when all the bad girls like Frieda were back in Weimar Berlin.

He ushered me into his little office and closed a frosted-glass door, which left the two of us alone with a little wooden desk, a whole tank corps of gray metal filing cabinets, and a nice view of the Gestapo's back garden, where a man was carefully tending the flower beds.

"Coffee?"

"Sure."

Schuchardt dropped a heating element into a jug of tap water. He seemed amused to see me, which is to say his hawkish face had the look of one who had eaten several sparrows for lunch.

"Well, well," he said. "Bernie Gunther. It's been two years, hasn't it?"

"Must be."

"Arthur Nebe is here, of course. He's the assistant commissioner. And I daresay there are many others you'd recognize. Personally, I could never understand why you left KRIPO."

"I thought it best to leave before I was pushed."

"You're quite wrong about that, I think. The Party much prefers pure criminalists such as yourself to a bunch of March violets who have climbed on the Party's bandwagon for ulterior motives." His razor-sharp nose wrinkled with displeasure. "And of course there are still a few in KRIPO who have never joined the Party. Indeed, they are respected for it. Ernst Gennat, for example."

"I daresay you're right." I might have mentioned all the good cops who'd been kicked out of KRIPO in the great police purge of 1933: Kopp, Klingelhöller, Rodenberg, and many others. But I wasn't there to have a political argument. I lit a Muratti, smoked my lungs for a second, and wondered if I dared mention what had brought me to Otto Schuchardt's desk.

"Relax, old friend," he said and handed me a surprisingly tasty cup of coffee. "It was you who helped me to get out of uniform and into KRIPO. I don't forget my friends."

"I'm glad to hear it."

"Somehow I don't get the feeling you're here to denounce someone. No, I don't see you as the type ever to do that. So what is it that I can do for you?"

"I have a friend who is a Jew," I said. "She's a good German. She even represented Germany at the Paris Olympiad. She's not religious. And she's married to a Gentile. She wants to leave Berlin. I'm hoping I can persuade her to change her mind. I wondered if there might be a way in which her Jewishness might be forgotten, or perhaps ignored. I mean, you hear of these things happening sometimes."

"Really?"

"Well, yes, I think so."

"I wouldn't repeat that hearsay if I were you. No matter how true it might be. Tell me, how Jewish is your friend?"

"Like I said, in the Olympiad of—"

"No, I mean by blood. You see, that's what really counts these days. Blood. Your friend could look like Leni Riefenstahl and be married to Julius Streicher, and none of that would matter a damn if she was of Jewish blood."

"Her parents are both Jewish."

"Then there's nothing I can do to help. What's more, my advice to you is to forget about trying to help her. You say she's planning to leave Berlin?"

"She thinks she might go and live in Hamburg."

"Hamburg?" Schuchardt really was amused this time. "I don't think living there is going to be the solution to her problem, somehow. No, my advice to her would be to leave Germany altogether."

"You're joking."

"I'm afraid not, Bernie. There are some new laws being drafted that will effectively denaturalize all Jews in Germany. I shouldn't be telling you this, but there are many old fighters who joined the Party before 1930 who believe that not enough has yet been done to solve the Jewish problem in Germany. There are some, myself included, who believe that things might get a little rough."

"I see."

"Sadly, you don't. At least not yet. But I think you will. In fact, I'm certain of it. Let me explain. According to my boss, Assistant Commissioner Volk, this is how it's going to work: A person will be classified as German only if all four of his grandparents were of German blood. A person will be officially classified as Jewish if he is descended from three or four Jewish grandparents."

"And if that person has just one Jewish grandparent?" I asked.

"Then that person will be classified as being of mixed blood. A crossbreed."

"And what will all of that mean, Otto? In practical terms."

"Jews will be stripped of German citizenship and forbidden to marry or have sexual relations with pure Germans. Employment in any public capacity will be completely forbidden, and property ownership restricted. Crossbreeds will be obliged to apply to the Leader himself for reclassification or Aryanization."

"Jesus Christ."

Otto Schuchardt smiled. "Oh, I very much doubt that he'd be in with any sort of a chance for reclassification. Not unless you could prove his heavenly father was a German."

I sucked the smoke from my cigarette as if it were mother's milk, and then stubbed it out in a nipple-sized foil ashtray. There was probably a compound, jigsaw-puzzle word—assembled from odd bits of German—to describe the way I was feeling, only I hadn't yet figured one out. But I was pretty sure it was going to involve words like "horror" and "astonishment" and "kick" and "stomach." I didn't know the half of it. Not yet.

"I appreciate your candor," I said.

Once again his face took on a look of pained amusement. "No, you don't. But I think you're about to appreciate it."

He opened his desk drawer and took out an oversized beige file. Pasted on the top left corner of the cover was a white label containing the name of the subject of the file and the name of the agency and department responsible for maintaining the file. The name on the file was mine.

"This is your police personnel file. All police have one. And all ex-policemen, such as yourself." Schuchardt opened the file and removed the first page. "The index sheet. Every item added to the file is given a number on this sheet of paper. Let's see. Yes. Item twenty-three." He turned the pages of the file until he found another sheet of paper, and then handed it to me.

It was an anonymous letter denouncing me as someone with a Jewish grandparent. The handwriting seemed vaguely familiar, but I hardly felt up to the task of trying to guess the author's identity in front of Otto Schuchardt. "There seems to be little point in me denying this," I said, handing it back.

"On the contrary," he said, "there's every point in the world." He struck a match, put the flame to the letter, and let it drop into the wastepaper bin. "Like I said before, I don't forget my friends." Then he took out his fountain pen, unscrewed the top, and wrote in the "Remarks" section of the index sheet. "No further action possible," he said as he wrote. "All the same, it might be best if you were to try and fix this."

"It seems a bit late now," I said. "My grandmother has been dead for twenty years."

"As someone of second-grade mixed race," he said, ignoring my facetiousness, "you may well find, in the future, that certain restrictions are imposed on you. For example, if you were to try and start up a business, you could be required, under the new laws, to make a racial declaration."

"Matter of fact, I'd been thinking of starting up as a private investigator. Assuming I can raise the money. Being the house detective at the Adlon is kind of slow after working Homicide at the Alex."

"In which case you would be well advised to make your one Jewish grandparent disappear from the official record. Believe me, you wouldn't be the first one to do this. There are many more crossbreeds around than you might think. In the government there are at least three that I know of."

"It's a crazy, mixed-up world we live in, for sure." I took out my cigarettes, put one in my mouth, thought better of it, and returned it to the pack. "Exactly how would you go about doing something like that? Making a grandparent disappear."

"Frankly, Bernie, I wouldn't know. But you could do worse than speak to Otto Trettin, at the Alex."

"Trettin? How can he help?"

"Otto is a very resourceful man. Very well connected. You know that he took over Liebermann von Sonnenberg's department at the Alex when Erich became the new head of KRIPO."

"Which was Counterfeiting and Forgery," I said. "I'm beginning to understand. Yes, Otto was always a very enterprising sort of fellow."

"You didn't hear it from me."

I stood up. "I was never even here."

We shook hands. "Tell your Jewish friend what I said, Bernie. To get out now, while the going's good. Germany's for the Germans now." Then he raised his right arm and added an almost rueful "Heil Hitler" that was a mixture of conviction and, perhaps, habit.

Anywhere else I might have ignored it. But not at Gestapo House. Also I was grateful to him. Not just for my own sake but for Frieda's, too. And I didn't want him to think me churlish. So I returned his Hitler greeting, which made twice in one day I'd had to do it. At this rate I was well on my way to becoming a thoroughgoing Nazi bastard before the week was out. Three-quarters of me, anyway.

Schuchardt walked me downstairs, where several policemen were now loitering excitedly in the hall. He stopped and spoke to one as we went to the front door.

"What's all the commotion?" I asked when Schuchardt caught up with me again.

"A cop's been found dead in the Kaiser Hotel," he said.

"That's too bad," I said, trying to keep in check the sudden wave of nausea I was feeling. "What happened?"

"No one saw anything. But the hospital said it looks like he might have suffered some kind of blow to his stomach."

4

RIEDA'S DEPARTURE FOR HAMBURG seemed to herald an exodus of Jews from the Adlon. Max Prenn, the hotel's chief reception clerk and a cousin of the country's best tennis player, Daniel Prenn, announced that he was following his relative out of Germany in the wake of the latter's expulsion from the German LTA, and said that he was going to live in England. Then Isaac somebody-or-other, one of the musicians in the hotel orchestra, went to work at the Ritz, in Paris. Finally there was the departure of Ilse Szrajbman, a stenographer who used to do typing and secretarial work for hotel guests: she went back to her hometown of Danzig, which was either a city in Poland or a free city in old Prussia, depending on how you looked at it.

I preferred not to look at it, the way I tried not to look at a lot of things in the autumn of 1934. Danzig was just another reason to have one of those Treaty of Versailles arguments about the Rhineland and the Saarland and Alsace-Lorraine and our African colonies and the size of our military forces. To that extent, anyway, I was much less of a typical German than the three-quarters that were to be allowed to me in the new Germany.

The hotel business leader—to give Georg Behlert, the Adlon's manager, his proper title—took businessmen and their capacity to do business in the Adlon very seriously; and the fact that one of the hotel's most important and highest-spending guests, an American in suite 114 named Max Reles, had come to rely on Ilse Szrajbman, meant that it was her departure, among all the Jewish departures from Adlon, that disturbed Behlert the most.

"The convenience and satisfaction of the guests at the Adlon always come first," he said in a tone that implied he thought this might be news to me.

I was in his office overlooking the hotel's Goethe Garden, from which, every day in summer, Behlert took a buttonhole. At least he did until the gardener told him that, in Berlin at least, a red carnation was a traditional sign that you were a communist and, therefore, illegal. Poor Behlert. He was no more a communist than he was a Nazi; his only ideology was the superiority of the Adlon over all other Berlin hotels, and he never wore a boutonniere again.

"A desk clerk, a violinist, yes, even a house detective help the hotel to run smoothly. Yet they are also relatively anonymous, and it seems unlikely that a guest will be greatly inconvenienced by any of their departures. But Fräulein Szrajbman saw Herr Reles every day. He trusted her. It will be hard to find a replacement whose typing and shorthand are as reliable as her good character."

Behlert wasn't a high-toned sort of man, he just looked and sounded that way. A few years younger than me—too young to have fought in the war—he wore a tailcoat, a collar as stiff as the smile on his face, spats, and a line-of-ants mustache that looked as if it had been grown especially for him by Ronald Colman.

"I suppose I shall have to put an advertisement in *The German Girl*," he said.

"That's a Nazi magazine. You put an ad in there and I guarantee you'll get yourself a Gestapo spy."

Behlert got up and closed the office door.

"Please, Herr Gunther. I don't think it's advisable to talk like that. You could get us both into trouble. You're speaking as if there's something wrong with employing someone who is a National Socialist."

Behlert thought himself too refined to use a word like "Nazi."

"Don't get me wrong," I said. "I just love Nazis. I've a sneaking suspicion that ninety-nine point nine percent of Nazis are giving the other point one percent an undeservedly bad reputation."

"Please, Herr Gunther."

"I expect some of them are excellent secretaries, too. Matter of fact, I saw several just the other day when I was at Gestapo headquarters."

"You were at Gestapo headquarters?" Behlert adjusted his shirt collar to accommodate an Adam's apple that was going up and down his neck like an elevator car.

"Sure. I used to be a cop, remember? Anyway, this pal of mine runs a Gestapo department employing a whole pit of stenographers. Blond, blue-eyed, a hundred words a minute, and that's just the confessions obtained without duress. When they start using the rack and thumbscrews, the ladies have to type even faster than that."

Acute discomfort continued to hover like a hornet in the air in front of Behlert.

"You're an unusual man, Herr Gunther," he said, weakly.

"That's what my friend in the Gestapo said. Something like that, anyway. Look, Herr Behlert, forgive me for knowing your business better than you, but it seems to me that the last thing we want at the Adlon is someone who might scare the guests with a lot of talk about politics. Some of these people are foreigners. Quite a few are also Jews. And they're a bit more particular about things like freedom of speech. Not to mention the freedom of Jews. Why don't you leave it to me to find someone suitable? Someone who has no interest in politics whatsoever. Whoever we find, I'll have to check her out anyway. Besides, I enjoy looking for girls. Even ones who can earn an honest living."

"All right. If you would." He smiled ruefully.

"What?"

"What you said just now, you reminded me of something," said Behlert. "I was remembering what it was like to speak without looking over your shoulder."

"You know what I think the problem is? That before the Nazis, there was never any free speech worth listening to."

THAT EVENING I WENT to one of the bars at Europa Haus, a geometric pavilion of glass and concrete. It had rained, and the streets were black and shiny, and the huge assemblage of modern offices—Odol, Allianz,

Daimler—looked like a great passenger liner cruising across the Atlantic, with every deck lit up. A taxi dropped me near the bow end, and I went into the Café-Bar Pavilion to splice the main brace and look for a suitable crew member to replace Ilse Szrajbman.

Of course, I had an ulterior motive in volunteering for such hazardous duty. It gave me something to do while I was drinking. Something better to do while I was drinking than feeling guilty about the man I had killed. Or so I hoped.

His name was August Krichbaum, and most of the newspapers had reported his murder, for, it transpired, there had been a witness of sorts who had seen me deliver the fatal blow. Fortunately the witness had been leaning out of an upper-floor window of the Kaiser Hotel at the time of Krichbaum's death and had seen only the top of my brown hat. The doorman described me as a man of about thirty with a mustache, and upon reading all of this, I might have shaved off my mustache if I had worn one. My only consolation was that Krichbaum had not left behind a wife and family. There was that and the fact that he was ex-SA and a Nazi Party member since 1929. Anyway, I had hardly meant to kill him. Not with one punch, even if it was a punch that had lowered Krichbaum's blood pressure, slowed his heart, and then stopped it altogether.

As usual, the Pavilion was full of cloche-hatted stenographers. I even spoke to a few, but there wasn't one who struck me as having what guests of the hotel needed most in a secretary beyond the ability to type and take good shorthand. And I knew what this was, even if Georg Behlert didn't: The girl needed to have a little bit of glamour. Just like the hotel itself. Quality and efficiency were what made the Adlon good. But glamour was what made the place famous, and why it was always full of the best people. Of course, this also made it attractive to some of the worst people. But that was where I came in and, of late, slightly more often in the evenings since Frieda had left. Because while the Nazis had closed nearly all of the sex clubs and bars that once made Berlin a byword for vice and sexual depravity, there was still a considerable number of joy girls who worked a more discreet trade in the Friedrichstadt *maisons* or, more commonly, in the bars and lobbies of the bigger hotels. And upon leaving the Pavilion, I decided to drop in at the Adlon on my way home. Just to see what was what.

The doorman, Carl, saw me getting out of a taxi and came forward with an umbrella. He was pretty good with an umbrella and a smile and the door and not much else. It wasn't what I'd have called a career, but with tips, he made more than I did. A lot more. Frieda had strongly suspected Carl was in the habit of taking tips from joy girls to let them into the hotel, but neither of us had ever been able to catch him or prove it. Flanked by two stone columns each bearing a lantern as big as a forty-two-centimeter howitzer shell, Carl and I remained on the pavement for a moment to smoke a cigarette and generally exercise our lungs. Above the door was a laughing stone face. No doubt the face had seen the hotel room rate. At fifteen marks a night, it was almost a third of what I made in a week.

I went inside the entrance hall, tipped my damp hat to the new desk clerk, and winked at the page boys. There were about eight of them. They sat yawning on a polished wooden bench like a colony of bored apes, waiting for a light that would summon them to duty. In the Adlon there were no bells. The hotel was always as quiet as the great reading room in the Prussian State Library. I expected the guests liked it that way, but I preferred a bit more action and vulgarity. The bronze bust of the Kaiser on top of a sienna marble chimney piece as big as the nearby Brandenburg Gate seemed to recognize as much.

"Hey."

"Who? Me, sir?"

"What are you doing here, Gunther?" said the Kaiser, tweaking the end of a mustache shaped like a flying albatross. "You should be in business for yourself. The times we're living in were made for scum like you. With all the people who go missing in this city, an enterprising fellow like you could make an excellent living as a private investigator. And the sooner the better, I'd say. After all, you're hardly cut out to work in a place like this, are you? Not with those feet. To say nothing of your manners."

"What's wrong with my manners, sir?"

The Kaiser laughed. "Listen to yourself. That accent, for one thing.

It's terrible. What's more, you can't even say 'sir' with any proper conviction. You have absolutely no sense of servility. Which makes you more or less useless in the hotel business. I can't imagine why Louis Adlon employed you. You're a thug. Always will be. Why else would you have murdered that poor fellow, Krichbaum? Take my word for it. You don't belong here."

I glanced around the sumptuously appointed entrance hall. At the square pillars of marble the color of clarified butter. There was even more marble on the floors and on the walls, as if a quarry had been running a sale of the stuff. The Kaiser had a point. If I stayed there much longer I might turn to marble myself, like some muscle-bound, trouserless Greek hero.

"I'd like to leave, sir," I told the Kaiser, "only I can't afford to. Not yet. It takes money to set up in business."

"Why don't you go to someone of your tribe? And borrow some money?"

"My tribe? You mean—?"

"One-quarter Jew? Surely that counts for something when you're trying to raise some ready cash?"

I felt myself fill up with indignation and anger, as if I'd been slapped on the face. I might have said something rude back to him. Like the thug I was. He was right about that much. Instead I decided to ignore his remarks. After all, he was the Kaiser.

I went up to the top floor and began a late-night patrol of the no-man's-land that was, at this late hour, the dimly lit landings and corridors. My feet were big, it was true, but they were quite silent on the thick Turkish carpets. Except for a small squeak of leather coming from my best Salamanders, I might have been the ghost of Herr Jansen, the assistant hotel manager who'd shot himself after a scandal involving a Russian spy, way back in 1913. It was said that Jansen had wrapped the revolver in a thick bath towel to avoid disturbing the hotel's guests with the sound of the gunshot. I'm sure they appreciated his consideration.

Entering the Wilhelmstrasse extension, I turned a corner and saw the figure of a woman wearing a light summer coat. She knocked gently at a door. I stopped, waiting to see what would happen. The door remained closed. She knocked again, and this time pressed her face against the wood and spoke:

"Hey, open up in there. You called Pension Schmidt for some female company. Remember? So here I am." She waited for a moment and then added, "Do you want me to suck your cock? I like sucking cock. I'm good at it, too." She let out a sigh of exasperation. "Look, mister, I know I'm a bit late, but it's not easy getting a taxi when it's raining, so let me in, eh?"

"You got that right," I said. "I had to hunt around for one myself. A taxi."

She swung around to face me nervously. Putting her hand on her chest, she let out a gasp that turned into a laugh. "Oh, you gave me such a fright," she said.

"I'm sorry. I didn't mean to startle you."

"No, it's all right. Is this your room?"

"Sadly not." I meant it, too. Even in the low light I could tell she was a beauty. She certainly smelled like one. I walked toward her.

"You'll probably think me very stupid," she said. "But I seem to have forgotten my room number. I was having dinner downstairs with my husband, and we had a row about something, and he walked off in a huff. And now I can't remember if this is our room or not."

Frieda Bamberger would have thrown her out and called the police. And, in all normal circumstances, so would I. But somewhere between the Pavilion and the Adlon I had resolved to become a little bit more forgiving, a little less quick to judge. Not to mention a little less quick to punch someone in the stomach. I grinned, enjoying her pluck. "Maybe I can help," I said. "I work for the hotel. What's your husband's name?"

"Schmidt."

It was a sensible choice of name, given the fact that I might have heard her use it already. The only trouble was I knew Pension Schmidt to be the most upscale brothel in Berlin.

"Mmm-hmm."

"Perhaps we'd better go downstairs, and then we can ask the desk clerk if he can tell me what room I'm supposed to be in." This was her, not me. Cool as a cucumber.

"Oh, I'm sure you got the right room. Kitty Schmidt was never known to make a mistake about something as elementary as giving the right room number to one of her joy girls." I jerked the brim of my hat toward the door. "It's just that the fleas change their minds sometimes. They think of their wives and their children and their sexual health and then they lose the nerve for it. He's probably in there listening to every word and pretending to be asleep and getting ready to complain to the manager if I knock on the door and accuse him of soliciting the services of a girl."

"I think there's been some sort of a mistake."

"And you made it." I took hold of her by the arm. "I think you'd better come with me, Fräulein."

"Suppose I start screaming."

I grinned. "Then you'll wake the guests. You wouldn't want to do that. The night manager would come, and then I'd be forced to call the polenta, and they'd put your pretty little ass in cement for the night." I sighed. "On the other hand, it's late, I'm tired, and I'd rather just throw you out on your ear."

"All right," she said brightly, and let me lead her back along the corridor to the stairs, where the light was better.

When I got a proper look at her, I saw that the full-length coat she was wearing was nicely trimmed with fur. Underneath she wore a violet-colored dress made of some gossamer-thin material, opaque shiny white silk stockings, a pair of elegant gray shoes, a couple of long pearl strings, and a little violet cloche hat. Her hair was brown and quite short, and her eyes were green, and she was beautiful in a thin, boyish way that was still the fashion, despite everything the Nazis were doing to persuade German women that it was all right to look and dress and, for all I know, probably smell like a milkmaid. The girl on the stairs next to me couldn't have looked less like a milkmaid if she'd arrived there on a shell blown along by some zephyrs.

"You promise you're not going to hand me over to the bulls," she said on the way downstairs.

"So long as you behave yourself, yes, I promise."

"Because if I go up before a magistrate, he'll put me in the tobacco jar and I'll lose my job."

"Is that what you call it?"

"Oh, I don't mean the sledge," she said. "I just slide a bit when I need a bit of extra money to help my mother. No, I mean my proper job. If I lost that, I'd have to become a full-time joy lady, and I wouldn't like that. It might have been different a few years ago. But things are different now. A lot less tolerant."

"What ever gave you that idea?"

"Still, you seem like a decent sort."

"There are some who might disagree with you," I said bitterly.

"What ever do you mean?"

"Nothing."

"You're not a Jew, are you?"

"Do I look like a Jew?"

"No. It was just the way you said—what you said. You said what a Jew says, sometimes. Not that it matters a damn to me what a man is. I can't see what all the fuss is about. I've yet to meet a Jew who looks like one of those silly cartoons. And I should know. I work for a Jew who's just the sweetest man you could ever hope to meet."

"Doing what, exactly?"

"You don't have to say it like that, you know. I'm not sitting on his face, if that's what you mean. I'm a stenographer, at Odol. The toothpaste company." She smiled brightly as if showing off her teeth.

"At Europa Haus?"

"Yes. What's so funny?"

"Nothing. I've just come from there. As a matter of fact, I was looking for you."

"Looking for me? What do you mean?"

"Forget it. What does your boss do?"

"Runs the legal department." She smiled. "I know. It's quite a contradiction, isn't it? Me working in legal."

"So, what, selling your mouse is just a hobby?"

She shrugged. "I said I needed the extra money, but that's only part of it. Did you see *Grand Hotel*?"

"The movie? Sure."

"Wasn't it wonderful?"

26

"It was all right."

"I'm a bit like Flaemmchen, I think. The girl Joan Crawford plays. I just love big hotels like that one in the movie. Like the Adlon. 'People come. People go. Nothing ever happens.' But it's not like that at all, is it? I think a lot happens in a place like this. A lot more than happens in the lives of most ordinary people. I love the atmosphere of this particular hotel. I love the glamour. I love the feel of the sheets. And the big bathrooms. You've no idea how much I love the bathrooms in this hotel."

"Isn't it a little dangerous? Joy ladies can get hurt. There are plenty of men in Berlin who like to dole out a little pain. Hitler. Goering. Hess. To name but three."

"That's another reason to come to a hotel like the Adlon. Most of the Fritzes who stay here know how to behave themselves. They treat a girl nicely. Politely. Besides, if anything went wrong, I'd only have to scream, and someone like you would turn up. What are you anyway? You don't look like you work on the front desk. Not with those mitts on you. And you're not the house copper. Not the one I've seen before."

"You seem to have it all worked out," I said, ignoring her questions.

"In this line of work it pays to do the algebra."

"And are you a good stenographer?"

"I've never had any complaints. I have shorthand and typing certificates from Kürfurstendamm Secretarial College. And before that, my school *Abitur*."

We reached the entrance hall, where the new desk clerk eyed us suspiciously. I steered the girl down another flight, to the basement.

"I thought you were going to throw me out," she said, glancing back at the front door.

I didn't answer. I was thinking. I was thinking, Why not replace Ilse Szrajbman with this girl? She was good-looking, well dressed, personable, intelligent, and, if she was to be believed, a good stenographer, too. Something like that was easy to prove. All I had to do was sit her down in front of a typewriter. And after all, I told myself, I could easily have gone to the Europa Haus, met the girl, and offered her a job, completely unaware of the way in which she chose to earn a little extra money.

"Any convictions?"

Most Germans thought whores were little better than criminals, but I'd known enough joy ladies in my life to recognize that many of them were much better than that. Often they were thoughtful, cultured, clever. Besides, this one wasn't exactly a grasshopper. She was quite used to behaving herself in a big hotel like the Adlon. She wasn't a lady, but she could pass herself off as one.

"Me? None so far."

And yet. All my experience as a policeman told me not to trust her. Then again, my recent experience as a German told me not to trust anyone.

"All right. Come to my office. I have a proposition for you."

She stopped on the stairs. "I don't do a soup kitchen, mister."

"Relax. I'm not after one. Besides, I'm the romantic kind. At the very least I expect to be taken to dinner at the Kroll Garden. I like flowers and champagne and a box of chocolates from von Hövel. Then, if I like the lady, I might let her take me shopping at Gersons. But I have to warn you. It could be a while before I feel sufficiently comfortable to spend the weekend with you in Baden-Baden."

"You have expensive taste, Herr . . . ?"

"Gunther."

"I approve. It coincides with my own, almost exactly."

"I had a feeling it would."

We went into the detectives' office. It was a windowless room with a camp bed, an empty fireplace, a chair, a desk, and a washbasin. There were a razor and a shaving mug on a shelf above the basin, and an ironing board and a steam iron so that one could press a shirt and look vaguely respectable. Fritz Muller, the other house detective, had left a strong smell of sweat in the room, but the smell of cigarettes and boredom was all mine. Her nose wrinkled with disgust.

"So this is life belowstairs, huh? No offense, mister, but by the standard of the rest of the hotel, it's kind of crummy in here."

"By that standard, so is the Charlottenburg Palace. Now, about that proposition, Fräulein . . . ?"

"Bauer. Dora Bauer."

"Your real name?"

"You wouldn't like it if I gave you another."

"And you can prove that."

"Mister, this is Germany."

She opened her bag to display several documents. One of them, in red pigskin, caught my eye.

"You're a Party member?"

"Doing what I do, it's always advisable to have the best documentation. This one turns away all sorts of unwelcome questions. Most cops leave you alone as soon as they see a Party card."

"I don't doubt it. What's the yellow one?"

"My Reich Chamber of Culture card. When I'm not typing or selling mouse, I'm an actress. I figured being a Party member might get me a few parts. But not so far. Last play I had was *Pandora's Box* at the Kammerspiele on Schumannstrasse. I was Lulu. That was three years ago. So I type for Herr Weiss at Odol and dream of something better. So what's the pitch?"

"Only this. We get a lot of businessmen here at the Adlon. Quite a few of them need the services of a temporary stenographer. They pay well. Much more than the going rate in an office. Maybe not as good as what you'd make on your back in an hour, but a lot better than Odol. Plus, it's honest, and above all, it's safe. And it would mean you could come in and out of the Adlon quite legitimately."

"Are you serious?" There was real interest and excitement in her tone of voice. "Work here? At the Adlon? Really?"

"Of course I'm serious."

"On the level?"

I smiled and nodded.

"You smile, Gunther, but believe me, these days there's something dodgy about nearly all jobs a girl is offered."

"Do you think Herr Weiss would give you a reference?"

"If I asked him nicely he'd give me anything." She smiled vainly. "Thanks. Thanks a lot, Gunther."

"Just don't let me down, Dora. If you do—" I shook my head. "Just don't, all right? Who knows? You might even end up marrying the minister of the interior. With what's in your handbag I wouldn't be at all surprised."

"Hey, you're one of the workers, do you know that?"

"I wish I was, Dora, I wish to God I was."

5

THE VERY NEXT DAY the guest in suite 114 reported a theft. This was one of the VIP corner rooms, right over the offices of North German Lloyd, and, accompanied by Herr Behlert, the hotel manager, I went along to interview him.

Max Reles was a German American from New York. Tall, powerful, balding, with feet like shoe boxes and fists as big as two basketballs, he resembled a cop more than a businessman—at least, a cop who could afford to buy silk ties from Sparmann and his suits (assuming he didn't pay attention to the Jewish boycott) from Rudolf Hertzog. He wore cologne and diamond cuff links that were almost as polished and shiny as his shoes.

Behlert and I advanced into the suite, and Reles looked at him and then at me with eyes as narrow as his mouth. His bare-knuckle features seemed to wear a permanent scowl. I'd seen less pugnacious faces on a church wall.

"Well, it's about fucking time," he said gruffly, giving me an up-and-down look as if I were the rawest recruit in his platoon. "What are you? A cop? Hell, you look like a cop." He looked at Behlert with something close to pity and added, "God damn it, Behlert, what kind of flea circus are you chumps running here, anyway? Jesus Christ, if this is Berlin's best hotel, then I'd hate to see the worst. I thought you Nazis were supposed to be tough on crime. That's your big boast, isn't it? Or is that just so much bullshit for the masses?"

Behlert tried to calm Reles, but to no avail. I decided to let him sound off for a while.

Through a set of tall French windows there was a large stone balcony, where, depending on your inclination, you could wave to your adoring public or rant about the Jews. Maybe both. I went over to the window, pulled aside the net curtain, and stared outside, waiting for him to cool off. If ever he cooled off. I had my doubts about that. He spoke excellent German for an American, although he sang his words a bit more than we Berliners do, a bit like a Bayer, which gave it away.

"You won't find the thief out there, fellow."

"Nevertheless, that's probably where he is," I said. "I can't imagine the thief is still in the hotel. Can you?"

"What's that? German logic? God damn it, what's the matter with you people? You might try and look a little more concerned."

He hurled a gas grenade of a cigar at the window in front of me. Behlert sprang forward and picked it up. It was that or let the rug burn.

"Perhaps if you were to tell us what's missing, sir," I said, facing him squarely. "And exactly what makes you think it's been stolen?"

"What makes me think? Jesus, are you calling me a liar?"

"Not at all, Herr Reles. I wouldn't dream of doing that until I had ascertained all of the facts."

Reles's scowl turned to puzzlement as he tried to figure out if I was being insulting or not. I wasn't exactly sure about that myself.

Meanwhile, Behlert was holding the crystal ashtray in front of Reles like an altar boy preparing to help a priest give communion. The cigar itself, wet and brown, resembled something left there by a small dog, and perhaps that was why Reles himself seemed to think better of putting it back in his mouth. He sneered biliously and waved the thing away with the back of his hand, which was when I noticed the diamond rings on his little fingers, not to mention his perfectly manicured, pink fingernails. It was like discovering a rose at the bottom of a boxer's spittoon.

With Behlert standing between me and Reles, I half expected him to remind us of the rules of the ring. I didn't much like loudmouthed Amis, even the ones who were loud in perfect German, and outside of the hotel I would hardly have minded showing it.

"So what's your story, Fritz?" Reles asked me. "You look too young to be a house detective. That's a job for a retired cop, not a punk like you. Unless, of course, you're a commie. The Nazis wouldn't want a cop that was a commie. Fact is, I'm none too fond of the reds myself."

"I'd hardly be working here if I was a red, Herr Reles. The hotel flower arranger wouldn't like that. She prefers white to red. And so do I. Besides, it's not my story that matters right now, it's yours. So let's try to concentrate on that, eh? Look, sir, I can see you're upset. Helen Keller could see that you're upset, but unless we can all keep calm and establish what happened here, we won't get anywhere."

Reles grinned and then snatched the cigar back just as Behlert was taking away the ashtray. "Helen Keller, eh?" He chuckled and put the cigar back in his mouth, puffing it back into life. But the tobacco seemed to smoke the traces of good humor out of him, and he returned to his resting state, which seemed to be that of low rage. He pointed at a chest of drawers. Like most of the furniture in his suite, it was blond Biedermeier and looked as if it had been baked in a glaze of honey.

"On top of that cabinet was a little basketry-and-lacquer Chinese box. It was early seventeenth century, Ming dynasty, and it was valuable. I had it parceled up and ready to send to someone in the States. I'm not exactly sure when it disappeared. Might have been yesterday. Might have been the day before."

"How big was this box?"

"About twenty inches long, about a foot wide, three or four inches deep."

I tried to work that out in metric and gave up.

"There's a distinctive scene painted on the lid. Some Chinese officials sitting around on the edge of a lake."

"Are you a collector of Chinese art, sir?"

"Hell, no. It's too . . . Chinese for my tastes. I like my art to look a little more homegrown."

"Since it was parceled, do you think you might have asked the concierge to have it collected and forgotten about it? Sometimes we're too efficient for our own good."

"Not so, as I've noticed," he said.

"If you could answer the question, please."

"You were a cop, weren't you?" Reles sighed and combed his hair with the flat of his hand, as if checking it was still there. It was, but only just. "I checked, okay? No one sent it."

"Then I have one more question, sir. Who else has access to this room? It could be someone with a key, perhaps. Or someone you've invited up here."

"Meaning?"

"Meaning just what I said. Can you think of someone who might have taken the box?"

"You mean apart from the maid?"

"Naturally, I'll be asking her."

Reles shook his head. Behlert cleared his throat and lifted his hand to interrupt.

"There is someone, surely," he said.

"What are you talking about, Behlert?" snarled Reles.

The manager pointed at a desk by the window, where, between two sheaves of notepaper, sat a shiny new Torpedo portable typewriter. "Wasn't Fräulein Szrajbman coming in here every day to do some shorthand and typing for you? Until a couple of days ago?"

Reles bit his knuckle. "Goddamn bitch," he said, and flung away his cigar again. This time it flew through the door of the en-suite bathroom, hit the porcelain-tiled wall, and landed safely in the U-boat-sized bath. Behlert lifted his eyebrows clean off his forehead and went to retrieve it once again.

"You're right," I said. "I was a cop. I worked Homicide for almost ten years until my allegiance to the old republic and the basic principles of justice made me surplus to the new requirements. But along the way

I developed a pretty good nose for criminal investigation. So. It's clear to me you think she took it and, what's more, that you've got a pretty good idea why. If we were in a police station I might ask you about that. But since you're a guest in this hotel, it's up to you whether you tell us or not. Sir."

"We argued about money," he said quietly. "About the number of hours she'd worked."

"Is that all?"

"Of course. What are you implying, mister?"

"I'm not implying anything. But I knew Fräulein Szrajbman quite well. She was very conscientious. That's why the Adlon recommended her to you in the first place."

"She's a thief," Reles said, flatly. "What the hell are you going to do about it?"

"I'll put the matter into the hands of the police right away, sir, if that's what you want."

"You're damn right I do. Just tell your old pals to swing by, and I'll swear out a warrant or whatever you flatfoots do in this sausage factory you call a country. Soon as they like. Now, get the hell out of here before I lose my temper."

At that I almost told him he'd have to keep his temper before he could ever lose it, and that while his parents might have taught him to speak good German, they certainly hadn't taught him any good German manners to go with it. Instead I kept my mouth shut, which, as Hedda Adlon was fond of telling me, is a large part of running a good hotel.

The fact that it was now also a large part of being a good German was neither here nor there.

6

A COUPLE OF SCHUPOS wearing puttees and rubber macs against the driving rain were standing on duty by the main entrance of the Police Praesidium on Berlin's Alexanderplatz. The word "praesidium" comes from the Latin meaning "protection," but given that the Alex was now under the control of a bunch of thugs and murderers, it was hard to see who was protecting whom from whom. The two uniformed cops had a similar problem. Recognizing my face, they didn't know whether to salute or batter me to the ground.

As usual, the main entrance hall smelled of cigarettes, cheap coffee, unwashed bodies, and sausage. I was arriving just as the local wurst seller had turned up to sell boiled sausage to those cops who were lunching at their desks. The Max—they were always known as Max— wore a white coat, a top hat, and, as was traditional, a little mustache he'd drawn onto his face with an eyebrow pencil. His mustaches were longer than I remembered and probably would continue to be that way while Hitler continued with a postage stamp on his own upper lip. But I often wondered if anyone had ever dared ask Hitler if he could smell gas, because that was what he looked like: a gas sniffer. Sometimes you saw these men fitting long pipes into holes in the road and then sniffing the open ends for escaping gas. It always gave them the same telltale smudge on the upper lip.

"Haven't seen you in a while, Herr Commissar," said the Max. The large square metal boiler hanging from a strap around his neck looked like a steam-powered accordion.

"I've been away for a while. It must have been something I ate."

"Very amusing, sir, I'm sure."

"You tell him, Bernie," said a voice. "We've got more than enough sausage at the Alex, but not nearly enough laughs."

I looked around and saw Otto Trettin coming through the entrance hall.

"What the hell are you doing back here?" he asked. "Don't say you're another March violet."

"I came to report a crime at the Adlon."

"The biggest crime at the Adlon is what they charge for a plate of sausage, eh, Max?"

"Too right, Herr Trettin."

"But after that," I said, "I was planning to buy you a beer."

"Beer first," said Otto. "Then report the crime."

Otto and I went across the road to the Zum, in the arches of the local S-Bahn station. Cops liked it there because with a train passing overhead every few minutes it was hard to be overheard. And I imagined this was especially important in Otto Trettin's case, since it was generally known that he fiddled his expenses and, probably, was not averse to having his bread spread with some very dodgy butter. He was still a good cop, however, one of the Alex's best from the days before the police purge, and although he wasn't a Party member, the Nazis seemed to like him. Otto had always been a bit heavy-handed: he had famously handed out a beating to the Sass brothers, which, at that time, was a serious breach of police ethics, although they had certainly deserved it, and, doubtless, this was one of the reasons that had helped him to find favor with the new government. The Nazis liked a bit of rough justice. To that extent it was perhaps surprising I wasn't working there myself.

"I'll have a Landwehr Top," said Trettin.

"Make that two," I told the barman.

Named after Berlin's famous canal in which the water's surface was often polluted with a layer of oil or gasoline, a Landwehr Top was a beer with a brandy in it. We hurried them down and ordered two more.

"You're a bastard, Gunther," said Otto. "Now that you've left, I've got no one to talk to. No one I can trust, that is."

"What about your beloved coauthor, Erich?"

Trettin and Erich Liebermann von Sonnenberg had published a book together the previous year. *Criminal Cases* was little more than a series of stories cobbled together from a trawl through KRIPO's oldest files. But no one doubted that the two had made money from it. Fiddling his expenses, ramping up the overtime, taking the odd back-hander, and now with a book already translated into English, Otto Trettin always seemed to know how to make money.

"Erich? We don't see much of each other now that he's head of Berlin KRIPO. Head's up his arse with his own self-importance these days. You left me sitting in the ink, do you know that?"

"I can't feel sorry for you. Not after I read your lousy book. You wrote up one of my cases and you didn't even give me the credit. You gave the bracelets on that one to von Bachman. I could have understood it if he was a Nazi. But he's not."

"He paid me to write him up. A hundred marks, to make him look good."

"You're joking."

"No, I'm not. Not that it matters now. He's dead."

"I didn't know."

"Sure you did. You've just forgotten, that's all. Berlin's like that these days. All sorts of people are dead and we forget about it. Fatty Arbuckle. Stefan George. Hindenburg. The Alex is no different. Take that cop who got murdered the other day. We've already forgotten his name."

"August Krichbaum."

"Everyone except you." He shook his head. "See what I mean? You're a good copper. You shouldn't ever have left." He raised his glass. "To the dead. Where would we be without them?"

"Steady on," I said as he drained his glass a second time.

"I've had a hell of a morning. I've been to Plötzensee Prison with a load of Berlin's top polenta, and the Leader. Now ask me why."

"Why?"

"Because his nibs wanted to see the falling ax in action."

The falling ax was what we Germans quaintly called the guillotine. Otto waved the barman back a third time.

"You've seen an execution, with Hitler?"

"That's right."

"There wasn't anything about an execution in the newspaper. Who was it?"

"Some poor communist. Just a kid, really. Anyway, Hitler watched it happen and pronounced himself very impressed. So much so that he's ordered twenty new falling-ax machines from the manufacturer in Tegel. One for every big city in Germany. He was smiling when he left. Which is more than I can say for that poor commie. I've never seen it before. Goering's idea that we should, apparently. Something about us all recognizing the gravity of the historic mission we've set ourselves— or some such nonsense. Well, there's a lot of gravity involved with a falling ax, let me tell you. Have you ever seen one at work?"

"Just once. Gormann the Strangler."

"Oh, right. Then you'll know what it's like." Otto shook his head. "My God, I'll never forget it as long as I live. That terrible sound. Took it well, though, the commie. When the lad saw that Hitler was there, he started to sing the Red Flag. At least he did until someone slapped him. Now ask me why I'm telling you all this."

"Because you enjoy scaring the shit out of people, Otto. You always were the sensitive type."

"I'm telling you, Bernie, because people like you need to know."

"People like me. What does that mean?"

"You've got a smart mouth, son. Which is why you have to be told that these bastards are not playing games. They're in power and they mean to stay in power, with whatever it takes. Last year there were just four executions at the Plot. This year there have already been twelve. And it's going to get worse."

A train thundered overhead, rendering all conversation meaningless for almost a minute. It sounded like a very large, very slow falling ax.

"That's the thing about things getting worse," I remarked. "Just as you're thinking they can't, they usually do. That's what the fellow on the Jewish Desk at the Gestapo told me, anyway. There are some new laws on the way that mean my grandmother wasn't quite German enough. Not that it matters much to her. She's dead, too. But it seems as if it's going to matter to me. If you follow my meaning."

"Like Aaron's rod."

"Exactly. And you being an expert on forgers and counterfeiting, I was wondering if you knew someone who might help to fix it for me to lose the yarmulke. I used to think an Iron Cross was all the evidence I needed to be a German. But it would seem not."

"A German's worst problems always start when he starts to think of what it means to be a German." Otto sighed and wiped his mouth with the back of his hand. "Cheer up, yiddo. You're not the first to need an Aryan transfusion. That's what they call it these days. My paternal grandfather was a gyppo. That's where I get my Latin good looks from."

"I've never understood what they have against Gypsies."

"I think it's something to do with fortune-telling. Hitler just doesn't want us to know the future he has planned for Germany."

"It's that or the price of clothespins, I suppose." Gypsies were always selling clothespins.

Otto produced a nice gold Pelikan from his coat pocket and started to write a name and address on a piece of paper. "Emil is expensive, so try not to let your tribe's reputation for driving a hard bargain lead you to suppose that he's not worth every penny, because he is. Make sure you tell him I sent you and, if necessary, remind him that the only reason he's not cooling his heels in the Punch is because I lost his file. But I lost it in a place where I can certainly find it again."

The Punch was what Berlin's police and underworld called the courthouse and jail complex in Moabit; because Moabit was a heavily working-class district, someone had once described the prison there as "an imperial punch in the face of the Berlin proletariat." Certainly a punch in the face was more or less guaranteed when you went there, regardless of your social class. It was without question Berlin's hardest concrete.

He told me what was in Emil Linthe's file, so that I might make proper use of it when I spoke to him.

"Thanks, Otto."

"This crime at the Adlon," he said. "Anything there for me? Like a nice young girl who's been passing dud checks?"

"It's small fry for a bull like you. An antique box belonging to one of the guests got stolen. Besides, I already figured out who probably did it."

"Even better. I can get the credit. Who did do it?"

"Some Ami blowhard's stenographer. Jewish girl who's already left Berlin."

"Good-looking?"

"Forget it, Otto. She went home to Danzig."

"Danzig is good. I could use a trip somewhere nice." He finished his drink. "Come on. We'll go back across the road. As soon as you've reported it I can be on my way. I wonder why she went to Danzig. I thought Jews were leaving Danzig. Especially now that it's gone Nazi. They don't even like Berliners in Danzig."

"Like everywhere else in Germany. We buy the rest of the country a beer, and still they hate us." I finished my brandy. "Your neighbor's field of corn is always better, I guess."

"I thought everyone knew that Berlin is the most tolerant city in Germany. For one thing, it's always been the only place that would tolerate the German government living here. Danzig. I ask you."

"Then we'd better hurry before she realizes her mistake and comes back."

7

THE FRONT DESK AT THE ALEX was the usual crowd scene from Hieronymus Bosch. A woman with a face like Erasmus and a pink pig's bladder of a hat was reporting a burglary to a duty sergeant whose outsized ears looked as if they had belonged to someone else before being sliced off and stuck on the sides of his dog-shaped skull with a pencil and an unsmoked roll-up. Two spectacularly ugly thugs—their bloodied mugs stamped with the atavistic stigmata of criminality, their hands manacled behind their twisting backs—were being pushed and pulled into a dimly lit corridor that led down to the cells and a probable job offer from the SS. A cleaning woman, with a cigarette clamped firmly in her mouth against the smell, who was badly in need of a shave, was mopping a pool of vomit on the shit-brown linoleum floor. A lost-looking boy, his dirty face streaked with tears, was sitting fearfully in a corner underneath an enormous spiderweb and rocking on his stringy buttocks, and probably wondering if he'd make bail. A pale, rabbit-eyed attorney, carrying a briefcase as big as the well-fed sow whose hide had been used to fashion it, was demanding to see his client, except that no one was listening. Somewhere, someone was adducing his previous good character and his innocence of everything. Meanwhile a cop had removed his black leather shako and was showing a fellow SCHUPO the large purple bruise on his closely shaven head: it was probably just a thought making a futile bid to escape from his rusticated skull.

It felt awkward being back at the Alex. Awkward and exciting. I figured Martin Luther must have felt the same way when he turned up at the Diet of Worms to defend himself against a charge of spoiling the church door in Wittenberg. So many faces that were familiar. A few looked at me as if I were the prodigal son, but rather more seemed to regard me as the fatted calf.

Berlin Alexanderplatz. I could have told Alfred Döblin a thing or two.

Otto Trettin led me behind the desk and told a young uniformed cop to record my statement.

The cop was in his mid-twenties and, unusually by SCHUPO standards, was as bright as the badge on his ammunition pouch. He hadn't been typing my statement very long when he stopped, bit his already well-bitten fingernails, lit a cigarette, and silently went over to a filing cabinet as big as a Mercedes that stood in the center of the huge room. He was taller than I'd expected. And thinner. He hadn't been there long enough to get a taste for beer and get himself a pregnant belly, like a true SCHUPO man. He came back reading, which, in the Alex, was something of a miracle in itself.

"I thought so," he said, handing Otto the file, but looking at me. "This object you're reporting stolen was reported stolen yesterday. I took the particulars myself."

"Chinese lacquer-and-basketry box," said Otto, glancing over the report. "Fifty centimeters by thirty centimeters by ten centimeters."

I tried to work that out in imperial measurement and gave up.

"Seventeenth century, Mong dynasty." Otto looked at me. "That sound like the same box, Bernie?"

"Ming dynasty," I said. "It's Ming."

"Ming, Mong, what's the difference?"

"Either it's the same box or they're as common as pretzels. Who made the report?"

"A Dr. Martin Stock," said the young cop. "From the Asiatic Museum. He was pretty exercised about it."

"What kind of fellow was he?" I asked.

"Oh, you know. Kind of how you'd imagine someone from a museum would look. Sixtyish, gray mustache, white goatee, bald, myopic, overweight—he reminded me of the walrus at the zoo. He wore a bow tie—"

"I've seen that before," said Otto. "A walrus wearing a bow tie."

The cop smiled and then continued. "Spats, nothing in his lapel—I mean no Party badge or anything. And it was a Bruno Kuczorski suit he was wearing."

"Now he's just showing off," said Otto.

"I saw the label on the inside of his coat when he took out his handkerchief to mop his brow. An anxious sort of fellow. But you would have gathered that from the handkerchief."

"On the level?"

"Like he swallowed a geometry set."

"What's your name, son?" Otto asked him.

"Heinz Seldte."

"Well, Heinz Seldte, it's my opinion that you should leave this fat man's desk job you've got here and become a cop."

"Thank you, sir."

"So what's the deal, Gunther?" said Otto. "You trying to make a monkey out of me?"

"I'm the one who feels like a monkey." I tugged the sheet and the carbons off Seldte's typewriter and crushed them up. "I think maybe I should go and yodel in a few ears, like Johnny Weissmuller, and see what comes running out of the jungle." I took Dr. Stock's crime sheet from the police file. "Mind if I borrow this, Otto?"

Otto glanced at Seldte, who shrugged back at him. "It's okay with us, I guess," said Otto. "But you will let us know what you find out, Bernie. Ming Mong dynasty theft is a special investigative priority for KRIPO right now. We have our reputation to think of."

"I'll get right on it, I promise."

I meant it, too. It was going to be a pleasure to feel like a real detective again instead of a hotel carpet creeper. But, as Immanuel Kant once said, it's funny how categorically wrong you can be about a lot of stuff you think just has to be true.

MOST OF BERLIN'S MUSEUMS stood on a little island in the center of the city, surrounded by the dark waters of the River Spree, as if the people who built them had decided that Berlin needed to keep its culture separate

43

from the state. As I was about to discover, there should have been a lot more importance attached to this idea than anyone might have thought.

The Ethnographical Museum, however, formerly in Prinz-Albrecht-Strasse, was now located in Dahlem, in the far west of Berlin. I traveled there on the underground railway—on the Wilmersdorf line as far as Dahlem-Dorf—and then walked southeast to the new Asiatic Museum. It was a comparatively modern three-story redbrick building surrounded by expensive villas and manor houses with large gates and even larger dogs. Laws were made for the protection of suburbs such as Dahlem, and it was hard to see why there should have been two Gestapo men parked in a black W out front of the nearby confessing church until I remembered there was a priest in Dahlem called Martin Niemöller who was well known for his opposition to the so-called Aryan paragraph. Either that or the two men just had something to confess.

I went into the museum, opened the first door marked PRIVATE, and found myself looking down at a rather fetching stenographer sitting behind a three-bank Carmen, with Maybelline eyes and a mouth that was painted better than Holbein's favorite portrait. She wore a checked shirt; a whole souk's supply of brass bangles, which tinkled on her wrist like tiny telephones; and a rather severe expression that almost had me checking the knot on my tie.

"Can I help you?"

I felt sure she could, but I hardly liked to mention exactly how. Instead, I sat on the corner of her desk and folded my arms, just to keep my hands off her breasts. She didn't like that. Her desk looked as neat as a display in a department-store window.

"Herr Stock about?"

"I guess if you had an appointment you'd know it was Dr. Stock."

"I don't. Have an appointment."

"So he's busy." She glanced involuntarily at a door on the other side of the room, as if hoping I would be gone before it opened again.

"I bet he does that a lot. Is busy. Men like him always are. Now, if it was me, I'd be giving you a little dictation or maybe signing a few letters you'd just typed with those lovely hands of yours."

"You *can* write, then?"

"Sure. I can even type. Not as well as you, I'll bet. But you can be judge of that." I reached into my jacket and took out the crime sheet I'd borrowed from the Alex. "Here," I said, handing it over. "Take a look and tell me what you think."

She glanced at it and her eyes widened a few f-stops.

"You're from the Police Praesidium, on Alexanderplatz?"

"Didn't I say? I just came from there on the underground." This was true, but only as far as it went. If she or Stock asked to see a warrant disc, I wasn't going to get anywhere, which was the main reason I was behaving the way a lot of real cops from the Alex behave. A Berliner is someone who believes it's best to be just a little less polite than other people might think is necessary. And most Berlin cops fall a long way short of that high standard. I lit a cigarette, blew the smoke her way, and then nodded at a chunk of rock on a shelf behind her well-coiffed head.

"Is that a swastika on that bit of stone?"

"It's a seal," she said. "From the Indus Valley civilization. From around 1500 B.C. The swastika used to be a significant religious symbol of our own remote ancestors."

I grinned at her. "Either that or they were trying to warn us about something."

She stood up from behind the typewriter and quickly walked across the office to fetch Dr. Stock. It gave me enough time to study her curves and the seams in her stockings, so perfect they looked as if they'd been done in a technical drawing class. I always disliked technical drawing, but I might have been a lot better at it had I been asked to sit behind a nice girl's legs and try to make a couple of straight lines on her calves.

Stock was less easy on the eye than his secretary but exactly as Heinz Seldte had described him back at the Alex. A Berlin waxwork.

"This is most embarrassing," he wailed. "There has been an awful mistake for which I'm most dreadfully sorry." He came close enough for me to smell the peppermint lozenges on his breath, which was a nice change from most of the people who spoke to me, and then bowed an abject apology. "Dreadfully sorry, sir. It would seem that the box I reported stolen was not stolen at all. Merely mislaid."

"Mislaid? How's that possible?"

"We've been moving the Fischer collections from the old Ethnographical Museum, in Prinz-Albrecht-Strasse, to our new home, here in Dahlem, and everything is in disarray. The official guide to our collections is out of print. Many objects were misplaced or wrongly attributed. I'm afraid you've had a wasted journey. On the underground, you said? Perhaps the museum could pay for a taxicab to take you back to the Police Praesidium. It's the least we can do to make up for the inconvenience."

"So you have the box back in your possession?" I said, ignoring his bleatings.

Stock looked awkward again.

"Perhaps I might see it for myself," I said.

"Why?"

"Why?" I shrugged. "Because you reported it stolen, that's why. And now you're reporting that it has been found. The thing is, sir, I have to fill out a report, in triplicate. Proper procedures have to be followed. And if this Ming dynasty box can't be produced, I don't see how I can very well close the file on its disappearance. You see, sir, in a sense, the moment I type that it's been found, I make myself responsible for it. I mean, that's logical, isn't it?"

"Well, the fact is—" He looked at his stenographer and twitched a couple of times, as if someone had a fishing line in him somewhere.

She stared at me with hat pins in her eyes.

"Perhaps you'd better come into my office, Herr—"

"Trettin. Criminal Commissar Trettin."

I followed him into his office, and he closed the door behind me straightaway. But for the size and opulence of the room, I might have felt sorry for him. Everywhere there were Chinese artifacts and Japanese paintings, although it could just as easily have been Chinese paintings and Japanese artifacts. That year I was a little weak on my knowledge of Asiatic antiquities.

"Must be interesting, working in a place like this."

"Are you interested in history, Commissar?"

"One thing I've learned is that if our history were a little less interesting, then we might be a lot better off. Now, what about that box?"

"Oh, dear," he said. "How am I going to explain this without making it sound suspicious?"

"Don't try to finesse it," I told him. "Just tell it like it is. Just tell the truth."

"I always endeavor to do that," he said pompously.

"Sure you do," I said, toughening on him now. "Look, stop wasting my time, Herr Doctor, have you got the box or not?"

"Please don't rush me."

"Naturally, I've got all day to waste on this case."

"It's a little complicated, you see."

"Take my word for it, the truth is rarely complicated."

I sat down in an armchair. He hadn't asked me to. But that didn't matter now. I wasn't selling anything. And I wasn't buying anything while I was still standing on my size large. I took out a notebook and tapped a pencil on my tongue. Taking notes of a conversation always puts people on their heels.

"Well, you see the museum falls under the control of the Ministry of the Interior. And while the collections remained at Prinz-Albrecht-Strasse, the minister, Herr Frick, happened upon them and decided that a few of the objects might serve a more useful purpose as diplomatic gifts. Do you understand what I mean by that, Commissar Trettin?"

I smiled. "I think so, sir. It's kind of like bribery. Only it's legal."

"I can assure you it's perfectly normal practice in all foreign relations. The wheels of diplomacy often have to be oiled. Or so I'm told."

"By Herr Frick."

"No. Not by him. By one of his people. Herr Breitmeyer. Arno Breitmeyer."

"Mmm-hmm." I took note of the name.

"Naturally I'll be speaking to him, as well," I said. "But let me try to straighten this pretzel. Herr Breitmeyer removed an item from the Fischer collections—"

"Yes, yes. Adolph Fischer. A great collector of Asian artifacts. Now dead."

"Namely one Chinese box. And gave it to a foreigner?"

"Not just one object. I believe there were several."

"You believe." I paused for more effect. "Am I right in thinking that all of this happened without your knowledge or approval?"

"That is correct. You see, it was thought at the ministry that the collections left at the original museum were not wanted for exhibition." Stock colored with embarrassment. "That while being of great historical significance . . ."

I stifled a yawn.

"That, perhaps, they were unsuitable within the meaning of the Aryan paragraph. You see, Adolph Fischer was a Jew. The ministry had formed the impression that, under these circumstances, the true origins of the collection made it impossible to exhibit. That it was—in their words, not mine—'racially tainted.' "

I nodded, as if all this sounded perfectly reasonable. "And when they did all this, they neglected to tell you, is that right?"

Stock nodded unhappily.

"Someone at the ministry didn't think you sufficiently important to keep you informed about this," I said, rubbing it in a little. "Which is why, when you found the object missing from the collection, you assumed it had been stolen, and reported it immediately."

"That's it," he said with some relief.

"Do you happen to know the name of the person to whom Herr Breitmeyer gave the Ming box?"

"No. You would have to ask him that question."

"I will, of course. Thank you, Doctor, you have been most helpful."

"Do I take it the matter is now closed?"

"As far as your own involvement is concerned, yes, sir, you can."

Stock's relief turned to euphoria, or at least as near to euphoria as someone so dry was ever going to get.

"Now, then," I said, "about that taxicab back into the city."

8

I TOLD THE TAXI DRIVER to drop me at the Ministry of the Interior on Unter den Linden. Next to the Greek embassy, it was a dull, dirty gray building just around the corner from the Adlon. It was crying out for some climbing ivy.

I went inside and, at the desk in the cavernous main entrance hall, handed my business card to one of the clerks on duty. He had one of those startled animal faces that makes you think God has a wicked sense of humor.

"I wonder if you can help me," I said unctuously. "The Adlon Hotel wishes to invite Herr Breitmeyer—that's Arno Breitmeyer—to a gala reception in a couple of weeks. And we should like to know the correct way to address him and to which department we should send the invitation."

"I wish I was going to a gala reception at the Adlon," the clerk admitted, and consulted a thick leather-bound department list on the desk in front of him.

"To be honest, they can be rather stiff affairs. I don't particularly like champagne. Give me beer and sausage any day."

The clerk smiled ruefully as if he were not quite convinced, and found the name he was looking for. "Here we are. Arno Breitmeyer. He's an SS-Standartenführer. That's a colonel to you and me. He's also the deputy Reich sports leader."

"Is he, now? Then I expect that's why they want to invite him. If he's merely the deputy, then perhaps we should invite his boss as well. Who would that be, do you think?"

"Hans von Tschammer und Osten."

"Yes, of course."

I'd heard the name and seen it in the newspapers. At the time I'd thought it typical of the Nazis that they should have appointed an SA thug from Saxony to be Germany's sporting leader. A man who had helped beat to death a thirteen-year-old Jewish boy. I guess it was the fact that the boy had been murdered in a Dessau gym that had really bolstered von Tschammer und Osten's sporting credentials.

"Thank you. You've been most helpful."

"Must be nice working at the Adlon."

"You might think that. But the only thing that stops it from being exactly like hell are the locks on the bedroom doors."

It was one of the many maxims I'd heard from Hedda Adlon, the owner's wife. I liked her a lot. We shared a sense of humor, although I think she had more of it than I did. Hedda Adlon had more of everything than I did.

Back in the hotel, I called Otto Trettin and told him some of what I'd discovered at the museum.

"So this fellow Reles," said Otto. "The hotel guest. It looks as if he might have been in possession of the box quite legitimately."

"That all depends on your notion of legitimacy."

"In which case this little stenographer, the one who went back to Danzig—"

"Ilse Szrajbman."

"Maybe she did steal the box, after all."

"Maybe. But she'll have had a good reason."

"Like that, is it?"

"No. But I know the girl, Otto. And I've met Max Reles."

"So what are you saying?"

"I'd like to find out more before you go charging off to Danzig."

"I'd like to pay less tax and make more love, but it's not going to happen. What's it to you if I go to Danzig?"

"We both know that if you go you'll have to make an arrest to justify your expenses, Otto."

"It's true, the Deutsches Haus hotel in Danzig is quite expensive."

"So why not telephone the local KRIPO first? See if you can get someone local to go and see her. If she really does have the box, then perhaps he can persuade her to return it."

"What's in it for me?"

"I don't know. Nothing, probably. But she's a Jew. And we both know what's going to happen to her if she's arrested. They'll send her to one of their concentration camps. Or they'll put her in that Gestapo prison, near Tempelhof. Columbia Haus. She doesn't deserve that. She's just a kid, Otto."

"You're turning soft, you know that, don't you?"

I thought of Dora Bauer and how I had helped her get off the sledge. "I suppose I am."

"I was looking forward to some sea air."

"Drop by the hotel sometime, and I'll have the chef fix you a nice plate of Bismarck herrings. I swear, you'll think you were on Rügen Island."

"All right, Bernie. But you owe me."

"Sure I do. And, believe me, I'm glad about that. I'm not sure our friendship could take the strain if it was you who owed me. Call me when you hear something."

MOST OF THE TIME THE ADLON ran like a big state Mercedes—a Swabian colossus with handcrafted coachwork, hand-stitched leather, and six outsized Continental AGs. I can't claim that any of this was attributable to me, but I took my duties—which were largely routine—seriously enough. I had a maxim of my own: Running a good hotel is about predicting the future, and then preventing it from happening. So every day I would look over the hotel register, just in case there were any names that leaped out at me as likely to cause trouble. There never were. Unless you count King Prajadhipok and his request that the chef prepare him a dish of ants and grasshoppers; or the actor Emil Jannings and his predilection for loudly spanking the bare bottoms of young actresses with a hairbrush.

The events diary was a different story, however. Corporate hospitality given at the Adlon was frequently lavish, often alcoholic, and sometimes things got a bit out of hand. On that particular day there were two groups of businessmen that were booked in. Representatives of the German Labor Front were meeting all day in the Beethoven Room; and, in the evening—by a coincidence that was not lost on me after my visit to the Ministry of the Interior—the members of the German Olympic Organizing Committee, including Hans von Tschammer und Osten and SS colonel Breitmeyer, were to convene for drinks and dinner in the Raphael Room.

Of the two, I was expecting trouble only from DAF—the Labor Front, which was the Nazi organization that had taken over Germany's trade-union movement. This was led by Dr. Robert Ley, a former chemist who was given to bouts of heavy drinking and womanizing, especially when the taxpayer was picking up the bill. Prostitutes were frequently invited into the Adlon as the guests of Labor Front regional leaders, and the sight and sound of heavy men making love to whores in the lavatories was not uncommon. Their light brown tunics and red armbands made them easy to spot, which made me think that Nazi officials and pheasants had something in common. You didn't have to know anything about them personally to want to shoot one.

As things turned out, Ley didn't show, and the DAF delegates behaved themselves more or less impeccably, with only one of them being sick on the carpet. I ought to have been pleased by that, I suppose. As a hotel worker I was a member of the Labor Front myself. I wasn't exactly sure what I got for my fifty pfennigs a week, but it was impossible to get any kind of job in Germany without being a member. I was looking forward to the day when I could parade proudly at Nuremburg with a brightly polished shovel over my shoulder and, in front of the Leader, dedicate myself and my hotel work to the concept of labor, if not the reality. No doubt the Adlon's other house detective, Fritz Muller, felt much the same way. When he was around, it was impossible not to consider the true importance of work in German society. Or for that matter when he wasn't around, because Muller seldom did any work himself. He had been tasked by me with keeping an eye on the Raphael Room, which looked like the easier detail, but when trouble broke out he was nowhere to be found, and it was to me that Behlert came seeking assistance.

"There's trouble in Raphael," he said, breathlessly.

As we swiftly walked through the hotel—no member of the staff was ever permitted to run in the Adlon—I tried to get Behlert to paint a picture of exactly who all these men were and what their meeting had been about. Some of the names on the Olympic Organizing Committee were not the sort of men you went up against without first reading the life of Metternich. But Behlert's picture came out as poorly painted as von Menzel's copy of a Raphael mural that had given the function room its name.

"I believe there may have been one or two members of the organizing committee who were present earlier on in the evening," he said, mopping his brow with a napkin-sized handkerchief. Perhaps it was a napkin. "Funk from Propaganda, Conti from the Ministry of the Interior, Hans von Tschammer und Osten, the sports leader. But now it's mostly businessmen from all over Germany. And Max Reles."

"Reles?"

"He's the host."

"Well, that's all right," I said. "For a moment there, I thought one of them might try to give us some trouble."

As we neared the Raphael Room we heard shouts. Then the double doors were flung open and two men stormed out. You can call me a Bolshevik if you like, but from the size of their stomachs I knew they were German businessmen. One of them had a black bow tie that had been twisted halfway around what was laughably called his neck. Above his neck was a face as red as the little paper Nazi flags that were pinned among several paper Olympic flags to an easel beside the doors. For a moment I considered asking him what had happened, but that would only have resulted in my being trampled, like a tea plantation trying to resist a rampaging bull elephant.

Behlert followed me through the doors and, as my eyes caught those of Max Reles, I heard him say something about Laurel and Hardy before his tough face opened into a smile and his thick body took on an apologetic, placating, almost diplomatic aspect that would hardly have disgraced Prince Metternich himself.

"It was all a big misunderstanding," he said. "Wouldn't you agree, gentlemen?"

But for the fact that his hair was messed up and there was some blood on his mouth, I might have believed him.

Reles looked around the dinner table for support. Somewhere under a cumulonimbus cloud of cigar smoke, several voices murmured wearily like a papal conclave that had neglected to pay the Sistine Chapel's chimney sweep.

"You see?" Reles lifted his big hands in the air, as if I'd pointed a gun at him, and for some reason I got the feeling that if I had, he'd hardly have reacted differently. He'd have kept his nerve under the drill of a drunken dentist. "Storm in a teacup." It didn't sound right in German and, snapping his thick, stubby fingers, he added, "I mean, a storm in a water glass. Right?"

Behlert nodded eagerly. "Yes, that's right, Herr Reles," he said. "And may I say, your German is excellent."

Reles looked uncharacteristically sheepish. "Well, it's a hell of a language to speak well," he said. "Considering it must have been invented to let trains know when it's time to leave a station."

Behlert smiled unctuously.

"All the same," I said, picking one of several broken wineglasses off the tablecloth, "it does look like there was a storm. A Bohemian one, I think. This stuff is fifty pfennigs a time."

"Naturally I'll pay for any breakages." Reles pointed at me and grinned at his complacent-looking guests. "Can you believe this guy? He wants me to pay for the breakages."

There's nothing that looks as pleased with itself as a German businessman with a cigar.

"Oh, there's no question of that, Herr Reles," Behlert said, and looked at me critically as if I had mud on my shoes, or something worse. "Gunther. If Herr Reles says it was an accident, then there's no need to take this any further."

"He didn't say it was an accident. He said it was a misunderstanding. Which is how a mistake often falls just short of being a crime."

"Is that out of this week's *Berlin Police Gazette*?" Reles found a cigar and lit up.

"Maybe it ought to be. Then again, if it was, I might still be a Berlin policeman."

"But you're not. You're working here in this hotel, in which I am a guest. And, I might add, a big-spending guest. Herr Behlert, tell the sommelier to bring us six bottles of your finest champagne."

Around the table there was a loud murmur of approval. But none of them wanted to meet my eye. Just a lot of well-fed and -watered faces intent on getting back to the trough. A Rembrandt group portrait with everyone looking the other way: *The Syndics of the Clothmakers Guild*. It was then that I saw him, seated at the far end of the room, like Mephisto waiting patiently for a quiet word with Faust. Like the others, he was wearing a tuxedo and, but for his satirically grotesque saddlebag of a face, and the fact that he was cleaning his fingernails with a switch-blade, he looked almost respectable. Like the wolf dressed up as Little Red Riding Hood's grandmother.

I never forget a face. Especially the face on a man who'd once led a group of SA to carry out a gun attack against the members of a workers' social club who were holding a dance party at the Eden Palace in Charlottenburg. Four dead, including a friend from my old school. Probably there were other killings for which he was responsible, but it was that one, on November 23, 1930, that I particularly recalled. And then I had his name: Gerhard Krempel. He'd served some time for that murder, at least until the Nazis got into government.

"Come to think of it, make it a dozen bottles."

Ordinarily I might have said something to Krempel—a witty epithet, perhaps, or something worse—but Behlert wouldn't have liked that. Punching a guest in the throat wasn't the kind of hotel-keeping that read well in Baedeker. And, for all either of us knew, Krempel was the new minister for level playing fields and good sportsmanship. Besides, Behlert was already steering me out of the Raphael Room. That is, when he wasn't bowing and apologizing to Max Reles.

At the Adlon, a guest is always given an apology rather than an excuse. That was another of Hedda Adlon's maxims. But it was the first time I'd seen anyone in the hotel apologizing for interrupting a fight. Because I didn't doubt that the man who had left earlier had been hit by Max Reles. And that he had hit Reles back. I certainly hoped that was the case. I wouldn't have minded punching him myself.

Outside the Raphael Room, Behlert faced me irritably. "Please, Herr Gunther, I know you think you are doing your job, but do try to remember that Herr Reles occupies the Ducal suite. As such he is a very important guest."

"Oh, I know. I just heard him order a dozen bottles of champagne. All the same, he's keeping some very ugly company."

"Nonsense," Behlert said, and walked away to find the sommelier, shaking his head. "Nonsense, nonsense."

He was right, of course. After all, we were all of us keeping some very ugly company in Hitler's new Germany. And perhaps the Leader was the ugliest of them all.

9

ROOM 210 WAS ON THE SECOND FLOOR in the Wilhelmstrasse extension. It cost sixteen marks a night, and came with an en-suite bathroom. It was a nice room and a few meters bigger than my apartment.

I got there at long past midday. Hanging on the door was a DO NOT DISTURB card and a pink form informing the room's occupant that there was a message awaiting him at the front desk. His name was Herr Doctor Heinrich Rubusch, and the chambermaid usually would have left him alone, except that he was supposed to check out of the hotel at eleven. When she knocked at the door there was no reply, at which point she tried to enter the room, and found the key was still in the lock. After a great deal more fruitless knocking, she informed Herr Pieck, the assistant manager, who, fearing the worst, summoned me.

I went to the hotel safe to fetch one of the key turners that we kept in there—a simple piece of metal about the size of tuning fork designed to fit an Adlon keyhole and turn a key from the other side. There were supposed to be six turners, but one was gone, which probably meant Muller, the other hotel detective, had it and had forgotten to put it back. This would have been quite typical. Muller was a bit of a drunk. I took another key turner from the safe and went up to the second floor.

Herr Rubusch was still in bed. I hoped he'd wake up and shout at us to get out and let him get some sleep, but he didn't. I put my fingers on the big vein on his neck, but there was so much fat on him that I soon gave up and, having opened his pajama jacket, pressed my ear to his cold ham of a chest.

"Shall I call Dr. Küttner?" asked Pieck.

"Yes. But tell him not to hurry. He's dead."

"Dead?"

I shrugged. "Staying in a hotel is a bit like life. At some stage you have to check out."

"Oh, dear me, are you sure?"

"Baron Frankenstein couldn't make this character move."

The chambermaid standing in the doorway started crossing herself gravely. Pieck told her to go and fetch the house doctor at once.

I sniffed the water glass on his bedside table. It had water in it. The dead man's fingernails were clean and polished as if he'd just had a manicure. There was no blood visible anywhere on his person or on his pillow. "Looks like natural causes, but we'd better wait for Küttner. I don't get paid any extra for an on-the-spot diagnosis."

Pieck walked toward the window and started to open it.

"I wouldn't do that if I were you," I said. "The police won't like it."

"The police?"

"When a dead body's found, they like it if you tell them. That's the law. Or at least it used to be. But, considering the number of bodies that turn up dead these days, who knows? In case you hadn't noticed, there's a strong smell of perfume in the room. Blue Grass by Elizabeth Arden, if I'm not mistaken. Somehow I don't see this gentleman choosing to wear it himself, which means there might have been someone with him when he stepped off the pavement. And that means the police will prefer things to be left the way they are now. With the window closed."

I went into the bathroom and glanced over a neat array of men's toiletries. It was the usual out-of-town crap. One of the hand towels was smeared with makeup. In the wastebasket was a tissue with a lipstick mark. I opened his toilet bag and found a bottle of nitroglycerin pills and a packet of three Fromms. I opened up the packet, saw that one was missing, and took out a little folded slip on which was printed: "Please discreetly hand me a packet of Fromms." I lifted the lid on the toilet seat and checked the water in the lavatory. There was nothing in the water. In a wastepaper basket by the desk I found an empty Fromm wrapper. I did all the things a real detective would have done except make a tasteless joke. I was going to leave that to Dr. Küttner.

By the time he came through the door I was about to ready to toss him a probable cause, but professional courtesy made me hang on to it until he'd earned his retainer.

"People in expensive hotels are seldom ever really ill, you know," he said. "At sixteen marks a night they usually wait until they're back home to be really ill."

"This one won't be going home," I said.

"Dead, is he?" said Küttner.

"It's beginning to look that way, Herr Doctor."

"Makes a change to be doing something for my fee, I suppose."

He took out a stethoscope and set about looking for a heartbeat.

"I had better go and inform Frau Adlon," Pieck said, and left the room.

While Küttner worked his trade, I took another look at the body. Rubusch was a big, heavy man with short, fair hair and a face as fat as a hundred-kilo baby. In bed, from the side, he looked like a foothill in the Harz Mountains. Without his clothes it was hard to place him, but I was sure there was a reason other than the fact that he was staying in the hotel why he seemed familiar to me.

Küttner leaned back and nodded with what looked like satisfaction. "He's been dead for several hours I should say." Looking at his pocket watch, he added, "Sometime between the hours of midnight and six o'clock this morning."

"There are some nitro pills in the bathroom, Doc," I said. "I took the liberty of looking through his things."

"Probably an enlarged heart."

"An enlarged everything, by the look of him," I said, and handed the doctor the little slip of folded paper. "And I do mean everything. There's a packet of three minus one in the bathroom. That, plus some makeup on the towel and the smell of perfume in the air, leads me to suggest that, perhaps, the last few hours of his life may have included a very happy few minutes."

By now I had noticed a clip of brand-new banknotes on the desk and was liking my theory more and more.

"You don't think he died in her arms, do you?" asked Küttner.

"No. The door was locked from the inside."

"So this poor fellow could have had sex, shown her out, locked the door, gone back to bed, and then expired after all the exertion and excitement."

"You've got me convinced."

"The useful thing about being a hotel doctor is that people such as yourself don't ever get to see that my surgery is full of sick people. Consequently, I look like I actually know what I'm doing."

"Don't you?"

"Only some of the time. Most medicine comes down to just one prescription, you know. That you'll feel a lot better in the morning."

"He won't."

"There are worse ways to hit the slab, I suppose," said Küttner.

"Not if you are married, there aren't."

"Was he? Married?"

I lifted the dead man's left hand to show off a gold band.

"You don't miss much, do you, Gunther?"

"Not much, give or take the old Weimar Republic and a proper police force that catches criminals instead of employing them."

Küttner was no liberal, but he was no Nazi, either. A month or two earlier I had found him in the men's room, weeping at the news of Paul von Hindenburg's death. All the same, he looked alarmed at my remark, and for a moment he glanced down at Heinrich Rubusch's body as if he might report my conversation to the Gestapo.

"Relax, Doc. Even the Gestapo haven't yet worked out a way of making an informer out of a dead man."

I WENT DOWNSTAIRS to the front and picked up the message for Rubusch, which was only from Georg Behlert expressing the hope that he had enjoyed his stay at the Adlon. I was checking the duty roster when, out of the corner of my eye, I saw Hedda Adlon coming through the entrance hall talking to Pieck. This was my cue to hurry up and find out more before she could talk to me. Hedda Adlon seemed to have a high opinion of my abilities, and I wanted to keep it that way. The passkey to what I did for a living was having snappy answers to the questions other people hadn't even thought about. An air of omniscience is a very useful quality in a god or, for that matter, a detective. Of course, with a detective, omniscience is just an illusion. Plato knew that. And it's one of the things that made him a better writer than Sir Arthur Conan Doyle.

Unseen by my employer, I stepped into the elevator car.

"Which floor?" asked the boy. His name was Wolfgang, and he was a boy of about sixty.

"Just drive."

Smoothly, Wolfgang's white gloves went into motion, like a magician's, and I felt my stomach lower inside my torso as we ascended into Lorenz Adlon's idea of heaven.

"Is there something on your mind, Herr Gunther?"

"Last night, did you see any joy ladies go up to the second floor?"

"A lot of ladies go up and down in this elevator car, Herr Gunther. Doris Duke, Barbara Hutton, the Soviet ambassador, the Queen of Siam, Princess Mafalda. It's easy to see who and what they are. But some of these actresses, movie stars, showgirls, they all look like joy ladies to me. I guess that's why I'm the elevator boy and not the house detective."

"You're right, of course."

He grinned back at me. "A smart hotel's a bit like a jeweler's shop window. Everything is on show. Now that reminds me. I did see Herr Muller talking to a lady on the stairs at about two a.m. It's possible she was a joy lady. Except for the fact she was wearing diamonds. Tiara, too. That makes me think she wasn't a joy lady. I mean, if she could afford to be wearing mints, then why would she be letting people stroke her mouse? At the same time, if she was a little pinkie in the air, then what was she doing speaking to a sow's bladder like Muller? No offense intended."

"None taken. He is a sow's bladder. Was this lady blond or brunette?"

"Blond. And plenty of it, too."

"I'm relieved to hear it," I said, mentally eliminating from my list of possible suspects Dora Bauer. She had short brown hair and was hardly the type to afford a tiara.

" Anything else?"

"She wore a lot of perfume. Smelled real nice. Like she was Aphrodite herself."

"I get the picture. Did you drive her?"

"No. She must have used the stairs."

"Or maybe she just climbed on the back of a swan and flew straight out of the window. That's what Aphrodite would have done."

"Are you calling me a liar, sir?"

"No, not at all. Just an incurable romantic and lover of women in general."

Wolfgang grinned. "That I am, sir."

"Me, too."

MULLER WAS IN THE OFFICE we shared, which was about all we shared. He hated me and, if I'd cared enough, I might have hated him back. Before coming to the Adlon he'd been a leather hat with the Potsdam police—a uniformed bull with an instinctive dislike of detectives from the Alex like me. He was also ex-Freikorps and more right wing than the Nazis, which was another reason he hated me: he hated all Republicans the way a wheat farmer hates rats. But for his drinking, he might have remained in the police. Instead he took early retirement, climbed on the temperance wagon for as long as it took to find himself the job at the Adlon, and started drinking again. Most of the time he could hold it, too, I'll say that for him. Most of the time. I might have figured it was part of my job to put him out of a job, but I didn't. Leastways, I hadn't done it yet. Of course, we both knew it wouldn't be long before Behlert or one of the Adlons found him drunk on the job. And I hoped it would happen without any help from me. But I knew I could probably live with the disappointment if this turned out not to be the case.

He was asleep in the chair. There was a half bottle of Bismarck on the floor beside his foot and an empty glass in his hand. He hadn't shaved, and the sound of a heavy chest of drawers being rolled across a wooden floor was coming out of his nose and throat. He looked like an uninvited guest at a Brueghel peasant wedding. I slipped my hand into his coat pocket and took out his wallet. Inside were four new five-mark notes with a serial number that matched the notes I'd found on the desk in Rubusch's room. I figured Muller had either procured the joy lady for him or taken a bribe off her afterward. Perhaps both, but it hardly mattered. I put the leaves back in the wallet, returned it to his pocket, and then kicked him on the ankle.

"Hey. Sigmund Romberg. Wake up."

Muller stirred, took a sniff of air, and then let out a deep breath that smelled like a wet malting floor. Wiping his sandpaper chin with the back of his hand, he looked around thirstily.

"It's by your left foot," I said.

He glanced down at the bottle and pretended to ignore it, only he wasn't very convincing. He could have pretended he was Frederick the Great and he would have looked more persuasive.

"What do you want?"

"Thanks, but it's a little early for me. But you go right ahead and have one if it makes thinking any easier. I'll just stand here and watch and have fun imagining what your liver must look like. You know, I'll bet it's an interesting shape. Maybe I should paint it. I do a little abstract painting now and then. Let's see, now. How about *Still Life with Liver and Onions*? We can use your brains for the onions, okay?"

"What do you want?"

His tone was darker now, as if he were getting ready to hit me. But I was on my toes, moving around the room like a dancing master just in case I had to slug him. I almost wanted him to try it so I could. A solid right to the jaw might have helped sober him up.

"Since we're talking of interesting shapes, why don't we talk about that joy lady who was in here last night? The one wearing the tiara. The one visiting the man in 210. Name of Rubusch, Heinrich Rubusch. Did he give you the four leaves, or did you take it off the pussycat in the corridor? Incidentally, if you're wondering why it's any of my damn business, it's because Rubusch is dead."

"Who says I took four leaves off anyone?"

"Your concern for the welfare of the hotel's guests is most touching, Muller. The serial numbers on those four new bills in your wallet match the numbers on a fold of notes lying on a table in the dead man's room."

"You've been in my wallet?"

"You might ask yourself why I'm telling you that I've been in your wallet. The fact is I could have brought Behlert or Pieck or even one of the Adlons along here and found those leaves in front of an audience. But I haven't. Now ask me why."

"All right. I'll take a card from your pack. Why?"

"I don't want to see you fired, Muller. I just want you out of this hotel. I'm offering you a chance to leave under your own steam. Who knows? That way, you might even leave with a reference."

"Suppose I don't want to leave."

"Then I'll go and fetch them anyway. Of course, by the time we get back, you'll have got rid of the leaves. But that won't matter, because that's not why they'll fire you. They'll fire you because you're stinking drunk. In fact, you stink of it so bad, the city's thinking of sending a gas sniffer here to check it out."

"Drunk, he says." Muller picked up the bottle and then drained it.

"What do you expect, in a job like this, with so much hanging around? What's a man to do with himself all day if he doesn't drink?"

I was almost ready to agree with him there. The job *was* boring. I was bored myself. I felt like a calf's foot in aspic jelly.

Muller looked at the empty bottle and grinned. "Looks like I need another leg to stand on." Then he looked at me. "You think you're so clever, don't you, Gunther?"

"With the intellectual equipment you have, Muller, I can see that it might seem that way. But there's still a lot I don't know. Take that joy girl. Did you bring her into the hotel, or did Rubusch?"

"He's dead, you say?"

I nodded.

"I ain't surprised. Big fat man, right?"

I nodded again.

"I saw the girl on the stairs and reckoned I could tap the tree for a little trickle-down, you know?" He shrugged. "Who can live on twenty-five marks a week? She said her name was Angela. I don't know if that's true or not. I didn't ask to see her papers. Twenty marks was good enough ID as far as I was concerned." He grinned. "She was pretty good, too. You don't see many snappers as good-looking as that one. A real peach, so she was. So, like I said, I ain't surprised the fat man is dead. I felt my arteries tighten like clams just looking at her."

"Was that when you saw him? When you saw her?"

"No. I saw him earlier on that evening. In the bar. And then in the Raphael Room."

"He was one of the Olympic Committee's party?"

"Yes."

"And where were you? You were supposed to be keeping an eye on them?"

"What can I tell you?" he said irritably. "They were businessmen, not students. I left them to get on with it. I went to that beer house on the corner of Behrenstrasse and Friedrichstrasse—Pschorr Haus—and got soaked. How was I to know there was going to be trouble?"

"Hope for the best but expect the worst. That's the job, pal." I took out my cigarette case and flicked it open in front of his ugly face. "So. What's it to be? A letter of resignation or Louis Adlon's Oxford toe cap buried up your arse?"

He took a cigarette. I even lit it for him, just to be sociable.

"All right, you win. I'll resign. But we ain't friends."

"That's okay. I'll probably cry a little when I get home tonight, but I think I can live with it."

I WAS HALFWAY ACROSS THE ENTRANCE HALL when Hedda Adlon winged me with a tilt of her jaw and the sound of my name in full. Hedda Adlon was the only person who ever pronounced my first name as if it really meant what it means: brave bear, although actually there's some debate that the "hard" part actually means "foolhardy."

I followed her and the two Pekingese dogs that were always with her into the office of the hotel's assistant managing director. This was her office, and when her husband, Louis, wasn't around—and he wasn't around much when the hunting season got under way—Hedda Adlon was very much in charge.

"So," she said, closing the door, "what do we know about poor Herr Rubusch? Have you telephoned the police?"

"No, not yet. I was on my way to the Alex when you caught me. I wanted to tell them in person."

"Oh? Why is that?"

In her early thirties, Hedda Adlon was much younger than her husband. Although she had been born in Germany, she'd spent much of her youth living in America, and she spoke German with a slight American accent. Like Max Reles. Only that was as far as the similarity went. She was blond, with a full German figure. But it was a healthy figure. As healthy as several million marks. You don't get a healthier figure than that. She enjoyed entertaining and riding—she had been an enthusiastic member of the Berlin fox hunt until Hermann Goering had banned hunting with dogs in Germany—and was very gregarious, which was, I suspected, one of the reasons why the close-lipped Louis Adlon had married her in the first place. She added an extra touch of glamour to the hotel, like a mother-of-pearl inlay on the gates of paradise. She smiled a lot and was good at putting people at their ease and could hold a conversation with anyone. I remembered a dinner at the Adlon in which she was seated next to a Red Indian chief wearing his full native headdress: she spoke to him all evening, as if she'd been talking to the French ambassador. Of course, it's always possible that he was the French ambassador. The French—especially the diplomats—do like their feathers and their decorations.

"I was going to ask the police if they might handle the matter discreetly, Frau Adlon. On the face of it, Herr Doctor Rubusch, who was married, had been entertaining a young lady in his room shortly before he died. No wife could ever like the news of her widowhood to be delivered with that kind of postscript. Not in my experience. So, for her sake, and the sake of the reputation of the hotel, I was hoping to put the matter straight into the hands of a homicide detective who's an old friend of mine. Someone who's equipped with enough human skills to deal sensitively with the case."

"That's very thoughtful of you, Bernhard. We're grateful to you. But you said homicide? I thought his death was natural."

"Even if he died in his sleep with a Bible in his arms, there has to be a homicide inquiry. That's the law."

"But you do agree with Dr. Küttner that his death was from natural causes."

"Probably."

"Only it wasn't with a Bible in his arms, but a young lady. Am I to assume you mean a prostitute?"

"Very likely. We chase them out of the hotel like cats where and when we can. But it's not always easy. This one was wearing a tiara."

"That's a nice touch." Hedda put a cigarette into a holder. "Clever. Who's ever going to challenge someone in a tiara?"

"I might do it if it was a man wearing one."

She smiled, lit the cigarette, sucked at the holder, and then blew out the smoke, not inhaling the stuff at all, like a child pretending to smoke, pretending to be a grown-up. It reminded me of me, pretending to be a detective, going through the motions with just the taste of a proper investigation on my lips and not much more. Hotel detective. Really it was a contradiction in terms. Like national socialism. Racial purity. Aryan superiority.

"Well, if that's all, I'll be getting along to the Alex. The boys in Homicide are a little different from most people. They like to hear bad news as soon as possible."

10

A LOT OF WHAT I'D TOLD Hedda Adlon was nonsense, of course. I had no old friends in Homicide. Not anymore. Otto Trettin was in Counterfeiting and Forgery. Bruno Stahlecker was part of Inspectorate G: the Juvenile Section. Ernst Gennat, who ran Homicide, was no longer a friend. Not since the purge of 1933. And there was certainly no one with any human skills who worked in Homicide. What good were they when you were arresting Jews and communists—when you were busy building the new Germany? All the same, there were some Homicide cops who were worse than others, and these were the bulls I hoped to avoid. For the sake of Frau Rubusch. And Frau Adlon. And the reputation of the hotel. And all of it courtesy of Bernie Gunther, Ring-cycle hero and good guy, dragon slaying a specialty.

Near the front desk in the Alex I saw Heinz Seldte, the young cop who seemed too intelligent to be wearing a SCHUPO uniform. It was a good start. I waved him over, amiably.

"Who are the duty detectives in Homicide?" I asked.

Seldte didn't answer. He didn't even look at me. He was too busy coming to attention and looking over my shoulder.

"You turning yourself in for a murder, Bernie?"

Given the fact that I had actually murdered someone, and quite recently, too, I turned around and tried to look as nonchalant as I was able to. But my heart was beating, as if I'd run all the way along Unter den Linden.

"That all depends on who I'm supposed to have murdered, sir. I can think of one or two people I'd be happy to put my hands up for. Might be worth it at that. As long as I knew they were actually dead."

"Police officers, perhaps."

"Well, now, that would be telling, sir."

"Still the same young bastard, I see."

"Yes, sir. Only not so young. Not anymore."

"Come to my office. Let's talk."

I didn't argue. It's never a good idea to disagree with the head of the Berlin Criminal Police. Erich Liebermann von Sonnenberg was still just a criminal director when I'd been a detective at the Alex, back in 1932. That was the year von Sonnenberg had joined the Nazi Party, and this had guaranteed his preferment by the Nazis after 1933. I respected him in spite of that. For one thing, he had always been an effective police-man and, for another, he was a good friend of Otto Trettin, as well as the coauthor of his stupid book.

We went into his office and he closed the door behind me.

"I don't have to remind you whose office this was when you were last here."

I glanced around. The office had been painted, and there was a new carpet instead of linoleum on the floor. The map on the wall showing the incidence of SA versus red violence was gone, and in its place was a glass case full of mottled brown moths that matched the color of von Sonnenberg's hair.

"Bernard Weiss."

"A good policeman."

"I'm pleased to hear you say so, sir, given the circumstances of his departure."

Weiss, a Jew, had been forced to leave the police and to flee Germany in 1932.

"You were a good cop, too, Bernie. The difference is, you could probably have stayed on here."

"It didn't feel like that at the time."

"So what brings you back here?"

I told him about the dead man in the Adlon.

"Natural causes?"

"Looks like. I was hoping the investigating detectives might spare the widow the full circumstances of the man's death, sir."

"Any particular reason?"

"All part of the Adlon's high-class service."

"Like fresh towels in the en-suite bathroom every day, is that it?"

"There's the hotel's reputation to consider as well. It wouldn't do for people to get the idea that we're Pension Schmidt."

I told him about the joy lady.

"I'll put some men on it. Right away." He picked up the telephone and barked a few orders and waited, covering the candlestick with his hand. "Rust and Brandt," he said. "The duty detectives."

"I don't remember them."

"I'll tell them to watch their umlauts." Von Sonnenberg added some instructions into the candlestick, and when he had finished speaking, he hooked the earpiece and shot me a questioning look. "Fair enough?"

"I'm grateful, sir."

"That remains to be seen." He eyed me slowly and leaned back in his chair. "Just between the two of us, Bernie, most of the detectives here in KRIPO aren't worth a spit. And that includes Rust and Brandt. They're strictly by the book because they wouldn't have the nerve or the experience to know that there's a lot more to the job than what's written in there. A good detective needs to have imagination. These days the trouble is that that sounds like it has a subversive, undisciplined aspect to it. And no one wants to be thought of as being subversive. Do you see what I mean?"

"Yes, sir."

He lit a cigarette quickly.

"What would you say were some of the characteristics of a good detective?"

I shrugged. "The feeling that you're right, when everyone else is wrong." I smiled. "I can see how that might not go down too well, either." I hesitated.

"You can speak freely. It's just you and me in here."

"Dogged persistence. When people tell you to lay off, you don't lay off. I never could walk away from something because of politics."

"Then I take it you're still not a Nazi."

I said nothing.

"Are you anti-Nazi?"

"A Nazi is someone who follows Hitler. To be anti-Nazi is to listen to what he says."

Von Sonnenberg chuckled. "It's refreshing speaking to a man like you, Bernie. You remind me of how things used to be here. Of how cops used to talk. Real cops. I assume you had your own informers."

"You can't do the job without keeping your ear on the toilet door."

"The trouble is, everyone's an informer now." Von Sonnenberg shook his head gloomily. "And I do mean everyone. Which means there's much too much information. By the time any of it's been assessed, it's useless."

"We get the police force we deserve, sir."

"You of all people could be forgiven for thinking that. But I can't sit back and do nothing about it. I wouldn't be doing my job properly. Under the republic, the Berlin police force enjoyed a reputation as one of the best in the world."

"That's not what the Nazis said, sir."

"I can't help that. But I can try to arrest the decline."

"I get the feeling my gratitude is about to be sorely tested."

"I have one or two detectives here who might, in time, amount to something."

"You mean apart from Otto."

Von Sonnenberg chuckled again. "Otto. Yes. Well, Otto is Otto, isn't he?"

"Always."

"But these cops are lacking in experience. Your kind of experience. One of them is Richard Bömer."

"I don't know him, either, sir."

"No, well, you wouldn't. He's my sister's son-in-law. I was thinking he might benefit from a little avuncular advice."

"I really don't think I'd make much of an uncle, sir. I haven't got a brother, but if I had, he'd probably have died of criticism by now. The only reason they took me out of uniform and put me in plainclothes was because I was so short with the traffic on Potsdamer Platz. Advice from me sounds like a ruler across the knuckles. I even avoid my own shaving mirror in case I tell myself to go and get a proper job."

"A proper job. For you? Like what, for instance?"

"I've been thinking I might try to set myself up as a private investigator."

"To do that you'll need a license from a magistrate. In which case, you would need to show police consent. It might be useful to have a senior policeman on your side for something like that."

He had a point, and there seemed to be no use in wriggling. He had me just where he wanted, as if I were a moth pinned in the glass case on his office wall.

"All right. But don't expect white gloves and silver service. If this fellow Richard doesn't like boiled sausage from the Wurst Max, I'll be wasting his time and mine."

"Naturally. All the same, it might be a good idea if you were to meet him somewhere outside the Alex. And that better include the bars around here. I'd like to avoid anyone pulling his chain about the low company he's keeping."

"Suits me. But I'd rather not have your sister's son-in-law in the Adlon. No disrespect to you or her, but they generally prefer it if I'm not teaching a class when I'm there."

"Sure. We'll think of a spot. Somewhere halfway. How about the Lustgarten?"

I nodded.

"I'll get Richard to bring you the files on a couple of cases he's looking at. Cold ones. Who knows? Maybe you can warm them up for him. A floater from the canal. And that poor dumb cop who got himself murdered. Maybe you read about him in the *Beobachter*? August Krichbaum."

11

ONCE A HUGE, LANDSCAPED GARDEN, the Lustgarten was enclosed by the old royal palace—to which it had formerly belonged—and the Old Museum and the Cathedral, but in recent years it had been used not as a garden at all but for military parades and political rallies. I'd been part of a rally there myself, in February 1933, when two hundred thousand people had filled the Lustgarten to demonstrate against Hitler. Perhaps that was why, when they came to power, the Nazis ordered the gardens to be paved over and the famous equestrian statue of Frederick William III removed—so that they could stage even larger military parades and rallies in support of the Leader.

Arriving in that great empty space, I realized I had forgotten about the statue and was obliged to guess where it had been so that I might stand there myself and give Kriminalinspector Richard Bömer half a chance to find me in accordance with Liebermann von Sonnenberg's arrangements.

Before he saw me, I saw him—a tallish man in his late twenties, fair-haired, carrying a briefcase under his arm, and wearing a gray suit and a pair of shiny black boots that might have been made to measure for him at the police school in Havel. Deep laugh lines bracketed a wide, full mouth that seemed on the edge of a smile. His nose was bent slightly out of shape, and a thick scar ran through one eyebrow like a little bridge over a golden stream. Except for his ears, which were unscarred, he looked like a promising, young light middleweight who had forgotten to remove his gum shield. Seeing me, he approached unhurriedly.

"Hey."

"Are you Gunther?"

He pointed southeast, in the direction of the palace. "I think he used to face this way. Frederick William the Third, I mean."

"Sure about that?"

"Yes."

"Good. I like a man who holds on to his opinions."

He turned and pointed to the west. "They moved him over there. Behind those trees. Which is where I've been waiting for the last ten minutes. I decided to come over here when it occurred to me that you might not know that he'd moved."

"Who expects a granite horseman to go anywhere?"

"They've got to march somewhere, I guess."

"That's a matter of opinion. Come on. Let's sit. A cop never stands when he can sit."

We walked up to the Old Museum and sat on the steps in front of a long façade of Ionic columns.

"I like coming here," he said. "It makes you think of what we used to be. And what we will be again."

I looked at him blankly.

"You know, German history," he said.

"German history is nothing more than a series of ridiculous mustaches," I said.

Bömer smiled a crooked, bashful smile, like a schoolboy. "My uncle would love that one," he said.

"I take it you don't mean Liebermann von Sonnenberg."

"He's my wife's uncle."

"As if having the head of KRIPO holding a sponge in your corner wasn't enough. So *your* uncle. Who's he? Hermann Goering?"

He looked sheepish. "I just want to work homicides. To be a good policeman."

"One thing I learned about being a good policeman. It doesn't pay nearly as well as being a bad one. So who's your uncle?"

"Does it matter?"

"It's only that Liebermann wanted me to be your uncle, so to speak. And I'm the jealous type. If you've got another uncle as important as me, I want to know about it. Besides, I'm nosy, too. That's why I became a detective."

"He's someone at the Ministry of Propaganda."

"You don't look like Joey the Crip, so you must be talking about someone else."

"Bömer. Dr. Karl Bömer."

"These days it seems everyone needs a doctorate to lie to people."

He grinned again. "You're just doing this, aren't you? Because you know I'm a Party member."

"Isn't everyone?"

"You're not."

"Somehow I never got around to it. There was always a big line of people outside Party headquarters when I went to apply."

"It should have told you something. That there's safety in numbers."

"No, there isn't. I was in the trenches, my young friend. A battalion can be killed just as easily as a single man. And it was the generals, not the Jews, who made sure of that. They're the ones who stabbed us in the back."

"The chief said I should try to avoid talking politics with you, Gunther."

"That's not politics. That's history. You want to know the real truth of German history? It's that there's no truth in German history. Like me at the Alex. None of what you've heard about me is true."

"The chief said you were a good detective. One of the best."

"Apart from that."

"He said it was you who caught Gormann, the strangler."

"If that had been difficult, the chief would have put me in his book. Did you read it?"

He nodded.

"What did you think?"

"It wasn't written for other cops."

"You're in the wrong job, Richard. You should be working in the diplomatic corps. It was a lousy book. It tells you nothing about being a detective. Not that I can tell you much. Except this, perhaps. It's easy for a cop to recognize when a man is lying. What's harder is to know when he's telling the truth. Or maybe this: A policeman is just a man who's a little less dumb than a criminal."

"Your investigative method, perhaps? You could tell me something about that."

"My method was a bit like what Field Marshal von Moltke said about a battle plan. It never survives contact with the enemy. People are different, Richard. It stands to reason that homicides are different, too. Perhaps if you were to tell me about a case you're working on now. Better still, if you brought me the file, I could take a look at it and offer my thoughts. The chief mentioned one case that needed warming up. The murder of that cop. August Krichbaum, wasn't it? Perhaps I could suggest something there."

"That's no longer a cold case," said Bömer. "Looks like there may be a lead, after all."

I bit my lip. "Oh? What's that?"

"Krichbaum got himself murdered in front of the Kaiser Hotel, right? Pathologist reckoned someone clouted him in the gut."

"Must have been quite a punch."

"I guess if you're not ready for it, it might be. Anyway, the hotel doorman got a look at the main suspect. Not much of a look, but he's an ex-cop. Anyway, he's looked at the photograph of every crook in Berlin, and no luck. Since then he's been racking his brains and now reckons that the fellow who hit Krichbaum might have been another cop."

"A cop? You're joking."

"Not at all. They've got him looking over the personnel files of the entire Berlin police force, past and present. As soon as he thumbs the right mug, they'll have the guy, for sure."

"Well, that's a relief."

I lit a cigarette and rubbed the back of my neck uncomfortably, as if I could already feel the blade of the falling ax. It's said that all you ever feel is a sharp bite, like the angry nip of the electric clippers in a gentlemen's hairdressers. It took me a moment or two to remind myself that the hotel doorman's description of the suspect had been of a man with a mustache. And it took me a while longer to remember that in the original photograph on my own police personnel file I had been wearing a mustache. Did that make it more or less likely that he could identify me? I wasn't sure. I took a deep breath and felt my head swim a little.

"But I brought the file on something else I've been working on," said Bömer, unbuckling his saddle-leather briefcase.

"Good," I said, without enthusiasm. "Oh, good."

He handed me a buff-colored file.

"A few days ago, there was a body found floating in the Mühlen-damm Lock."

"A Landwehr Top," I said.

"I beg your pardon?"

"Nothing. So why didn't the Mühlendamm Murder Commission deal with it?"

"Because there was some mystery about the man's identity and about the cause of death. The man drowned. But the body was full of seawater, see? So he couldn't possibly have drowned in the River Spree." He handed me some photographs. "Plus, as you can see, an attempt had been made to weigh the body down. The rope around the ankles prob-ably slipped the weight."

"How deep is it there?" I asked, leafing through the pictures taken at the scene and in the morgue.

"About nine meters."

I was looking at the body of a man in his late fifties. Big, blond, and typically Aryan, except for the fact that there was a photograph of his penis, which had been circumcised. Among German men that was a little unusual.

"As you can see, he might have been a Jew," said Bömer. "Although from the rest of him, you wouldn't say he looks like a Jew at all."

"The strangest people are, these days."

"I mean to say, he looks more typically Aryan, don't you think?"

"Sure. Like a poster boy for the SA."

"Well, let's hope so."

"Meaning?"

"Meaning this: If it should turn out he's German, then obviously we'd like to find out as much as we can. But if it should turn out that he's Jewish, then my orders are that we don't bother to investigate. That it's understandable these things should happen in Berlin and not to waste any police time investigating it."

I marveled at the calm way he said this. As if it were the most natural distinction in the world. I didn't speak. I didn't have to. I was looking at the pictures of a dead man. But I was still thinking about my own neck.

"Broken nose, cauliflower ear, big hands." I flicked my cigarette away and tried to concentrate on what I was looking at, if only to get my mind off the death of August Krichbaum. "This fellow was no choirboy. Maybe he was a Jew, after all. Interesting."

"What is?"

"That triangular mark on his chest. What is it? A bruise? The pathologist doesn't say. Which is sloppy. Wouldn't have happened in my day. I could probably tell a lot more from the actual body. Where is it now?"

"At the Charité Hospital."

Suddenly, I figured that looking at Bömer's Landwehr Top was the best way of taking my mind off August Krichbaum.

"Have you got a car?"

"Yes."

"Come on. Let's go and take a look. If anyone in there asks what we're doing, you're helping me to look for my missing brother."

WE DROVE NORTHWEST in an open-top Butz. There was a two-wheel trailer attached to the back, almost as if Bömer were planning to go camping after he was through with me. This wasn't so far from the truth.

"I lead a Hitler Youth troop of boys aged ten to fourteen," he explained. "We were camping last weekend, which is why I still have the trailer attached to the car."

"I sincerely hope they're all still in there."

"Go ahead and laugh. Everyone else at the Alex laughs. But I happen to believe in Germany's future."

"So do I, which is why I also hope you locked them in. The members of your youth troop, I mean. Nasty little brutes. I saw some the other day playing piggy in the middle with some old Jew's hat. Still, I guess we should forget about it. I mean, it's understandable that these things happen in Berlin."

"I don't have anything against the Jews myself."

"But. There's always a 'but' after that particular sentiment. It's like a stupid little trailer attached to the car."

"But I do believe our nation has become weak and degenerate. And that the best way of turning that around is to make being German seem like something important. To do that properly, we have to make ourselves a special thing, a race apart. To make ourselves seem exclusively German, even to the extent of saying that it's no good being a Jew first and a German second. There's no room for anything else."

"You make camping sound fun, Bömer. Is that what you tell the boys around the campfire? Now I understand what the trailer's for. I suppose it's full of degenerate literature to get the bonfire going."

He grinned and shook his head. "Christ, did you speak like this when you were a detective at the Alex?"

"No. Back then we could all still say what the hell we liked."

He laughed. "All I'm trying to do is explain why I think we need the government we have now."

"Richard. When Germans look to their governments to fix things, you know we're really in the shit. If you ask me, I think we're an easy people to govern. All you have to do is make a new law once a year that says, do as you're damn well told."

We drove across Karlsplatz and onto Luisenstrasse, passing the monument to Rudolf Virchow, the so-called father of pathology and an early advocate of racial purity, which was probably the only reason why his statue hadn't been moved. Next to the Charité Hospital was the Pathological Institute. We parked the car and went inside.

A red-haired intern wearing a white jacket showed us down to the ancient morgue, where a man armed with a pump-action spray gun was making short and pungent work of what remained of that summer's insect life. I wondered if the stuff worked on Nazis. The man with the spray gun led us into the cold store, which, from the smell, wasn't quite cold enough. He hit the air with some insecticide and walked us around a dozen, sheet-covered bodies laid out on slabs like a tented village, until we found the one we were looking for.

I took out my cigarettes and offered one to Bömer.

"I don't smoke."

"Too bad. A lot of folks still believe we all smoked in the war to calm our nerves, but mostly it was to cover the smell of the dead. You should take up smoking, and not just to help out in a smelly situation like this. Smoking is essential for a detective. It helps convince us we're doing something, even when we're doing nothing much at all. You'll find there's a lot of nothing much at all that happens when you're a detective."

I threw off the sheet and stared hard at a man's body the size of Schmeling's bigger brother and the color of uncooked dough. Looking at him, you almost expected someone to shovel him into an oven and bake him back to life. The skin on his face looked like a hand left too long in the bathwater. It was crinkled like an apricot. Even his optician wouldn't have recognized him. What was more, the pathologist had already been at work. A crudely sewn thoracic scar crossed the body from the chin to the pubic hair like a length of toy railway track. The scar traversed the center of the triangular mark on the man's broad chest. Pinching the cigarette from my mouth, I went down for a closer look.

"Not a tattoo," I said. "A burn mark. It looks a little like the tip of a flatiron, don't you think?"

Bömer nodded. "Tortured?"

"Are there any similar marks on his back?"

"I don't know."

I took hold of a big shoulder. "Then let's turn him over. You take the hip and the legs. I'll turn the body. We'll pull him toward us, and I'll lean over and take a look."

It was like moving a wet sandbag. There was nothing on his back except some lank hair and a birthmark, but as the body rested against our abdomens, Bömer swore uncomfortably.

"Too much for you, Richard?"

"Something just leaked out of his prick and onto my shirt," he said, quickly stepping away from the slab and then staring in horror at a large brown-yellow wound in the center of his belly. "Shit."

"Close. But not quite."

"That was a new shirt. Now what am I going to do?" He pulled the material away from the skin of his belly and sighed.

"Haven't you got a brown one in that trailer of yours?" I joked. Bömer looked relieved. "Yes, I have."

"Then shut up and pay attention. Our friend here wasn't tortured, that much I'm sure of. Anyone using a hot iron on him would have used it more often than once if he'd meant to hurt him."

"So why do it?"

I lifted one of the hands and bent the fingers into a fist as big as the fuel tank on a small motorcycle.

"Look at the size of these mitts. The scar tissue on the knuckles. Especially here, at the base of each small finger. And do you see this bump?" I let Bömer take a look at a bump that curled all the way around the back of the palm to a point just below the knuckle of the little finger. Then, lowering the left, I lifted the man's right. "This one's even more pronounced. This is a common fracture in boxers. I'd say this guy was a southpaw, too, which should help narrow it down a bit. Except that he hadn't boxed in a while. See the dirt under these fingernails? No boxer would tolerate that. Only the pathologist here didn't scrape them out, and no detective ought to tolerate that. If the medicine man doesn't do his job, it's up to you to put him straight."

I took out my pocketknife and an Adlon envelope containing Muller's resignation letter and scraped out what was underneath the dead man's nails.

"I don't see what a few crumbs of dirt are going to tell us," said Bömer.

"Probably nothing. But evidence rarely comes in a large size. And it's nearly always dirty. Remember that. Now all I need is to see the dead man's clothes. And I need the use of a microscope for a few minutes." I glanced around. "As I recall, there's a laboratory somewhere on this floor."

He pointed. "In there."

While Bömer went to fetch the dead man's clothes, I put the contents of his fingernails into a Petri dish and stared at them for a while underneath a microscope. I was no scientist and no geologist, either, but I knew gold when I saw it. There was just a tiny crumb, but it was enough to catch the light and my attention. And when Bömer came into the lab carrying a cardboard box, I went ahead and told him what I'd found, even though I knew what he was going to say.

"Gold, huh? A jeweler, maybe? That might also be evidence that the man was a Jew."

"I told you, Richard. This man was a boxer. Most likely he was working on a building site. That would account for the dirt under the nails."

"And the gold?"

"Generally speaking, outside of a goldsmith's, the best place to look for gold is in the dirt."

I opened the cardboard box and found myself looking through the clothes of a workingman. At a pair of strong boots. At a thick leather belt. At a leather cap. The cheap flannel shirt interested me more, as there were no buttons on it, and there were small tears on the material where they should have been.

"Someone tore this man's shirt open in a hurry," I said. "Most likely when his heart stopped beating. It looks as though someone tried to revive him after he drowned. That would certainly explain the shirt. It was ripped open so that an attempt could be made to start his heart again. With a hot iron. It's an old boxing trainer's trick. Something about the heat and the shock, I think. Anyway, that explains the burn."

"Are you saying someone threw this man in the water and then tried to revive him?"

"Well, it wasn't the Spree. You told me that yourself. He drowned somewhere else. *Then* someone tried to revive him. Then they dumped him in the river. That's the chain of causation, but I can't attach any whys to that. Not yet."

"Interesting."

I looked at the man's jacket. It was a cheap corduroy from C&A.

Except the lining had been opened and then restitched, and, squeezing the material under the breast pocket, I felt something crumple in my fingers. I took out my knife again, cut away some of the stitches on the lining, and picked out a folded piece of paper. Carefully I unfolded it until I was able to spread a strip of paper about the size of a schoolboy's ruler on the bench beside the microscope. After being in the waters of the River Spree, whatever it was that had been printed on the strip of paper was gone forever. The paper was quite blank. But there was no mistaking its meaning.

Bömer's face was equally blank. "Could this have been his name and address?"

"It might have been, if he was a ten-year-old boy and his mother worried about him getting lost."

"Well, then. What does it mean?"

"It means that what you first suspected is now confirmed. I believe this strip of paper was probably a fragment from the Torah."

"The *what*?"

"If God is German, I for one won't be at all surprised. Apparently he enjoys being worshipped, issuing people with ten commandments at a time, and has even written his own unreadable book. But the God that this man worshipped was the Hebrew God. Jews sometimes sew a piece of the word of God into their clothes, next to their heart. Yes, that's right, Richard. He was a Jew."

"Shit. God damn it all."

"You really mean that, don't you?"

"I told you, Gunther. The chief is never going to authorize me to investigate the death of a Jew. Damn it all. I thought this might have been a chance to prove myself. To lead a proper murder investigation, you know?"

I said nothing. It wasn't that I was speechless, but I certainly didn't feel like making a speech. What would be the point?

"I don't make police policy, Gunther," said Bömer. "Even Liebermann von Sonnenberg doesn't do that. If you really want to know, the policy comes down from the Ministry of the Interior. From Frick. And Frick gets it from Goering, who probably gets it from—"

"The devil himself. I know."

Suddenly I badly wanted to be away from Richard Bömer and his vaulting forensic ambition. And it was now obvious in a way it hadn't been obvious before that being a policeman had changed a lot more than I had supposed. I couldn't ever go back to the Alex even if I had wanted to.

"I expect there will be other murders, Richard. In fact, I'm sure of it. In that respect at least, you can rely on the Nazis."

"You don't understand. I want to be a detective, like in the stories. It's all I've ever wanted to be. A proper detective, like you were, Gunther. But police states are bad for crime and bad for criminals. Because everyone's a policeman in Germany now. And if they're not yet, they soon will be." He kicked the laboratory workbench and swore again.

"Richard. You almost make me feel sorry for you." I picked up the dead man's file and handed it back. "Well, I can't say it's not been fun. I've missed the job. I've even missed the customers. Can you believe that? But from now on I'm going to miss the job the way I miss the Lustgarten. Which is to say, not at all. Because it's not the same. It's not like it used to be. When someone gets murdered—it doesn't matter who it is—you investigate. You investigate, because that's what you do when you live in a decent society. And when you don't, when you say that someone's death isn't worth the candle, then the job's not worth having anyway. Not anymore."

I held the file out to him. But he stared at it as if it wasn't there.

"Go ahead," I said. "Take this. It's yours."

But we both knew it wasn't.

Ignoring the file, he turned and walked out of the laboratory, and although I wasn't there to see it, the Pathological Institute, as well.

A few months later Erich Liebermann von Sonnenberg told me that Richard Bömer had left KRIPO and joined the SS. At the time it looked like the better career move.

12

THE TWO OFFICERS FROM KRIPO were very polite," Georg Behlert told me. "Frau Adlon couldn't have been more grateful for the way you've handled this whole affair. Excellent. Well done."

We were seated in Behlert's office overlooking the Goethe Garden. Through the open doors of the adjoining Palm Court, a piano trio was doing its best to ignore a statue of Hercules that seemed to demand something rather more muscular than a selection of Mozart and Schubert. I felt a little like Hercules myself, returning to Mycenae after carrying out some pointless labor.

"Perhaps," I said. "But I can't think it was a good idea for me to get involved like this. I should just have let them get on with it. I might have known they would extract some sort of price."

Behlert looked puzzled. "What price? You don't mean—?"

"Not from the hotel," I added. "A price from me." And just to see the look of horror on his smooth, shiny face, I told Behlert about Liebermann von Sonnenberg and the dead man in the Charité.

"Next time," I said. "If there is a next time. I shan't try to influence a police investigation. It was naive of me to think I could. And for what? Some fat guy in room 210 I never even met. Why should I worry about his wife? Maybe she hated him. If she didn't, she ought to have. It would serve him damn well right if the cops put their feet right through her feelings when they gave her the bad news. He should have thought of her when he started monkeying around with a Berlin joy lady."

"But you were doing what you did for the sake of the good reputation of the Adlon Hotel," said Behlert, as if that was all the justification required.

"Yes, I suppose so."

He was on his feet now, removing a stopper from a decanter of the good stuff and pouring us each a thimble-sized glass.

"Here. Drink this. It looks like you need it."

"Thanks, Georg."

"What's going to happen to him?"

"To Rubusch?"

"No, I mean, to the poor fellow in the morgue?"

"You really want to know?"

He nodded.

"With an unidentified body, what usually happens is, they take him around to the university anatomical institute and let the students loose on him."

"But suppose the investigation reveals his true identity."

"I didn't make that clear, did I? There isn't going to be an investigation. Not now that we—I mean, I—not now that I've established that he was a Jew. The Berlin police don't want to know about dead Jews. It's not considered a proper use of police time and resources. As far as the cops are concerned, his murderer—if indeed he was murdered, I'm not at all sure about that—that person is more likely to be congratulated than prosecuted."

Behlert drained his glass of the excellent schnapps and shook his head with disbelief.

"I'm not making this up," I said. "I know it seems incredible, but it's all true. Hand on heart."

"I believe you, Bernie. I believe you." He sighed. "One of the guests has just returned from Bavaria. He's a British Jew. From Manchester. Apparently he saw a road sign that said something like DANGEROUS BEND, SPEED LIMIT 50. JEWS HURRY UP. What could I tell him? I said it was probably a sick joke. But I knew it wasn't. In my own hometown of Jena, there is a similar sign outside the Zeiss Planetarium that suggests a new homeland for Jews on the planet Mars. And the terrible thing is, they mean it. Some of the guests are saying they're never coming back to Germany. That we're no longer the considerate people we were. Even in Berlin."

"These days a considerate German is someone who doesn't knock at your door early in the morning in case you think it's the Gestapo."

I handed him the letter containing Muller's resignation as an Adlon Hotel detective. He read it and then laid it on his desk.

"I can't say I'm surprised or sorry. I've had my suspicions about that man for some time. Of course, for you it will mean there's more to do. At least until we can find a replacement. Which is why I'm going to increase your salary. How does an extra ten marks a week sound?"

"It's not Handel, but I guess I like it."

"Good. Perhaps you can find a replacement. After all, you were very helpful with Fräulein Bauer. The stenographer? She's been doing a lot of work for Herr Reles in 114. Apparently he's very pleased with her."

"Good."

"You might know someone else. An ex-policeman. Someone like yourself. Someone reliable. Someone discreet. Someone smart."

I nodded slowly and poured the drink down my throat.

Georg Behlert seemed to think he knew me, but I wasn't sure I knew myself. Not anymore. Certainly not since my visit to see Otto Schuchardt on the Jewish Desk at Gestapo House.

It was, perhaps, time I did something about that.

I CAUGHT A NUMBER 10 TRAM WEST, across Invalidenstrasse and into Old Moabit, past the criminal courts and the prison. Next to Bolle's Dairy—from which a strong smell of horse manure blew down the street toward the Lessing Bridge—was a dilapidated tenement. It was a crummy sort of area—even the trash in the street looked like something someone had thrown away.

Emil Linthe was on the top floor, and through the open window on the landing in front of his door, one could hear noise from the machine-tool factory on Huttenstrasse. It had been silent for almost a year during the Great Depression, but since the Nazis had come into government, the place was constantly active. There were just three iron beats, over and over again, like a waltz conducted by Thor, the god of thunder.

I knocked on the door, and eventually it opened, to reveal a tall, slim man in his thirties with a plentiful head of hair that was high at the front and almost nonexistent at the back. It was like finding a chaise longue on top of someone's head.

"Do you ever get used to that noise?" I asked.

"What noise?"

"I guess you do. Emil Linthe?"

"Gone away. On holiday. Rügen Island."

There was ink on his fingers. Enough to make me suspect I was talking to the right man after all.

"My mistake," I said. "Maybe you're going by a different name these days. Otto Trettin said it might be Maier, or maybe Schmidt. Walter Schmidt."

Linthe's persona deflated like a balloon. "A copper."

"Relax. I'm not here to squeeze your wrists. I'm here on business. Your kind of business."

"And why would I want to do business with the Berlin polenta?"

"Because Otto still hasn't found your file, Emil. And because you don't want to give him any reason to start looking for it again. Or you might find yourself back in the Punch. His words, not mine. But I'm like a brother to that man."

"I always thought coppers killed their brothers when they were still in their cradles."

"Ask me in. There's a good fellow. It's a bit noisy out here, and you wouldn't want me to raise my voice, now, would you?"

Emil Linthe stepped aside. At the same time he drew up his suspenders and picked up a cigarette he'd left burning in an ashtray on a ledge inside the door. As I came inside, he closed the door and then quickly moved ahead of me along the corridor to close the sitting room door. But not soon enough to prevent me from seeing what looked like a printing press. We went into the kitchen.

"I told you, Emil. I'm not here to squeeze your wrists."

"The leopard doesn't change its spots."

"As a matter of fact, that's exactly what I wanted to talk to you about. I hear you can do exactly that. For the right money. I want you to give me what Otto Trettin called an Aryan transfusion."

I told him the problem about my grandmother.

He smiled and shook his head. "It makes me laugh," he said. "All those people who got on the Nazi train, now running back down the aisle to look for the station they started from."

I might have told him I wasn't one of those people. I might have admitted I wasn't a cop, but I didn't want to deliver myself into his potentially blackmailing hands. Linthe was a crook after all. I needed to hold on to the whip, or else I might lose control of a horse I planned to ride for as long as I needed it.

"You Nazis are all the same." He laughed again. "Hypocrites."

"I'm not a Nazi. I'm a German. And a German is different from a Nazi. A German is a man who manages to overcome his worst prejudices. A Nazi is a man who turns them into laws."

But he was too busy laughing to listen to what I was saying.

"It wasn't my intention to amuse you, Emil."

"Nevertheless, I am amused. It is rather amusing."

I grabbed him by the braces and drew them tight in opposite directions so that I was half strangling him, and then shoved him hard up against the kitchen wall. Through the window, just north of Moabit, I could make out the shape of Plötzensee Prison, where recently Otto had seen the falling ax in action. It reminded me to be gentle with Emil Linthe. But not too gentle.

"Am I laughing?" I slapped him on one cheek and then the other. "Am I?"

"No," he yelled irritably.

"Perhaps you think that file of yours really is lost, Emil. Perhaps I need to remind you what's in it. You're a known associate of the Hand in Hand, a very nasty little criminal ring. Also of Salomon Smolianoff, a Ukrainian counterfeiter who's currently doing three years in the Dutch cement for forging British banknotes. You did three in the Punch for the same offense. Which is why you've developed a profitable little sideline forging documents. Of course, if they ever catch you forging currency again they'll throw away the key. And they will, Emil. They will. I can guarantee it. Because if you don't help me I'll walk straight round to the Charlottenburg Police Praesidium and tell them about the printing press in your living room. What is it, a platen?"

I let him go. "I mean, I'm a fair man. I would offer to pay you, but what would be the point? You could probably print more in ten minutes than I could earn in a year."

Emil Linthe grinned, sheepishly. "You know about printing presses?"

"Not really. But I know what one looks like when I see it."

"Actually it's a Kluge. Better than a platen. The Kluge is the best for running any type of job work, including die cutting, foil stamping, and embossing." He lit a cigarette. "Look, I didn't say I wouldn't help you. Any friend of Otto's, yes? I just said it was amusing, that's all."

"Not to me, Emil. Not to me."

"Well, then you're in luck. I happen to know what the hell I'm doing. Unlike most of the people Otto could have recommended. You say your maternal grandmother, surname—?"

"Adler."

"Right. She was Jewish by birth? But was brought up as a Roman Catholic?"

"Yes."

"In the parish of?"

"Neukölln."

"I'll have to fix it in the church registry and in the town hall. Neukölln's good. A lot of officials there are old lefties and very easily corrupted. If it was more than two grandparents I probably couldn't help you. But one is relatively straightforward, if you know what you're doing. Which I do. But I'll need birth certificates, death certificates, all you've got."

I handed him an envelope from my coat pocket.

"It's probably best I redo everything from scratch. All records fixed."

"How much will it cost me?"

Linthe shook his head. "Like you said. In ten minutes I can print more than you can make in a year. So. We'll call it a favor to you and Otto, all right?" He shook his head. "It's no sweat. Adler easily becomes Kugler, or Ebner, or Fendler, or Kepler, or Muller, see?"

"Not Muller," I said.

"It's a good German name."

"I don't like it."

"All right. And just to make things that little bit more plausible, we'll turn your grandmother into your great-grandmother. Just put the Jew in you back a generation so that it becomes inconsequential. By the time I've finished, you'll look more German than the Kaiser."

"He was half English, wasn't he? His grandmother was Queen Victoria."

"True. But she was half German. And so was the Kaiser's mother." Linthe shook his head. "No one is ever one hundred percent anything. That's what's so stupid about this Aryan paragraph. We're all of us a mixture. You, me, the Kaiser, Hitler. Hitler, most of all, I shouldn't wonder. They say Hitler is one-quarter Jewish. What do you think of that?"

"Maybe he and I have something in common after all."

For his sake I just hoped Hitler had a friend on the Jew Desk in the Gestapo, like I did.

13

HEDDA ADLON HAD A FRIEND, TOO, but not the kind you find anywhere south of paradise. Her name was Mrs. Noreen Charalambides and, a couple of days before I was introduced to her, I had already committed her face and her backside and her calves and her bosom to a space in the flask of my Faustian memory previously reserved for Helen of Troy.

It was my job to keep an eye on the guests, and whenever I saw Mrs. Charalambides in and around the hotel, I kept all eight of them on her, waiting for her to brush against the silken thread that marked the outer limits of my darker, spidery world. Not that I would ever have tried to "fraternize" with a guest, if that was what you called it. That was what Hedda Adlon and Georg Behlert called it, but something as brotherly as fraternity was a very long way from what I wanted to do with Noreen Charalambides. Whatever you called it, the hotel took a dim view of that kind of thing. It did happen, of course, and several chambermaids were not above selling it for the right price. When Erich von Stroheim or Emil Jannings were staying at the hotel, the chief reception clerk was always careful to have them attended by a rather elderly chambermaid named Bella. Then again, Stroheim wasn't that particular. He liked them young. But he liked them old, too.

It sounds ridiculous, and of course it is—love is ridiculous, that's what makes it fun—but I suppose I was a little in love with Noreen Charalambides before I even met her. Like some schoolgirl with a Ross postcard of Max Hansen in her satchel. I looked at her the way I some-times look at an SSK in the window of the Mercedes-Benz showroom on Potsdamer Platz: I don't ever expect to drive that car, let alone own one, but a man can dream. While she was there, Mrs. Charalambides looked like the fastest and most beautiful car in the hotel.

She was tall, an impression enhanced by her choice of hat. The weather had cooled of late. She wore a gray Astrakhan shako that she may have bought in Moscow, her previous port of call, although she was in fact an American who lived in New York. An American who was on her way back home from some kind of literary or theatrical festival in Russia. Maybe she had bought the sable coat in Moscow, too. I'm sure the sable didn't mind. Mrs. Charalambides looked better in it than any sable I'd ever seen.

Her hair, which she wore in a bun, was also sable-colored and, I imagined, every bit as nice to stroke. Nicer, probably, as it wasn't likely to bite. All the same, I wouldn't have minded being bitten by Noreen Charalambides. Any proximity to her pouting, cherry-red Fokker Alba-tross of a mouth would have been worth losing a fingertip or a piece of my ear. Vincent van Gogh wasn't the only fellow who could make that kind of heady, romantic sacrificial gesture.

I took to hanging around in the entrance hall like a page boy in the hope of laying eyes on her. Even Hedda Adlon remarked on the similarity.

"I'm thinking of asking you to read Lorenz Adlon's rulebook for page boys," she joked.

"I read that. It'll never sell. For one thing, there are too many rules. And for another, most of these page boys are too busy running errands to have the time to read anything longer than *War and Peace*."

She laughed at that. Hedda Adlon usually liked my jokes. "It's not that long," she said.

"Try telling that to a page boy. Anyway, the jokes in *War and Peace* are better."

"Have you read it? *War and Peace?*"

"I've started it several times, but after four years of war I usually declare an armistice and then sell the book down the river."

"There's someone who'd like to meet you. And it so happens she's a writer."

Naturally, I knew exactly whom Hedda was talking about. Writers, especially lady writers from New York, were thin on the ground at the Adlon that month. It probably had a lot to do with the fifteen-mark-a-night room rate. This was slightly cheaper if you didn't have a bath, and a lot of writers don't, but the last American writer who'd stayed at the Adlon had been Sinclair Lewis, and that was in 1930. The Depression hit everyone, of course. But no one gets depressed quite like a writer.

We went upstairs to the little apartment the Adlons kept in the hotel. I say "little," but only by the standards of the large hunting estate they also kept in the countryside, away from Berlin. The apartment was nicely decorated—a fine example of late Wilhelmine wealth. The carpets were thick, the curtains heavy, the bronze hulking, the gilt abundant, and the silver solid; even the water in the carafe looked like it had extra lead in it.

Mrs. Charalambides was seated on a little birch-wood sofa with white cushions and a music-stand back. She was wearing a dark blue wraparound dress, a triple string of good pearls, diamond clip earrings, and immediately below her cleavage, a matching sapphire brooch that must have fallen off a maharajah's best turban. She hardly looked like a writer—that is, unless she'd been a queen who'd given up her throne to write novels about the grand hotels of Europe. She spoke German well, which was fine with me since, for several minutes after shaking her gloved hand, I could hardly speak German myself and I was more or less obliged to let these two women talk across me like a Ping-Pong table.

"Mrs. Charalambides—"

"Noreen, please."

"Is a playwright and journalist."

"Freelance."

"For the *Herald Tribune*."

"In New York."

"She's just returned from Moscow, where one of her plays—"

"My only play, so far."

"Was being produced by the famous Moscow Art Theater, after a very successful run on Broadway."

"You should be my agent, Hedda."

"Noreen and I were at school together. In America."

"Hedda used to help me with my German. Still does."

"Your German is perfect, Noreen. Don't you agree, Herr Gunther?"

"Yes. Perfect." But I was looking at Mrs. Charalambides' legs. And her eyes. And her beautiful mouth. Now, that was what I called perfect.

"Anyway, her newspaper has asked her to write an article about the forthcoming Berlin Olympiad."

"There's been a lot of opposition in America to the idea of our taking part in these Olympics, given your government's racial policies. The AOC president, Avery Brundage, was over here in Germany just a few weeks ago. On a fact-finding mission. To see if Jews are being discriminated against. And, incredibly, he reported back to the AOC that they were not. As a result of which the AOC has now voted, unanimously, to accept Germany's invitation and to attend the Berlin Olympiad in 1936."

"Any Olympiad that doesn't include the United States," said Hedda, "would be completely meaningless."

"Exactly," said Mrs. Charalambides. "Since the AOC president returned to the U.S., the boycott movement has collapsed. But my newspaper is puzzled. No, it's astonished that Brundage could have arrived at the conclusions he did. The American ambassador, Mr. Dodd; the chief consul, Mr. Messersmith; and the vice consul, Mr. Geist, have all written to my government expressing their utter dismay at the president's report. And reminding it of their own report, sent to the State Department last year, which highlighted the systematic exclusion of Jews from German sports clubs. Brundage—"

"He's the president of the American Olympic Committee," said Hedda, interrupting, redundantly.

"He's a bigot," said Mrs. Charalambides, becoming angrier. "And an anti-Semite. You'd have to be, to ignore what's happening in this country. The many instances of open racial discrimination. The signs in the parks. In the public baths. The pogroms."

"Pogroms?" I frowned. "Surely that's an exaggeration. I haven't heard of any pogroms. This is Berlin, not Odessa."

"In July, four Jews were murdered by SS men, in Hirschberg."

"Hirschberg?" I sneered. "That's in Czechoslovakia. Or Poland. I forget which. It's troll country. Not Germany."

"It's the Sudetenland," said Mrs. Charalambides. "The people there are ethnic Germans."

"Well, don't tell Hitler," I said. "Or he'll want them back. Look, Mrs. Charalambides, I don't agree with what's happening in Germany. But is it really any worse than what's happening in your own country? The signs in the parks? In the public baths? The lynchings? And I hear it's not just Negroes who get strung up by white people. Mexicans and Italians also go carefully in certain parts of the United States. And I don't recall anyone suggesting a boycott of the Los Angeles Games, in 1932."

"You're well informed, Herr Gunther," she said. "And right, of course. As a matter of fact, I wrote an article about just such a lynching I saw in Georgia, in 1930. But I'm here and I'm Jewish, and my newspaper wants me to write about what's happening in this country, and that's what I intend to do."

"Well, good for you," I said. "I hope you can change the AOC's mind. I'd like to see the Nazis take a blow to their prestige. Especially now that we've started spending money on it. And I'd love it, of course, if that Austrian clown got some egg on his face. But I fail to see what any of this has to do with me. I'm a hotel detective, not a press attaché."

Hedda Adlon opened a silver cigarette box the size of a small mausoleum and pushed it toward me. There were English cigarettes on one side of the box and Turkish on the other. It looked like Gallipoli in there. I chose the winning side—at least in the Dardanelles—and let her light me. The cigarette, just like the service, was better than I was used to. I looked hopefully at the decanters on the sideboard, but Hedda Adlon didn't drink much herself and probably thought I felt the same way about the stuff. Apart from that, she was doing a fine job of making me look nice. After all, she'd had plenty of practice doing it.

"Herr Behlert told me what happened when you went to the Alex," said Hedda. "About that poor Jewish man and how the police are refusing to investigate his death. Because of his race."

"Mmm-hmm."

"Apparently you thought he might have been a boxer."

"Mmm-hmm." Neither of them was smoking. Not yet. Perhaps they hoped to make me light-headed. The Turkish cigarette in my mouth was strong enough, but I had the feeling I was going to need more than one to go along with whatever it was they wanted from me.

Noreen Charalambides said, "I was thinking that the dead man's story might be the basis of an interesting article in my newspaper. In the same way I wrote about that lynching in Georgia. It occurred to me that the dead man might have been murdered by the Nazis because he was Jewish. It also occurred to me that there might be an important sports angle that could tie his story in with the Olympics. Did you know that the German Boxing Federation was the first German sports organization to exclude Jews?"

"It doesn't surprise me. Boxing's always been an important sport to the Nazis."

"Oh? I didn't know that."

"Sure. The SA has been punching people in the face since before 1925. Those beer-hall brawlers always liked a good fight. Especially after Schmeling became world champion. Of course, when he went and lost the title to Max Baer, that didn't exactly do the cause of Jewish boxers in Germany any favors."

Mrs. Charalambides looked at me blankly. I guessed that her remark about the German Boxing Federation had probably emptied the spit bucket of what she knew about the sweet science.

"Max Baer is half Jewish," I explained.

"Oh, I see. Herr Gunther, I'm sure you must have already considered the possibility that the dead man—let's call him Fritz—that Fritz was a member of a gym or a sporting association and was expelled because he was Jewish. Who knows what happened after that?"

I hadn't considered the possibility at all. I'd been too busy thinking about what might happen to me. But now that I did, what she said made some sense. Still, I wasn't about to admit that. Not yet. Not while these two wanted something from me.

"I was wondering," said Mrs. Charalambides. "I was wondering if you might care to help me find out some more about Fritz. Kind of like a private investigator. I speak pretty good German, as you can see, but I don't know my way around this city. Berlin is a bit of a mystery to me."

I shrugged. "If all the world is a stage, then most of Berlin is just beer and sausage."

"And the mustard? That's my problem. I'm afraid if I go around asking questions on my own, I'll run into a large dollop of Gestapo and get myself kicked out of Germany."

"There is that possibility."

"You see, I also plan to interview someone on the German Olympic Organizing Committee. Von Tschammer und Osten, Diem, or possibly Lewald. Did you know he's a Jew? I wouldn't like them to find out what I'm about until it's too late for them to stop me." She paused. "Naturally, I'd pay you. A fee for helping me."

I was about to remind them that I already had a job when Hedda Adlon took over the sales pitch.

"I'll clear it with my husband and with Herr Behlert," she said. "Herr Muller can cover for you."

"He resigned," I said. "But there's a fellow in the juvenile section at the Alex who can probably use the overtime. Name of Stahlecker. I've been meaning to give him a call."

"Please do." Hedda nodded. "I'd count it as a personal favor, Herr Gunther," she said. "I don't want Mrs. Charalambides to come to any harm, and it seems to me that having you alongside her is the best way of ensuring her safety."

I toyed with the idea of suggesting her safety might be better enhanced by forgetting the whole idea; but the prospect of spending time with Noreen Charalambides was not an unattractive one. I'd seen comet tails that were less attractive.

"She's determined to do this, regardless of what you decide," added Hedda, reading half of my mind. "So don't waste your breath, Herr

Gunther. I've already tried to dissuade her. But she's always been a stubborn woman."

Mrs. Charalambides smiled.

"You can borrow my car, of course."

It was clear they had the whole thing worked out between them and all I had to do was go along with it. I wanted to ask about the fee, but neither of them seemed inclined to return to the subject. That's the thing about people with money. It's only the absence of money that ever makes it seem relevant. Like having a sable coat. The sable probably paid no attention to it until the day it wasn't there.

"Of course. I'd be delighted to help in any way I can, Frau Adlon. If that's what you want."

I kept my eyes on my employer while I said this. I didn't want Hedda thinking that my delight in her friend's glamorous company might be anything other than rhetorical. Not when her friend was so very beautiful. Not when my own excitement at the proximity of her person seemed to me so very obvious. I felt like a porcupine in a room full of toy balloons.

Mrs. Charalambides crossed her legs, and it was like someone striking a match. To hell with the Gestapo, I thought, it's me, Gunther, she needs protection from. It's me who wants to strip her naked and to stand her in front of me and then think of some extra things she can do with her sweet behind than only sitting on it. Just the idea of being alone in a car with her put me in mind of a novice father confessor in a convent populated with nuns who were ex–chorus girls. Mentally I slapped myself across the mouth a couple of times and then once more to make sure I really got the message.

This woman is not for the likes of you, Gunther, I told myself. You're not even going to dream about her. She's a married woman and she's your employer's oldest friend, and you're going to sleep with Hermann Goering before you lay a finger on her.

Of course, as Samuel Johnson reminds us, sex is usually what happens when you're busy resurfacing the autobahn with good intentions. Perhaps it loses something in the translation. But it was true enough in my case.

14

HEDDA ADLON'S CAR was a Mercedes SSK—the type of car I never expected ever to drive. K stood for "short," but with its enormous fenders and six external cylinders, the white sports car looked about as short as a castle drawbridge and was just as hard to handle. Like any other car, it had four tires and a steering wheel, but there the similarity ended. Starting the supercharged seven-liter engine was like turning the prop for Manfred von Richthofen, and only the addition of twin 7.92-millimeter machine guns could have made it any louder. The car drew attention like a spotlight in a colony of stage-struck moths. Undeniably it was exhilarating to drive the car—I gained a new admiration for Hedda's abilities behind the wheel, to say nothing of her husband's willingness to indulge his younger wife with expensive toys—but it was of less use for private investigation work than a pantomime horse. At least a pantomime horse would have provided two people with a sort of anonymity. And I might have appreciated the intimate practicalities of bringing up the rear behind Mrs. Charalambides.

We used the car for a day and then gave it back, and thereafter borrowed Herr Behlert's rather more discreet W.

Berlin's wide roads were almost as busy as the sidewalks. Trams rattled up the center, their steady clockwork progress invigilated by white-sleeved traffic policemen who prevented cars and taxis from cutting in front of them like so many potbellied linesmen in a metropolitan football match. With the traffic cops' whistles, the car Klaxons, and the bus horns, the road system was almost as noisy as a football match, too, and the way Berliners drove, you might have believed they thought someone stood a good chance of winning. Things looked calmer inside the trams: sober-suited clerks faced men in uniform like two delegations signing a peace treaty in a French siding. But the injustices of the armistice and the Depression already seemed a long way behind us. The city's famous air was thick with the smell of gasoline and the smell of blooms from the baskets of the many flower women, not to mention a growing self-confidence. Germans were good about themselves again; at least those of us who were properly, noticeably German. Like the eagle on the Kaiser's helmet.

"Do you ever think of yourself as Aryan?" Mrs. Charalambides asked me. "As more German than the Jews?"

I hardly wanted to tell her about my Aryan transfusion. For one thing, I hardly knew her; for another, it seemed rather a shameful thing to tell someone who, as far as I was aware, was one hundred percent Jewish. So I shrugged and said, "A German is a man who can feel enormously proud of being a German while wearing a pair of tight leather shorts. In other words, the whole idea is ridiculous. Does that answer your question?"

She smiled. "Hedda said you had to leave the police because you were a well-known Social Democrat."

"I don't know about well known. If I had been well known, things would be different for me now, I guess. These days you recognize a man who was a prominent Social Democrat by the arrows on his pajamas."

"Do you miss being a policeman?"

I shook my head.

"But you were a policeman for more than ten years. Did you always want to be a policeman?"

"Maybe. I don't know. When I was a little boy I used to play cops and robbers on the green outside our apartment building, and I wasn't sure which I enjoyed being most: a cop or a robber. Anyway, I told my father that when I grew up I was probably going to be a cop or a robber, and he said, 'Why not be like most cops and do both?'" I grinned. "He was a respectable man, but he didn't much like the police. No one did. I wouldn't say we lived in a tough neighborhood, but when I was growing up we still called a story with a happy ending an alibi."

FOR SEVERAL DAYS WE DOODLED our way across a street map of Berlin with me telling her jokes and keeping her amused while we went visiting the city's gyms and sporting clubs, and I showed around the photograph of "Fritz" from the police file Richard Bömer had left with me. It's true Fritz wasn't looking his best, on account of the fact that he was dead, but no one seemed to recognize him. Maybe they didn't at that, but it was hard to tell, given their greater interest in Mrs. Charalambides. A well-dressed, beautiful woman visiting a Berlin gym wasn't unheard of, but it was unusual. I tried to tell her that I might get more out of the men in these places if she stayed in the car, but she wasn't having it. Mrs. Charalambides wasn't the kind of woman you told to do anything very much.

"If I do what you say," she said, "how am I going to get my story?"

I might have agreed with her except for the fact that it was always the same three-word story we came upon: NO JEWS ALLOWED. I felt sorry for Mrs. Charalambides seeing that kind of thing whenever we went inside a gym. She didn't show it, but I guessed it might be upsetting for her.

The T-gym was the last place on my list. With the benefit of hindsight it ought to have been the first.

In the heart of West Berlin, just south of the Zoological Garden Station, is the Kaiser Wilhelm Memorial Church. With its many spires of differing heights, it looks more like the castle of the Swan Knight Lohengrin than any place of religious worship. Grouped around the church were cinemas, dance halls, cabarets, restaurants, smart shops, and, at the western end of the Tauentzienstrasse, sandwiched between a cheap hotel and the Kaufhaus des Westens, was the T-gym.

I parked the car, got Mrs. Charalambides out, and then turned to gaze in the KaDeWe's shop window. "This is a pretty good department store," I said.

"No."

"Oh, it is. The restaurant's good, too."

"I mean, no, I'm not going shopping while you go in that gym."

"How about you go in the gym and I go shopping? There's a mark on this tie I'm wearing."

"Then you'd hardly be doing your job. You don't know much about women if you think I'm not coming into the gym with you."

"Who said I know anything about women?" I shrugged. "The one thing I know for sure about women is that they walk along the street with their arms folded. Men don't do that. Not unless they're queer."

"You wouldn't be doing your job, and I wouldn't pay you. How about that?"

"I'm glad you mentioned that, Mrs. Charalambides. How much are you paying me? We never actually agreed on a fee."

"Tell me what you think would be fair."

"That's a difficult one. I've not had much practice at being fair. Fair's a word I use for what's on a barometer or perhaps to describe a maiden who's in distress."

"Why don't you think of me like that and then suggest a price."

"Because if I ever did think of you like that, then I'd have to charge you nothing at all. I don't recall Lohengrin asking Elsa for ten marks a day."

"Maybe he should have done. Then he might not have left her."

"True."

"Well, then, ten marks a day plus expenses it shall be."

She smiled, enough to let me know that her dentist loved her, and then took my arm. She could have taken the other one to match, and I wouldn't have objected. Not that ten marks a day had anything to do with it. Just being near enough to smell her and get the odd snapshot of her garters when she climbed out of Behlert's car was payment enough. We turned away from the department-store window and went along to the T-gym door.

"The place is owned by an ex-boxer called the Terrible Turk. People call him the Turk for short and because they don't want to hurt his feelings. He hurts people who hurt his feelings. I never used to come to this place very much because it was the kind of gym that was more popular with businessmen and actors than with Berlin's rings."

"Rings? What are they?"

"Nothing to do with the Olympics, that's for sure. The rings are what we Berliners call the criminal fraternities that more or less used to run this city during the Weimar Republic. There were three main rings: the Big, the Free, and the Free Alliance. All of them were officially registered as benevolent societies or sports clubs. Some of them were registered as gyms, and everyone used to pay them tribute: doormen, bootblacks, prostitutes, toilet attendants, newspaper vendors, flower sellers, you name it. All of it backed up by muscle from a gym. The rings still exist, but they themselves have to pay up now to a new gang in town. A gang with more muscle than anyone. The Nazis."

Mrs. Charalambides smiled and tightened her grip on my arm, which was the first time I realized her eyes were as blue as an ultramarine panel in an illuminated manuscript, and just as eloquent. She liked me. That much was obvious.

"How have you stayed out of prison?" she asked.

"By not being honest," I said, and pushed open the T-gym's door.

I never yet walked through the door of a boxing gym that didn't remind me of the Depression. Mostly it was the smell, and a fresh coat of puke-green paint, and a grimy open window did nothing to hide that. Like every other gym we'd been inside that week, the T-gym smelled of physical hardship, of high hopes and low disappointments, of urine and cheap soap and disinfectant, and above all of sweat. Sweat on the ropes and on the hand wraps; sweat on the heavy bags and on the focus mitts; sweat on the towels and on the head protectors. A valley-shaped stain on a boxing poster for a forthcoming fight at the Bock Brewery might have been sweat, too, but rising damp looked a better bet than any of the muscle-bound prospects who were sparring or working high-speed bags. In the main ring, a man with a face like a medicine ball was washing some blood off the canvas floor. In a little office, in front of an open door, a Neanderthal type who might have been a cornerman was showing a fellow troglodyte how to use a bruising iron. Blood and iron. Bismarck would have loved the place.

Two new things about the T-gym since I was last there were signs on the wall next to the poster. One read: UNDER NEW MANAGEMENT; the other: GERMANS! DEFEND YOURSELVES. JEWS NOT WELCOME.

"That would seem to cover pretty much everything," I said, looking at the signs.

"I thought you said this place was owned by a Turk," she said.

"No, he just called himself a Turk. He's German."

"Correction," said a man walking toward me. "He's a Jew." The man was the Neanderthal I'd seen before—a little shorter than I had supposed but as broad as a farm gate. He was wearing a white roll-neck, white gym slacks, and white gym shoes, but his eyes were small and as black as two lumps of coal. He looked like a medium-sized polar bear.

"That explains the sign, I suppose," I said to nobody in particular. And then, to the nobody in the roll-neck, "Hey, Primo, did the Turk sell the place, or did someone just steal it off him?"

"I'm the new owner," said the man, lifting his belly into his chest and poking a jaw as big as a toilet seat toward me.

"Well, I guess you answered my question, Primo."

"I didn't catch your name."

"Gunther, Bernhard Gunther. And this is my aunt Hilda."

"Are you a friend of Solly Mayer's?"

"Who?"

"I guess you answered my question. Solly Mayer was the Turk's real name."

"I was hoping he could help me to identify someone, that's all. Someone who used to be a fighter, like the Turk. I've got a photograph here." I took the picture of Fritz out of the file and showed it to the roll-neck. "Maybe you'd care to take a look at it yourself, Primo."

To give him credit, he looked at the photograph as if he really was trying to help.

"I know, he's not looking his best. When this was taken, he'd spent several days floating in the canal."

"Are you a cop?"

"Private."

Still looking at the picture, he started to shake his head.

"Are you sure? We think he might have been a Jewish fighter."

He handed the picture back immediately. "Floating in the canal, you say?"

"That's right. Aged about thirty."

"Forget it. If your floater was a Jew, then I'm glad he's dead. That sign on the wall isn't for show, you know, snooper."

"No? It'd be a strange kind of sign that isn't for show, don't you think?"

I slipped the picture back in the file and handed it to Mrs. Charalambides, just in case. Roll-neck had the look of a man who was building up steam to hit someone, and that someone was me.

"We don't like Jews, and we don't like the kind of people who would waste other people's time looking for them. And, by the way, I don't like you calling me Primo, neither."

I grinned back at him and then at Mrs. Charalambides. "I'll lay you good money that the president of the AOC never came in this dump," I said.

"Is he another dirty Jew?"

"I think we'd better leave," said Mrs. Charalambides.

"Maybe you're right," I said. "It does smell kind of bad in here."

The next second, he took a swing at me with his right, but I was ready for it, and his scarred fist whistled past the tip of my ear like a Hitler salute gone awry. He ought to have used the jab first—tested me out with it before throwing the kitchen sink my way. Now I knew everything there was to know about him—as a fighter, anyway. The man was made for the corner, not the ring. When I'd been a criminal commissar, I'd had a sergeant who was quite an accomplished pugilist, and he'd taught me one or two things. Enough to stay out of harm's way. Half of winning any fight is not getting hit. The punch that had put August Krichbaum on a slab had been a lucky punch; or an unlucky one, depending on the way you looked at it. For that reason I hoped I could avoid hitting this man harder than he probably needed to be hit. He swung again and missed again. So far I was doing just fine.

Meanwhile, Mrs. Charalambides had the good sense to take several steps back and look embarrassed. That was how it seemed to me, anyway.

His third punch connected, but only just, like a flat stone landing on the surface of a lake. At the same time, he growled something that sounded like "Jew lover," and for a moment I thought he might actually be right. I was damned if Mrs. Charalambides wasn't very lovable indeed. And it angered me that she should have to witness this close-up display of rabid anti-Semitism.

I was also feeling a certain obligation to the small crowd that had stopped what they were doing in the gym to see what happened next. So I let go with a left jab to Primo's nose. It brought him up short, as if he'd found a scorpion in his nightshirt pocket. A second demoralizing jab and then a third rocked his head on his shoulders like an old teddy bear's.

By now there was blood on his face where his nose had been, and, seeing my client head for the door, I resolved to roll the credits, and I hit him just a little too hard with my right. Too hard for my fist, that is. Even as Primo was going down like a telegraph pole, I was shaking my hand. It already showed a degree of swelling. Meanwhile, something hit the floor of the gym like a coconut falling off a docker's hoist—his head, probably—and the fight, such as it was, had ended.

For a moment I stood over my latest victim like the Colossus at Rhodes, but I might as easily have looked like the outsized doorman at the Rio Rita bar down the street. There was a short murmur of approval, not for my triumph, but for the delivery of a well-executed hook, and, still flexing my hand, I knelt down anxiously to see what damage I had caused. Another man got there before me. It was the man with the face like a medicine ball.

"Is he all right?" I asked, genuinely concerned.

"He'll be fine," was the reply. "You just knocked some sense into him, that's all. Give him a couple of minutes, he'll be telling us all how you caught him with a lucky one."

He took hold of my hand and looked at it.

"Sure, it's some ice you'll be needing on that handle, and no mistake. Here. Come with me. But make it quick. Before that idiot comes around. Frankel's the boss here."

I followed my Samaritan into a small kitchen, where he opened a refrigerator and then handed me a canvas bag full of ice cubes.

"Keep your hand in there for as long as you can bear it," he ordered.

"Thanks." I put my hand in the bag.

He shook his head. "You were looking for the Turk, you said."

I nodded.

"He's not in any trouble, is he?" In the corner of his mouth was a ten-pfennig Lilliput, which he now removed and inspected critically.

"Not from me. I just wanted him to look at a picture and see if he recognizes the guy."

"Yeah. I saw the mug. Familiar. But I couldn't fix him." He thumped the side of his head as if trying to dislodge something. "I'm a bit punchy these days. Memory's all screwed up. Solly's your man for the memory. He used to know every fighter that ever put on a pair of German gloves, and plenty others besides. It was a shame what happened here. When the Nazis announced that new law of theirs, forbidding Jews from all sporting clubs, Solly had no choice but to sell. And because he had to sell, he had to take what he was offered by that bastard Frankel. Which wasn't even enough to cover what he owed the bank. These days he doesn't have a pot to piss in."

Finally I could bear the cold no longer and withdrew my hand from the bag of ice.

"How's the hand?" He put the cigar back in his mouth and took a look.

"Still swollen," I said. "With pride, probably. I hit him harder than I should have done. At least that's what this hand says."

"Nonsense. You hardly hit him at all. Big fellow like you. If you'd put your shoulder into it, you could have broke his jaw, maybe. But relax, he had it coming. Only no one thought it would be gift-wrapped so neatly. A real sweet punch, that's what it was you dropped him with, my friend. You should take it up. The fight game, I mean. Fellow like you could make a real go of it. With the right trainer, of course. Me, perhaps. You might even make some money doing it."

"Thanks, but no, thanks. Making money might take away the fun of it. I'm strictly an amateur when it comes to hitting people, and that's the way I want it to stay. Besides, while the Nazis are around, I'll always be second best."

"Got that right." He grinned. "It doesn't look broken. Might feel sore for a couple of days, though." He gave me my hand back.

"Where does Solly live these days?"

The man looked sheepish. "It used to be here. In a couple of rooms above the gym. But when he lost this place, he lost his home as well. The last I heard of the Turk, he was living in a tent in the Grunewald Forest, along with some other Jews who've lost out under the Nazis. But that was six, maybe nine months ago, so he might not still be there." He shrugged. "Then again, where else can he go? It's not like there's any Jewish welfare agency in this country, is there? And these days the Salvation Army's almost as bad as the SA."

I nodded and handed back the ice bag. "Thanks, mister."

"Give him my regards if you see him. The name's Buckow. Like the town, but uglier."

15

I FOUND MRS. CHARALAMBIDES STANDING in front of the KaDeWe, staring intently at a new Bosch gas-engine washing machine with a built-in wringer-roller. She wasn't the kind of woman I could ever imagine using a washing machine. She probably thought it was a phonograph. It looked a lot like a phonograph.

"You know, when reason fails, a fist comes in very handy," I said.

She met the reflection of my eyes in the window glass for a moment and then stared some more at the washing machine.

"Maybe we should buy it so that fellow in the gym can wash his mouth," I offered feebly.

Her mouth stayed tight, as if she were trying not to spill what was really on her mind. I turned my back on the window, lit a cigarette, and stared across Wittenbergplatz.

"This used to be a civilized place, where people always behaved with courtesy and politeness. Well, most of the time. But it's people like him who make me remember that Berlin is just an idea that a Polabian Slav had in a swamp."

I snatched the cigarette from my mouth and stared up at the blue sky. It was a beautiful day. "Hard to believe on a day like this. Goethe had his own theory about why the sky is blue. He didn't believe in Newton's idea that light is a mixture of colors. Goethe thought it was something to do with the interaction of white light and its opposite: darkness." I puffed hard for a moment. "Plenty of darkness in Germany, eh? Maybe that's why the sky is so blue. Maybe that's why they call this Hitler weather. Because it contains so much darkness."

I laughed at my own idea. But I was babbling.

"You know, you really should see the Grunewald Forest at this time of year. In the autumn, it's very beautiful. I thought we might take a drive out there now. As it happens, I also think it would be very useful for your newspaper story. Apparently the Turk is living there now. In a tent. Like a lot of other Jews, it seems. Either they're just hardened naturalists or the Nazis are planning to build another ghetto. Maybe both. Tell you what. If you're willing to try naturalism for a while, then so am I."

"Do you have to make a joke about everything, Herr Gunther?"

I threw away the cigarette. "Only the things that really aren't very funny, Mrs. Charalambides. Unfortunately, that's pretty much every-thing these days. You see, I'm worried that if I don't make jokes, then someone will mistake me for a Nazi. I mean, have you ever heard Hitler tell a joke? No, neither have I. Maybe I'd like him better if he did."

She continued staring at the washing machine. It seemed she wasn't ready to smile yet. She said, "You provoked him." She shook her head. "I don't like fighting, Herr Gunther. I'm a pacifist."

"This is Germany, Mrs. Charalambides. Fighting is our favorite means of diplomacy, everyone knows that. But as it happens, I'm a pacifist, too. As a matter of fact, I was trying to turn the other cheek to that fellow, just like it says in the Bible, and, well, you saw what happened. I did it twice before he actually managed to put a hand on me. After that I had no choice. According to the Bible, anyway. Render unto Caesar that which is Caesar's. That's another thing it says. So I did. I rendered him. Unconscious. Hell, no one likes violence less than I do."

She tried to keep her mouth steady, but it wasn't working now.

"Besides," I added, "you can't tell me that you didn't want to hit him yourself."

She laughed. "Well, all right, I did. He was a bastard, and I'm glad you hit him. All right? But isn't it dangerous? I mean, you could get into trouble. I wouldn't want to get you into any trouble."

"I certainly don't need your help for that, Mrs. Charalambides. I can manage it quite well on my own."

"I'll bet you can."

She smiled properly and took my injured hand. It wasn't exactly tiny, but it was still frozen.

"You're cold," she said.

"You should see the other fellow."

"I'd rather see the Grunewald."

"It'll be my pleasure, Mrs. Charalambides."

We got back into the car and drove west along the Kurfürstendamm.

"Mr. Charalambides . . ." I said, after a minute or two.

"Is a Greek American and a famous writer. Much more famous than I am. At least in America. Not so much here. He's a far better writer than I am. At least that's what he tells me."

"Tell me about him."

"Nick? When you've said he's a writer, you've said all there is to know about him. Except maybe his politics. He's quite active in the American left. Right now he's in Hollywood, trying to write a script and hating every minute of it. It's not that he hates the movies or even the studios. It's just that he hates being away from New York. Which is where we met, about six years ago. Since then we've had three good years and three bad ones. A bit like Joseph's prophecy to Pharaoh, except that none of the good and the bad are consecutive. Right now we're going through one of the bad years. Nick drinks, you see."

"A man should have a hobby. Me, I like model train sets."

"It's more than a hobby, I'm afraid. Nick's made a whole career out of drinking. He even writes about it. He drinks for a year and then he gives up for a year. You'll think I'm exaggerating, probably, but I'm not. He can stop drinking on January the first and start again on New Year's Eve. Somehow he has the willpower to last for exactly three hundred sixty-five days doing one or the other."

"Why?"

"To prove he can do it. To make life more interesting. To be bloody-minded. Nick's a complicated man. There's never an easy explanation for anything he does. Least of all, the simple things in life."

"So now he's drinking."

"No. Now he's sober. That's what makes this a bad year. For one thing, I like a drink myself and I hate drinking alone. And for another, Nick's a pain in the ass when he's sober and perfectly charming when he's drunk. That's one of the reasons I came to Europe. To have a drink in peace. Right now I'm sick of him and I'm sick of myself. Do you ever get sick of yourself, Gunther?"

"Only when I look in the mirror. To be a policeman you need a good memory for a face—your own, most of all. The job changes you in ways you don't expect. After a while you can look in a mirror and see a man who looks no different from any of the scum you've put in jail. But lately I also get sick when I tell someone the story of my life."

At Halensee I turned south, onto Königsallee, and pointed north out of the window. "They're building the Olympic Stadium just up there," I said. "Beyond the S-Bahn railway to Pichelsberg. From here on in Berlin is just forest and little lakes and exclusive villa colonies. Your friends the Adlons used to have a place down here, but Hedda didn't like it, so they bought a place near Potsdam, in the village of Nedlitz. They use it as a weekend place for extra-special guests who want to escape the rigors of life at the Adlon. Not to mention their wives. Or their husbands."

"I suppose the price of employing a proper detective is his knowing everything there is to know about you," she said.

"Take my word for it. The price is a lot cheaper than that."

About eight kilometers southwest of Halensee Station I stopped in front of the prettily situated Hubertus Restaurant.

"Why are we stopping?"

"An early lunch and a little information. When I said the Turk was living in the Grunewald, I neglected to mention that the forest covers almost eight thousand acres. If we're ever going to find him, we're going to have to pick up some local knowledge."

The Hubertus was something out of a Lehar operetta: an ivy-clad, cozy villa with a garden where a crown prince and his young baroness might stop for a quick knuckle of veal on their way to some grand but doom-laden hunting lodge. Surrounded by a chorus of rather well-fed Berliners, we did our best to look like a leading man and his lady, and to hide our disappointment at our waiter's ignorance of the local area.

After lunch we drove farther to the south and west, and asked at a village shop on the Reitmeister See, then at the post office in Krumme Lanke, and finally at a garage in Paulsborn, where the attendant told us he'd heard of some people living in tents along the left bank of the Schlachtensee, in a place that could best be reached by water. So then we drove to Beelitzhof and hired a motorboat to continue our search.

"I've had a lovely day," she said as the boat cut through the chill Prussian blue waters. "Even if we don't find what we're looking for."

And then we did.

We saw their smoke first, rising above the thick coniferous trees like a pillar of cloud. It was a small village of army-surplus tents, about six or seven of them. During the Great Depression, a large tent shantytown for the poor and unemployed had been built rather nearer home, in the Tiergarten.

I cut the engine and we approached carefully. A small, ragged group of men, several of them obviously Jewish, came out of their shelters.

They were carrying clubs and slingshots. If I'd been alone, it's possible I might have met with a more hostile reception, but, seeing Mrs. Charalambides, they appeared to relax a little. You don't go looking for trouble wearing a set of pearls and a sable coat. I tied up the boat and helped her to step ashore.

"We're looking for Solly Mayer," she said, smiling pleasantly. "Do you know him?"

No one spoke.

"My married name is Noreen Charalambides," she said. "But my maiden name is Eisner. I'm Jewish. I'm telling you that so you can be sure we're not here to spy on you or to inform on you, or on Herr Mayer. I'm an American journalist and I'm in search of some information. We think Solly Mayer might be able to help us. So please don't be afraid. We mean you no harm."

"We're not afraid of you," said one of the men. He was tall and bearded. He wore a long black coat and a broad-brimmed black hat. Two long curls of hair were hanging off the sides of his forehead like lengths of seaweed. "We thought you might be Hitler Youth. There's a troop of them camped around here somewhere and they've been attacking us. For fun."

"That's terrible," said Mrs. Charalambides.

"Mostly we try to ignore it," said the Jew with the earlocks. "There's a limit to what the law allows us to do in the way of self-defense. But lately their attacks have been increasing in violence."

"We just want to live in peace," said another man.

I glanced around their encampment. Several rabbits hung off a pole next to a couple of fishing rods. A large kettle stood steaming on a metal grate laid over a fire. A line of washing was strung between two threadbare tents. With winter fast approaching I didn't give much for their survival chances. I felt cold and hungry just looking at them.

"I'm Solly Mayer."

He was tallish, with a short neck, and, like the rest of them, heavily sunburned from months of living in the open air. But I ought to have picked him out immediately. Most boxers have their noses broken horizontally, but the Turk's had been stitched vertically as well. It looked like a small pink upholstered cushion lying in the center of a wide expanse called his face. I could imagine a nose like that doing a lot of things. Ramming a Roman trireme. Breaking down a castle door. Finding a white truffle. But I couldn't imagine anyone breathing through it.

Mrs. Charalambides told him about the article she was planning to write and about her hope that the Americans might still boycott the Berlin Olympiad.

"You mean they haven't done that already?" said the tall man with the beard. "The Amis really mean to send a team?"

"I'm afraid so," said Mrs. Charalambides.

"Surely Roosevelt can't ignore what's happening here," said the tall man. "He's a Democrat. And what about all those Jews in New York? Surely they won't let him ignore it."

"I kind of think that's exactly what he wants to do at the moment," she said. "You see, among his opponents, his administration already has a reputation of being too friendly with American Jews. He probably imagines that it's better for him politically to have no position on the matter of whether or not the American team comes here in thirty-six. My newspaper would like to change that position. And so would I."

"And you think," said the Turk, "that writing an article about some dead Jewish boxer might help?"

"Yes. It think it might."

I handed the Turk the photograph of "Fritz." He settled a pair of glasses on what was laughingly called the bridge of his nose and, holding the photo at arm's length, stared at it critically.

"What did this fellow weigh?" he asked me.

"When they fished him out of the canal, about ninety kilos."

"So maybe he was about nine or ten kilos lighter when he was in training," said the Turk. "A middleweight. Or maybe a light heavyweight." He looked again and then smacked the picture with the back of his hand. "I dunno. After they've been in the ring for a while, a lot of these pugs start to look the same. What makes you think he was Jewish? To me he looks like a goy."

"He was circumcised," I said. "Oh, and by the way, he was a southpaw, too."

"I see." The Turk nodded. "Well, maybe, just maybe, it could be that this is a fellow by the name of Erich Seelig. A few years ago he was a light heavyweight champion, from Bromberg. If it is him, this is the Jew who beat some pretty good fighters like Rere de Vos, Walter Eggert, and Gypsy Trollmann."

"Gypsy Trollmann?"

"Yeah. You know him?"

"I've heard of him, of course," I said. "Who hasn't? Whatever happened to that guy?"

"He's the doorman at the Cockatoo, last I heard."

"And Seelig? What's his story?"

"We don't get the newspapers here, friend. Everything I know is months old. But what I heard was that some SA thugs turned up at his last fight. A title defense against Helmut Hartkopp, in Hamburg. They put the frighteners on him. Because he was Jewish. After that he disappears. Maybe he leaves the country. Maybe he stays and ends up in the canal. Who knows? Berlin is a long way from Hamburg. But not as far as Bromberg. That's in the Polish corridor, I think."

"Erich Seelig, you say."

"Maybe. I never had to look at no corpse before. Unless it was in the ring, of course. How'd you find me, anyway?"

"Fellow named Buckow at the T-gym. He said to say hello."

"Bucky? Yeah, he's all right, is Bucky."

I took out my wallet and thumbed a leaf at him, but he wouldn't take it, so I gave him all but one of my cigarettes, and Mrs. Charalambides did the same.

We were about to get back in the boat when something flew through the air and struck the man wearing the big hat. He dropped to one knee with one bloody hand pressed to his cheek.

"It's those little bastards again," spat the Turk.

In the distance, about thirty meters away, I saw a collection of khaki-clad youths now occupying a clearing in the forest. A stone flew through the air, narrowly missing Mrs. Charalambides.

"Yiddos," they chanted in a singsong sort of way. "Yidd-os!"

"I've had enough of this," said the Turk. "I'm going to sort those little bastards out."

"No," I said. "Don't. You'll only land yourself in trouble. Let me handle it."

"What can you do?" said Mrs. Charalambides.

"We'll see. Give me your room key."

"My room key? What for?"

"Just do it."

She opened an ostrich-leather bag and handed over the key. It was attached to a big brass oval fob. I threaded the key off the fob and handed it back. Then I turned and walked toward our attackers.

"Be careful," she said.

Another stone sailed over my head.

"Yidd-os! Yidd-os! Yidd-os!"

"That's enough," I shouted at them. "The next boy who throws a stone will be under arrest."

There were maybe twenty of them, aged between ten and sixteen. All blond, with young, hard faces and heads full of the nonsense they heard from Nazis like Richard Bömer. Germany's future was in their hands. And so were several large stones. When I was about ten meters away I flashed the key fob in the palm of my hand hoping that, from a distance, it might pass for a policeman's warrant disc. I heard one of them gasp, "He's a copper," and I smiled, realizing my trick had worked. They were just a bunch of kids, after all.

"That's right, I'm a policeman," I said, still holding the disc out. "Criminal Commissar Adlon, from the Westend Praesidium. And you can all count yourselves lucky that none of these other police officers you attacked are more seriously hurt."

"Police officers?"

"But they look like yids. Some of them do, anyway."

"What kind of cops go around dressed as yids?"

"Secret policemen, that's who," I said, and slapped the oldest-looking boy hard on his freckled cheek. He started to cry. "These are Gestapo officers on the lookout for a vicious killer who's been murdering boys in this forest. That's right. Boys like you. He cuts their throats and then dismembers their bodies. The only reason it hasn't been in the papers is that we don't want to cause a panic. And then you mugs come along and nearly blow the whole operation."

"You can't blame us, sir," said another boy. "They looked like yids."

I slapped him, too. I thought it best they formed an accurate impression of what the Gestapo was really like. That way Germany might have some kind of future, after all.

"Shut up," I snarled. "And don't speak unless you're spoken to. Got that?"

The members of the Hitler Youth troop nodded sullenly.

I took hold of one by his neckerchief.

"You, what have you got to say for yourself?"

"Sorry, sir."

"Sorry? You could have had that officer's eye out. I've a good mind to tell your fathers to leather the lot of you. Better still, I've a good mind to have you all arrested and thrown into a concentration camp. How would you like that, eh?"

"Please, sir. We didn't mean any harm."

I let the boy go. By now all of them were looking contrite. They were looking less like Hitler Youth and more like a group of schoolboys. I had them where I wanted them now. I might have been handling a squad back at the Alex. After all, cops do all the same stupid juvenile things that schoolboys do, except the homework.

"All right. We'll say no more about it this time. And that goes for you, too. Tell no one about this. No one. Do you hear? This is an undercover operation. And the next time you feel inclined to take the law into your own hands, don't. Not everyone who looks like a Jew really is a Jew. Remember that. Now go home before I change my mind and run you all in for assaulting a police officer. And remember what I said. There's a vicious murderer at work in these woods, so you'd best stay away from here until you read that he's been caught."

"Yes, sir."

"We'll do that, sir."

I walked back to the little group of tents on the edge of the lake. The light was beginning to fade. The bullfrogs were opening up shop. Fish were jumping in the water. One of the Jews was already casting a line at a widening ripple. The man with the hat wasn't badly injured. He was smoking one of my cigarettes to steady his nerves.

"What did you say to get rid of them?" asked the Turk.

"I told them all you were undercover cops," I said.

"And they believed you?" asked Mrs. Charalambides.

"Of course they believed me."

"But why?" she said. "It's such an obvious lie."

"And when did that ever stop the Nazis?" I nodded at the boat. "Get in," I told her. "We're leaving."

I fetched my last cigarette from behind my ear and lit it from a piece of firewood that the Turk brought to me. "I think they'll leave you alone," I told him. "I didn't exactly put the fear of God in them. Just the fear of the Gestapo. But to them that probably means more."

The Turk laughed. "Thanks, mister," he said, and shook my hand.

I untied the rope and climbed into the boat alongside Mrs. Chara-lambides. "That's one thing I've learned in the last few years," I said, starting the engine. "To lie like you mean it. As long as you can convince yourself of something first, no matter how outrageous, there's no telling what you can get away with these days."

"And I thought you had to be a Nazi to be that cynical," she said.

I think she meant it as a joke, but it didn't feel good hearing her say it. At the same time, I knew of course that she was right. I was a cynic. In my defense I might have told her I was an ex-cop and that being a cop is to know but one truth, which is that everything you're told is a lie, but that wouldn't have sounded good, either. She was right, and it was no good brushing it off with another cynical remark about how the Nazis probably put something in the water, like bromide, that made all of us Germans believe the worst about everyone. I was a cynic. Who wasn't that lived in Germany?

Not that I could have believed anything bad about Noreen Chara-lambides. And I certainly didn't want her to think anything bad about me. There wasn't a dog muzzle handy, so I folded one lip under another to keep my mouth under control for a while, and then pushed the throttle forward. It's one thing biting your enemies. It's quite another when it looks like you might bite your friends. To say nothing of the woman you are falling for.

16

WE RETURNED THE BOAT and got back into the car. We drove east, into Berlin, along streets full of silent people who probably wanted nothing to do with one another. It had never been a particularly friendly city. Berliners are not known for their great hospitality. But now it was like the town of Hamelin after the children had left. We still had the rats, of course.

Respectable men in well-brushed felt hats and cake-box collars were scurrying home after yet another day spent trying, respectably, to ignore the uniformed and licensed louts who persisted in resting their dirty boots on the country's best furniture. Bus conductors leaned precariously off their platforms so as to avoid any possibility of conversation with their passengers. These days nobody wanted to speak his mind. They didn't put that in Baedeker.

At the taxi rank on the corner of Leibnizstrasse, the cabbies were putting up their checkered hoods—a sure sign that the weather was getting cooler. It wasn't yet cold enough, however, to deter the trio of SA men bravely continuing with their vigilant boycott of a Jewish-owned jewelry store next to the synagogue on Fasanenstrasse.

Germans! Defend Yourselves! Don't Buy from Jews! Buy Only from German Shops!

With their brown leather boots, brown leather cross belts, and brown leather faces, and lit up by the green neon of the Kurfürstendamm, the three Nazis looked prehistoric, reptilian, dangerous, like a bask of hungry crocodiles that had escaped from the aquarium in the Zoological Gardens.

I felt vaguely cold-blooded myself. Like I needed a drink.

"Are you sulking?" she asked.

"Sulking?"

"As in silent protest."

"It's the only kind that's safe these days. Anyway, it's nothing a drink can't fix."

"I could use a drink myself."

"Only not at the Adlon, eh? Someone will ask me to do something if we go there." As we neared the junction with Joachimstaler Strasse, I pointed. "There. The Cockatoo Bar."

"Is that one of your regular haunts, Gunther?"

"No, but it's someone else's. Someone you should speak to for your article."

"Oh? Who?"

"Gypsy Trollmann."

"That's right, I remember. The Turk said he's the doorman at the Cockatoo, didn't he? And he's the one who fought Erich Seelig."

"The Turk didn't sound like he was one hundred percent positive that Seelig is our Fritz. So perhaps Trollmann can confirm it. When you spend time in the ring with a fellow who's trying to hit you, you probably get to know his face pretty well."

"Is he really a Gypsy, or is he just a Gypsy the way Solly Mayer is a Turk?"

"Unfortunately for Trollmann, he is the real thing. You see, it's not just the Jews the Nazis don't like. It's Gypsies, too. And pansies. And Jehovah's Witnesses. And communists, of course, we mustn't forget the Reds. So far the Reds have had it toughest of all. I mean, I haven't yet heard of anyone who's been executed for being Jewish."

I thought about repeating Otto Trettin's story about the falling ax at Plötzensee and rejected the idea. Since I was already going to have to tell her about Gypsy Trollmann, I figured one sad story was all she could handle that evening. Stories certainly didn't come any sadder than Gypsy Trollmann's.

WE WERE EARLIER than the main crowd at the Cockatoo, and this meant that "Rukelie," as Trollmann was known to those working at the club, hadn't yet arrived. No one causes trouble at seven o'clock in the evening. Not even me.

Some parts of the Cockatoo were done up to look like a bar in French Polynesia, but for the most part it was velvet bucket chairs, flock wallpaper, and red lights, like any other place in Berlin. The blue-and-gold bar was said to be the longest in the city, but clearly only by those who didn't own a measuring tape or thought that it was a long way to Tipperary. The ceiling looked as if it had been iced like a wedding cake. There were a dull cabaret, a dance floor, and a small orchestra that managed to dance around the Nazi disapproval of decadent music by playing jazz as if it had been invented not by black men, but by a church organist from Brandenburg. With nude dancing girls now strictly forbidden in all clubs, the Cockatoo's gimmick was to have a parrot perched on every table. This only served to remind everyone of another great advantage of having dancing girls: they didn't shit on your dinner plate. Not unless they were Anita Berber, anyway.

While I drank schnapps, Mrs. Charalambides sipped martinis like a geisha drinking tea and with as little obvious effect, and I quickly formed the impression that it wasn't just a talent for writing she shared with her husband. The woman managed her drink the way the gods could handle their daily dose of ambrosia.

"So, tell me about Gypsy Trollmann," she said, taking out her reporter's notebook and pencil.

"Unlike the Turk, who's no more Turkish than I am, Trollmann is a real Gypsy. A Sinti. That's like a subset of Roma, only don't ask me to explain how, because I'm not Bruno Malinowski. When we were still a republic, the papers all made quite a thing out of Trollmann being a gyppo, and because he was also good-looking, not to mention an excellent fighter, it wasn't long before he was doing great. Promoters couldn't get enough of the kid." I shrugged. "I don't suppose he's older than about twenty-seven even now. Anyway, by the middle of last year he was ready for a shot at the German light heavyweight title, and there being no other obvious candidates, he was matched against Adolf Witt for the vacant belt, here in Berlin.

"Of course, the Nazis were hoping that Aryan superiority would win out and that Witt would beat his racially inferior opponent to a pulp. That was one of the reasons they let him fight in the first place. Not that this stopped them from trying to fix the judges, of course, only they hadn't counted on the crowd, who were so impressed by Trollmann's heart and completely dominant display that there was a riot when the judges gave the fight to Witt, and the authorities were obliged to declare Trollmann the winner, after all. The kid wept for joy. Unfortunately, his happiness was short-lived.

"Six days later the German Boxing Federation stripped the kid of the title and his license on the grounds that his style of hit-and-run boxing, and his 'unmanly' tears, made him unfit to hold the belt."

By now her neat shorthand covered several pages of her notebook. She sipped her drink and shook her head. "They took it off him because he cried?"

"It gets worse," I said. "This is a very German story. As you might expect, the kid gets death threats. Poison-pen letters. Shit in his mailbox. You name it. His wife and kids are intimidated. It gets so bad he makes her ask him for a divorce and change her name so that she and the kids can live in peace. Because Trollmann's not beaten yet. He still thinks he can box his way out of trouble. Reluctantly, the German federation gives him a license to fight again on two conditions: One is that he gives up the hit-and-run style that made him such a great fighter—I mean he was fast, no one could lay a glove on him. And the other condition was that his first fight would be against a much heavier opponent, Gustav Eder."

"They wanted to see the kid humiliated," she said.

"They wanted to see the kid get killed is what," I said. "The two meet in July 1933, at the Bock Brewery, here in Berlin. In order to send up the new racial restrictions, Trollmann turns up for the fight looking like a caricature of an Aryan man, with his body whitened with flour and his hair dyed blond."

"Oh, Lord. You mean like some poor Negro trying to disguise himself in order to escape a lynching?"

"Kind of, I suppose. Anyway, the fight takes place, and forced to abandon the style that had made him a champion, Trollmann stands toe-to-toe with Eder and trades the heavier man punch for punch. He takes a terrible beating until, in round five, he's battered into submission and loses the fight on a knockout. After which he's never the same fighter again. Last I heard, he was taking monthly fights against bigger, stronger fellows and taking regular beatings just to make the payments to his wife."

She shook her head. "It's a modern Greek tragedy," she said.

"If you mean that there are not many laughs in it, then you're right. And for sure, the gods deserve a kick in the ass, or worse, for letting shit like that happen to someone."

"From what I've seen so far, they've got their work cut out in Germany."

"Isn't that the point? If they're not there for us now, then maybe they're just not there at all."

"I don't believe that, Bernie," she said. "It's bad for a playwright to believe that man is all there is. No one wants to go to a theater to be told that. Especially now. Maybe now most of all."

"Could be I should start going to the theater again," I said. "Who knows, it might restore my faith in human nature. Then again, here comes Trollmann, so I'd best not build up my hopes."

Even as I spoke, I knew that if my faith in human nature had come with a bookmaker's ticket, then just laying eyes on Trollmann again would have had me tearing it into pieces. Gypsy Trollmann, once as handsome as any leading man, was now the caricature of a ring-damaged pug. It was like clapping eyes on Mr. Hyde immediately after a home visit from Dr. Jekyll, so grotesquely were his features coarsened by his many beatings. His nose, previously small and combative, was now the size and shape of a sandbag on a poorly built redoubt, and this seemed to have shifted his dark eyes to opposite sides of his head, like something bovine. His much-enlarged ears were entirely without con-tours and might have fallen onto his head from a pork butcher's bacon slicer. His mouth now seemed impossibly wide, and when he stretched his scarred lips into a smile to reveal several missing teeth, it was like sharing a joke with King Kong's little brother. The worst of it was his disposition, which was sunnier than a picture wall in a school kinder-garten, as if he hadn't a care in the world.

Trollmann picked up a seat as if it were a bread stick and put it down again with its back to our table.

We introduced ourselves. Mrs. Charalambides flashed him a smile that could have lit up a coal mine, and then fixed him with blue eyes a Persian cat would have envied. Trollmann kept on nodding and grin-ning, as if we were his oldest and dearest friends. Considering the way the world had treated him until now, perhaps we were.

"To tell the truth, I do remember you, Herr Gunther. You're a cop. Sure, I remember now."

"Never tell the truth to a policeman, Rukelie. That's how you get caught. It's true, I used to be a cop. Only not anymore. These days I'm the carpet creeper at the Adlon Hotel. It seems the Nazis don't like republican-minded cops any more than they like Gypsy fighters."

"Hey, you got that right, Herr Gunther. Sure, I remember you now. You came to see me fight. You was with another cop. A cop who could fight a bit, right?"

"Heinrich Grund."

"Sure, I remember him. He used to work out at the same gym as me. Right."

"We came to see you fight Paul Vogel, at the Sportpalast, here in Berlin."

"Vogel, yeah. I won that fight on points. He was a tough customer, was Paul Vogel." He looked at Mrs. Charalambides and shrugged apol-ogetically. "Looking at me now—it's hard to believe, ma'am, I know—but I used to win a lot of fights in those days. Now they just want to use me as a punching bag. You know, put me up in front of someone for target practice. I could beat some of these fellows, too. Only they won't let me fight my own way." He raised his fists and went through the motions of ducking and diving on the chair. "You know?"

She nodded and laid her hand on top of his welder's mitt.

"You're a pretty lady, ma'am. Isn't she pretty, Herr Gunther?"

"Thank you, Rukelie."

"That she is," I said.

"I used to know a lot of pretty ladies on account of how I was a good-looking guy for a fighter. Isn't that right, Herr Gunther?"

I nodded.

"None better."

"On account of the fact that I used to dance around so that none of these other fellows could land a glove on me. See, boxing's more than just hitting people. It's about not getting hit, too. But them Nazis don't want me to do that. They don't like my style." He sighed, and a tear appeared in the corner of his bovine eye. "Well, it's all over for me now as a professional fighter, I guess. I ain't fought since March. Six defeats in a row, I figure it's time to hang up the gloves."

"Why don't you leave Germany?" she asked. "If they won't let you fight your own way."

Trollmann shook his head. "How could I leave? My kids live here. And my ex-wife. I couldn't leave them behind. Besides, it takes money to set up in a new place. And I can't earn like I used to. So I work here. And sell fight tickets. Hey, you want to buy some? I got tickets for Emil Scholz against Adolf Witt at the Spichernsaele. November sixteenth. Should be a good fight."

She bought four. After her remarks outside the T-gym, I wasn't sure she actually wanted to see a fight, and I imagined it was her way of kindly putting some money in Trollmann's pocket.

"Here," she said, handing them to me. "You look after them."

"Do you remember fighting a fellow named Seelig?" I asked Trollmann. "Erich Seelig?"

"Sure, I remember Erich. I remember all my fights. It's all the boxing I got now. My memories. I fought Seelig in June 1932. And lost. On points, at the Brewery. Sure, I remember Seelig. How could I forget, right? He had a pretty rough time of it himself, did Erich. Just like me. On account of the fact that he's Jewish. The Nazis took his titles away, and his license. Last I heard, he fought Helmut Hartkopp in Hamburg and won on points. In February last year."

"What happened to him?" She offered him a cigarette, but he shook his head.

"I dunno. But he ain't fighting in Germany no more, that's for a hundred percent."

I showed Trollmann the picture of Fritz and told him the circumstances of the man's death. "Do you think perhaps this might be Erich Seelig?"

"This ain't Seelig," said Trollmann. "Seelig is younger than me. And younger than this guy was, for sure. Who told you this was Seelig?"

"The Turk."

"Solly Meyer? That explains it. The Turk is blind in one eye. Detached retina. You give him a chess set and he couldn't tell black from white. Don't get me wrong, the Turk is an okay guy. But he don't see so good no more."

The place was filling up now. Trollmann waved at a girl on the opposite side of the bar; for some reason she had pieces of silver paper in her hair. All sorts of people waved at Trollmann. Despite the best efforts of the Nazis to dehumanize him, he remained a popular man. Even the parrot on our table seemed to like Trollmann and let him smooth its gray feathered breast without trying to take a piece out of his finger.

Trollmann looked at the photograph again and nodded.

"I know this guy. And it ain't Trollmann. How'd you figure him for a fighter anyway?"

I told him about the healed fractures on the knuckles of the dead man's little fingers and the burn mark on his chest, and he nodded sagely.

"You're a clever man, Herr Gunther. And you were right. This guy is a pug. Name of Isaac Deutsch. A Jewish boxer, sure. You were right about that."

"Stop it," said Mrs. Charalambides. "You're going to make his head swell." But she was writing now. The pencil was moving across the page of her notebook with the sound of an urgent whisper.

Trollmann grinned but kept on talking. "Zak was in the same workers' sports club as me. The Sparta, back in Hannover. Poor old Zak. Somewhere at home I got me a photograph of all the fighters at the Sparta. The ones who were contenders, anyway. And Zak is standing right in front of me. Poor guy. He was a nice fellow and a pretty good fighter, with a lot of heart. We was never matched, though. I wouldn't have liked to have fought him. Not from fear, you understand, although he was plenty tough. But because he was a real nice fellow. His uncle, Joey, used to train him, and he looked like a prospect for the Olympics until he got kicked out of the federation and the Sparta." He sighed and shook his head again. "So poor old Zak's dead. That's sad."

"So he wasn't a professional fighter?" I said.

"What's the difference?" asked Mrs. Charalambides.

I groaned. But patiently, like he was talking to a little girl, Trollmann explained it to her. He had a good, kind way about him. Except for the memory of seeing him fight, I might have had a hard time believing he'd ever been a professional boxer.

"Zak, he wanted a medal before he turned professional," he said. "Might have won one, too, if he'd not been Jewish. Which makes it ironic, I suppose. If 'ironic' means what I think it means."

"What do you think it means?" she asked.

"Like when there's a difference between what is supposed to happen to a man and what actually happens to him."

"That covers it pretty well in this case," she agreed.

"Like the fact that Zak Deutsch couldn't box at the Olympics for Germany because he was a Jew. But he ended up being a construction worker at Pichelsberg, helping to build the new stadium. Even though he wasn't supposed to be working there. See, only Aryan Germans are allowed to get jobs on the Olympic construction site. That's what I heard, anyway. And that's what I meant about it being ironic, see? Because there are lots of Jews working at the Pichelsberg site. I was going to have to work there myself before I got this job. You see, there's so much pressure to get the stadium finished in time that they can't afford to turn any able-bodied man away. Be he Jew or Gentile. That's what I heard."

"This is beginning to make some sense," I said.

"You've got a strange idea of sense, Herr Gunther." Trollmann grinned his big, toothy grin. "Me, I think it's crazy."

"Me, too," murmured Mrs. Charalambides.

"What I meant was that I'm beginning to understand a few things," I said. "But you are right, too, Rukelie. It is crazy." I lit a cigarette. "During the war I saw a lot of stupid things. Men getting killed for no good reason. The sheer waste of life. And quite a bit of stupidity after the war, as well. But this business with the Jews and the Gypsies is just madness. How else can you explain the inexplicable?"

"I been giving this some thought," said Trollmann. "A lot of thought. And from what I seen in the fight game, the conclusion I come to is this: Sometimes, if you want to win a contest at all costs, it helps to hate the other guy." He shrugged. "Roma people. Jewish people. Homos and commies. The Nazis need someone to hate, that's all."

"I guess you're right," I said. "But it makes me worry if there's another war. I worry what will happen to all these poor bastards the Nazis don't like."

17

MOST OF THE WAY BACK to the Adlon, I was thinking about what we had learned. Gypsy Trollmann had promised to mail me the Sparta Club photograph, but I didn't doubt his identification of the dead man found floating in Mühlendamm Lock or his information about Isaac Deutsch's having been a construction worker on the Olympic Stadium site. Say one thing, do another, that was typical of the Nazis. All the same, Pichelsberg was a long way from Mühlendamm; the opposite end of the city. And nothing I had yet learned explained how Deutsch had drowned in salt water.

"You talk too much, Gunther."

"I was thinking, Mrs. Charalambides. What you must think of us? We seem to be the only people in the world who are actively trying to live up to everyone else's worst impression of us."

"Please call me Noreen. Charalambides is such a long name, even in Germany."

"I don't know if I can do that now that you're my employer. Ten marks a day demands a certain amount of professional courtesy."

"You can hardly go on calling me Mrs. Charalambides if you're going to kiss me."

"Am I going to kiss you?"

"This morning you mentioned something about Isaac Newton. Which certainly encourages me to think you are."

"Oh? How's that?"

"Newton came up with three laws to describe the relationships between two bodies. I'd say he might also have come up with a fourth if he'd ever met me and you, Gunther. You're going to kiss me, all right. There's absolutely no doubt about it."

"You mean there's algebra and stuff to prove it?"

"Pages of it. Impulse, unbalanced force, equal and opposite reaction. Between us, we've got almost enough equations to cover a bedsheet."

"Then I guess there's no point in my trying to resist the laws of planetary motion, Noreen."

"Absolutely none at all. In fact, it would be best if you gave in to the impulse right now, in case you put the whole damned universe out of joint."

I stopped the car, pulled on the hand brake, and leaned toward her. For a moment she turned away.

"Hermann-Goering-Strasse," she said. "Didn't it used to be called something else?"

"Budapester Strasse."

"That's better. I want to remember where it was you first kissed me. I don't want that memory to include Hermann Goering."

She turned toward me expectantly, and I kissed her hard. Her breath was charged with cigarettes and ice-cold liquor and lipstick and a little something special from inside her pants. She tasted better than lightly salted butter on freshly baked bread. I felt her eyelashes brush my cheeks like the wings of tiny hummingbirds, and after a minute or so she began to breathe like a medium who was trying to get in touch with the spirit world. Maybe she did at that. And, keen to possess her whole body, I pushed my left hand underneath her fur coat and let it slide awhile up and down her thigh and torso, as if I'd been trying to generate static electricity. Noreen Charalambides wasn't the only one who knew physics. There was a thud as her handbag slid off her lap and hit the floor of the car. I opened my eyes and drew away from her mouth.

"Gravity still works, then," I said. "The way my head feels, I was beginning to wonder. I guess Newton knew a thing or two, after all."

"He didn't know everything. I bet he didn't know how to kiss a girl like that."

"That's because he never met a girl such as you, Noreen. If he had, he might have done something useful with his life. Like this."

I kissed her again, only this time I put my whole back into it, like I really meant what I was doing. And maybe I did. A lot of time had passed since I'd felt this way about a woman. I glanced out of the window and, seeing the name of the street, I was reminded of what I had told myself the first time I'd talked to Noreen back in Hedda Adlon's apartment at the hotel: that Noreen was my employer's oldest friend, and that I was going to sleep with Hermann Goering before I ever laid a finger on her. The way things were going, it looked as if the Prussian prime minister was in for a Hermann-sized surprise.

Her tongue was in my mouth now, alongside my heart and the misgivings I kept trying to swallow. I was losing control, but mostly of my left hand, which was now under her dress and making itself familiar with her garter and the cool thigh it was stretched across. Only when the hand slipped into the secret space between her thighs did she move to arrest the wrist commanding it. I let her move my hand away and then brought my fingers up to my mouth and licked them.

"This hand. I don't know what gets into it sometimes."

"You're a man, Gunther. That's what gets into it." She took my fingers and brushed them with her lips. "I like you kissing me. You're a good kisser. If kissing was in the Olympics, you'd be a medal prospect. But I don't like to be hurried. I like to be walked around the ring for a while before being mounted. And don't even think of using the whip if you want to stay in the saddle. I'm the independent sort, Gunther. When I run it'll be because my eyes are open and because I want to. And I won't be wearing any blinkers if and when we reach the wire. I might not be wearing anything at all."

"Sure," I said. "I never figured you any other way. No blinkers. Not even a tongue strap. How do you feel about me giving you an apple sometimes?"

"I like apples," she said. "Just watch out you don't get your fingers bitten."

I let her bite me, hard. It was painful, but I enjoyed it. Pain from her felt good, like something primordial, something that was always meant to be. Besides, we both knew that when our clothes were lying on the floor beside our sweating, naked bodies, I was going to pay her back in kind. That's always how it is between a man and a woman. A man takes a woman. A woman gets taken. It isn't always marked by a due consideration of what is fair and decent and well mannered. Sometimes human nature can leave you looking just a little shamefaced.

I DROVE US BACK to the hotel and parked the car. As we went through the door and into the entrance hall, we met Max Reles, who was on his way out somewhere. He was accompanied by Gerhard Krempel and Dora Bauer, and they were all wearing evening clothes. Reles spoke to Noreen first and in English, which left me with the opportunity to say something to Dora.

"Good evening, Fräulein Bauer," I said politely.

"Herr Gunther."

"You look lovely."

"Thank you." She smiled warmly. "And I really mean that. I'm very grateful to you for helping me to get this job."

"It was my pleasure, Fräulein. Behlert tells me you're now working almost exclusively for Herr Reles."

"Max keeps me very busy, yes. I don't think I've ever done so much typing. Not even when I was at Odol. But right now, we're off to the opera."

"To see what?"

She smiled ingenuously. "I haven't the faintest idea. I don't know anything about opera."

"Me neither."

"I expect I shall hate it. But Max wants me to take some dictation during the interval."

"And what about you, Herr Krempel? What do you do during the interval? Murder a good tune? In the absence of anything else."

"Do I know you?" he asked, hardly looking at me. His whispered growl of a voice sounded as if it had been rubbed down with sandpaper and then marinated in burning kerosene.

"No, you don't. But I know you."

Krempel was tall, with flying-buttress shoulders and dead black eyes. Thick yellow hair grew on top of a head that was as big as a Galápagos tortoise and probably about as quick. His mouth resembled an ancient scar on a footballer's knees. Fingers like scrap-yard grapples were already bunching into fists the size of wrecking balls. He looked like a real thug's thug, and if the German Labor Front included a section for employees in the field of intimidation and coercion, then Gerhard Krempel might reasonably have expected to be elected as a workers' representative.

"You must be confusing me with someone else," he said, stifling a yawn.

"My mistake. I expect it's those evening clothes. I thought you were an SA bullyboy."

Max Reles must have caught that, because he scowled at me and then at Noreen.

"Is this dishwasher giving you any trouble?" he asked her, speaking German now for my benefit.

"No," she said. "Herr Gunther's been very helpful."

"Really?" Reles chuckled. "Must be his birthday or something. How about it, Gunther? Did you take a bath today?"

Krempel thought that was hilarious.

"Tell me, did you find my Chinese box yet? Or the girl who stole it?"

"The matter is in the hands of the police, sir. I'm sure they're doing all they can to bring it to a satisfactory conclusion."

"That's very reassuring. Tell me, Gunther, what kind of a cop were you, anyway, before you started peeping through hotel keyholes? You know, I'll bet you were one of those cops who wear that stupid leather helmet with the flat top. Is that because all of you kraut cops have flat heads or because some of you do a little moonlighting carrying trays of fish at Friedrichshain Market?"

"I think it's both," said Krempel.

"You know, in the States some people call coppers 'flatfoots' because a lot of them have flat feet," said Reles. "But I think I like 'flatheads' a whole lot better."

"We aim to please, sir," I said patiently. "Ladies. Gentlemen." As I turned to leave, I even tipped my hat. It seemed more diplomatic than punching Max Reles on the nose and a lot less likely to leave me without a job. "Enjoy your evening, Fräulein Bauer."

I strolled over behind the front desk where Franz Joseph, the concierge, was in conversation with Dajos Béla, the leader of the hotel orchestra. I checked my pigeonhole. I had two messages. One was from Emil Linthe informing me that his work was completed. The other message was from Otto Trettin, asking me to call him back, urgently. I picked up the phone and had the hotel operator connect me with the Alex and then with Otto, who often worked late, since he seldom worked early.

"So what's the story in Danzig?" I asked.

"Never mind that now," he said. "Remember that cop who got murdered? August Krichbaum?"

"Sure," I said, making a fist and biting my knuckles, calmly.

"The witness is an ex-cop. Seems like he reckons the killer is an ex-cop, too. He's been going through the police files and has got himself a short list of suspects."

"I heard that."

Otto paused for a moment. "You're on the list, Bernie."

"Me?" I said, as coolly as I was able. "How do you figure that?"

"Maybe you did it."

"Maybe I did. On the other hand, maybe it's a frame. Because I was a republican."

"Maybe," admitted Otto. "They've framed people for less."

"How long is the list?"

"I hear just ten men."

"I see. Well, thanks for the tip, Otto."

"I thought you'd want to know."

I lit a cigarette. "It happens I think I've got an alibi for when it happened. But I hardly want to use him. You see, it's the fellow on the Jew Desk at the Gestapo. The one who tipped me off about my grandmother. If I mention him, they'll want to know what I was doing at Gestapo House. And I might drop him in it."

A simple lie often saves a lot of time-consuming truth. I hardly wanted to put sand in Otto's eye bath, but I didn't seem to have much choice in the matter.

"Then it's fortunate you were with me at the time of Krichbaum's murder," said Otto. "Having a beer in the Zum. Remember?"

"Sure, I remember."

"We talked about you helping me with a chapter in my new book. A case you once worked on. Gormann the Strangler. You'd think I know all about it, the number of times you've bored me with that story."

"I'll remember that. Thanks, Otto."

I breathed a sigh of relief. Trettin's name and word still counted for something at the Alex. Half a sigh, anyway.

"By the way," he added. "Your Jewish stenographer, Ilse Szrajbman, had the guest's Chinese lacquer box, all right. She says she took it on an impulse because Reles behaved like a shit and refused to pay what he owed for her work."

"Knowing Reles, I can easily believe that." I tried to gather my trembling thoughts. "But why didn't she speak to the hotel manager about it? Why didn't she tell Herr Behlert?"

"She said it's not so easy for a Jew to complain about things. Or about a man who is as well connected as this Max Reles. She told the Danzig KRIPO that she was afraid of him."

"So afraid that she was prepared to steal from him?"

"Danzig is a long way from Berlin, Bernie. Besides, it was an impulse thing, like I said. And she regretted it."

"The Danzig KRIPO is being unusually sensitive about this, Otto. Why?"

"As a favor to me, not the Jewess. A lot of these local cops want to come and work crime in the big city, you know that. I'm a somebody to these morons. Anyway, I got the box back. And to be frank, I can't see what all the fuss was about. I've seen more obvious-looking antiques in Woolworth's. What do you want me to do with it?"

"Perhaps you could drop it by the hotel sometime. I'd rather not come by the Alex, unless I'm asked to. Last time I was there, your old pal Liebermann von Sonnenberg collared me for a favor."

"He told me."

"Although from the sound of things, it's me who might need to ask him for a favor."

"It's me you owe, not him, Bernie."

"I'll try to remember that. You know, Otto, there's a lot more to this thing with Max Reles than some stenographer trying to get even with her boss. Just a few weeks ago that Chinese box was in a museum here in Berlin. Next thing, Reles has the box and it's being used by him to bribe some Ami on their Olympic Committee with the full knowledge of the Ministry of the Interior."

"Please bear in mind I have sensitive ears, Bernie. There are things I want to know. But there are just as many things I don't want to know."

I put the phone down and looked at Franz Joseph. His real name was Gustav, but with his bald head and muttonchop whiskers, the Adlon concierge bore a marked resemblance to the old Austrian emperor Franz Joseph, and was so nicknamed by almost everyone in the hotel.

"Hey, Franz Joseph. Did you get Herr Reles tickets for the opera tonight?"

"Reles?"

"The American in suite 114."

"Yes. Alexander Kipnis is singing Gurnemanz in *Parsifal*. The tickets were hard to get, even for me. Kipnis is a Jew, you see. These days it's not often you can hear a Jew singing Wagner."

"I imagine Kipnis has one of the least disagreeable voices to be heard in German right now."

"They say Hitler doesn't approve."

"Where is this opera?"

"The German Opera House. On Bismarckstrasse."

"Can you remember the seat numbers? Only, I need to find Herr Reles and give him a message."

"The curtain goes up in an hour. He has a box on the grand tier, stage left."

"You make that sound like a big deal, Franz."

"It is. It's the same box Hitler has when he goes to the opera."

"But not tonight."

"Obviously."

I walked back into the entrance hall. Behlert was speaking to two men. I hadn't ever seen them before, but I knew they were cops. For a start there was Behlert's manner to identify them: he looked like he was speaking to two of the most interesting men in the world; and then there was theirs: they looked indifferent to almost everything he was saying, except the part about me. And I knew that much because Behlert pointed my way. Another reason I knew they were cops was their thick coats and their heavy boots and their body odor. During the winter, Berlin cops always dressed and smelled as if they were in the trenches. Backed by Behlert's rolling eyeballs, they came toward me, flashing their warrant discs and sizing me up with narrowed eyes—almost as if they hoped I was going to make their day and run for it; that way they could have had a little fun trying to shoot me. I could hardly blame them. A lot of Berlin crime gets cleaned up that way.

"Bernhard Gunther?"

"Yes."

"Inspectors Rust and Brandt, from the Alex."

"Sure, I remember. You two were the detectives Liebermann von Sonnenberg assigned to investigate the death of Herr Rubusch, in 210, weren't you? Say, what did he die of anyway? I never did find out."

"Cerebral aneurysm," said one.

"Aneurysm, eh? Never can tell with that kind of thing, can you? One minute you're hopping around like a flea, and the next you're lying on the floor of the trench looking up at the sky."

"We'd like to ask you a few questions down at the Alex."

"Sure."

I followed them outside into the cold night air.

"Is that what this is about?"

"You'll find out when we get to the Alex," said Rust.

BISMARCKSTRASSE WAS STILL CALLED BISMARCKSTRASSE and ran all the way from the western tip of the Tiergarten to the eastern edge of the Grunewald. The German Opera House, formerly called the Municipal Opera House, was about halfway along the street, on the north side, and was comparatively recent in its design and construction. Not that I'd ever really noticed it much before. At the end of a working day I need something a little less bogus than the sight of a lot of very fat people pretending to be heroes and heroines. My idea of a musical evening is the Kempinski Waterland Chorus: a revue of buxom girls in short skirts playing ukuleles and singing vulgar songs about Bavarian goatherds.

I was hardly in the mood for anything that took itself as seriously as opera in German, not after a couple of uncomfortable hours spent at the Alex waiting to be asked questions about the cop I had killed, and then for them to find Otto Trettin—he was in the Zum—and have him corroborate my story. When finally they let me go I wondered if that was the end of it. But somehow I suspected it was not, with the result that I hardly felt like celebrating. All in all it had been quite an experience, which is often the lesson you get from life when you need it least.

In spite of that, I was still keen to see who Max Reles might be sharing a box with. And arriving at the opera in time for the interval, I bought a standing pass that afforded me an excellent view of the stage and, more important, the occupants of Hitler's usual box on the grand tier. Before the lights went down I was even able to borrow a pair of opera glasses from a woman sitting close to where I was standing, so that I might take a closer look at them.

"He's not in the house tonight," said the woman observing where my attention was directed.

"Who?"

"The Leader."

That much was obvious. But it was clear that there were others in the box, guests of Max Reles, who were senior figures in the Nazi Party. One of these was a man in his late forties with silver hair and thick, dark eyebrows. He wore a brown, military-style tunic with several decorations, including an Iron Cross and a Nazi armband, a white shirt, a black tie, brown riding breeches, and leather jackboots.

I handed back the opera glasses. "I don't suppose you know who the party leader is?"

The woman peered through the glasses and then nodded. "That's Von Tschammer und Osten."

"The Reich sports leader?"

"Yes."

"And the general standing behind him?"

"Von Reichenau." She had answered without a moment's hesitation. "The bald one is Walther Funk, from the Propaganda Ministry."

"I'm impressed," I said, with genuine admiration.

The woman smiled. She wore spectacles. Not a beauty, but she looked intelligent in an attractive way. "It's my job to know who these people are," she explained. "I'm a photographic editor at the *Berlin Illustrated News*." Still scrutinizing the box, she shook her head. "I don't recognize the tall one, though. The one with the face like a blunt instrument. Or for that matter the rather attractive girl who seems to be with him. They seem to be the host and hostess, but either she's too young for him or he's too old for her. I'm not quite sure which it is."

"He's an American," I said. "His name is Max Reles. And the girl is his stenographer."

"You think so?"

I borrowed the opera glasses and looked again. I could see no sign that Dora Bauer was anything more to Reles than a secretary. She had a notepad in her hand and seemed to be writing something. Then again, she was looking extremely attractive and hardly like a stenographer. The necklace she was wearing glittered like the huge electric chandelier above our heads. As I watched, she put down the pad and, picking up a bottle of champagne, proceeded to fill everyone's glass. Another woman appeared. Von Tschammer und Osten drained his glass and then held it out for another refill. Reles lit a large cigar. The general laughed at his own joke and then leered at the second woman's cleavage. This was worth the cost of a set of opera glasses on its own.

"It looks like quite a party," I said.

"It might be, if this wasn't *Parsifal*."

I looked at her blankly.

"*Parsifal* lasts for five hours." The lady with the glasses looked at her watch. "And there are still three hours of it left to go."

"Thanks for the tip," I said, and left.

I RETURNED TO THE ADLON, borrowed a passkey from the desk, and climbed the stairs to suite 114. The rooms smelled strongly of cigars and cologne. The closets were full of tailor-made suits, and the drawers with neatly folded shirts. Even his shoes were handmade by a company in London. Just looking at his wardrobe, I felt I was in the wrong job. Then again, I didn't have to look at a pair of shoes owned by Max Reles to know that. Whatever the American did for a living, it was obviously paying him very well. The way I imagined everything did. He had that look about him. A selection of gold watches and rings on his bedside table only served to underline the impression of a man who was almost indifferent to his personal security or the Adlon's Matterhorn-high room rates.

The Torpedo on the table in the window had a cover on it, but the alphabetical accordion file on the floor underneath told me it was getting plenty of use. The thing was full of correspondence to and from construction companies, gas companies, timber companies, rubber companies, plumbers, electricians, engineers, carpenters—and from all over Germany, too: everywhere from Bremen to Würzburg. Some of the letters were in English, of course, and several of these were addressed to the Avery Brundage Company in Chicago, which seemed like it ought to have meant something to me, but didn't.

I raked through the wastepaper basket and smoothed out a few carbon copies to read before folding these and putting them in my pocket. I told myself Max Reles would hardly miss some correspondence from his wastepaper basket, although in truth I hardly cared if, on the face of it, Reles was helping to fix Olympic contracts. In a Germany governed by an ill assortment of murderers and fraudsters, I could see no point in trying to persuade an understandably reluctant Otto Trettin to take on a case that probably involved senior Nazi officials. I was looking for something more obviously criminal. I had no real idea of just what this might amount to. All the same, I thought I might recognize this if ever I saw it.

Of course, I was motivated by not much more than my own dislike and distrust of the man. These were feelings that had always served me well enough in the past. At the Alex we always said that an ordinary cop's job is to suspect the man who everyone else thinks is guilty, but a detective's job is to suspect the man who everyone else thinks is innocent.

Something caught my eye. The idea of Max Reles having such a thing as a ratchet screwdriver in a suite at the Adlon seemed a little out of place. It was lying on the window ledge in the bathroom. I was about to conclude that it might have been left there by a maintenance man, when I noticed what was written on the handle: *Yankee No. 15 North Bros. Mfg. Co. Phil. Penna. USA.* Reles must have brought the screwdriver from America. But why? The proximity of four screwheads in a marble-tiled panel concealing the lavatory cistern seemed to command investigation, and these were much easier to undo than perhaps they ought to have been.

With the panel removed, I peered into the space underneath the cistern and saw a canvas bag. I picked it up. The bag was heavy. I lifted it out of the cavity, placed it on the lavatory seat, and unlaced the neck.

While the ownership of firearms, especially pistols, was restricted in Germany, people with a legitimate reason to own one were permitted to do so, and for a three-mark fee, a weapons license could easily be obtained from any magistrate. A rifle, a revolver, even an automatic pistol could be owned quite legally by almost anyone. But I didn't think there was a magistrate anywhere in the country who would have signed a permit for a Thompson submachine gun with a drum magazine. The bag also contained several hundred rounds of ammunition, two Colt semi-automatic pistols with rubberized grips, and a folding switchblade. Inside the bag was another, smaller leather bag holding five thick bundles of thousand-dollar bills featuring a portrait of President Cleveland, and several thinner packets of German marks. There was also a leather wallet containing about a hundred Swiss gold francs and several dozen benzedrine inhalers still in their Smith Kline & French boxes.

All of it—especially the Chicago typewriter—looked like prima facie evidence that Max Reles was some kind of gangster.

I put everything back in the canvas bag, returned it to the hiding place under the cistern, and then replaced the tiled panel. When everything was exactly as I had found it, I slipped out of the suite and walked back along the corridor, pausing at the foot of the stairs, and wondering if I dared go up to 201 and use the passkey to let myself into Noreen's suite. For a moment I let my imagination throw me in the back of a fast car and run along the AVUS speedway as far as Potsdam. Then I stared hard at the key for almost ten seconds before dropping it into my jacket pocket and pointing my libido downstairs.

Steady on, Gunther, I told myself. You heard what the lady said. She doesn't like to be hurried.

But behind the desk there was another message waiting for me. It was from Noreen and more than a couple of hours old. I went back upstairs and pressed my ear to her door. In view of what was in the note, I might legitimately have used the passkey and let myself in. But German good manners got the better of me and I knocked.

A very long minute passed before she opened the door.

"Oh. It's you." She sounded almost disappointed.

"Were you expecting someone else?"

Noreen was wearing a brown chiffon peignoir and, underneath, a matching nightgown. She smelled like honeysuckle, and there was enough sleep still in her blue eyes to persuade me that she might want to go back to bed again, only this time with me. Maybe. She hustled me inside and closed the door.

"What I meant was, I left that note for you a couple of hours ago. I thought you'd come straightaway. I must have fallen asleep."

"I went out for a while. To cool down."

"Where did you go?"

"*Parsifal*. The opera."

"You're all surprises, you know that? I never figured you for a music lover."

"I'm not. I stayed for five minutes and then felt an irresistible urge to come here and search for you."

"Hmm. So what does that make me? A flower maiden? Klingsor's slave—what's her name? The one in *Parsifal*?"

"I haven't a clue." I shrugged. "Like I said, I only stayed five minutes."

Noreen put her arms around my neck. "I hope you brought Parsifal's holy spear with you, Gunther, because I don't happen to have one here." She backed me across the room to the bed. "At least not yet, I don't."

"You think I should stay with you tonight?"

"In my humble opinion, yes." She shrugged off the peignoir and let it fall onto the thick carpet with a whisper of chiffon.

I said, "You never held a humble opinion in your life," and kissed her. This time she allowed my hands to roam the contours of her body as if they belonged to an impatient masseur. Mostly they stayed on her bottom, my fingers gathering chiffon until I could pull her into my groin. My right hand seemed to be making a miraculous recovery.

"So it's true," she said. "Adlon room service is the best in Europe."

"The key to running a good hotel," I said, cupping one of her breasts in my hand, "is to eliminate boredom. Nearly all of our problems are caused by the innocent curiosity of our guests."

"I don't think I've been accused of that," she said. "Innocence.

Not in a long time." She shook her head. "I'm not the innocent type, Gunther."

I grinned.

"I guess you don't believe me," she said, pulling a length of hair through her mouth. "Because I'm still wearing clothes."

She pushed me down to sit on the edge of the bed and then stepped back in order to make a performance out of taking off her nightgown. Nude, she was worth a private room in Pompeii, and as far as performances go, it had *Parsifal* beat by several lewd acts. Looking at Noreen, you wondered why anyone ever bothered to draw or paint anything else but a woman's naked body. Cubes might have done it for Braque, but I liked curves, and Noreen's were good enough to satisfy Apollonius of Perga and probably Kepler, too. She drew my head against her belly and, pulling my hair, like the coat on a favorite dog, she teased me with the absence of all that made me a man.

"Why don't you touch me?" she said softly. "I want you to touch me. Right now."

She came and sat on my augmented lap and patiently permitted my impudent curiosities with eyes that were closed to anything else but her own pleasure. With nostrils flared, she breathed deeply, like a yogi concentrating her breath.

"So what changed your mind?" I asked, bending to kiss her hardening nipple. "About tonight?"

"Who says I changed my mind?" she said. "Maybe I planned this all along. Like this is a scene in a play I've written." She pushed off my jacket and started to undo my tie. "This is just what I want your character to do. Maybe you've got very little choice in the matter. Do you really feel you have a choice here, Gunther?"

"No." I bit her nipple. "Not now. But I got the impression earlier on that you were playing a little hard to get."

"I am hard to get. Only not to you. You're the first in a long time."

"I could say the same."

"You could. But it would be a lie. You're one of the principal characters in my play, remember? I know all about you, Gunther." She started to unbutton my shirt.

"Is Max Reles another character? You do know him, don't you?"

"Do we have to talk about him now?"

"It can wait."

"Good. Because I can't wait. I never could, not since I was a little girl. Ask me about him later, when the waiting is over."

18

THE CEILINGS IN THE SUITES at the Adlon were just the right distance from the floor. When you lay on the bed and blew a column of cigarette smoke straight up, the crystal chandelier looked like a remote and icy mountaintop surrounded with an ermine collar of cloud. I'd never paid the ceilings much attention before. Previous erotic encounters with Frieda Bamberger had been furtive, hurried affairs, conducted with one eye on the clock and the other on the door handle, and certainly I'd never felt sufficiently relaxed to fall asleep afterward. But now that I was looking at the lofty heights of this room, I found my soul climbing up the silky walls to sit on the picture rail, like some invisible gargoyle, and then to stare down with forensic fascination on the naked aftermath of what had gone before.

Our bare limbs still entwined, Noreen and Gunther lay side by sweating side, like Eros and Psyche fallen from some other, more heavenlike ceiling—although it was hard to imagine anything much more heavenly than what had just occurred. I felt like Saint Peter taking vacant possession of a smart new basilica.

"I bet you've never even been in one of these beds," said Noreen, taking the cigarette from my fingers and smoking it with the exaggerated gestures of a drunk or someone onstage. "Have you?"

"No," I lied. "It feels strange."

She hardly wanted to hear about my private trysts with Frieda. Certainly not as much as I wanted to hear about Max Reles.

"He doesn't seem to like you very much," she said after I mentioned his name again.

"Why is that? After all, I've been doing a swell job of hiding how much I dislike him. No, really, I despise the man, but he's a guest of this hotel, which obliges me not to punch him down six flights of stairs and then kick him out the door. That's what I'd like to do. And I'd do it, too, if I had another job to go to."

"Be careful, Bernie. He's a dangerous man."

"That much I already know. The question is, how do you know it?"

"We met on the SS *Manhattan*," she said. "On the voyage from New York to Hamburg. We were introduced at the captain's table, and occasionally we met up to play gin rummy." She shrugged. "He wasn't a good player. Anyway, it was a longish voyage, and a single woman has to expect that she will become the focus of attention for single gentlemen. Maybe even a few married ones. There was another man, besides Max Reles. A Canadian lawyer called John Martin. I had a drink with him, and he got the wrong idea about me. The fact is, he started to believe that he and I—well, to use his words, that he and I had something special going on. Well, we didn't. No, really we didn't. But he couldn't accept that and became something of a nuisance. He told me he loved me and that he wanted to marry me, and I didn't like it. I tried to avoid him, only that's not so easy on a boat.

"One night, off the coast of Ireland, I mentioned some of this to Max Reles over a game of gin rummy. He didn't say very much. And it's quite possible that I'm completely mistaken about this, but the very next day, this man Martin was reported missing, and it was presumed he must have fallen overboard. I believe they carried out a search, but it was for appearance's sake, since there was no way he could have survived after several hours in the sea.

"Anyway, soon after, I formed the impression that Reles had

something to do with the poor man's disappearance. It was something he said. I can't remember the exact words he used, but I do remember he was smiling when he said it." Noreen shook her head. "You must think I'm crazy. I mean, this is all completely circumstantial. Which is the main reason I never mentioned this to anyone."

"Not at all," I said. "There's nothing wrong with evidence that's circumstantial. In the right circumstances, that is. What did he say?"

"He said something like, 'It sounds very much as if your irritating little problem has been taken care of, Mrs. Charalambides.' And then he asked me if I'd pushed him off the boat. Which he seemed to think was funny. I told him I didn't think it was at all funny and asked him if he thought there was any chance that Mr. Martin might still be alive. To which he then replied, 'I very much hope not.' Well, after that, I kept away from him."

"What exactly do you know about Max Reles?"

"Not very much. Just what he told me over cards. He said he was a businessman in that way men do when they want to give the impression that what they do isn't very interesting. He speaks excellent German, of course. And I think some Hungarian. He told me he was on his way to Zurich, so I hardly expected to see him again. And certainly not here. I saw him again for the first time about a week ago. In the library. I had a drink with him, just to be polite. Apparently he's been here for a while."

"That he has."

"You do believe me, don't you?"

She said it in a way that made me think she might not be telling the truth. Then again, I'm just built that way. Some people like to believe in a pot of gold at the end of a rainbow. I'm the type who thinks the pot of gold is being watched by four cops in a car.

"You don't think I imagined it, do you?"

"Not at all," I said, although I did wonder why any man would murder another for a woman who was nothing more than a partner for a game of cards. "From what you've told me, I think you came to a very reasonable conclusion."

"You think I should have told the ship's captain, don't you? Or the police, when we got to Hamburg."

"With no real evidence to corroborate your story, Reles would only have denied it and made you look a fool. Besides, it's not like it would have helped the man who drowned."

"All the same, somehow I feel responsible for what happened."

She rolled across the bed, reaching for the ashtray on the bedside table, and stabbed out the cigarette. I rolled after her and caught up only an hour or two later. It was a big bed. I started to kiss her behind, then the small of her back, and then her shoulders. I was just about to sink my fangs into her neck when I noticed the book next to the ashtray. It was the book written by Hitler.

She saw that I noticed it, and said, "I'm reading it."

"Why?"

"It's an important book. But reading it doesn't make me a Nazi, any more than reading Marx makes me a communist. Although, as it happens, I do consider myself to be a communist. Does that surprise you?"

"That you think you're a communist? No, not particularly. The best people are these days. George Bernard Shaw. Even Trotsky, I hear. I like to consider myself a Social Democrat, but since democracy no longer exists in this country, that would be naive."

"I'm glad you're a democrat. That it's something that is still important to you. The fact is, I wouldn't have slept with you if you'd been a Nazi, Gunther."

"Like a lot of people, I might like them a bit more if it was me who was in charge and not Hitler."

"I'm trying to get an interview with him. That's one of the reasons I'm reading Hitler's book. Not that I think he will agree to meet me. Most likely I'll have to make do with seeing the sports minister. I'm meeting him tomorrow afternoon."

"You won't mention our friend Zak Deutsch, will you, Noreen? Or me, for that matter."

"No, of course I won't. Tell me something. Do you think he was murdered?"

"Maybe. Maybe not. We'll have a much better idea after we've spoken to Stefan Blitz. He's that geologist I was telling you about. I'm hoping he can shed some light on how a man can drown in salt water in the center of Berlin. You see, it's one thing when it happens off the coast of Ireland, in the Atlantic Ocean. It's quite another when it happens in the local canal."

UNTIL THE SPRING OF 1934, Stefan Blitz had been a teacher of geology at Frederick William University, in Berlin. I knew him because sometimes he had helped KRIPO to identify the clay found on the shoes of murder suspects or their victims. He lived in Zehlendorf, in Berlin's southwest, in a modern housing development called Uncle Tom's Hut, named after a local tavern and subway shop that were themselves named after the book by Harriet Beecher Stowe. Noreen was intrigued.

"I can't believe they called it that," she said. "In the States, people would never have dared give it a name like that in case people thought the houses were fit only for Negroes."

I parked the car in front of a four-story apartment building that was as big as a city block. The smooth, modern façade was very slightly curved and pockmarked with different-sized, recessed windows, none of which was on the same level. It looked like a face recovering from a dose of smallpox. There were hundreds, perhaps thousands of these Weimar-built homes in Berlin, and they were about as distinguished as packets of Persil. And yet, although they despised modernism, the Nazis had more in common with its mostly Jewish architects than they might have thought. Nazism and modernism were both products of the inhuman, and when I looked at one of those neat, standardized gray concrete buildings, it wasn't hard to imagine a neat, standardized detachment of gray storm troopers living in one, like so many rats in a box.

It wasn't like that inside, however—at least not inside Stefan Blitz's apartment. In contrast to the carefully planned modernism of the exterior, his furniture was old mahogany, tattered upholstery, chipped Wilhelmine ornaments, table oilcloths, and Eiffel Towers of books, with all of the shelves given over to slices of rock.

Blitz himself was as tattered as his upholstery and, like any other Jew who was forbidden his way of making a living, he was as thin as a maquette in an artist's garret and hardly living at all. A hospitable, kind, and generous man, he displayed character traits that made him the very opposite of the grasping bogeyman Jew so often caricatured in the Nazi press. Nevertheless, that was what he looked like: a lecher in the stews of Damascus. He offered us tea, coffee, Coca-Cola, alcohol, something to eat, a more comfortable chair, chocolates, and his last cigarettes before finally, having refused them all, we were able to come to the point of our visit.

"Is it possible that a man could drown in seawater in the center of Berlin?" I asked.

"I assume you've discounted the possibility of a swimming pool, otherwise you wouldn't be here. The Admiral's Garden baths on Alexanderplatz is a brine bath. I used to swim there myself before they stopped Jews from going there."

"The victim is Jewish," I said. "And so, for that reason, yes, you're right, I think I have discounted that possibility."

"Why, if you don't mind my asking, is a Gentile bothering to investigate the death of a Jew in the new Germany?"

"It's my idea," Noreen said, and told Blitz about the Olympiad and the failed U.S. boycott and the newspaper she hoped would put that to rights, and how she herself was a Jew.

"I suppose it would be something if an American boycott were to succeed," Blitz admitted. "Although I have my doubts. The Nazis won't be so easy to dislodge, with or without a boycott. Now that they have power, they mean to hang on to it. The Reichstag will sink before they have another election, and, believe me, I know what I'm talking about. It was built on posts because of all the swampy spots that exist between it and the Old Museum."

Noreen smiled her neon smile. Her glamour seemed to warm the apartment, as if someone had lit a fire in the empty grate. She lit a cigarette from a little gold case, which she pushed toward him. He took one and slid it behind his ear like a pencil.

"Could a man drown in Berlin seawater, he asks," said Blitz. "Two hundred sixty million years ago this whole area was an ancient sea— the Zechstein Sea. Berlin itself was founded on a series of islands that appeared in a river valley during the last Ice Age. The substrata are mostly sand. And salt. A lot of salt from the Zechstein Sea. The salt formed several islands on the land surface, and quite a few deepwater groundwater chambers all over the city and the surrounding area."

"Seawater chambers?" asked Noreen.

"Yes, yes. In my opinion, there are some places in Berlin where men should not be digging. Such a chamber might easily be ruptured, with potentially disastrous consequences."

"Could such a place include Pichelsberg?"

"It could happen almost anywhere in Berlin," said Blitz. "For someone in a hurry, who didn't carry out a proper geological survey—boreholes and that kind of thing—it would not just be the old lies that the new Germany obliged him to swallow, but a considerable quantity of salt water, also." He smiled carefully, like a man playing a card game whose rules he was still uncertain of.

"Including Pichelsberg?" I persisted.

Blitz shrugged. "Pichelsberg? What is this interest in Pichelsberg? I'm a geologist, not a town planner, Herr Gunther."

"Come on, Stefan, you know why I'm asking."

"Yes, and I don't like it. I have enough problems without adding Pichelsberg as well. Where exactly are you going with this? You mentioned a drowned man. A Jew, you said. And a newspaper article. Forgive me, but it seems to me that one dead Jew is quite enough."

"Dr. Blitz," said Noreen, "I promise you. Nothing you say will be attributed to you. I won't quote you. I won't mention Uncle Tom's Cabin or that I even spoke to a geologist."

Blitz removed the cigarette from behind his ear and studied it like a core of white rock. When he lit it, his satisfaction could be seen and heard. "American cigarettes. I'm so used to cheap ones I'd forgotten how good tobacco can taste." He nodded thoughtfully. "Perhaps I should try to go to America. I'm damned sure the meaning of life in Germany doesn't include liberty and the pursuit of happiness. Not if you're Jewish, anyway."

Noreen emptied her case on the table. "Please," she said, "keep them. I have more back at the hotel."

"If you're sure," he said.

She nodded, and pulled the sable coat closer to her chest.

"A good engineering company," he said, carefully. "It would first drill, not dig. You understand? The Ice Age left behind a real mixture of substrata that would make construction here very unpredictable. Especially somewhere like Pichelsberg. Does that answer your question?"

"Is it possible that the people building the Olympic Stadium don't know this?" she asked.

Blitz shrugged. "Who mentioned the Olympics? I know nothing about the Olympics, and I tell you I don't want to know. We're told it's not for Jews, and I for one am very happy about this." It was chilly in his apartment, but he wiped some sweat off his forehead with a ragged handkerchief. "Look, if you don't mind, I think I've said enough."

"One more question," I said, "and then we'll leave."

Blitz stared momentarily at the ceiling as if calling on his maker to give him patience. His hand was trembling as he put the cigarette back between his cracked lips.

"Is there any gold in Berlin's substrata?"

"Gold, yes, gold. But only trace amounts. Believe me, Bernie, you won't get rich looking for gold in Berlin." He chuckled. "At least not unless you take it from those who already have it. This is a Jew telling you, so you can take that to the bank. Even the Nazis aren't stupid enough to look for gold in Berlin."

We didn't stay much longer. We both knew we'd unsettled Blitz. And in view of what he'd said, I didn't blame him for being circumspect and nervous. The Nazis would hardly have taken kindly to what he was surely saying about the construction site at Pichelsberg. When we left, we didn't offer him money. He wouldn't have taken it. But when his back was turned to lead us out of the apartment, Noreen slipped a leaf under the coffeepot.

BACK IN THE CAR, Noreen let out a loud sigh and shook her head. "This town is beginning to get me down," she said. "Tell me you don't get used to it."

"Not me. I've only just got used to the idea that we lost the war. Everyone says the Jews were to blame for that, but I always thought it was the navy's fault. It was them who got us into it and their mutiny that forced us to quit. But for them we might have fought on, to an honorable peace."

"You sound like you regret that."

"Only the fact that the wrong people signed the armistice. The army should have done it instead of the politicians, which let the army off the hook rather, and which is why we're in the state we're in. D'you see?"

"Not really."

"No? Well, that's half the problem. Nobody does. Least of all us Germans. Most mornings I wake up and think I must have imagined the last two years. The last twenty-four hours most of all. What does a woman like you see in a man like me?"

She took my left hand and squeezed it. "A man like you. You make that sound as if there's more than one. There isn't. I know. I've looked. And in all kinds of places. Including the bed we slept in. Last night I was wondering how I'd feel in the morning. Well, now I know."

"How do you feel?"

"Scared."

"Of what?"

"The way I feel, of course. Like you're driving the car."

"I am driving the car." I wiggled the steering wheel for effect.

"At home no one ever drives me anywhere. I like to drive myself. I prefer to decide when to start and when to stop. But with you, I really don't mind. I wouldn't mind if you decided to drive us all the way to China and back."

"China? It'd be enough for me just to have you stay on in Berlin for a while."

"So what's stopping me?"

"Perhaps Nick Charalambides. And your newspaper article. And maybe this. That it's my honest opinion that Isaac Deutsch wasn't murdered at all. That his death was an accident. No one drowned him. He drowned. Without any help from anyone else. Right here in the center of Berlin. I know, it's not as good a story if he wasn't murdered. But what can I do?"

"Damn."

"Exactly."

For a moment I was reminded of Richard Bömer and his disappointment at discovering that Isaac Deutsch was Jewish. And now here was Noreen Charalambides, disappointed to discover the poor guy hadn't been murdered. It's a hell of a world.

"Are you sure?"

"Here's what I think happened. After his career as a boxer was outlawed by the Nazis, Isaac Deutsch and his uncle got a job on the Olympic building site. In spite of the official policy about hiring only Aryan workers. Given how much there is to do before the Olympiad starts, in 1936, someone decided it might be best to cut a few corners. And not just with the racial origins of the workforce. With safety, too, I suspect. Isaac Deutsch was probably involved in some kind of underground excavation when he ruptured one of those water chambers Blitz told us about. He had an accident, and he was drowned in seawater, only no one knew it was seawater. Someone figured it might be best if his body was found drowned a long way from Pichelsberg. Just in case some nosy cop started asking questions about illegal Jewish workers. Which is how the body ended up in a freshwater canal, on the other side of Berlin."

Noreen searched her empty cigarette case for a smoke. "Damn," she said again.

I gave her mine. "Much as I'm reluctant to admit it, Noreen, this little investigation is over. Nothing would give me more pleasure than to spin this out and keep on driving you around Berlin. But I think honesty's best. Especially since I'm a little out of practice in that area, what with one thing and another."

She lit the cigarette and stared out of the window as we came into Steglitz.

"Pull up," she said, sharply.

"What?"

"Pull up, I said."

I stopped the car close to the town hall, at the corner of Schlossstrasse, and started to apologize on the assumption that she had taken offense at something I had said. Even before I had switched off the engine, she had got out of the car and was walking swiftly back down the street. I followed.

"Hey, I'm sorry," I said. "But there's still a story you can write here.

Maybe if you found Isaac Deutsch's uncle Joey—the guy who was his trainer—then perhaps he'd talk. You could get his story. That would be a good angle. How Jews are forbidden to compete in the Olympics but how one who gets an illegal job building the stadium ends up dead. That could be a great story."

Noreen didn't look like she was listening. And I was more than a little horrified to see that she was heading toward a large group of SA and SS men standing around a man and woman dressed in civilian clothes. The woman was blond and in her twenties; the man was older and Jewish. I knew he was Jewish, because, like her, he had a placard around his neck. The man's placard read: "I'm a dirty Jew who takes German girls to his room." The girl's placard read: "I go to this dirty swine's place to sleep with a Jew!"

Before I could do anything to stop her, Noreen threw away her cigarette, produced her Baby Brownie from her capacious leather handbag, and, looking down through the little viewfinder, took a photograph of the somber couple and the grinning Nazis.

I caught up with her and tried to take her by the arm. She pulled it away angrily.

"This is not a good idea," I said.

"Nonsense. They wouldn't have put those placards around their necks unless they wanted people to pay attention to them. And that's just what I'm doing." She wound her film and once again lined up the group.

One of the SS shouted at me, "Hey, Bubi. Leave her alone. She's right, your girlfriend. There's no point in making an example of bastards like these unless people see it and take note."

"That's exactly what I'm doing," said Noreen. "Taking note."

I waited patiently until Noreen had finished. Until now she'd photographed only anti-Semitic signs in the parks and some Nazi flags on Unter den Linden, and I hoped this rather more candid kind of photography wasn't about to become a habit with her. I doubt my nerves could have taken it.

We walked back to the car in silence, abandoning the miscegenating couple to their public disgrace and humiliation.

"If you'd ever seen them beat someone up," I said, "then you'd be more careful about doing something like that. You want to photograph something interesting, I'll run you over to the Bismarck Monument or the Charlottenburg Palace."

Noreen dropped the camera back in her bag. "Don't treat me like some goddamn tourist," she said. "I didn't take that picture for my album. I took it for the fucking newspaper. Don't you get it? A picture like that makes an absolute mockery of Avery Brundage's claims that Berlin is a proper place to hold an Olympic Games."

"Brundage?"

"Yes, Avery Brundage. Weren't you listening? I told you before. He's the president of the American Olympic Committee."

I nodded. "What else do you know about him?"

"Almost nothing beyond the fact that he must be a real asshole."

"Would it surprise you to learn that he's in correspondence with your old friend Max Reles? And that he owns a construction company in Chicago?"

"How do you know that?"

"I'm a detective, remember? I'm supposed to know things I'm not supposed to know about."

She smiled. "Sonofabitch. You searched his room, didn't you? That's why you were asking me about him last night. I'll bet that's when you did it, too. Right after that little scene in the lobby, when you knew he'd be out for a while."

"Almost right. I followed him to the opera first."

"Five minutes of *Parsifal*. I remember. So that's why you went."

"His guests included the sports leader. Funk from Propaganda. Some army general called von Reichenau. The rest I didn't recognize. But I'll bet they were all Nazis."

"Those you mentioned are all on the German Olympic Organizing Committee," she said. "And I'll bet the rest were, too." She shook her head. "So you went back to the Adlon and searched his room while you knew he was safely otherwise engaged. What else did you find?"

"A lot of letters. Reles employs a stenographer I found for him, and it seems he keeps her very busy writing to companies who are bidding for Olympic contracts."

"Then he must be on a kickback. Maybe lots of kickbacks. The GOC, too, maybe."

"I took some carbon copies from his wastepaper basket."

"Great. Can I see them?"

When we were in the car once again I handed them over. She started to read one. "Nothing incriminating here," she said.

"That's what I thought. At first."

"It's just a bid for a contract to supply cement to the Ministry of the Interior."

"The other one is a bid for a contract to supply propane gas for the Olympic flame." I paused. "Don't you get it? That's a carbon. It means that it was typed by the Adlon's own stenographer in his suite. Contracts are supposed to be for German companies only. And Max Reles is an American."

"Maybe he bought these companies."

"Maybe. I think he's probably got enough money. Probably that's why he went to Zurich before he came here. There's a bag in his room containing thousands of dollars and gold Swiss francs. Not to mention a submachine gun. Even in Germany you don't need a machine gun to run a company these days. Not unless you have some serious problems with your labor force."

"I need to think about this."

"We both do. I've a feeling we're getting in over our heads, and I'm kind of attached to mine. I mention that only because we have the falling ax in this country, and it's not just criminals who get haircuts. It's communists and republicans and probably anyone the government doesn't like. Look, you really won't mention any of this to von Tschammer und Osten, will you?"

"No, of course I won't. I'm not ready to get thrown out of Germany just yet. Especially since last night."

"I'm glad to hear it."

"While I'm thinking about Max Reles, that idea you had. About looking for Isaac Deutsch's uncle and basing my story on him. It's a good one."

"I only said that to get you back in the car."

"Well, I'm back in the car, and it's still a good idea."

"I'm not so sure. Suppose you did write a story about Jews helping to build the new stadium. Maybe all those Jews will end up losing their jobs as a result of that. And what happens to them then? How are they going to feed their families? It might even be that some of them end up in concentration camps. Have you thought about that?"

"Of course I've thought about it. What do you take me for? I'm a Jew, remember? The human consequences of what I might write are always on my mind. Look, Bernie, the way I see it is this: There's a much bigger issue at stake here than a few hundred people losing their jobs. The USA is by far the most important country in any Olympics. In L.A., we won forty-one gold medals, more than any other country. Italy, which was next, won twelve. An Olympiad without America would be meaningless. That's why a boycott is important. Because if the games are not held here, it would be just about the most serious blow that Nazi prestige could suffer inside Germany. Not to mention it being one of the most effective ways that the outside world has of showing the youth of Germany its true opinion of Nazi doctrine. That has to be more important than whether a few Jews can feed their families. Wouldn't you agree?"

"Maybe. But if we go to Pichelsberg looking for answers about Isaac Deutsch, we might find ourselves asking questions of the very people who tossed him into the canal. They might not take kindly to being written about. Even if it is in a New York newspaper. Looking for Joey Deutsch could turn out to be just as dangerous as investigating Max Reles."

"You're a detective. An ex-cop. I'd have thought a certain amount of danger is written into your job description."

"A certain amount, yes. But that doesn't make me bulletproof. Besides, when you're back in New York collecting a Pulitzer Prize for reporting, I'll still be here. That's the hope, at least. I can float in the canal just as easily as Isaac Deutsch."

"If it's a question of money."

"Given what happened last night, I might tell you it's not a question of money. At the same time, I have to admit that money is always a very persuasive answer."

"Money talks, huh, Gunther?"

"Sometimes it seems you just can't shut it up. I'm a hotel detective because I have to be, Noreen, not because I want to be. I'm broke, angel. When I quit KRIPO, I left behind a reasonable salary and a pension, not to mention what my father used to call 'good prospects.' I don't see myself rising to the rank of hotel manager, do you?"

Noreen smiled. "Not in the kind of hotel I'd ever want to stay in."

"Exactly."

"How does twenty marks a day sound?"

"Generous. Very. But it's a different kind of dialogue I'm looking for."

"Pulitzer Prizes don't pay that much, you know."

"I'm not after a slice. Just a loan. A business loan, with interest. What with the Depression, the banks aren't lending. Not even to each other. And I can hardly ask the Adlons to stake me enough to hand in my notice."

"To do what?"

"To do this. Be a private investigator, of course. It's about the one thing I'm good at. I figure about five hundred marks would let me set up on my own."

"How do I know you'd stay alive long enough to pay me back?"

"That would be an incentive, of course. I'd hate to lose my life. And I'd hate to see you lose your money as a result of that, of course. Fact is, I could probably pay you a twenty-percent return on your investment."

"You've obviously given this some thought."

"Ever since the Nazis came into power. Human tragedies like the one we just witnessed in front of the town hall back there are happening all over this city. And it's going to get worse before it gets better. A lot of people—Jews, Gypsies, Freemasons, communists, homosexuals, Jehovah's Witnesses—they already figure they can't go to the cops and get a hearing from anyone. So they're going to go somewhere else. Which just has to be good for someone like me."

"So you could end up making a profit under the Nazis?"

"That's always a possibility. At the same time, it's just possible I might actually end up helping someone as well as myself."

"You know what I like about you, Gunther?"

"I sure could use a bit of reminding."

"It's that you can make Copernicus and Kepler look so very short-sighted and impractical and yet still cut a convincingly romantic figure."

"Does that mean you still find me attractive?"

"I don't know. Ask me later when I've forgotten that I'm no longer just your employer but your banker, too."

"Does that mean you're going to give me the loan?"

Noreen smiled. "Why not? But on one condition. You never tell Hedda that you got the money from me."

"It'll be our secret."

"One of two, it now looks like."

"You do realize you're going to have to sleep with me again," I said. "To guarantee my silence."

"Of course. In fact, as your banker, I was banking on it. With interest."

19

I DROPPED NOREEN OFF at the Ministry of the Interior for her interview with von Tschammer und Osten, and drove back to the hotel and then kept on driving, west, again. Now that she was out of the way, I wanted to nose around the Olympic site at Pichelsberg on my own. The fact was I had only the one pair of gum boots; and then there was the fact that I didn't want to draw any attention while I was doing the nosing, which was almost impossible when Noreen was on my arm. She commanded attention like a nudist playing the trombone.

Pichelsberg Racecourse was at the north end of the Grunewald. In the center of the racecourse was the stadium, laid out from a design by Otto March and opened in 1913. Encircling the course were running and cycling tracks, while to the north was a swimming pool—all built for the canceled Berlin Olympiad of 1916. In stands that could accommodate almost forty thousand people were sculptures, including a goddess of victory and a Neptune group. Except that none of them were there anymore. Nothing was. Everything—the racecourse, the stadium, and the pool—had been demolished and replaced by an enormous earthwork: a huge mass of soil had been created from the excavation of a vaguely circular pit, where I assumed the new stadium was going to be built. As assumptions go, this one seemed unlikely. The Berlin Olympics were less than two years away and nothing had been built. Indeed, a perfectly serviceable and recently constructed stadium had been knocked down to make way for the Battle of Verdun as imagined by D. W. Griffith. As I got out of the car I half expected to see the French front lines, our own line, and heavy shell bursts in the air.

For a moment I was back in uniform and feeling fairly sick with fear at the sudden recollection of that earlier dun-colored wilderness. And then the shakes were on me, as if I had just woken up from the same nightmare I always had, which was about being back there . . .

. . . carrying a box of ammunition through the mud and clay while shells were falling all around. It took me two hours to move 150 meters up to our front line. I kept throwing myself on the ground or simply falling over until I was soaked to the skin and caked with earth, like a man made of mud.

I had almost reached our redoubt when I stepped into a shell hole and found myself waist deep in mud and sinking. I shouted for help, but the noise of the barrage was too loud for anyone to hear. Struggling only seemed to make me sink more quickly, and in less than five minutes I was up to my neck and facing the horrible fate of being drowned in a small sea of brown glue. I'd seen horses stuck in the mud, and nearly always they were shot, such was the effort of pulling one out. I struggled to take hold of my pistol so that I might shoot myself in the head before being drowned, but that was hopeless, too. The mud held me tightly now. I tried to lean back so that I might "float" on the surface, but that was no use, either.

And then, just as the mud was up to my jaw, there was an enormous explosion a few meters away as a shell hit the ground and, miraculously, I was lifted right out of the morass and high into the air to land twenty meters away, winded but uninjured. Had it not been for the mud enveloping me, the shock of the blast would certainly have killed me.

That was my recurring nightmare, and I never had it without waking up, soaked with perspiration and out of breath, as if I had just sprinted across no-man's-land. Even now, in broad daylight, I had to drop down on my haunches and take several deep breaths in an effort to pull myself together. A few spots of color in the once fertile but now devastated landscape served my mental recovery: some blue thistle at the edge of the distant tree line; red dead nettle close to where I'd left the car; some yellow-flowered tansy ragwort; a robin redbreast picking a juicy pink worm out of the ground; the empty blue sky; and finally an army of workmen and a railway line conveying a small red train of earthmoving wagons from one end of the site to the other.

"Are you all right?"

The man wore a workman's peaked cap and a quilted jacket as voluminous as a smock. His black trousers ended several centimeters above boots doubled in size by several kilos of clay. Over a shoulder as big as Jutland rested a sledgehammer. His blond hair was almost white, and his eyes were as blue as the thistle flowers. His chin and cheekbones might have been sketched by one of those Nazi artists, like Josef Thorak.

"I'm okay." I stood up, lit a cigarette, and waved it at the landscape. "When I saw no-man's-land, I went off a bit like August Stramm, you know? 'Yielding clod lulls iron off to sleep, Blood clots the patches where they oozed, Rust crumbles, flesh is slime, Sucking lusts around decay.'"

To my surprise, he completed the verse: "'Murder on murder blinks in childish eyes.' Yes, I know that poem. Me, I was Second Royal Württemburg, Twenty-seventh Division. You?"

"Twenty-sixth Div."

"Then we were in the same battle."

I nodded. "Amiens. August 1918."

I offered him a cigarette, and he took a light from my own, trench style, not to waste a match.

"Two graduates of the university of mud," he said. "Scholars of human evolution."

"Ah, yes. The ascent of man." I grinned, remembering the old saying. "When someone kills you not with a bayonet, but with a machine gun; not with a machine gun, but with a flamethrower; not with a flamethrower, but with poison gas."

"What are you doing here, friend?"

"Just looking around."

"Well, you're not allowed. Not anymore. Didn't you see the sign?"

"No," I answered truthfully.

"We're way behind schedule as it is. We're already working three shifts. So we don't have time for visitors."

"It doesn't look too busy here."

"Most of the lads are on the other side of that earthwork," he said, pointing to the west of the site. "You sure you're not from the ministry?"

"Of the Interior? No. Why do you ask?"

"Because they've threatened to replace any construction companies that aren't pulling their weight, that's why. I thought you might be spying on us."

"I'm no spy. Hell, I'm not even a Nazi. The truth is, I came out here to look for someone. A fellow by the name of Joey Deutsch. Maybe you know him."

"No."

"Maybe the site foreman's heard of him."

"That would be me. The name's Blask, Heinrich Blask. Why are you looking for this fellow, anyway?"

"It's not like he's in trouble or anything. And I'm not about to tell him he's won a fortune on the lottery." I was wondering exactly what I was going to tell him, until I remembered the fight tickets in my pocket:

the ones we'd bought off Gypsy Trollmann. "The fact is, I manage a couple of fighters, and I want Joey to train them. I don't know what he's like with a pick and a shovel, but Joey's a pretty good trainer. One of the best. He'd be in the game right now, but for the obvious reason."

"Which is?"

"With a name like Deutsch? He's a kike. And kikes aren't allowed in gyms. At least not the gyms that are open to the public. Me, I've got my own gym. So no one's offended, right?"

"Maybe you don't know, but we're not allowed to employ non-Aryan labor here," said Blask.

"Sure I know that. I also know that it happens. And who can blame you with the ministry breathing down your neck about getting this stadium built in time? Pretty tall order if you ask me. Listen, Heinrich, I'm not here to make trouble for you. I just want to find Joey. Maybe his nephew's working with him. Isaac. He used to be a fighter himself."

I took two tickets out of my pocket and showed them to the foreman. "Maybe you'd like some tickets to a fight yourself. Scholz versus Witt at the Spichernsaele. How about it, Heinrich? Can you help me here?"

"If there were kikes working on this site," said Blask, "and I'm not saying that there are, but you would do best to speak to the hiring boss. A man called Erich Goerz. He's not on site very much. Mostly he works out of a bar on the Schildhorn." He took one of the tickets. "There's a monument there."

"The Schildhorn Column."

"'Sright. From what I heard, if you want to work, no questions asked, that's where you go. Every morning around six there's a whole crowd of illegals that waits there. Jews, gyppos, you name it. Goerz turns up, decides who works and who doesn't. Mostly on account of how they each pay him a commission. He calls the names, gives them a work tab, they report to wherever they're needed most." He shrugged. "They're good workers, he finds, so what am I going to do, me with my schedule? He doesn't tell me, and I don't need to be told, right? I just do what the bosses order me to do."

"Any idea what the bar's called?"

"Albert the Bear or something." He took the other ticket. "But let me give you some free advice, comrade. Be careful. Erich Goerz wasn't in the Royal Württemburg, like me. His idea of comradeship owes more to Al Capone than the Prussian army. You follow me? He's not as big as you, but he's pretty handy with his fists. Maybe you'll like that. You look like a fellow who can take care of himself. But Erich Goerz also carries a gun. And not where you'd expect him to carry one. It's strapped to his ankle. If ever he stops to tie up his shoelaces, don't hesitate. Kick him in the teeth before he shoots you."

"Thanks for the warning, friend." I flicked my cigarette into no-man's-land. "You already said he's not as big as me. Anything else you can tell me about what he looks like?"

"Let me see." Blask dropped the sledgehammer and stroked his anvil-sized chin. "For one thing, he smokes Russian cigarettes. I think they're Russian, anyway. Flat ones that smell like a nest of burning weasels. So when he's in the room, you'll know about it. Otherwise he's a pretty regular guy, at least to look at. Aged about thirty, thirty-five, pimp mustache, bit swarthy—looks like he should be wearing a fez. Owns a new Hanomag with a Brandenburg license plate. Matter of fact, that might be where he's from, originally. The driver's from somewhere south of there. Wittenberg, I think. He's a slugger, too, with a reach like the Palace Bridge, so mind you watch out for him as well."

TO THE SOUTH OF PICHELSBERG, a high road affording pretty views but now much used by construction traffic skirted the Havel River and led to Beelitzhof and the two-kilometer peninsula of Schildhorn. Close to the riverbank were a little group of bars and ivy-covered restaurants, and a series of stone steps that rose steeply up to a group of pine trees that hid the Schildhorn monument and whatever else went on there at six o'clock in the morning. The monument was well chosen as a place for picking up illegal workers. From the road it was impossible to see anything that happened around the monument.

Albert the Bear was shaped a bit like a boot or a shoe and was of such an age that it looked as if the shoe might have an old woman who lived in it with so many children she didn't know what to do. Outside the door was a new Hanomag with an IE license plate. It looked as if I'd arrived at the right time.

I drove on for about three or four hundred meters and parked. In the trunk of Behlert's car was a pair of overalls. Behlert was always messing around under the hood of the W. I put on the overalls and walked back into the village, stopping only to push my hands into some damp soil to give myself a workingman's manicure. A cold easterly wind was blowing off the river and carried a strong hint of the coming winter, not to mention a whiff of something chemical from the Hohenzollerndamm Gasworks on the edge of Wilmersdorf.

Outside the Albert, a tall man with a courtroom artist's idea of a face was leaning on the Hanomag reading the *Zeitung*. He was smoking a Tom Thumb and probably keeping an eye on the car. As I pushed open the door, a little bell rang above my head. It didn't seem like a good idea, but I went inside anyway.

I was greeted by a large stuffed bear. The bear's jaws were open and its paws were in the air, and I guess a person coming through the door was supposed to feel under attack or something, but to me the bear looked as if he were conducting an ursine choir to sing "The Teddy Bears' Picnic." Otherwise the place was almost empty. The floor was a checkerboard of cheap linoleum. Tables with neat yellow cloths were ranged around the orange-colored walls that were a picture gallery of river scenes and characters. In the far corner, underneath a large photograph of the River Spree logjammed with Sunday canoeists, sat a man in a cloud of foul-smelling cigarette smoke. He was reading a newspaper that was spread over the whole table, and he hardly looked up as I came over and stood in front of him.

"Hey," I said.

"Don't make the mistake of pulling out that chair," he murmured. "I'm not the type who likes to jaw with strangers."

He wore a mid-green suit and a dark green shirt with a brown woolen tie. On the bench next to him were a leather coat and hat and, for no reason I could see, a substantial-looking dog lead. The flat, yellowish cigarettes he was smoking were not Russian, however; they were French.

"I understand. Are you Herr Goerz?"

"Who wants to know?"

"Stefan Blitz. I was told you were the man to speak to about getting work on the Olympic site."

"Oh? Who told you that?"

"Fellow named Trollmann. Johann Trollmann."

"Never heard of him. Does he work for me?"

"No, Herr Goerz. He said he heard it from a friend of his. I can't remember his name. Trollmann and I, we used to box together." I paused. "I say 'used to,' because now we can't. Not anymore. Not now that there are rules about non-Aryans in sporting contests. Which is how I come to be looking for a job."

"I've never been a sporting man myself," said Goerz. "I was too busy earning a living." He looked up from his newspaper. "I can see the boxer in you, maybe. But somehow I can't see the Jew."

"I'm a mischling. Half and half. But that doesn't seem to make much difference to the government."

Goerz laughed. "No, it certainly doesn't. Let me see your hands, Stefan Blitz."

I held them out in front of him, showing off my dirty fingernails.

"Not the backs of your hands. The palms."

"Are you going to tell my fortune?"

His eyes narrowed as he pulled on the last few centimeters of the foul-smelling cigarette. "Maybe." Not touching my hands, just looking, he added, "These hands look strong enough. But they don't look like they've done much real work."

"Like I said, mostly I've worked with my knuckles. But I can handle a pick and a shovel. During the war I did my fair share of digging trenches. Quite a few graves, too."

"Sad." He put out the cigarette. "Tell me, Stefan, do you know what a tithing is?"

"It's in the Bible. It means a tenth part, doesn't it?"

"'Sright. Now, then. I'm just the hiring boss. I get paid by the construction company to find them men. But I also get paid by you, to find you a job, see? A tenth of what you make at the end of the day. You can think of it as being like your union dues."

"A tenth seems a little high for any union I've ever been in."

"I agree. But then beggars can't be choosers, now, can they? Jews aren't allowed to be in German workingmen's unions. So, under those circumstances, a tenth is what you're asked to pay. And you can take it or leave it."

"I'll take it."

"I thought you would. Besides, like I said. It's in your holy book. Genesis, chapter fourteen, verse twenty. 'And he gave him tithes of all.' That's the best way to look at it, I think. As your holy duty. And if you can't work your head around that, then just remember this: I only pick the men who pay me the tithing. Clear?"

"Clear."

"Six o'clock sharp, at the monument outside. Maybe you'll work, maybe you won't. It all depends on how many are needed."

"I'll be here."

"As if I care." Goerz looked back down at his newspaper. The interview was over.

I HAD ARRANGED TO MEET NOREEN at the Romanisches Café on Tauentzienstrasse. Formerly popular with Berlin's literati, the café resembled an airship that had made an unscheduled landing on the pavement in front of a four-story Romanesque building that might have been the sibling of the Kaiser Wilhelm Memorial Church opposite. Or perhaps it was the modern equivalent of a Hohenzollern hunting lodge—somewhere for the princes and emperors of the first German empire to get a coffee or a kummel after spending a long morning on their knees to a God who, by comparison with them, must have seemed rather vulgar and ill bred.

Under the glass ceilings of the café she was easy to see, like an exotic species of hothouse flower. But, as with any vivid tropical bloom, something dangerous was close at hand. A young man wearing a smart black uniform was seated at her table, like Miss Muffet's spider. Less than six months after the demise of the SA as a political force independent of the

Nazis, the impeccably dressed SS had already established itself as the most feared uniformed organization in Hitler's Germany.

I was none too pleased to see him myself. He was tall and blond and handsome with an easy smile and manners as polished as his boots—lighting Noreen's cigarette as urgently as if her life had depended on it, and standing up with a click of heels that was as loud as a champagne cork when I presented myself at their table. The SS officer's matching black Labrador shifted uncertainly on his haunches and uttered a low growl. Master and dog looked like a warlock and his familiar, and before Noreen had even begun the introductions, I was hoping he might disappear in a puff of black smoke.

"This is Lieutenant Seetzen," she said, smiling politely. "He's been keeping me company and practicing his English."

I fixed a rictus smile to my jaw, affecting pleasure in our new friend's company, but I was glad when he finally made his excuses and left.

"That's a relief," she said. "I thought he'd never go."

"Oh? You looked like you were getting on very well."

"Don't be an ass, Gunther. What could I do? I was reading through my notes, and he just sat down and started speaking to me. All the same, it was kind of fascinating in a sort of creepy way. He was telling me that he's applied to join the Prussian Gestapo."

"Now, there's a job with prospects. If only I didn't have any scruples, I might just do the same."

"Right now he's on a training course in the Grunewald."

"I wonder what they teach them. How to use a rubber hose on a man without killing him? Where do they get these bastards?"

"He's from Eutin."

"Ah, so that's where they get them."

Noreen tried to stifle a yawn with the back of her elegantly gloved hand. It was easy to see why the lieutenant had spoken to her. She was easily the best-looking woman in the café. "I'm sorry," she said. "But it's been a hell of an afternoon. First von Tschammer und Osten, and then that young lieutenant. For a clever people, you Germans can be awfully dumb." She glanced down at her reporter's notebook. "Your leader of German sports is so full of bullshit."

"That's how he got the job, angel." I lit a cigarette.

She turned some of the pages of shorthand, shaking her head.

"Listen to this. I mean, he said a lot of things that sounded sort of unhinged to me, but this took the biscuit. When I asked him about Hitler's promise that, in the selection of its Olympic team, Germany would observe Olympic statutes and recognize neither race nor color, he said—and I quote, 'But it is being observed. At least, in principle. Technically, nobody is being excluded on any of those grounds.' And listen to this, Bernie. This is the best bit. 'By the time the games are held, Jews will probably no longer be German citizens, or at least first-class German citizens. They may be admissible as guests. And in view of all the international agitation on behalf of the Jews, it may even happen that, at the last moment, the government will accede to there being a small quota of Jews on the team, albeit in those sporting events in which Germany stands only a slight chance of winning, such as chess or croquet. Because the fact remains that there are certain sports in which it cannot be denied, a German-Jewish victory would present us with a political, not to say philosophical, question.' "

"Is that so?" I put out my cigarette. It was still only half smoked, but I felt something sticking in my throat, as if I had swallowed the little silver death's-head badge from the lieutenant's black cap.

"Depressing, isn't it?"

"If I've given you the impression that I'm a tough guy, then I should tell you now, I'm not. I appreciate a little bit of warning before anyone punches me in the stomach."

"There's more. Von Tschammer und Osten said that all Roman Catholic and Protestant youth organizations are, like all Jewish organizations, to be expressly forbidden to pursue any sport. As far as the Nazis are concerned, people are going to have to make a choice between religion and sports. The point being that all sports training is to be done under Nazi auspices. He actually said that the Nazis are conducting a cultural war against the church."

"He said that?"

"Any Catholic or Protestant athletes who don't join Nazi sports clubs will lose their chance of representing Germany."

I shrugged. "So let them. Who cares about a few idiots running around a track anyway?"

"You're missing the point, Gunther. They've purged the police. Now they're purging sports. If they succeed, there will be no aspect of German life in which they won't be able to exert their authority. In all aspects of German society, Nazis will be preferred. If you want to get on in life, you will have to become a Nazi."

She was smiling, and it annoyed me that she was smiling. I knew why she was smiling. She was pleased because she thought she had a scoop for her newspaper article. But it still annoyed me that she was smiling. To me this was more than just a story, this was my country.

"It's you who's missing the point," I said. "You think it was an accident that SS lieutenant decided to speak to you? You think he was just passing the time of day?" I laughed. "The Gestapo marked your card, angel. Why else would he have told you he was joining the Gestapo? After your interview with the sports leader they probably followed you here."

"Oh, that's nonsense, Bernie."

"Is it? Most likely Lieutenant Seetzen was told to charm you, to find out what kind of person you are. Who your associates are. And now they know about me." I glanced around the café. "They're probably watching us right now. Perhaps the waiter is one of theirs. Or that man reading the newspaper. It could be anyone. That's what they do."

Noreen swallowed nervously and lit another cigarette. Her lovely blue eyes flicked one way and then the other, examining the waiter and then the man with the newspaper for some sign that they were spying on us. "You really think so?"

Noreen was beginning to look convinced, and I might have smiled and told her I was joking but for the fact that I'd also succeeded in convincing myself. Why wouldn't the Gestapo have followed an American journalist who had just finished interviewing the sports leader? It made perfect sense. It's what I'd have done if I'd been in the Gestapo. I told myself I ought to have seen this coming.

"So now they know about you," I said. "And they know about me."

"I've put you in danger, haven't I?"

"Like you said this morning. A certain amount of danger is written into the job description."

"I'm sorry."

"Forget it. Then again, maybe you shouldn't forget it, after all. I like your feeling guilty on my part. It means I can blackmail you with a clear conscience, angel. Besides. As soon as I saw you I knew you were trouble. And it just so happens that's just the way I like my women. With big fenders, polished coachwork, lots of chrome, and a supercharged engine, like that car Hedda drives. The kind of car where you find yourself in Poland the moment you touch the gas. I'd be on the bus if I was interested in sleeping with librarians."

"All the same, I've been thinking about this story and not thinking at all about the impact it might have on you. I can't believe I've been so stupid as to bring you to the attention of the Gestapo."

"Maybe I didn't mention it before, but I've been in their sights for quite a while. Ever since I quit the force, as a matter of fact. There are several good reasons I can think of why the Gestapo or for that matter KRIPO could arrest me if they wanted to. It's the reasons I can't think of that are the ones I worry about most."

20

N OREEN WANTED TO SPEND THE NIGHT with me at my apartment, but I couldn't bring myself to bring her to what was little more than a room with a tiny kitchen and an even tinier bathroom. Calling it an apartment at all was a bit like describing a mustard seed as a vegetable.

There were smaller apartments in Berlin, but mostly it was the families of mice that got them first.

It was embarrassment that prevented me from showing her how I lived. But it was shame that prevented me from telling her that I was one-eighth Jewish. It's true I had been discomfited at the discovery my so-called mixed blood had been denounced to the Gestapo, but I felt no shame in being who and what I was. How could I? It seemed so insignificant. No, the shame I felt related to my having asked Emil Linthe to airbrush from the official record the very blood that connected me with Noreen, albeit in a small way. How could I tell her that? And, still nursing my secret, I spent another blissful night with Noreen in her suite at the Adlon.

Lying between her thighs, I slept only a little. We had better things to do. And early in the morning, when I made my nefarious exit from her room, I told her only that I was going home and that I would see her later that day, and nothing at all about catching the S-Bahn to Grunewald and Schildhorn.

I kept some working clothes in my office. As soon as I had changed, I went out into the predawn darkness and walked to Potsdamer Station. About forty-five minutes after that, I was walking up the steps to the Schildhorn monument with several other men, most of them Jewish-looking types with brown hair, dark melancholy eyes, bat ears, and beaks that made you wonder if God had chosen his people on the basis of their having noses they might not have chosen for themselves. This generalization was made easier by the certain knowledge that all these men shared a bloodline that was probably purer than my own. In the moonlight, one or two of them shot me a questioning look, as if wondering what the Nazis could possibly have against a tall, burly man with blond hair, blue eyes, and a nose like a baker's thumb. I didn't blame them. In that particular company I stuck out like Rameses II.

There were about 150 men gathered in the darkness under the invisible pine trees, which whispered their presence in an early-morning breeze. The monument itself was supposed to be a stylized tree crowned by a cross from which a shield was hanging. It probably meant something to someone who had a taste for unsightly religious monuments. To me it looked like a lamppost without a much-needed lamp. Or, perhaps, a stone stake for burning city architects. That would have been a worthwhile monument. Especially in Berlin.

I walked around this economy-sized obelisk, eavesdropping on a few conversations. Mostly they were to do with how many days each man had worked in the recent past. Or not worked, as seemed rather more common.

"I got one day last week," said a man. "And two the week before. I need to work today, or my family won't eat."

Another started to excoriate Goerz but was quickly silenced by someone else.

"Blame the Nazis, not Goerz. But for him none of us would work. He's risking as much as us. Maybe more."

"If you ask me, he gets well paid for the risk."

"It's my first time," I told the man standing next to me. "How do you get yourself picked?"

I offered him a cigarette, and he looked at me and my cigarettes strangely, as if suspecting that no one who really needed to work had money for such sensuous and expensive luxuries. He took it anyway and put it behind his ear.

"There's no method in it," he said. "I've been coming here for six months, and still it seems arbitrary. There are some days when he likes your face, and others when he doesn't even meet your eye."

"Maybe he's just trying to spread the work around," I said. "For the sake of fairness."

"Fairness?" The man snorted his derision. "Fairness has absolutely nothing to do with it. One day he'll take a hundred men. Another day he'll take seventy-five. It's a kind of fascism, I think. Goerz reminding us all of the power he wields."

Shorter than me by a head, the man was red-haired and sharply featured, with a face like a heavily rusted hatchet. He wore a thick pea jacket and a worker's cap, and around his neck was tied a bright green handkerchief that matched the color of the eyes behind his wire-framed glasses. Jutting out of his coat pocket was a book by Dostoevsky, and it was almost as if this young and studious-looking Jew had emerged, fully formed, from a space between the pages: neurotic, poor, undernourished, desperate. His name was Solomon Feigenbaum, which, to my mostly Aryan ears, was about as Jewish as a ghetto full of tailors.

"Anyway, if it's your first time, you almost always get picked," said Feigenbaum. "Goerz likes to give the new man a day, so that they get the taste."

"That's a relief."

"If you say so. Only you don't look like you're in desperate need of work. Matter of fact, you don't even look Jewish."

"That's what my mother said to my father. I always figured that's why she married him. It takes more than a hooked nose and a yarmulke to make a Jew, friend. What about Helene Mayer?"

"Who's she?"

"A Jewish fencer on the German Olympic team in 1932. Looks like Hitler's wet dream. She's got more blond hair than the floor in a Swedish barbershop. And what about Leni Riefenstahl? Surely you've heard the rumors."

"You're kidding."

"Not at all. Her mother was a Polish Jew."

Feigenbaum seemed vaguely amused by that.

"Listen," I said. "I haven't worked in weeks. A friend of mine told me about this *Plage*. As a matter of fact, I thought I'd see him here." As if hoping to see Isaac Deutsch, I looked around the crowd of men standing near the monument, and shook my head with disappointment.

"Did your friend tell you about the work?"

"Only that it's no questions asked."

"That all?"

"What else is there?"

"Like they use Jewish labor for work that maybe so-called German workers don't want to do because it's dangerous. On account of how they're cutting corners on safety so they can finish the stadium on time. Did your friend tell you that?"

"Are you trying to put me off?"

"I'm just telling you how it is. It seems to me that if your friend was really your friend, he might have mentioned that much. That you've got to be a bit desperate maybe to take some of the risks they expect you to take. It's not like anyone's gonna give you a hard hat, my friend. A rock falls on your head or you get buried in a cave-in, there isn't going to be anyone looking surprised or grief-stricken. There's no social welfare for illegally employed Jews. Maybe not even a headstone. Understand?"

"I understand that maybe you're trying to put me off. Increase your own chances of getting work."

"What I'm trying to say is we look after each other, see? If we don't, nobody else will. When we go down the pit, we're like the three musketeers."

"The pit? I thought we were on the stadium site."

"That's up top, for German workers. Nothing to it. Most of us here are working on the tunnel for a new S-Bahn that's going to run from the stadium all the way to Königgratzer Strasse. If you work today, you'll find out what it's like to be a mole." He glanced up at the still-dark sky. "We go down in the dark, we work in the dark, and we come up in the dark."

"You're right, my friend didn't tell me any of this," I said. "You would think he'd have mentioned it. Then again, it's been a while since I've seen him. Or his uncle. Hey, maybe you know them. Isaac and Joey Deutsch?"

"I don't know them," said Feigenbaum, but behind his glasses, his eyes had narrowed and were studying me carefully, as if maybe he had heard of them, after all. I didn't spend ten years at the Alex without getting an itch for when a man is lying. He pulled on his earlobe a couple of times and then glanced away, nervously. That was the clincher.

"But you must," I said firmly. "Isaac used to be a boxer. He was a real prospect until the Nazis excluded Jews from the fights and took away his license. Joey was his trainer. Surely you know them?"

"I tell you I don't know them." Feigenbaum spoke firmly.

I shrugged and lit a cigarette. "If you say so. I mean, it's nothing to me." I puffed the cigarette to let him get a whiff of it. I could tell he was desperate for a smoke, even though he still had the one I'd given him behind his ear. "I guess all that talk about the three musketeers and looking out for each other was just that. Talk."

"What do you mean?" His nostrils flared in front of the tobacco smoke and he licked his lips.

"Nothing," I said. "Nothing at all." I took another drag and dried his face with it. "Here. Finish it. You know you want one."

Feigenbaum took the cigarette from my fingers and went to work on it as if I'd offered him an opium pipe. Some people are just like that with a nail: they make you think that maybe there's something really harmful about a little thing like a cigarette. It's a little unnerving to watch an addiction at work like that sometimes.

I looked the other way, smiling nonchalantly. "Story of my life, I guess. I don't mean anything at all. Maybe none of us do, right? One minute we're here, and the next we're gone." I glanced at my wrist and then remembered I'd deliberately left my wristwatch back at the hotel. "Bloody wristwatch. I keep forgetting I pawned it. Where is this fellow Goerz, anyway? Shouldn't he be here by now?"

"He'll be here when he's here," said Feigenbaum, and then, still smoking my cigarette, he walked away.

Erich Goerz arrived a few minutes after that. He was accompanied by his tall driver and another, muscular-looking man. Goerz was smoking the same pungent French cigarettes and, under a gray gabardine coat, wearing the same green suit. A hat sat on the back of his head like a felt halo, and in his hand was the lead for the same invisible dog. Immediately after he appeared, men started to crowd around him as if he'd been about to deliver the Sermon on the Mount, and his two disciples extended their thick arms to prevent Goerz from being jostled. I pushed a bit closer myself, keen to seem like I was as needful of work as anyone else.

"Stand back, you kike bastards, I can see you," snarled Goerz. "What do you think this is, a beauty parade? Stand back, I said. I get pushed over like last week, and none of you yids will work today, got that?

Right. Listen to me, you kikes. I need just ten gangs today. Ten gangs. A hundred men, hear? You. Where's that money you owe me? I told you not to show your face back here until you can pay me."

"How can I pay you if I can't work?" said a plaintive voice.

"You should have thought of that before," said Goerz. "I don't know how. Sell your whore of a sister or something. What do I care?"

The two disciples grabbed the man and pushed him out of Goerz's line of sight.

"You." Goerz was speaking to someone else now. "How much did you get for those copper pipes?"

The man he'd spoken to mumbled something back.

"Give," Goerz snarled, and snatched some notes out of the man's hand.

With all this business concluded at last, he started to choose men for the work gangs, and as each gang was filled, the men left unpicked began to look more and more desperate, which only seemed to delight Goerz. He was like some capricious schoolboy selecting classmates for an important game of football. As the last gang came to be filled, one man said, "I'll give you an extra two for my shift."

"I'll kick in three," the man next to him said, and was promptly rewarded with one of the tickets a disciple handed to those lucky men whom Goerz had identified as those who would work that day.

"One day left," he said, grinning broadly. "Who wants it?"

Feigenbaum pushed his way to the front of the large crowd of men still encircling Goerz. "Please, Herr Goerz," he said. "Give me a break. It's been a week since I had a day. I need a day real bad. I've got three kids."

"That's the trouble with you Jews. You're like rabbits. No wonder people hate your guts."

Goerz looked at me. "You. Boxer." He snatched the last ticket from the hand of his disciple and then thrust it at me. "Here's a job."

I felt bad, but I took the ticket all the same, avoiding Feigenbaum's eye as I followed the rest of the men who'd been picked back down the steps to the riverbank. There were about thirty or forty steps, and they were as steep as Jacob's ladder, which was, perhaps, the intention of the Prussian emperor William IV, whose romantic ideas of chivalry had brought that peculiar monument into being. I was almost two-thirds of the way down the steps when I caught sight of the truck that was waiting to drive Erich Goerz's illegal workforce to the site. At the same time I heard some footsteps closing behind me. This was no angel, it was Goerz. He took a swing at me with a cosh, which missed, and like Jacob, I was obliged to wrestle with him for a moment before I lost my footing and fell down the remainder of the steps and hit my head on the stone wall.

I felt as if I had been lying on a concert-sized harp while someone had struck it hard with a sledgehammer. Every part of me seemed to vibrate wildly. For a moment I lay there, staring up at the early-morning sky with the certain knowledge that, unlike Hitler, God has a sense of humor. It was in the Psalms, after all. He who sits in the heavens shall laugh. How else was I to explain the fact that in order to claim for himself the shift given to me, Feigenbaum, a Jew, had almost certainly informed the anti-Semitic Goerz that I had been asking questions about Isaac and Joey Deutsch? He who sits in the heavens was laughing, all right. That was enough to make me split my sides. I closed my eyes in prayer to ask Him if there was something He had against Germans, but the answer was all too obvious, and opening my eyes again, I found there was no perceptible difference between having them open and having them closed, except that my eyelids now seemed like the heaviest thing in the world. So heavy, they felt like they were made of stone. Perhaps the stone over a deep, dark, cold tomb. The kind of stone that even Jacob's angel could not have wrestled away. Forever and ever. Amen.

21

HEDDA ADLON ALWAYS SAID that for her to run a truly great hotel, the guests needed to be asleep for sixteen hours a day; during the other eight they should be resting quietly in the bar. That sounded just fine with me. I wanted to sleep for a long time, and preferably in Noreen's bed. I might have done, too, except for the fact that she was trying to put out her cigarette in the small of my back. That's what it felt like, anyway. I tried to shift away, and then something struck me hard across the head and shoulders. I opened my eyes to discover that I was sitting on a wooden floor, covered with sawdust and tied with my back to a freestanding faience stove—one of those ceramic heaters shaped like a public drinking fountain that sits in the corner of many a German living room, like some senile relation in a rocking chair. Since I was seldom ever home, the stove in my own living room was seldom lit and was therefore seldom ever warm, but even through my jacket this one felt hotter than the smokestack on a busy steam tug. I arched my back trying to minimize the point of contact with the hot ceramic and succeeded only in burning my hands; hearing my cry of pain, Erich Goerz once again set about lashing me with the dog lead. At least now I knew why he carried it. No doubt he saw himself as a sort of overseer, like that Egyptian slave driver murdered by Moses in Exodus. I wouldn't have minded murdering Goerz myself.

When he stopped beating me, I looked up and saw that he had my identity card in his hands, and cursed myself for not leaving it back at the hotel in the pocket of my suit. Standing a few feet behind him were Goerz's tall, cadaverous-looking driver and the square-sized man from the monument. He had a face like an unfinished piece of marble sculpture.

"Bernhard Gunther," said Goerz. "It says here you're a hotel employee but that you used to be a cop. What's a hotel employee doing around here, asking questions about Isaac Deutsch?"

"Untie me and I'll tell you."

"Tell me and then I'll untie you. Maybe."

I saw no reason not to tell him the truth. No reason at all. Torture will do that to you sometimes. "One of the guests at the hotel is an American reporter," I said. "She's writing a newspaper article about Jews in German sports. And Isaac Deutsch in particular. She wants to bring about a U.S. boycott of the Olympiad. And she's paying me to help her do the research."

I grimaced and tried to ignore the heat in my back, which was a little like trying to ignore a minor imp in hell, armed with a hot pitchfork and my name on his day's work sheet.

"That's bullshit," said Goerz. "It's bullshit, because I read the newspapers, which is how I happen to know that the American Olympic Committee already voted against a boycott." He raised the dog lead and started to beat me again.

"She's a Jew," I yelled through the blows. "She thinks that if she writes the truth about what's happening in this country, to people like Isaac Deutsch, then the Amis will have to change their minds. Deutsch is the focus of her piece. How he got kicked out of his local boxing association and how he ended up working here. And how there was an accident. I don't know what happened exactly. He drowned, didn't he? In the S-Bahn tunnel, was it? And then someone dumped him in the canal on the other side of the city."

Goerz stopped beating me. He looked out of breath. He swept his hair out of his eyes, straightened his tie, swung the leash around his neck, and then hung on it with both hands. "And how did you find out about him?"

"An ex-colleague, a bull at the Alex, showed me the body in the morgue and gave me the file. That's all. I used to work Homicide, see? They'd run out of ideas on who the guy might be and figured I might offer a new perspective."

Goerz looked at his driver and laughed. "Shall I tell you what I think?" he said. "I think you used to be a cop. And I think you still are. A secret cop. Gestapo. I've never seen anyone who looked less like a hotel employee than you do, my friend. I'll bet that's just a cover story so you can go around spying on people. And more important, on us."

"It's the truth, I tell you. Look, I know you didn't kill Deutsch. It was an accident. That much was clear from the autopsy. You see, he couldn't have drowned in the canal, because his lungs were full of sea-water. That's what made the polenta suspicious in the first place."

"There was an autopsy?" It was the square-looking man—the living sculpture—who spoke. "You mean they cut him open?"

"Of course there was an autopsy, you dumb schmuck. That's the law. Where do you think this is? The Belgian Congo? When a body's found, a body has to be investigated. Surgically and circumstantially."

"But when they finished with him, they'd have given him a proper burial, right?"

I groaned with pain and shook my head. "Burials are for Otto Normals," I said. "Not unidentified bodies. There' s been no identification. Not formally. No one claimed him, see? I'm only investigating it because the Ami woman wanted to find out about the guy. The polenta doesn't know shit about him. As far as I know, the body went to the Charité Hospital. To the anatomy class. The kids with the forceps and the lancets got to play with him."

"You mean medical students?"

"I don't mean students of political economy, you stupid bastard. Of course medical students."

I was beginning to see that this was a sensitive subject to the man with the jaw that looked as if it had been cut from a piece of marble. But with my tongue loosened from the pain I was feeling from the heat of the stove, I kept on talking regardless. "By now they'll have sliced him open and used his dick to make an oxtail soup. His skull's probably an ashtray on some student's desk. What do you care, Hermann? You're the people who dumped the poor bastard in the canal like a pail of restaurant garbage."

The square-looking man with the marble chin shook his head grimly. "I thought at least he'd get a decent burial."

"I told you, decent burials are for citizens. Not floaters. It seems to me that the only person who's tried to treat Isaac Deutsch with any respect is my client." I tried to twist away from the stove, but it was no good. I was beginning to feel like Jan Hus.

"Your client." Erich Goerz's voice was full of contempt, like some grand inquisitor. He started to beat me again. The dog lead whistled through the air like a flail. I felt like a dusty rug at the Adlon. "You're going. To tell us. Exactly. Who the hell. You are . . ."

"That's enough," said the square-looking man with the marble chin.

I didn't see what happened next. I was too busy pressing my chin into my chest and closing my eyes, trying to ride out the pain of the beating. All I know is that suddenly the beating stopped and Goerz hit the floor in front of me with blood pouring from the side of his mouth. I looked up just in time to see Marble Jaw neatly sidestep a big haymaker from Goerz's driver before lifting him off his toes with a fist that came flying up from the basement like an express elevator. The driver went down like a tower of wooden blocks, which was as satisfying to me as if I had toppled him myself.

Marble Jaw took a breath and then started to untie me.

"I'm sorry," I said.

"For what?"

"For what I said about your nephew, Isaac." I pulled the ropes away and wrestled my back clear of the stove. "I'm right, aren't I? You are Isaac's uncle Joey?"

He nodded and helped me to stand. "The back of your coat's scorched through," he said. "I can't see what your back looks like, but it can't be too bad. Otherwise we could probably smell it."

"There's a comforting thought. By the way, thanks. For helping me." I put my arm around his huge shoulder and straightened painfully.

"He's had that coming for a long time," said Joey.

"I'm afraid all of what I said was true. But I'm sorry you had to hear about it like that."

Joey Deutsch shook his head. "I suspected as much," he said. "Goerz told me different, of course, but in my guts I suppose I knew different. I wanted to believe him, for Isaac's sake. I guess I had to hear it from someone else for it sink in."

Erich Goerz rolled slowly onto his stomach and groaned.

"That's quite an uppercut you've got on you, Joey," I said.

"Come on. I'll get you home." He hesitated. "Can you stand by yourself?"

"Yes."

Joey bent down over the unconscious driver and retrieved a set of car keys from the man's waistcoat pocket. "We'll take Erich's car," he said. "Just in case these two bastards come after us."

Goerz groaned again and contracted, slowly, into a fetal position. For a brief second I thought he might be having some sort of convulsion until I remembered what Blask, the site foreman, had told me about the gun strapped to Goerz's ankle. Only it wasn't strapped to his ankle anymore. It was in his hand.

"Look out!" I yelled, and kicked Goerz in the head. I'd meant to kick his hand, but as I raised my foot I lost control and fell onto the floor again.

The pistol fired harmlessly, breaking a windowpane.

I crawled over to Goerz to look at him. I hardly wanted another man's death on my conscience. He was unconscious, but fortunately for me, and more especially him, Erich Goerz was still breathing. I retrieved my ID card from the floor, where he had tossed it angrily a few minutes earlier, and picked up the pistol. It was a Bayard semiautomatic 6.35-millimeter.

"French cigarettes, French gun," I said. "Makes sense, I suppose." I made the gun safe and pointed it at the door. "Anyone else out there, do you think?" I asked Joey.

"You mean, like him? No, it was just these two, the three truck drivers, and, I'm sorry to say, me. After Isaac got killed, they took me on the payroll. As extra muscle, they said, but I guess it was just as much about ensuring that I kept my mouth shut."

As Joey helped me walk to the door, I got a better look at him and saw a man who didn't look much more Jewish than I did. The hair on the side of a head as big as a watermelon was gray, but on top it was blond, and as curly as an Astrakhan coat. The huge face was both florid and pasty, like old bacon. Small brown eyes sat on either side of a broken nose that was sharp and pointy. The eyebrows were almost invisible, as were the teeth in his gaping mouth. Somehow he put me in mind of a man-sized baby.

We went downstairs, and I recognized that we were in the Albert the Bear. There was no sign of a proprietor, and I didn't ask. Outside, the fresh morning air helped revive me a little. I got into the passenger seat of the Hanomag and, almost destroying the gears, Deutsch quickly drove us away. He was a terrible driver and narrowly missed colliding with a water trough on the corner.

It turned out that he lived not so very far away from me in the southeastern part of the city. We dumped what was left of the Hanomag in the car park of the cemetery on Baruther Strasse. Joey wanted to take me to a hospital, but I told him I thought I'd probably be all right.

"How about you?" I asked him.

"Me? I'm all right. You don't have to worry about me, son."

"I just cost you a job."

Joey shook his head. "I shouldn't ever have taken it."

I lit us both a cigarette. "Feel up to talking about it?"

"How do you mean?"

"My Ami friend. The journalist. Noreen Charalambides. She's the one writing about Isaac. I imagine she'd like to speak to you. To get your story and Isaac's."

Joey grunted without much enthusiasm for the idea.

"Given that he's got no actual grave, it could be like a kind of memorial," I said. "To his memory."

While Joey considered this idea, he puffed at the cigarette. In his mallet-sized fist it looked more like a safety match.

"Not a bad idea at that," he said finally. "Bring her around this evening. She can get the whole story. If she doesn't mind slumming it."

He gave me an address in Britz, near the meat-canning factory. I jotted it down on the inside of my cigarette pack.

"Does Erich Goerz know this address?" I asked.

"Nobody does. There's just me that lives there now. If you can call it living. Since Isaac died I've let myself go a bit, you know? There doesn't seem to be much point in looking after the place now that he's gone. Not much point in anything at all, really."

"I know what that's like," I said.

"Been a while since I had any visitors. Maybe I could tidy up a bit. Put things in order before—"

"Don't put yourself to any trouble."

"It's no trouble," he said quietly. "No trouble at all." He nodded resolutely. "Matter of fact, I should have done it a while ago."

He walked away. I found a phone booth and telephoned the Adlon.

I told Noreen some of it but not all. The part about me spilling almost the whole story to Erich Goerz I didn't tell her. The only consolation there was that I hadn't mentioned the name of the hotel where she was staying.

She said she'd come right over.

22

I OPENED THE DOOR WIDE, but not as wide as Noreen's eyes. She stood there, wearing a red dress underneath her sable coat and looking at me with a mixture of shock and bewilderment, much as Lotte must have looked upon discovering she had arrived in time to find that young Werther had just succeeded in blowing his brains out. Assuming he had any brains.

"My God," she whispered, touching my face. "What happened to you?"

"I just read a portion of Ossian," I said. "Second-rate poetry always affects me this way."

She pushed me gently aside and closed the door behind her.

"You should see me when I'm really affected by something good. Like Schiller. I'm bedridden for days."

She shrugged off her coat and tossed it onto a chair.

"You might not want to do that," I said. I was trying not to feel embarrassed about the place, but it wasn't easy. "It's been a while since that chair was properly deloused."

"Do you have any iodine?"

"No, but I have a bottle of kummel. Matter of fact, I think I'll have one myself."

I went over to the sideboard to pour a couple of drinks. I didn't ask if she wanted one. I'd seen her drink before.

While she waited, she glanced around. The living room had a sideboard, an armchair, and a folding table. There was a high bookcase built into the walls, and it was full of books, several of which I'd read. There were a stove and a small fireplace with an even smaller fire. There was also a bed, since the living room happened also to be the bedroom. Through an open doorway was a garbage area that was also the kitchen. On the other side of the frosted kitchen window was a security grille and a fire escape, just to make the mice feel safe. Next to the front door was the door to the bathroom, only the bath was hanging upside down on the ceiling, right above the lavatory, where a man sitting there might contemplate the inconvenience of taking a bath in front of the fire. The floor was linoleum throughout, with a small collection of stamp-sized rugs. Some people might have thought it a bit of a dump, but to me it was a palace or, to be more accurate, the meanest room in a palace, the one where the servants kept their junk.

"I'm waiting for my interior decorator to come back with a portrait of the Leader," I said. "After that it should look nice and cozy."

She took the drink I offered her and stared closely at my face. "That weal," she said. "You should put something on it."

I pulled her closer. "How about your mouth?"

"Do you have any Vaseline?"

"What's that?"

"First-aid petroleum jelly."

"Hey, listen, I'll live. I was at the Battle of Amiens and I'm still here, and believe me, that takes some doing."

She shrugged and pulled away. "Go ahead. Be tough. But I had the funny idea I care for you, which means I don't like it that you've been whipped. If anyone's going to whip you it ought to be me, only I'll make sure I don't leave any marks."

"Thanks, I'll bear it in mind. Anyway, it wasn't a whip. It was a dog leash."

"You didn't mention a dog."

"There wasn't a dog. It's my impression that Goerz would prefer to carry a whip, but people on the tram look at you a bit strangely when you go around with one of those in your hand. Even in Berlin."

"Do you think he hits his Jewish workers with it?"

"I shouldn't be at all surprised."

I tossed back the kummel, held it on my tonsils for moment, and then let it roll, enjoying the warmth as it spread through my body. Meanwhile Noreen found some chamomile ointment and anointed my more obvious wounds with it. I think it made her feel better. I poured myself another kummel. Which made me feel better.

WE WALKED TO A TAXI RANK and took a cab to the address in Britz. South of another modern apartment building called the Horseshoe and next to the Grossmann Coburg canned-meat factory was a decayed archway that was the entrance to a series of courtyards and tenement buildings of the kind that might convince any architect that he was some kind of messiah come to save people from their squalor and poverty. Personally, I never minded a little squalor. To be honest, for a long time after the war I hardly noticed it.

Passing through another archway, we came upon a tatty sign for infrared health lamps painted onto the brickwork. That seemed a little optimistic, to say the least. We mounted a dark stairway that led up into the building's tomblike interior. Somewhere a barrel organ was churning out a melancholy tune that matched our lowering spirits. A German tenement building could have sucked all the light out of the second coming.

Halfway up the stairs we passed a woman who was on her way down. There was a bicycle wheel in her hand and a loaf of bread under her arm. A few steps behind her was a boy of about ten or eleven wearing the uniform of the Hitler Youth. The woman smiled and nodded a little bow in Noreen's direction or, as seemed more likely, at the sable coat she was wearing. This prompted Noreen to ask if we were on the right flight of stairs for Herr Deutsch. The woman with the bicycle wheel answered respectfully that it was, and we carried on up, stepping carefully around a second woman who was on her knees, scrubbing the stairs with a heavy brush and something noxious in a bucket. She had heard us ask about Joey Deutsch, and as we moved past, she said, "Tell that Jew it's his turn to clean the stairs."

"Tell him yourself," said Noreen.

"I did," said the woman. "Just now. But he paid no notice. Didn't even come to the door. Which is why I'm doing it myself."

"Perhaps he's not in," said Noreen.

"Oh, he's in there, all right. He must be. I saw him go up there a while ago and I haven't seen him come down. Besides, his door is open." She went at the steps with the brush for several seconds. "I expect he's avoiding me."

"Does he normally leave his front door open?" I asked, suddenly suspicious.

"What? Around here? Are you joking? But I think he must be expecting someone. You, perhaps, if your name is Gunther. There's a note stuck on the door."

We quickly went up the last two flights of stairs and stopped in front of a door once painted scarlet but now hardly painted at all unless you counted the yellow star and the words JEWS OUT with which someone had thoughtfully defaced it. There was a blue envelope tacked onto the door frame. It was addressed to me. And the door was open just as the woman cleaning the stairs had said. I put the envelope in my pocket and, taking out Erich Goerz's pistol, steered Noreen behind me.

"There's something not right here," I said, and pushed open the door.

As we went into the little apartment, Noreen reached up and touched a small brass plate on the door frame. "The mezuzah," she said. "It's a passage from the Torah. Most Jewish homes have one."

I worked the slide on the little automatic and stepped into the small hallway. The apartment comprised two largish rooms. To the left was a living room that was a shrine to boxing and one boxer in particular: Isaac Deutsch. In a glass cabinet were some ten or fifteen empty wooden trophy stands and several photographs of Joey and Isaac. I imagined the trophies had been pawned a long time ago. The walls were papered with boxing posters, and piles of fight magazines were heaped around the room. On a table were a very stale loaf of bread and a fruit bowl containing a couple of blackened bananas that were now a world's fair of tiny flies. A pair of ancient-looking boxing gloves hung from a nail on the back of the door, and a selection of rusting weights lay next to a bar that was leaning against a wall. Above it was a length of rope from which were hanging a shirt and a broken umbrella. There were a disemboweled armchair and, behind it, a full-length mirror with a crack in the glass. Everything else was just junk.

"Herr Deutsch?" My voice sounded tight in my chest, like I had a cuckoo nesting between my two lungs. "It's Gunther. Are you home?"

We went back through the hallway and into the bedroom, where the curtains were drawn. There was a strong smell of carbolic soap and disinfectant. Or so I thought, anyway. A big brass bed stood opposite a wardrobe the size of a small Swiss bank vault.

"Joey? Is that you?"

In the curtained gloom I saw the outline of a figure on the bed and felt my hair lift the back of my hat. You spend ten years as a cop, sometimes you know what you're going to see before you see it. And you know that it's not everyone who can look it straight in the eye.

"Noreen," I said. "I think Joey's killed himself. We'll only find out for sure when I draw the curtains and read that note. Maybe you're the kind of writer who feels she needs to see everything. Who thinks she has a duty to report everything, unflinchingly. I don't know. But it's my opinion that you need to brace yourself or leave the room. I've seen enough bodies in my time to know that it's never—"

"I've seen a dead body before, Bernie. I told you about that lynching in Georgia. And my father, he killed himself, with a shotgun. You don't forget that in a hurry, I can tell you."

Reflecting that it was interesting how quickly my concern to spare her feelings turned to something like sadism, I yanked the curtains open with no more argument. She wanted to play at being Turgenev, it was all right with me.

Joey Deutsch lay across his bed, still wearing the same clothes I had seen him in earlier. He was half twisted up off the mattress, as if some of the springs had burst out of the material under the small of his back. He was clean-shaven as before—only now it looked as if he were wearing a brown mustache and a small beard. These were corrosive burns and the result of whatever he had swallowed to poison himself. A bottle lay on the floor where he had dropped it, and next to this was a pool of bloody vomit. I picked the bottle up carefully and sniffed at the open neck.

"Lye," I told her, but she had already turned away and was leaving the room. I followed her into the hallway. "He drank lye. Jesus. What a way to kill yourself."

Noreen had pressed her face into a corner of the entrance hall like a disobedient child. Her arms were folded defensively across her chest and her eyes were closed. I lit a couple of cigarettes, tapped her on the elbow, and gave her one. I didn't say anything. Whatever I might have said would have sounded like "I told you so."

Still smoking, I went back into the living room. On top of a pile of fight magazines was a small leather writing folder. Inside were some envelopes and notepaper that matched the note addressed to me. So did the ink in the Pelikan he'd replaced in the little cylindrical leather sleeve. There was nothing that made me suspect anyone had forced him to write the note. The writing was neat and unhurried. I'd had love letters that were much less legible, although not for a long time. I read it carefully, as if Joey Deutsch had meant something to me. It seemed like the least I could do for a dead man. Then I read it again.

"What does it say?" Noreen was standing in the doorway. In her hand was a handkerchief, and in her eyes were some tears.

I held the note out to her. "Here." I watched her read it, wondering what was going through her mind. If she actually felt anything for the poor guy who'd just killed himself, or if she was just relieved to have found an end for her story and a good excuse to go home. If that sounds cynical, maybe it was, but the truth was that her leaving Berlin was all I could think about now because, for the first time, I realized I was in love with her. And when you're in love with someone you think might be about to leave you, it's easier to be cynical, just to protect yourself from the pain you know is coming.

She offered the note back.

"Why don't you keep it," I said. "Although he never met you, I think he really meant you to have it. For your newspaper article. I kind of sold him on the idea that your piece could be a kind of memorial to Isaac."

"It will be, I think. Why not?" She took the letter. "But what about the police? Won't they need this? It's evidence, isn't it?"

"What do they care?" I shrugged. "Maybe you've forgotten how anxious they were to find out what happened to Isaac. All the same, perhaps we ought to get out of here before we have to wait around and answer questions we might not want to answer. Like how come I've got a gun without a license, and why I've got the mark of a dog leash across my face."

"The neighbors," she said. "That woman on the stairs. Suppose they tell the police about us. The note. She knows your name."

"I'll square her on the way out. Ten marks buys a lot of silence in this part of Berlin. Besides, you saw the door. These neighbors don't exactly strike me as very neighborly. It's my impression that they'll be glad to see Joey dead and out of this building. And what do you think the polenta would do with a note like that? Print it in the newspaper? I don't think so. Most likely they'll destroy it. No, it's best you keep it, Noreen. For Joey's sake. And Isaac's, too."

"I guess you're right, Gunther. But I wish you weren't."

"I get that." I glanced around the miserable apartment and let out a sigh. "Who knows? Maybe he's better off out of it."

"You can't believe that."

"I don't see things improving for Jews in this country. There are a bunch of new laws coming that will make things even tougher for anyone who's not properly German, as they see it. That's what I've heard, anyway."

"Ahead of the Olympics?"

"Didn't I mention it?"

"You know you didn't."

I shrugged. "I suppose I didn't want to put a dent in your optimism, angel. That something can be done. Maybe I was hoping that some of your lefty idealism would rub off on me along with your pants and stockings."

"And did it?"

"Not this particular morning."

23

IN THE EARLY EVENING I accompanied Noreen back to the hotel. She went up to her room for a bath and an early night. The discovery of Joey Deutsch's body had left Noreen emotionally and physically exhausted. I had a good idea how she felt.

I was on my way to my office when Franz Joseph called me over and, after some polite inquiries about the marks on my face, told me he had a package for me, from Otto Trettin at the Alex. I knew it was the Chinese box belonging to Max Reles. Just the same, when I got to my desk, I opened it up to see what all the fuss had been about.

It looked like a paper-clip box for a Chinese emperor. I suppose it was quite attractive, if you like that kind of thing. I prefer something in sterling silver, with a matching table lighter. On a black lacquer lid, outlined in gold, was a brightly painted Arcadian scene featuring a lake, some mountains, a handsome weeping willow, a cherry tree, a fisherman, a couple of mounted archers, a coolie carrying a large bag of hotel laundry, and a group of Fu Manchu types in the local noodle house who seemed to be discussing the yellow peril and the finer points of white slavery. I expect you never got tired of looking at it if you lived in seventeenth-century China, unless there was some paint you could watch getting dry. It had the feel of a cheap souvenir from a day trip to Luna Park.

I opened it, and inside were a number of contract-tender letters from companies as far afield as Würzburg and Bremerhaven. I glanced over them without much interest. I put these in my pocket, to irritate Reles with their apparent loss in case they were important to him, and went up to his suite.

I knocked on the door. It was answered by Dora Bauer. She was wearing a light brown gingham pleated dress with a matching cape collar and a large pussycat bow on the shoulder. Her hair had a wave as big as a tsunami that swept all the way across her forehead and down to an eyebrow as thin as a spider's leg. A bow mouth that was more Clara than Cupid parted in a smile as wide as a welcome mat. The smile turned painful as she noticed the weal on my face.

"Oooh, what happened to you?"

Otherwise she seemed pleased to see me, unlike Reles, who ambled over behind her wearing his usual expression of contempt. I had the Chinese box at my back and was looking forward to handing it over after the usual litany of insults. I had the vain hope I might embarrass him or make him eat his words.

"If it isn't the Continental Op," he said.

"I don't have much time for detective stories," I said.

"I suppose you're too busy reading the Leader's book?"

"I don't have much time for his stories, either."

"You want to be careful saying disrespectful things like that. You could get hurt." He frowned and searched my face. "Maybe you already did. Or did you just pick a fight with another hotel guest? That's more your level, I'd say. Somehow I don't see you as the heroic type."

"Max, please." Dora sounded scolding, but that was as far as it went.

"You'd be surprised what I'm called to do in the line of duty, Herr Reles," I said. "Squeeze the eggs of a fellow who doesn't pay his bill. Flick the ear of some barfly. Slap a garter handler in the mouth. Hell, I've even been known to recover stolen property."

I brought my arm around and handed him the box, as if it had been a bunch of flowers. A bunch of five was what I felt like giving him.

"Well, I'll be damned. You found it. You really were a cop, weren't you?" He took the box and, backing away from the door, waved me in. "Come on in, Gunther. Dora, get Herr Gunther a drink, will you? What'll you have, Detective? Schnapps? Scotch? Vodka?" He pointed out a series of bottles on the sideboard.

"Thank you. Schnapps would be good."

I closed the door behind me, watching him carefully for the moment he opened the box. And when he did, I had the satisfaction of noticing a small wince of disappointment.

"That's a pity," he said.

"What is, sir?"

"Only that there was some money and correspondence in this box. And now it's not there."

"You didn't mention the contents before, sir." I shook my head. "Would you like me to inform the police, sir?" That was two "sirs" in a row: maybe it was still possible I could hold down a career in hotel keeping, after all.

He smiled irritably. "It really doesn't matter, I suppose."

"Ice?" Dora was standing over a bucket containing a piece of ice with a pick in her hand, looking more than a little like Lady Macbeth.

"Ice? In schnapps?" I shook my head. "No, I don't think so."

Dora stabbed the ice a couple of times and placed a few shards in a large tumbler glass, which she handed to Reles.

"American habit," said Reles. "We put ice in everything. But I kind of like it in schnapps. You should try it sometime."

Dora handed me a smaller glass of schnapps. I was watching her now for some sign that she might be up to her old whore's tricks, but there didn't seem to be anything between them that I could see. She even shied away a little when he came too close. The typewriter looked like it was still as busy as always. The wastepaper basket was overflowing.

I toasted Reles.

"Down the hatch," he said, and took a large mouthful of ice-cold schnapps.

I sipped mine like a dowager, and we faced each other in awkward silence. I waited a moment, then tossed back the rest.

"Well, if that's all, Detective," he said. "We have work to do, don't we, Fräulein Bauer?"

I handed Dora the glass and headed for the door. Reles was there ahead of me, to open it and speed me on my way.

"And thanks again," he said, "for recovering my property. I appreciate it. For what it's worth, you've restored my faith in the German people."

"I'll be sure to tell them that, sir."

He chuckled, thought of a retaliatory remark, appeared to think better of it, and then waited patiently for me to make my exit from his suite.

"Thanks for the drink, sir."

He nodded and closed the door behind me.

I hurried along the landing and down the stairs. Crossing the entrance hall, I went into the switchboard room, where, under a high window, four girls were sitting on high chairs in front of what looked like a double-sized upright piano. Behind them was a desk where Hermine, the switchboard supervisor, sat watching the hotel's "hello girls" as they went about the voluble business of connecting telephone calls. She was a prim woman, with short red hair and a complexion as pale as milk. Seeing me, Hermine stood up and then frowned.

"That mark on your face," she said. "It looks very much like a whip mark."

Several of her girls looked around and laughed.

"I went riding with Hedda Adlon," I said. "Listen, Hermine, the party in 114. Herr Reles. I want a list of everyone he calls this evening."

"Does Herr Behlert know you're asking?"

I shook my head. I went a little closer to the switchboard, and Hermine followed attentively.

"He wouldn't like you spying on the guests, Herr Gunther. I think you'll need to get his written permission."

"It's not spying, it's snooping. I'm paid to snoop, remember? To keep you and me and the guests safe, although not necessarily in that order."

"Maybe. But if he found you listening in on Herr Reles's calls, he'd have our hides."

"Putting you through now, Herr Reles," said Ingrid, who was one of the best-looking of the Adlon's hello girls.

"Herr Reles? He's on a call now? To whom?"

Ingrid exchanged a look with Hermine.

"Come on, ladies, this is important. If he's a crook—and I think he is—we need to know about it."

Hermine nodded her approval.

"Potsdam 3058," said Ingrid.

"Who's that?" I waited for a moment.

Hermine nodded again.

"That's Count von Helldorf's number," said Ingrid. "At the Potsdam Police Praesidium."

Anywhere else but the Adlon I might have persuaded them to let me eavesdrop on that call, but short of a spot lamp and a set of brass knuckles, I'd had all that I was going to get out of the hello girls: standards might have been compromised in other Berlin institutions such as the police, the courts, and the churches, but not at its best hotel.

So I went back to my office to smoke some cigarettes, have a couple of drinks, and take another look at the papers I had taken from the Chinese box. I had the curious idea these were more important to Max Reles than the box itself. But my mind was elsewhere. A telephone call made by Max Reles to von Helldorf so soon after I had seen the American was disturbing. Was it possible their topic of conversation had been me? And if so, to what effect? There were good reasons why von Helldorf might be useful to a man such as Max Reles, and vice versa.

Formerly the leader of Berlin's SA, Count Wolf-Heinrich Graf von Helldorf had been the police president of Berlin for just three months when a notorious scandal interrupted his progress to higher office. He had always been an enthusiastic gambler and a rumored pederast with a taste for the flagellation of young boys. He was also a close friend of Erik Hanussen, the famous clairvoyant who, it was supposed, had paid off the count's very substantial gambling debts in return for an introduction to the Leader.

Much of what happened thereafter was still the subject of speculation and mystery, but it seemed that Hitler was strongly impressed by the man Berlin's communists called "the people's stupefier." As a result of Hitler's open favor, Hanussen's influence over senior Party members, including von Helldorf, became even greater. Yet all was not quite what it seemed. Hanussen's leverage within the Party was, it was to be revealed, the result not of good advice, nor even of mesmeric power, but blackmail. At lavish sex parties he had hosted aboard his yacht, the *Ursel IV*, Hanussen had "hypnotized" several leading Nazis and subsequently filmed them taking part in sexual orgies. That was bad enough, but some of these orgies were homosexual orgies.

It is possible Berlin's famous clairvoyant might have survived all of this. But when Goebbels's newspaper, *Der Angriff*, revealed that Hanussen was a Jew, the shit really ended up on the conveyor belt, with most of it headed Hitler's way. Suddenly Hanussen had become an acute embarrassment, and von Helldorf, held largely responsible, was required to clean up the mess. Several days after Hermann Goering dismissed him as Berlin's police president, von Helldorf and some of his more murderous SA friends abducted Hanussen from his lavish apartment in Berlin's Westend, drove him to his yacht, and tortured him there until Hanussen gave them all of the compromising material he had amassed over several months: debt receipts, letters, photographs, and ciné film. Then they shot him and dumped the body on a field in Mühlenbeck. Somewhere north of Berlin, anyway.

Rumors persisted that von Helldorf had used some of the material he had obtained from Hanussen to secure himself a new position as police president of Potsdam—an unimportant town about an hour southwest of Berlin, where, it is said, beer goes to turn flat. Von Helldorf now spent most of his time there breeding horses and organizing the continuing persecution of those Social Democrats and German communists who had most offended the Nazis during the last days of the republic. And it was generally supposed that in this respect, von Helldorf was largely motivated by the hope he might eventually manage to restore himself to Hitler's full favor. I knew von Helldorf was also on the German Olympic Organizing Committee, of course, which said something about the success of his attempt to put himself back in favor with Hitler, although I wasn't quite sure exactly what he did on the committee. Possibly that was just payback from his old SA pal von Tschammer und Osten. Possibly, since Goering's departure from the Ministry of the Interior, he was in better odor there, too. In spite of everything, von Helldorf was not a man to be taken anything but seriously.

My attack of nerves lasted only a short while, however. As long as it took for the alcohol to kick in. After a few drinks I persuaded myself that since there was really nothing about the letters and business estimates I had taken from the Chinese box that could prove anything in a court of law, then there was no need for me to feel concerned. There wasn't anything I had seen that could have harmed a man like Max Reles. Besides, Reles couldn't know it had been I who had taken these papers, and not Ilse Szrajbman.

So I put the papers and the gun in my desk drawer and decided to head home, thinking, like Noreen, to have an early night myself. I was tired, and I ached in every conceivable part of my body.

Leaving Behlert's car where I had parked it earlier, I walked south down Hermann-Goering-Strasse to catch a tram on Potsdamer Platz. It was dark and a little windy, and the Nazi banners hanging on the Brandenburg Gate were flapping around like danger flags, as if our imperial past were trying to warn us about something in our Nazi present. Even a stray dog trotting along the pavement ahead of me stopped and turned to look at me dolefully, perhaps to ask if I had a solution to our country's problems. Then again, he might just have been trying to avoid the open door of the black W that had pulled up a few meters ahead. A man wearing a brown leather coat got out of the car and walked quickly toward me.

Instinctively, I turned to walk in the opposite direction and discovered my retreat blocked by a man wearing a thick, double-breasted overcoat and a low-brimmed hat, although it was the neat little bow tie I noticed most. At least until I noticed the beer token in his paw.

"Come with us, please."

The other man in the leather coat was right behind me now, so that, sandwiched between them, I couldn't very well have resisted. Like experienced window dressers moving a tailor's dummy, they folded me into the car and jumped in the backseat on either side of me. We were moving before they had even slammed the car doors.

"If this is about that cop," I said. "August Krichbaum, wasn't it? I thought we'd sorted out that bullshit. I mean, you checked my alibi. I had nothing to do with it. You know that."

After a few moments I realized we were going west, along Charlottenburger Strasse, in completely the opposite direction from Alexanderplatz. I asked where we were going, but neither of them spoke. The driver's hat was made of leather. So were his ears, probably. By the time we reached Berlin's famous radio tower and turned onto the AVUS—Berlin's fastest road—I had guessed where we were driving. The driver bought a ticket and we sped toward Wannsee Station. A few years before, Fritz von Opel had set a speed record on the AVUS, driving a rocket-powered car at almost 240 kilometers an hour. We weren't driving anything nearly as fast as that, but neither did I get the impression that we were likely to stop anywhere for coffee and cake. At the end of the AVUS, we drove through some woods onto the Glienecke Bridge and, although it was very dark, I could just make out that we had passed two castles. Shortly after that we entered Potsdam on New Königstrasse.

Surrounded by the Havel and its lakes, Potsdam wasn't much more than an island. And I couldn't have felt more lonely if I'd been marooned on some desert atoll with a solitary palm tree and a parrot. For more than a hundred years the town had been the headquarters of the Prussian army, but it might as well have been the headquarters of the Girl Guides for all the help the army was going to give me. I was about to become the prisoner of Count von Helldorf and there was nothing anyone could do about it. One of the buildings in Potsdam was the palace called Sanssouci, which is French for "without care." I was a long way from a state of mind like that.

As we drove past another castle and a parade ground, I caught a glimpse of a street sign. We were on Priest Strasse, and I was beginning to think I might have need of one as we turned into the courtyard of the local police praesidium.

Entering the building, we went up several flights of stairs and along a cold, dimly lit corridor to a handsomely appointed office with a nice view of the Havel, which I recognized only because there was an even more handsomely appointed motor yacht floating on it just below the leaded window and lit up like a ride at Luna Park.

In the office, a tree was burning in an open fireplace where you could have roasted a whole ox. There were a big hanging tapestry, a portrait of Hitler, and a suit of armor that looked about as stiff as the man standing beside it. He was wearing the uniform of a police general and an air of aristocratic superiority, as if he should have preferred that my shoes had been removed before I was allowed to walk on his park-sized Persian rug. I suppose he was about the same age as I, but there the similarity ended. When he spoke, his tone was careworn and exasperated, and he gave me the impression I had caused him to miss the beginning of an opera or, more likely in his case, a queerish cabaret turn. On a log cabin of a desk, a backgammon set was laid out for a game, and in his hand was a little leather cup containing a pair of dice that every now and then he would rattle nervously, like some mendicant friar.

"Please sit down," he said.

The man in the leather coat pushed me into a seat at a meeting table and then pushed a pen and a sheet of paper toward me. He seemed to be good at pushing things. "Sign it," he said.

"What is it?" I asked

"It's a D-11," said the man. "An order for protective custody."

"I used to be a cop myself," I said. "At the Alex. And I never heard of a D-11. What does it mean?"

Leather Coat glanced at von Helldorf, who replied, "If you sign it, it means you agree to be sent to a concentration camp."

"I don't want to go to a concentration camp. As a matter of fact, I don't want to be here, either. No offense, but it's been a hell of a day."

"Signing a D-11 doesn't mean you will be sent to a camp," explained von Helldorf. "What it means is that you agree to go."

"Forgive me, sir, but I don't agree."

Von Helldorf rocked on the heels of his jackboots and rattled the dice box behind his back.

"You could say that once it's signed, it acts as a guarantee of your good behavior," he said. "Your future good behavior. Do you see?"

"Yes. But equally, and with all due respect to yourself, General, it could just as easily result in my being taken from here to the nearest camp. Don't get me wrong. I could use a holiday. I'd like to sit around for a couple of weeks and catch up on my reading. But from what I've heard, there's not much concentration that's possible in a concentration camp."

"A lot of what you say is quite true, Herr Gunther," said von Helldorf. "However, if you don't sign, you will be kept here in a police cell until you agree to do so. So, as you can see, you really don't have much choice in the matter."

"So in other words, I'm damned if I do and damned if I don't."

"In a manner of speaking, yes."

"I don't suppose there's a piece of paper I have to sign before I can be kept in a police cell, is there?"

"I'm afraid not. But let me repeat, signing the D-11 doesn't mean you will go to a camp. The fact is, Herr Gunther, this government is doing its best to be more sparing with the use of protective custody. You may be aware that Oranienburg concentration camp has recently closed, for example. Also that the Leader has signed an amnesty affecting political prisoners, on August seventh this year. All of which makes perfect sense, given that almost everyone in the country is now inclined to favor his inspired leadership. Indeed, it is even hoped that in time all of the concentration camps will disappear, like Oranienburg.

"Nevertheless," continued von Helldorf, "there may come a stage in the future when, shall we say, the security of the state is endangered, at which time anyone subject to a D-11 will be arrested and incarcerated without recourse to the judicial system."

"Yes, I can understand how that might be useful."

"Good, good. Which leaves us with the subject of your own D-11."

"Perhaps if I knew the reason you feel I need to give a guarantee of my own good behavior," I said, "then I might be more inclined to sign such a thing."

Von Helldorf frowned and looked sternly at the three men who had brought me all the way from the Adlon. "Do you mean to tell me he hasn't been told why he's been brought here?"

Leather Coat shook his head. His hat was off now, and I had a clearer idea of him as a human being. He looked like a gorilla. "All I was told, sir, was that we should pick him up and bring him here immediately."

Von Helldorf rattled the dice box irritably, as if he wished it had been Leather Coat's skull. "It seems I have to do everything myself, Herr Gunther," he said, and walked toward me.

While I waited for him to arrive, I rolled my eyeballs around the room, which was set up for the playboy prince of Ruritania. On one wall was a geometry set of foils and sabers. Beneath this was an ocean-going sideboard that was home to a radio as big as a tombstone and a silver tray with more bottles and decanters than the cocktail bar at the Adlon. A double-front secretaire was full of leather-bound books, and a few of them were about the laws of criminal evidence and proce-dure, but mostly they were classics of German literature such as Zane Grey, P. C. Wren, Booth Tarkington, and Anita Loos. Police work never looked so leisured and comfortable.

Von Helldorf drew out one of the heavy dining chairs around the table, sat down, and leaned against a carved back that had more tracery than a window in a Gothic cathedral. Then he laid his hands on the desk as if he had been about to play the piano. Either way, he had my full attention.

"As you possibly know, I'm on the German Olympic Organizing Committee," he said. "It's my job to ensure the security not just of all the people who will be coming to Berlin in 1936, but also of all the people who are involved in making sure everything is ready in time. There are several hundred contractors, which presents something of a logistical nightmare if what looks like an almost impossible deadline is to be met. Now, given the fact that we have less than two years to get everything up and ready, I don't think anyone will be surprised to learn that there are times when mistakes get made or when standards have to be compromised. All the same, it's awkward for some of these contrac-tors when, in spite of doing their very best, they feel that they've become the subject of scrutiny by elements who lack the same enthusiasm for the Olympic project as everyone else. Indeed, it could be argued that some of these elements are behaving in a way that might easily be con-strued as unpatriotic and un-German. Do you see what I mean?"

"Yes," I said. "By the way, General, do you mind if I smoke?"

He nodded, and I tossed one onto my lip and lit it quickly, mar-veling at von Helldorf's talent for quietly spoken understatement. But

I wasn't about to mistake or underestimate him. Underneath the velvet glove was, I felt certain, a substantial fist, and even if the general wasn't prepared to hit me with it himself, I figured there were others in that absurdly large room who lacked his well-bred scruples about using violence.

"To put it bluntly, Herr Gunther, a number of people are upset that you and your Jewish lady friend, Mrs. Charalambides, have been asking a lot of awkward questions about this dead Jewish laborer, Herr Deutsch, and the unfortunate Dr. Rubusch. Very upset indeed. I'm told you actually assaulted a gang master who supplies labor for a new S-Bahn tunnel. Is that right?"

"Yes, that's quite correct," I said. "I did. However, in my defense I should point out that he assaulted me first. The mark on my face was given to me by him."

"He says this only happened because you attempted to subvert his workforce." Von Helldorf rattled the dice in the box impatiently.

"I'm not sure that 'subvert' is the right description of what I did, sir."

"How would you describe it?"

"I wanted to discover how Isaac Deutsch—that Jewish laborer you mentioned—met his death and if it was, as I had supposed, the result of his being illegally employed on the Olympic site."

"So that Mrs. Charalambides might write about it when she gets back home to America? Is that right?"

"Yes, sir."

Von Helldorf frowned. "You puzzle me, Herr Gunther. Don't you want your country to put on a good show in front of the rest of the world? Are you a patriotic German or not?"

"I like to think I'm as patriotic as the next man, sir. Only it strikes me that our policy with regard to the Jews is—inconsistent."

"And you want this exposed with what aim? So that all those Jewish workers might lose their jobs? Because they will. If Mrs. Charalambides writes about this in her American newspaper, I can guarantee it."

"No, sir, that's not what I want. It's just that I don't agree with our Jewish policy in the first place."

"That's neither here nor there. Most people in Germany do agree with it. Even so, that policy has to be tempered with what is practical. And the fact remains that it simply isn't feasible to get the project finished in time without employing a few Jewish workers."

He put it so matter-of-factly, I could hardly disagree. I shrugged. "I suppose not, sir."

"You suppose right," he said. "You simply can't go around making an issue about this. It's not realistic, Herr Gunther. And I simply can't allow it. Which is where the D-11 comes in, I'm afraid. As a guarantee that you will put an end to this habit you've developed of sticking your nose in where it isn't wanted."

It all sounded so reasonable I was actually tempted to sign his D-11, just in order to actually be able to return home and go to bed. I had to hand it to von Helldorf. He was a smooth operator. Quite possibly he had learned more from Erik Hanussen, the clairvoyant, than merely his own lucky number and color. Perhaps he had also learned how to persuade people to do something they didn't want to do. Such as signing a document saying that you agreed to be sent to a concentration camp. Maybe that just made von Helldorf a typical Nazi. Quite a few of them—Goebbels, Goering, and Hitler, most of all—seemed to have a flair for persuading Germans to go against their own common sense.

Reflecting that it might be a while before I got to smoke again, I took a couple of hurried puffs and then stubbed out my cigarette in a smoked-glass ashtray the same color as von Helldorf's lying eyes. And this was just enough time for me to remember the day I'd looked in on the Reichstag fire trial and how many Nazi liars I'd seen in court; and how everyone had loudly bravo'd the biggest liar of them all, Hermann Goering. Seldom had I found being a German so unattractive as on that particular day of lies. With all of that in mind, I felt obliged to tell von Helldorf to go to hell. Except that I didn't, of course. I was rather more polite about it. There's bravery, after all, and then there's downright stupidity.

"I'm sorry, General, but I can't sign that document. It'd be like a goose writing someone a Christmas card. Besides, I happen to know that all of those poor fellows who were in Oranienburg got sent on to a concentration camp in Lichtenberg."

The general upended the dice box onto the table in front of him and inspected the result, as if it mattered. Maybe it did, and I simply didn't know it. Maybe if he'd thrown a couple of sixes, that might have been lucky for me—he might have let me go. As it was, he'd thrown only a one and a two. He closed his eyes and sighed.

"Take him away," he told the man in the leather coat. "We'll see if a night in the cells can't change your mind, Herr Gunther."

His men picked me up by the shoulders on my suit and sleep-walked me out of von Helldorf's office. To my surprise we went up another floor.

"A room with a view, is that it?"

"All our cells have a nice view of the Havel," said Leather Coat. "Tomorrow, if you don't sign that paper, we'll give you a swimming lesson off the bow of the count's yacht."

"That's all right. I can swim already."

Leather Coat laughed. "Not off the yacht, you won't. Not after we tie you to the anchor."

THEY PUT ME IN A CELL and locked the door. A lock on the wrong side of the door is one of the things that remind you that it's a cell you're in and not a hotel room. That and a few bars on the window and a stinking mattress on a damp floor. The cell had all the usual amenities, like an en-suite bucket, but it was the little things that reminded me I wasn't staying at the Adlon. Little things like the cockroaches. Although really these were little only by the standard of the Zeppelin-sized roaches we'd encountered in the trenches. It's said that human beings will never starve on this planet if they can learn how to eat a cockroach. But try telling that to someone who's ever stepped on a roach or awoken in the night to find one crawling on his face.

Freud had invented a technique used in psychology called free association. Somehow I knew that if I got through this, I was forever after going to associate cockroaches with Nazis.

24

THEY LEFT ME ALONE for several days, which was better than a beating. Of course, this gave me plenty of time to think about Noreen and to worry that she would be worried about me. What would she think? What did anyone think when a loved one disappeared off the streets of Berlin and into a concentration camp or a police jail? The experience gave me a new understanding of what it was to be a Jew or a communist in the new Germany. But mostly I worried about myself. Did they really intend to throw me in the Havel if I refused to sign the D-11? And if I did sign it, could I trust von Helldorf not to send me to a camp straightaway?

When I wasn't worrying about myself, I reflected on how, thanks to von Helldorf, I knew something more about the death of Isaac Deutsch than I had before. I knew that his corpse was somehow connected with the corpse of Dr. Heinrich Rubusch. So was it possible that his death in a room at the Adlon Hotel had been the result of something other than natural causes? But what? I never saw a more natural-looking corpse. The two cops who had investigated the case, Rust and Brandt, had told me that the cause of death had been a cerebral aneurysm. Had they lied? And Max Reles—what was his involvement in all of this?

Since my incarceration in a Potsdam police cell seemed to owe everything to a telephone call Max Reles had placed to Count von Helldorf, I had to assume that the American was somehow implicated in the deaths of both men and that this had something to do with Olympic bids and contracts. Reles had somehow been informed of my interest in Deutsch and had assumed, incorrectly, that this was connected with my recovery of the stolen Chinese lacquer box—or, more accurately, with the contents of that Chinese box. Given the involvement of the notoriously corrupt von Helldorf, it seemed I had stumbled onto a conspiracy that involved a variety of people from the GOC and the Ministry of the Interior. How else could one explain how artifacts from Berlin's Ethnographical Museum were being given to Max Reles so that he might send them to Avery Brundage on the AOC in return for his continuing opposition to an American boycott of the Berlin games?

If all of this was true, then I was in a lot more trouble than I had realized when I'd been lifted off Herman Goering Strasse by von Helldorf's men. And by the fourth or perhaps the fifth day of my imprisonment, I was beginning to regret not taking a gamble on von Helldorf's word and signing the D-11—especially when I recalled his reasonable tone.

From my cell window I could see and hear the Havel. Between the south wall of the prison was a line of trees and beyond it the S-Bahn line to Berlin, which ran along the riverbank and across a bridge into Teltower. Sometimes the train and a steamboat traded hoots, like good-natured characters in a children's story. Once I heard a military band playing somewhere to the west, behind Potsdam's own Lustgarten. It rained a lot. Potsdam is green for a very good reason.

On the sixth day the door finally opened for longer than it took for me to slop out and be given a meal.

Leather Coat, smiling quietly, beckoned into the corridor outside my cell. "You're free to go," he said.

"What happened to your D-11?"

He shrugged.

"Just like that?" I said.

"Those are my orders."

I rubbed my face thoughtfully. I wasn't quite sure what was making it itch so much: my urgent need for a razor, or suspicion at this latest turn of events. I had heard stories of people being shot "while attempting to escape." Was this to be my fate? A bullet in the back of the head as I walked along the corridor?

Sensing my hesitation, Leather Coat's smile widened—as if he had guessed the reason for my hesitation in leaving. But he said nothing to reassure me. He looked as if he enjoyed my discomfort, as if he had just watched me eat a very hot chili pepper and was now looking forward to seeing me suffer an attack of hiccups. He lit a cigarette and stared at his fingernails for a moment.

"What about my stuff?"

"You'll get it downstairs."

"That's what I'm worried about." I picked up my jacket and put it on.

"Aw, now you've hurt my feelings," he said.

"You'll grow new ones when you get back under your stone."

He jerked his head down the corridor. "Get moving, Gunther, before we change our minds."

I walked ahead of him, and it was just as well that I hadn't eaten that morning—otherwise, it wouldn't have been only my heart that was in my mouth. My scalp was crawling, as if I had one of the praesidium's cockroaches in my hair. At any moment I expected to feel the cold barrel of a Luger pressed against my cranium and to hear the sound of a shot, abruptly curtailed as a hollow-point 9.5-gram round tunneled through my brain. For a second I recalled seeing a German officer in 1914 shooting a Belgian civilian suspected of leading an attack on our soldiers, and the way the bullet had left his head looking like a burst football.

My legs felt like jelly, but I forced them to march me along the corridor without stopping to look around and see if Leather Coat had a pistol in his hand. At the top of the stairs, the corridor kept on going and I paused awaiting his instructions.

"Downstairs," said the voice behind me.

I turned and tramped down the steps, my leather soles slapping against the stones like my heart on the walls of my chest. It felt pleasantly cool on the stairwell. A great blast of fresh air was coming up from the ground floor like a sea breeze. And arriving there at last, I saw a door open onto the central courtyard, where several more police cars and vans were parked.

To my relief, Leather Coat marched ahead of me now and led the way into a little office where my coat and hat, my tie, my braces, and the contents of my pockets were returned to me. I put a cigarette into my face and lit it before following him along another corridor and into a room the size of an abattoir. The walls were covered with white bricks, and on one was a large wooden crucifix; for a moment I thought we were in some kind of chapel. We turned a corner, and I stopped in my tracks, for there, like a strange-looking table and chair, was a shiny new falling ax. Constructed of dark polished oak and dull-colored steel, the machine was about eight feet high—just a bit taller than an executioner wearing his customary top hat. For a moment it sent such a chill through my body that I actually shivered. And I had to remind myself that it was unlikely Leather Coat would have attempted to execute me by himself. The Nazis were hardly short-staffed when it came to carrying out judicial murder.

"I bet this is where you bring Hitler Youth in lieu of a bedtime story," I said.

"We thought you'd like to see it." Leather Coat uttered a dry little chuckle and stroked the wooden frame of the falling ax fondly. "Just in case you were ever tempted to come back."

"Your hospitality overwhelms me. I suppose this is what they mean when they talk about the people who've lost their heads to Nazism. But it might be just as well to remember the fate of almost all the French revolutionaries who were so keen on their guillotine: Danton, Desmoulins, Robespierre, Saint-Just, Couthon. They ended up going for a ride on it themselves."

He scraped the blade with the flat of his thumb and said, "As if I care what happened to a bunch of francies."

"Maybe you should." I flicked my half-smoked cigarette at the terrible machine and followed Leather Coat through another door and into a corridor. This time I was pleased to see that it led out onto the street.

"As a matter of idle curiosity, why are you releasing me? After all, I never signed your D-11. Was it the thought of having to spell 'concentration camp'? Or was it something else? The law? Justice? Proper police procedure? I know that sounds unlikely, but I thought I'd ask anyway."

"If I was you, friend, I'd count myself lucky just to be walking out of here."

"Oh, I do. Only not as lucky as I count myself for the fact that you're not me. That really would be depressing."

I tipped my hat to him and walked out of there. A moment later I heard the door bang behind me. It sounded a lot better than a Luger, but it still made me jump all the same. It was raining, but the rain looked good because there was only the open sky above it. I took off my hat and lifted my unshaven face into the air. The rain felt even better than it looked, and I rubbed it across my chin and hair the same way I'd washed my face with it in the trenches. Rain: it was something clean and free that fell from the sky and wasn't going to kill you. But even while I celebrated the moment of my liberation, I felt a tug at my sleeve and turned around to find a woman standing behind me. She was wearing a long, dark dress with a high belt; a fawn-colored raincoat; and a small, shell-like hat.

"Please, sir," she said quietly, "were you a prisoner in there, perhaps?"

I rubbed my chin again. "Is it that obvious?"

"Did you by chance come across another man by the name of Dett-mann, Ludwig Dettmann? I'm his wife."

I shook my head. "I'm sorry, Frau Dettmann, no, I didn't see anyone at all. But what makes you think he's in there?"

She shook her head, sadly. "I don't. Not anymore. But when they arrested him, this is where he was taken. I'm sure of that, at least." She shrugged. "But afterward, who knows? No one thinks to tell his family anything. He could be anywhere for all I know. But no one thinks to tell his family anything. Several times I've been in that police station asking for information about my Ludwig, but they won't tell me what's happened to him. They've even threatened to arrest me if I go in there again."

"Might be one way of finding out," I said glibly.

"You don't understand. I have three children. And what's to become of them, eh? What is to become of them if I'm arrested, too?" She shook her head. "Nobody understands. Nobody wants to understand."

I nodded. She was right, of course. I didn't understand. No more than I understood what had persuaded von Helldorf to order my release.

I walked through the Lustgarten. In front of the state castle was a bridge that led across the Havel and over an island to the Teltower Tor Station, where I caught a train back to Berlin.

25

WASHED AND SHAVED and wearing a change of clothes, I walked back into the Adlon, encountering both surprise and delight, not to mention a certain amount of suspicion. It wasn't unknown for staff to pull a sicky for a few days and then return with the same explanation as me. Sometimes it was even true. Behlert greeted me much as he might have greeted a tomcat returning home after an absence of several days and nights: with a mixture of amusement and contempt.

"Where have you been?" he said, scolding. "We've been worried about you, Herr Gunther. Thank goodness your friend, Detective Sergeant Stahlecker, has been able to take on some of your duties."

"Good. I'm glad to hear it."

"But even he was unable to find out what had happened to you. No one at the police praesidium at Alexanderplatz seemed to know anything. It's not at all like you to disappear like that. What happened?"

"I've been staying at another hotel, Georg," I told him. "The one run by the police in Potsdam. And I didn't enjoy it. Not one bit. I'm thinking of walking around to that MER travel bureau on Unter den Linden and telling them not to recommend it any longer as a place to stay when you're in Potsdam. You can sleep much more comfortably in the river. In fact, I very nearly did."

Behlert glanced uncomfortably around the mausoleumlike entrance hall. "Please, Herr Gunther, keep your voice down or else someone will overhear, and then we'll both be in trouble with the police."

"I wouldn't be in trouble if it wasn't for the help of one of our guests, Georg."

"Who can you mean?"

I might have mentioned the name of Max Reles. But I saw no point in explaining exactly what had happened. Like the majority of law-abiding Berliners, Behlert preferred to know as little as possible about those things that might get him into trouble. And, in a way, I respected that. Given my own recent experiences, it was probably the more sensible way to be. So instead I said, "Frau Charalambides, of course. You know I've been working for her. Helping her write this article."

"Yes, I did know. And I can't say that I approved. In my opinion, it was wrong of Frau Adlon to ask you. It put you in a very difficult position."

I shrugged. "That can't be helped. Not now. Is she in the hotel?"

"No." He looked awkward. "I think perhaps you had better speak to Frau Adlon. As a matter of fact, she inquired about you only this morning. I believe she's in her apartment, upstairs."

"Has something happened to Frau Charalambides?"

"She's fine, I can assure you. Shall I telephone Frau Adlon and suggest an appointment for you?"

But sensing something was wrong, I was already running upstairs.

Outside Hedda's apartment I knocked and, hearing her voice, turned the handle and opened the door. She was sitting on the sofa, smoking a cigarette and reading a copy of *Fortune* magazine, which, given she had one, seemed only appropriate. Seeing me, she threw *Fortune* aside and stood up. She looked relieved to see me.

"Thank goodness you're all right," she said. "I've been worried about you."

I closed the door. "Where is she?"

"Gone home to New York," said Hedda. "She left on yesterday's boat from Hamburg."

"Then I guess she wasn't as worried as you."

"There's no need to be like that, Bernie. It's not how it is at all. Her leaving Germany and promising not to write about the Olympics was the price she paid to get you out of jail. And quite possibly to keep you out of jail as well."

"I see." I walked over to the sideboard and picked up one of her decanters. "Do you mind? It's been one of those—weeks."

"Please. Help yourself." Hedda went over to her desk and opened the lid.

I poured one out—quite a large one of whatever it was, I didn't much care—and sucked it down like it was a medicine I'd prescribed for myself. It tasted horrible, so I prescribed myself another and brought it back to the sofa.

"She left you this." Hedda handed me an Adlon envelope.

I slipped it into my pocket.

"It's my fault for getting you into this in the first place."

I shook my head. "I knew what I was doing. Even when I knew that what I was doing was, perhaps, ill advised."

"Noreen always did have that effect on people," said Hedda. "When we were both girls, it was nearly always I who got caught for some infraction of the school rules, and Noreen who got away with it. But I was never deterred by that. I was always up for our next escapade. Perhaps I should have warned you about her. I don't know. Maybe. Even now it feels like I'm the one who has to stay behind and make up her grades and offer an apology."

"I knew what I was doing," I repeated dully.

"She drinks too much," said Hedda, by way of an explanation. "She and Nick, her husband. I assume she told you all about him."

"Some."

"She drinks, and it doesn't seem to affect her in the least. Everyone who's around her drinks, and it affects them a great deal. That's what happened to poor Nick. Goodness, he never drank at all until he met Noreen."

"She's very intoxicating." I tried a smile, but it didn't come out right. "I expect I'll have a hangover before I get over it."

Hedda nodded. "Take a few days off, why don't you? The rest of the week, if you like. After five nights in jail you could probably use a break. Your friend Herr Stahlecker will cover for you." She nodded. "It's worked out very well with him. He doesn't have your experience, but—"

"Perhaps I will take some time off. Thanks." I finished my second drink. It didn't taste any better than the first. "Incidentally, is Max Reles still staying in the hotel?"

"Yes, I think so. Why?"

"No reason."

"He told me you got his property back for him. He was very pleased."

I nodded. "Maybe I'll go away somewhere. Würzburg, perhaps."

"Have you got family in Würzburg?"

"No. But I've always wanted to go there. It's the capital of Franconia, you know. Besides, it's the opposite end of Germany from Hamburg."

I didn't mention Dr. Rubusch, or the fact that the only reason I was going there was that he was from Würzburg.

"Stay at the Palace Hotel Russia House," she said. "I believe it's the best hotel in the state. Have a rest. Catch up on some sleep. You look tired. Put your feet up. If you like, I'll telephone the hotel manager and get you a special rate."

"Thanks. I will." But I didn't tell her that the last thing I intended to do was put my feet up. Not now that Noreen was gone out of my life for good.

26

L EAVING THE ADLON, I walked east to the Alex. The railway station was bristling with SS, and yet another military band was getting ready to welcome some self-important government bonzo. There are times when I swear I think we have more military bands than the French and the English put together. Maybe it's just a lot of Germans playing it safe. No one ever accused you of being unpatriotic when you were playing a flugelhorn or a tuba. Not in Germany.

Tearing myself away from the palpable excitement in the air around the station, I walked into the Alex. Seldte, the smart young fellow from SCHUPO, was still on duty at the front desk.

"I see your career is leaping ahead."

"Isn't it?" he said. "If I stay here for much longer, I'll turn into one of these freaks myself. If you're looking for Herr Trettin, I saw him head out of here about twenty minutes ago."

"Thanks, but I was hoping to see Liebermann von Sonnenberg."

"Would you like me to call his office?"

Fifteen minutes later I was sitting opposite the Berlin chief of KRIPO and smoking one of the Black Wisdom cigars Bernhard Weiss had been obliged to leave behind when he left.

"If this is about that unfortunate business involving August Krich-baum," said von Sonnenberg, "then you needn't worry, Bernie. You and the other cops who were in the frame as possible suspects are in the clear. Everything has been brought to a sort of conclusion. It was a lot of nonsense, of course."

"Oh? How's that?" I tried to contain the relief I felt. But after Noreen's departure, I hardly cared nearly as much. At the same time, I hoped they hadn't framed someone for the killing. That would really have given my conscience something indigestible to chew on for a while.

"Because we no longer have a reliable witness. The hotel doorman who saw the culprit was an ex-policeman, as you probably know. Well, it turns out that he is also a queer and a communist. It seems that this was why he left the police in the first place. Indeed, we now think his evidence may even have been motivated by malice against the police in general. Anyway, all of that's irrelevant, since the Gestapo has had him on an arrest list for several months. Not that he knew, of course."

"So where is he now?"

"In the concentration camp, at Lichtenberg."

I nodded, wondering if they'd made him sign a D-11.

"I'm sorry you had to go through all of that, Bernie."

I shrugged. "I'm sorry I wasn't able to do a bit more for your protégé, Bömer."

"You did all you could under the circumstances."

"I'd be glad to help out again."

"These young men today," said von Sonnenberg. "They're in too much of a hurry, if you ask me."

"I got that impression. You know, there's a bright young fellow wearing green on the desk in the entrance hall downstairs. Name of Heinz Seldte. You might give him a lick. Fellow's too smart to be left with his balls in a desk drawer like that."

"Thanks, Bernie. I'll have a look at him." He lit a cigarette. "So. Are you here to play the accordion, or is there some business you and I can do?"

"That all depends."

"On what?"

"On your opinion of Count von Helldorf."

"You might as well ask if I hate Stalin."

"I hear the count's trying to rehabilitate himself by tracking down anyone the SA ever had a grudge against."

"That would certainly look commendably loyal, wouldn't it?"

"Maybe he still wants to be your boss here in Berlin."

"Have you got a way of making sure that couldn't happen?"

"I might have." I puffed the strong cigar and aimed the smoke at the high ceiling. "You remember that stiff we had in the Adlon a while ago? The one you gave to Rust and Brandt."

"Sure. Natural causes. I remember."

"Suppose it wasn't?"

"What makes you think different?"

"Something von Helldorf said."

"I didn't know you were cozy with that queer, Bernie."

"For the last six days I've been his houseguest at the police prae-sidium in Potsdam. I'd like to repay his hospitality, if I can."

"They say he's still holding on to some of Hanussen's dirt, as an insurance policy against arrest. The films he shot on that boat of his. *The Ursel.* I've also heard that some of the dirt comes from underneath some very important fingernails."

"Like whose, for instance?"

"Ever ask yourself how he managed to get on that Olympic commit-tee? It's not his love of riding, I can tell you that much."

"Von Tschammer und Osten?"

"Small fry. No, it was Goebbels who got him the job."

"But he was the one who broke Hanussen."

"And it was Goebbels who saved von Helldorf. But for Joey, von Helldorf would have been shot alongside his warm friend, Ernst Röhm, when Hitler settled the SA's hash. In other words, von Helldorf is still connected. So I'll help you get him, if you can. But you'll have to find someone else to put the stake through his heart."

"All right. I'll leave your name out of it."

"What do you need from me?"

"The case file on Heinrich Rubusch. I'd like to check a few things out. Go and see the fellow's widow, in Würzburg."

"Würzburg?"

"It's near Regensburg, I believe."

"I know where the hell it is. I'm just trying to remember why I know where the hell it is." Liebermann von Sonnenberg flicked a switch on his desk intercom to speak to his secretary. "Ida? Why does Würzburg mean something to me?"

"You had a request from the Gestapo in Würzburg," said a woman's voice. "In your capacity as Interpol liaison officer. Requesting that you contact the FBI in America about a suspect living here in Germany."

"And did I?"

"Yes. We sent them what we got from the FBI a week or so ago."

"Wait a minute, Erich," I said. "I'm beginning to think this bone might make a lot more than just soup. Ida? This is Bernie Gunther. Can you remember the name of that suspect the Gestapo in Würzburg wanted to know about?"

"Wait a minute. I think I still have the Gestapo's letter in my tray. I haven't filed it yet. Yes, here we are. The suspect's name is Max Reles."

Von Sonnenberg flicked off the intercom and nodded. "You're smiling like that name means something, Bernie," he observed.

"Max Reles is a guest at the Adlon and a good friend of the count's."

"Is that so?" He shrugged. "Maybe it's just a small world."

"Sure it is. If it was any bigger, we'd have to hunt for clues like they do in the stories. You'd have a magnifying glass and a hunting hat and a definitive collection of cigarette ends."

Von Sonnenberg stubbed out his cigarette in the overflowing ashtray. "Who says I don't?"

"This information you had from the FBI. Any chance you kept a copy?"

"Let me tell you about being the Interpol liaison officer, Bernie. It's extra sauerkraut. I've got plenty of meat and potatoes on my plate already, and what I don't need is extra sauerkraut. I know it's on the table because Ida tells me it is. But mostly it's her that eats it, see? And the fact is that she wouldn't keep a copy of Luther's ninety-five theses unless I told her to. So."

"So now I've got two reasons to go to Würzburg."

"Three, if you include the wine."

"I never did before."

"Franconian wines are good," said von Sonnenberg. "If you like your wines sweet, that is."

"Some of these provincial Gestapo officers," I said. "They can be anything but sweet."

"I haven't noticed their big-city counterparts assisting old ladies to cross the road."

"Look, Erich, I hate to give you more sauerkraut, but a letter of introduction from you or even a telephone call would straighten this Gestapo man's tie for him. And keep it straight while I was squeezing his eggs."

Von Sonnenberg grinned. "It'll be a pleasure. There's nothing I like better than clipping the tails on some of these young pups in the Gestapo."

"I think that's a job I'd be good at."

"Maybe you'll be the first person who ever enjoyed going to Würzburg."

"That's always a possibility."

27

I READ HER LETTER ON THE TRAIN TO WÜRZBURG.

Adlon Hotel,
No. 1 Unter den Linden, Berlin

My dearest Bernie,
It grieves me more than words can tell you that I cannot be
there to say good-bye in person, but I've been told by someone

from the police chief's office in Potsdam that you won't be released from prison until I have left Germany.

It looks as if this has to be for good, I'm afraid—at least for as long as the Nazis are in government, anyway—as I've also been informed by someone in the Foreign Ministry that I won't be given a visa again.

And if all that wasn't bad enough, I've been told by an official in the Propaganda Ministry that if I publish the newspaper article I was planning to write and call upon the AOC to boycott the German Olympiad, then you could find yourself in a concentration camp; and since I have no wish to expose you to this kind of threat, you can rest assured, my dear Bernie, that no such article will now appear.

Perhaps you will consider that this will be a tragedy to me; but while I lament that I am now forbidden the chance to oppose the evil of national socialism in the way I know best, the greater tragedy, according to my understanding of that word, is the obligation I now have to give you up, and the utter improbability of seeing you at any time in the near future. Perhaps ever!

Given more time, I should have spoken to you of love and, perhaps, you would have done the same. Tempting as it is for a writer to put words in someone else's mouth, this is my letter and I must limit myself to what I myself can say. Which is this: I love you, right enough. And if I now seem to draw a line under that, it's only because the elation that I once might have felt at being in love with someone again—it's not easy for me to love anyone—is alloyed with the acute pain of our parting and separation.

There is a painting by Caspar David Friedrich that encapsulates the way I'm feeling right now. It's called The Wanderer above the Sea of Fog, and if you're ever in Hamburg, you should go to the local art gallery and take a look at it. If you don't know this painting, it depicts a solitary man standing on a mountaintop staring out over a landscape of distant peaks and jagged rocks. And you should picture me, similarly positioned on the stern of the SS Manhattan carrying me back to New York, and all the while staring back at a rocky, jagged, increasingly remote Germany that contains you, my love.

You might equally think of another Friedrich painting when you try to visualize my heart. This picture is called The Sea of Ice, and it shows a ship, hardly visible, crushed by great shards of ice upon a landscape more bleak than the surface of the moon. I'm not sure where this picture can be seen, as I only ever saw it myself in a book. Nevertheless, it represents very well the cold devastation that is my current situation.

It seems to me I might very easily curse the fortune that made me love you; and yet I know, in spite of everything, that I don't regret it one little bit, because, in the future, every time I read of some dreadful deed or criminal policy carried out by that big-talking man in his silly uniform, I will think of you, Bernie, and remember that there are many good Germans who have courageous, good hearts (although none, I think, could ever have a heart as courageous and good as yours). And this is good, for if Hitler teaches us anything, it is the stupidity of judging a whole race as one. There are bad Jews and there are good Jews, just as there are bad Germans and there are good Germans.

You are a good German, Bernie. You protect yourself with a thick coat of cynicism, but at heart I know that you are a good man. But I fear for all good men in Germany and I wonder what terrible choices now lie ahead of them and you. I wonder what awful compromises you will be called upon to make.

Which is why I want to help you to help others in the only way now open to me.

By now you will have found the enclosed check, and your first inclination on seeing that it is much more than you asked to borrow may be not to cash it at all. That would be a mistake. It seems to me that you should take it as my gift to you and start the private detective business you told me about. And for this good reason: in a society founded upon lies, the discovery of truth will

*become more and more important. Probably it will land you in
trouble, but, knowing you, I suspect you can handle that in your
own way. Most of all, I hope that you can come to the aid of
others in need of your help, as you tried to help me; and that you
will do what, because it is dangerous, you ought not to do because
it is also right.*

*I'm not sure I expressed that correctly. While I speak German
well enough I find I am out of practice writing it. I hope this
letter does not seem too formal. Emperor Charles V said he spoke
Spanish to God, Italian to women, French to men, and German
to his horse. But you know, I think that horse might just have
been the creature he loved best in the world and that, like you, his
horse was very bold and full of spirit; and I cannot think of any
other language that suits your temperament, Bernie. Certainly
not English, with its many shades of meaning! I never met a more
straightforward man than you, which is one of the reasons why I
love you so much.*

*These are ugly times and you will have to go to ugly places
and deal with people who have made themselves ugly, but you
are my knight of heaven, my Galahad, and I feel certain you can
endure all these tests without becoming ugly yourself. And you
must always tell yourself that you are not just sweeping leaves on
a windy day, although there will be times when that is what it will
feel like.*

I kiss you. Noreen. xx

WÜRZBURG WASN'T AN UGLY PLACE, although the Franconians had done their
best to make their state capital a virtual shrine to Nazism and had effectively uglified what was a pleasantly situated medieval red-roofed town
in an open part of a river valley. In almost every shop window there
was a photograph of Hitler or a sign advising Jews to keep out or risk
the consequences—sometimes both. The town made Berlin look like a
model of true representative democracy.

Dominating the landscape from the left bank of the river was the old castle of Marienberg, built by the prince-bishops of Würzburg who had been champions of the Counter-Reformation during another ugly time in German history. But it was just as easy to imagine the imposing white castle inhabited by some evil scientist who exercised a powerful and malign influence on Würzburg, unleashing an elemental force to make monsters of the town's unsuspecting peasants. These were mostly ordinary-looking folk, although there were one or two with boxy foreheads, vivid surgical scars, and ill-fitting coats who might have given even the most committed galvanist some pause for thought. I felt kind of inhuman myself and walked south from the railway station and onto Adolf-Hitler-Strasse with awkward, stiff legs, which might easily have belonged to a dead man, although that might have been the lingering effect of Noreen's letter.

Checking into the Palace Hotel Russia House helped to lift my spirits a little. After a week in police custody, I had the taste for a good hotel. Then again, I had the taste anyway, and now that I'd decided to overcome my scruples and cash Noreen's check, I also had the money. After a light supper in the hotel's Königs Café, I walked three quarters of a kilometer east, on Rottendorfer Strasse, to a quiet suburb near a reservoir to see the widow Rubusch.

It was a substantial two-story house—three if you counted the dormer window in the high mansard roof—with a curving bay-front door and a long white picket fence atop a substantial granite wall. It was painted the same color of yellowish beige that had been used to paint a small Star of David on the similar garden wall of the house on the opposite side of the street. There were one or two cars parked in front, both new and both made by Daimler-Benz. The trees had been recently pruned. It was a nice German neighborhood: quiet, well kept, solidly respectable. Even that yellow star looked as if it had been painted there by a professional decorator.

I mounted the front steps and tugged on a bell pull as big as a ship's cannon, and almost as loud.

A light came on and a maid appeared in the door—a big pig's-trotter of a girl with red braids and a stubborn, almost belligerent, cast to her jaw.

"Yes?"

"Bernhard Gunther," I said. "Frau Rubusch is expecting me."

"I wasn't told about it."

"Perhaps Hitler's telegram hasn't arrived yet. I'm sure he would have wanted to let you know."

"There's no need to be sarcastic," she said, and, taking a large step backward, opened the curved door. "If you only knew how much I'm expected to do around here."

I put down my briefcase and took off my hat and coat while she closed the front door and then locked it carefully.

"It sounds to me like you need a servant," I said.

She shot me a high-velocity look.

"You had better wait in here." She opened a door with the side of her foot and chopped at an electric light switch with the side of her hand. "Make yourself comfortable while I go and fetch her." Then, seeing my hat and coat, she sighed loudly and took them, shaking her head at the inconvenience of finding herself with yet another duty to perform.

I went over to the fireplace, where a blackened piece of log was almost burning, and picked up a long poker. "Want me to bring this back to life? I'm good with fire. Show me a shelf of decadent literature and I'll have you a blaze going in no time."

The maid smiled back at me bleakly, although it could just as easily have been a sneer. It crossed her mind to say something tart until she thought better of it. I had a poker in my hand, after all, and she looked just the type who gets hit by one. I probably would have done it, too, if I'd been married to her. Not that being struck about the head with a poker would have troubled that girl very much, especially when she was hungry. I've seen hippos that looked more vulnerable.

I turned the half-burned log, heaped some embers next to it, and fetched another log from the basket by the hearth. I even bent down and blew on it for a while. A flame reached around the little pile of wood I'd made and then took hold with a snap as loud as a Christmas cracker.

"You're good at that."

I turned to see a small, birdlike woman wearing a shawl, and an uncomfortable smile on a freshly lipsticked mouth.

I stood up, wiped my hands, and made the same lame joke I'd made earlier, about decadent books, which didn't sound any funnier the second time around. Not in that house. In the corner of the room was a table with a radio and a small photograph of Hitler, and a glass bowl of fruit.

"We're not really like that around here," she said with arms folded, watching the fire. "They did burn some books in front of the bishop's palace about eighteen months ago, but not here. Not in East Würzburg."

She made it sound like we were in Paris.

"And I suppose that yellow star painted on the house opposite is just mischievous children," I said.

Frau Rubusch laughed but covered her mouth politely while she did, so that I wouldn't have to look at her teeth, which were perfect and porcelain white, like a doll's. And indeed a doll was what she most reminded me of with her penciled eyebrows, her fine features, her dainty red cheeks, and her even finer hair. "That's not a Star of David," she said through her fingers. "The man who lives in that house is a director of Würzburger Hofbrau, the town brewery, and that star is the company's trademark."

"Maybe he should sue the Nazis for infringing his copyright."

"Which reminds me. Would you care for some schnapps?"

Next to the table was a three-tier wooden drinks trolley with bottles I was fond of. She poured a couple of large schooners, handed me one with her bony little hand, sat down on the sofa, kicked off her shoes, and tucked her feet under her skinny little backside. I'd seen folded laundry that looked less neat than she did.

"So your telegram said that you wanted to see me about my late husband."

"Yes. I'm sorry for your loss, Frau Rubusch. It must have been a terrible shock to you."

"It was."

I lit a cigarette, double-inhaled the smoke, and then swallowed half of my drink. I was nervous about telling this woman that I believed her husband might have been murdered. Especially when she had only just buried him with the belief that he'd died in his sleep of a cerebral aneurysm. I swallowed the other half.

She recognized my nervousness. "Help yourself to another," she said. "Perhaps then you'll feel up to telling me what's brought the Adlon Hotel detective all the way from Berlin."

I went over to the drinks trolley and refilled my glass. Next to the picture of Hitler was a photograph of a younger, thinner Heinrich Rubusch.

"I really don't know why Heinrich put that photograph there. Hitler's, I mean. We were never very political. And it's not like we used to entertain very much and try to impress people. I suppose he put it there in case anyone did visit. So that they would go away with the impression that we were good Germans."

"You don't have to be a Nazi to be that," I said. "Although it does help when you're a cop. Before I was a house detective at the Adlon, I was a Homicide cop at Berlin Alexanderplatz."

"And you think my husband might have been murdered. Is that it?"

"I think it's a possibility, yes."

"Well, that's a relief."

"I'm sorry?"

"Heinrich always stayed at the Adlon when he was in Berlin. I thought maybe you thought he'd stolen some towels." She waited for a moment and then smiled. "I was joking."

"Good. I hoped you were. Only, your being a widow, I assumed your sense of humor might have gone missing for a while."

"Before I met my husband, I ran a sisal farm in East Africa, Herr Gunther. I shot my first lion when I was fourteen. And I was fifteen when I helped my father put down a native rebellion during the Maji Maji War. I'm a lot tougher than I look."

"Good."

"Did you stop being a policeman because you weren't a Nazi?"

"I quit before I was pushed. Maybe I'm not as tough as I look. But I'd rather talk about your husband. I was reading the case notes on the train and was reminded that he had a heart condition."

"He had an enlarged heart, yes."

"It sort of makes you wonder why he didn't die of that instead of a cerebral aneurysm. Did he ever suffer from headaches?"

"No." She shook her head. "But his death wasn't exactly a surprise. He ate too much and drank too much. He loved his sausage and his beer, lots of cream, cigars, chocolate. He was a very German sort of German." She sighed. "He enjoyed life in every way. And I do mean every way."

"You mean besides his food and his drink and his cigars?"

"That's precisely what I mean. I haven't ever been to Berlin. But I hear it's changed quite a bit since the Nazis came into government. I'm told it's not the den of iniquity it used to be during the Weimar years."

"That's correct. It's not."

"Nevertheless, it's hard to believe that it's difficult to find the company of a certain kind of woman, if that is what one wants. One imagines that the Nazis can only do so much to change things. After all, it's not called the oldest profession for nothing."

I smiled.

"Did I say something amusing?"

"No, not at all, Frau Rubusch. It's just that after I found your husband dead, I went to a lot of trouble to persuade the police to spare you some of the details when they informed you that he was dead. To leave out the fact that he had been in bed with another woman. I had the quaint idea that it might upset you unnecessarily."

"That was very thoughtful of you. Perhaps you're right. You're not as tough as you look."

She sipped some of her schnapps and put the glass down on a flame birch coffee table: the X-shaped base made it look like something from Roman antiquity. Frau Rubusch had a sort of Roman air herself. Maybe it was just the way she was sitting, half reclined on her sofa, but it was easy to imagine her as the influential and steely wife of some fat senator who had, perhaps, outlived his usefulness.

"Tell me, Herr Gunther. Is it normal for ex-policemen to be in possession of a police file?"

"No. I've been helping out a friend in Homicide. And, to tell the truth, I miss the work. Your husband's case gave me an itch I simply had to scratch."

"Yes, I can see how that might happen. You said you were reading my husband's case file on the train. Is it inside that briefcase?"

"Yes."

"I would very much like to look at that file."

"Forgive me, but I don't think that would be a good idea. The file contains photographs of your husband's body as he was found in his hotel room."

"I was hoping it did. Those pictures are what I'd like to see. Oh, you needn't worry about me. Did you not think I would look at him before we buried him?"

I could see there was no point in arguing with her. Besides, as far as I was concerned, there were other things I wanted to discuss with her more important than the happy smile on her dead husband's face. So I opened my briefcase, took out the KRIPO file, and handed it over.

As soon as she saw the photograph, she started to cry, and for a moment, I cursed myself for taking Frau Rubusch at her word. But then she let out a breath, fanned herself with the flat of her hand, and, swallowing an almost visible lump in her throat, said, "And this is how you found him?"

"Yes. Exactly as we found him."

"Then I fear you are right to be suspicious, Herr Gunther. You see, my husband is wearing his pajama jacket in bed. He never wore a jacket when he was in bed. I used to pack him two pairs of pajamas, but he only ever wore the trousers. Someone else must have put the jacket on him. You see, he used to sweat a lot at night. Fat men often do. Which is why he never wore the jacket. Which reminds me. When the police returned his belongings, I received only one pajama jacket. Two pairs of pajama trousers but only one jacket. At the time I thought the police must have kept it or that perhaps they had lost it. Not that it seemed of any great importance. But now that I've seen this photograph, I rather think it must be important. Don't you?"

"Yes. I do." I lit another cigarette and stood up to help myself to a third drink. "If you don't mind."

She shook her head and carried on staring at the photograph.

"All right," I said. "Someone must have put the jacket on him after he was dead, in order to make his death seem as natural as possible. But what prostitute would do such a thing? If he died while or immediately

229

after having sex, any sensible party girl would have ripped a hole in the wall to get out of there."

"Also, my husband was very heavy. So it's hard to imagine a girl able to lift him up and put a jacket on him by herself. I know I couldn't have done that. Once, when he was drunk, I tried to get his shirt off him, and it was almost impossible."

"And yet there's the evidence of the autopsy. The cause of death appeared to be natural. What else but a strenuous bout of lovemaking could bring about a cerebral aneurysm?"

"All lovemaking was strenuous for Heinrich. I can assure you of that. But what was it that first made you think his death might be a murder, Herr Gunther?"

"Something someone said. Tell me, do you know a man named Max Reles?"

"No, I don't."

"Well, he knew your husband."

"And you think he might have had something to do with my husband's death?"

"It's not much more than a slight breeze I have, but yes. I do. Let me tell you why."

"Wait. Have you eaten dinner?"

"I had a light supper at the hotel."

She smiled kindly. "This is Franconia you're in now, Herr Gunther. We don't do light suppers in this state. What was it? That you ate?"

"Just a plate of cold ham and cheese. And a beer."

"I thought as much. You'll stay for dinner, then. Magda always cooks far too much anyway. It'll be nice to have someone eat properly in this house again."

"Now that I come to think of it, I am rather hungry. I've missed quite a few meals of late."

THE HOUSE WAS TOO BIG FOR ONE. It would have been too big for a basketball team. Her two sons were grown up and gone away, to university, she said, but my money was on Magda's cooking. Not that there was anything wrong with it. But any man there for any length of time was taking a big risk with his arteries. I was in that house for only a couple of hours, and I felt as fat as Hermann Goering. Every time I laid my knife and fork together, I was persuaded to have another helping. And if I wasn't eating food, I was looking at it. All over the place there were paintings of dead game and cornucopias, and bulging fruit bowls, just in case anyone got peckish. Even the furniture looked like they fed it extra beeswax. It was big and heavy, and whenever she sat or leaned on any of it, Angelika Rubusch resembled Alice down the rabbit hole.

I guessed she was in her mid-forties, but she might have been older. She was a handsome woman, which is just a way of saying that she was aging better than a pretty one. And there were several reasons for suspecting she found me attractive, which is just a way of saying I had probably drunk too much.

After dinner I tried to gather my thoughts on what I knew about her husband: "Your husband owned a quarry, didn't he?"

"That's right. We supplied a wide range of natural stone to builders all over Europe. But mainly limestone. This part of Germany is famous for it. We call it beige limestone on account of the honey color. Most of the public buildings in Würzburg are made of beige limestone. It's uniquely German, which makes it popular with the Nazis. Since Hitler came to power, business has been booming. They can't get enough of it. Every new public building in Germany seems to require beige Jura limestone. Before he died, Paul Troost, Hitler's architect, actually came down here to look at our limestone for the new chancellery building."

"What about the Olympics?"

"No, we didn't get that contract. Not that it matters now. You see, I'm selling the business. My sons don't have any interest in limestone. They are studying to become lawyers. I can't run the business by myself. I've had a very good offer from another company here in Würzburg. So I'm going to take the money and become a rich widow."

"But you did bid for an Olympic contract?"

"Of course. That's why Heinrich went to Berlin. He went several times, as a matter of fact. To discuss our tender with Werner March, the Olympic architect, and some other people from the Ministry of the Interior. The day before Heinrich died, he telephoned me from the Adlon to say we'd lost it. He was very agitated about losing it and said he was going to take the matter up with Walter March, who was keen on our stone. At the time, I remember telling him to watch his blood pressure. His face got very red when he was cross about something. So when he died, naturally, I already suspected it must have something to do with his health."

"Can you think why Max Reles should have been in possession of a contract tender from your company?"

"Is he someone at the ministry?"

"Actually, no, he's a German-American businessman."

She shook her head.

I took the letter I'd found in the Chinese box and unfolded it on the dinner table. "I'd half suspected Max Reles was taking something off the top of supplier contracts. Like a finder's fee, or a commission. But since your husband's company didn't actually get a contract, then I'm not so sure what the connection was. Or why Max Reles should have been worried that I was asking questions about your husband. Not that I ever was, you understand. Not until now. Not until someone else made a connection between Heinrich Rubusch and Isaac Deutsch. And assumed that I had already connected the two." I let out a yawn. "When I hadn't. Sorry, none of that is going to make any sense to you. I'm tired, I guess. And probably a little drunk."

Angelika Rubusch wasn't listening, and I didn't blame her. She didn't know anything about Isaac Deutsch and probably didn't care. I was making less sense than a blind football team. Bernie Gunther, stumbling around in the dark and kicking at a ball that wasn't even there. She was shaking her head, and I was about to apologize again when I saw that she was looking at her own letter of tender.

"I don't understand," she said.

"That makes two of us. I haven't understood anything for a while now. I'm just a guy to whom things happen. And I don't know why. Some detective, huh?"

"Where did you get this?"

"Max Reles had it. He seems to have his fingers in a lot of Olympic pies. I found that paper in something else that belonged to him. An antique Chinese box that was lost for a while. While it was missing, I formed the distinct impression that he was very keen to have it returned to him."

"I think I can understand why," said Angelika Rubusch. "This isn't our tender. It's on our notepaper, but these aren't our figures. This is way above the price we put in to supply this quantity of limestone. About twice as much. I'm looking at this and thinking that it's no wonder we didn't get the contract."

"Are you sure?"

"Of course I'm sure. I was my husband's secretary. That was to stop him from . . . you know. Well, that's not important now. I used to type all our correspondence, including the original letter of tender to the German Olympic Organizing Committee, and I can tell you that I certainly didn't type this. For one thing, there's a spelling mistake. There is no *e* in 'Würzburg.' "

"There isn't?"

"Not if you come from Würzburg, there isn't. Also, the letter *g* on this typewriter is riding a little higher than the other letters." She put the tender letter in front of me and placed a well-manicured fingernail under the offending *g*. "D'you see?"

In truth, my eyesight was feeling a little blurred, but I nodded all the same.

She held the notepaper up to the light. "And you know what? This isn't even our notepaper. It looks like it, only the watermark is different."

"I see." And now I really did.

"Of course," I said. "Max Reles must have been rigging bids. And I think that works like this: You put in a bid for something yourself and then make sure that competing bids are priced at an unreasonably high level. Either that or you chase off the other bidders, by whatever means necessary. If this is a fake bid, Max Reles must have an interest in the company that was awarded the contract to supply the limestone. Probably that was a high bid too, but crucially not as high as your husband's bid. As a matter of fact, who did win the contract?"

"Würzburg Jura Limestone," she said dully. "Our major competitor. The same company I've agreed to sell to."

"All right. Perhaps Reles had already asked Heinrich to put in a high bid so that your competitor would get the contract. If he'd agreed to do it, he'd have been paid a commission. And maybe even ended up supplying Würzburg Jura himself. The advantage being that he could have been paid twice."

"Heinrich may have been cheating on me as a husband," she said, "but he wasn't like that in business."

"In which case, Max Reles must have tried and failed to put the thumbscrews on him. Or simply faked the bid from your husband's company. Perhaps both. Either way, Heinrich found out about it. So Max Reles got rid of him. Quickly. Discreetly. But permanently. This all makes sense now. The first night I ever saw your husband was at a dinner hosted by Reles for a lot of businessmen where there was an argument. One of the other businessmen stormed out. Perhaps he was asked to supply an inflated bid for something else."

"What are we going to do now?"

"Tomorrow morning I have an appointment with the local Gestapo. It seems I'm not the only one who's interested in Max Reles. Perhaps they'll tell me what they know, and perhaps I'll tell them what I know, and maybe we'll figure out a way forward from there. But I'm afraid all of that might mean another autopsy. Obviously the Berlin pathologist missed something. These days they often do. Forensic standards are no longer as rigorous as they used to be. Nothing is."

28

Y OU WALK UP TO A DOOR that is guarded by two steel-helmeted men wearing black uniforms and white gloves. I'm not sure about the purpose of the white gloves. Are they meant to persuade the rest of us that the SS is pure in heart and deed? If so, then I'm not convinced: this is the militia that murdered Ernst Röhm and God knows how many other SA men.

Inside a heavy wood-and-glass door is a large hallway with a stone floor and a marble staircase. Next to the desk are a Nazi flag and a full-length portrait of Adolf Hitler. Behind the desk is another man wearing a black uniform and the same unhelpful expression you see all over Germany. It is the face of totalitarian bureaucracy and officialdom. This face does not seek to please. It is not there to serve you. It cares not if you live or die. It regards you not as a citizen but as an object to be processed, up the stairs or out the door. It is how a man looks when he stops behaving like a human being and becomes a kind of robot.

Unquestioning obedience. Orders to be carried out without a second thought. This is what they want. Ranks upon serried ranks of steel-helmeted automatons.

My appointment is checked off on a neatly typed list that lies on the well-polished desk. I am early. I should not be early any more than I should be late. Now I will have to wait, and the robot does not know what to do with someone who is early and has to wait. There is an empty wooden chair beside the elevator cage. Normally there is a guard sitting there, I am told, but until the appointed time I may sit there.

I sit. A few minutes pass. I smoke. At precisely ten o'clock the robot lifts the telephone receiver, dials a number, and announces my arrival. I am ordered into the elevator and up to the fourth floor, where another robot will meet me. I enter the elevator. The robot operating the machinery has heard the order and assumes temporary responsibility for my movement within the building.

On the fourth floor, a group of people are waiting to take the elevator down. One of these is a man whose arms are supported by two more robots. He is manacled and half conscious, and there is blood streaming from his nose and onto his clothes. No one looks at all ashamed or embarrassed at my being there or seeing any of this. This would be to admit the possibility that what has been done is wrong. And since what has been done to him has been done in the name of the Leader, this simply cannot be the case. The man is dragged into the elevator, and the third robot, who remains standing on the fourth-floor landing, now leads me down a long, wide corridor. He stops in front of a door numbered 43, knocks, and then opens it without waiting. When I enter, he closes the door behind me.

The room is furnished but empty. The window is wide open, but there is a smell in the air that makes me think that perhaps this is the place where the man with the bloody nose has just been interrogated. And when I see a couple of spots of blood on the brown linoleum, I know I am right about this. I go over to the window and look out onto Ludwigstrasse. My hotel is just around the corner, and although it is foggy outside, I can see its roof from here. On the other side of the street from Würzburg's Gestapo HQ is the office building of the local Nazi Party. Through an upper window I can see a man with his feet up on a desk, and I wonder what gets done in there, in the name of the Party, that doesn't get done in here.

A bell starts to toll. The sound drifts across the red rooftops from the cathedral, I presume, only it sounds more like something out at sea, something to warn ships approaching rocks in the fog. And I think of Noreen, somewhere on the North Atlantic, standing in the stern of the SS *Manhattan*, staring back at me through the thick fog.

The door opens behind me, and a strong smell of soap is carried into the room. I turn as a smallish man closes the door and rolls down the sleeves of his shirt. I guess that he has just washed his hands. Perhaps there was some blood on them. He says nothing until he has fetched his black SS tunic from a hanger in the closet and puts it on as if the uniform will help to compensate for his lack of centimeters.

"You're Gunther?" he said in a voice that sounded folksy and Franconian.

"That's right. And you must be Captain Weinberger."

He carried on buttoning his tunic without bothering to answer. Then he pointed at the chair in front of his desk. "Sit down, please."

"No, thanks," I said, sitting down on the windowsill. "I'm a bit like a cat. I'm very particular where I sit."

"What ever do you mean?"

"There's blood on the floor underneath that chair and, for all I know, there's some on it as well. I don't make enough money to risk spoiling a good suit."

Weinberger colored a little. "Please yourself."

He sat down behind the desk. His forehead was the only tall thing about him. On top of it was a shock of thick brown curly hair. His eyes were green and penetrating. His mouth was insolent. He looked like a defiant schoolboy. And it was hard to imagine him being rough with anything other than a collection of toy soldiers or a fairground coconut toss. "So, how can I help you, Herr Gunther?"

I didn't like the look of him. But that hardly mattered. A display of good manners would have struck the wrong note. Clipping the tails of young pups in the Gestapo was, as Liebermann von Sonnenberg had said, almost a sport among senior police officers.

"An American called Max Reles. What do you know about him?"

"And you're asking in what capacity?" Weinberger put his boots up onto the desk like the man in the office across the street and clasped his hands behind his head. "You're not Gestapo, and you're not KRIPO. And I think we can take it you're not SS."

"I'm conducting an undercover investigation for Berlin's assistant police commissioner, Liebermann von Sonnenberg."

"Yes, I got his letter. And his telephone call. It's not often that Berlin pays much attention to a place like this. But you still haven't answered my question."

I lit a cigarette and flicked the match out of the window. "Don't piss me around. Are you going to help me, or am I going back to my hotel to call the Alex?"

"Oh, I wouldn't dream of pissing you off, Herr Gunther." He smiled, affably. "Since this doesn't appear to be an official matter, I just want to know why I'm going to help you. That is right, isn't it? I mean, if this was an official matter, the assistant commissioner's request would have come down through my superiors, wouldn't it?"

"We can do it that way if you'd prefer," I said. "But then you'd be wasting my time. And yours. So why don't you just count this as a favor to the head of Berlin KRIPO."

"I'm glad you mentioned that. A favor. Because I'd like a favor in return. That's fair, isn't it?"

"So what do you want?"

Weinberger shook his head. "Not here, eh? Let's go for a coffee. Your hotel is not far. Let's go there."

"All right. If that's how you want this."

"I think it might be best. Given what you're asking about." He stood up and grabbed his belts and his cap. "Besides, I'm already doing you a favor. The coffee here is terrible."

He said nothing more until we were out of the building. But then I could hardly stop him.

"This isn't a bad town. I should know, I went to university here. I studied law, and when I graduated, I joined the Gestapo. It's a very Catholic town, of course, which meant that, in the beginning, it wasn't particularly Nazi. I can see that surprises you, but it's true—when I first joined the Party, this town had one of the smallest Party memberships in the whole of Germany. It just shows you what can be achieved in a short period of time, eh?

"Most of the cases we get in the Würzburg Gestapo office are denunciations. Germans having sexual relations with Jews, that kind of thing. But here's the anomaly: the majority of denunciations come not from Party members, but from good Catholics. Of course, there is no actual law against Germans and Jews conducting their sordid love affairs. Not yet. But that doesn't stop the denunciations, and we're obliged to investigate them if only to prove that the Party disapproves of these obscene relationships. Occasionally we parade a couple accused of race defilement around the town square, but it seldom goes much further than that. Once or twice we have run a Jew out of town for profiteering, but that's it. And it goes almost without saying that most of the denunciations are groundless and the product of stupidity and ignorance. Naturally. Most of the people who live here are not much more than peasants. This place is not Berlin. Would that it were.

"My own situation is a case in point, Herr Gunther. Weinberger is not necessaily a Jewish name. I am not a Jew. None of my grandparents is a Jew. And yet I myself have been denounced as a Jew, and on more than one occasion, I might add. Which is not exactly helping my career here in Würzburg."

"I can imagine." I allowed myself a smile, but that was all. I hadn't yet got the information I needed, and until then, I hardly wanted to upset the young Gestapo man walking along the street beside me. We turned onto Adolf-Hitler-Strasse and walked north, toward my hotel.

"Well, yes, it's funny. Of course it is. Even I can see that. But somehow I feel it wouldn't be happening in a more sophisticated place, such as Berlin. After all, there are people there with Jewish-sounding names who are Nazis, aren't there? Liebermann von Sonnenberg? I ask you. Well, I'm sure he would understand my predicament."

I hardly liked to tell him that Berlin's assistant police commissioner might have been a Party member but he also despised the Gestapo and all that it stood for.

"What I feel is this," he said earnestly. "That my name wouldn't hold me back in a place like Berlin. Here in Würzburg there will always be the faintest suspicion that I'm not completely Aryan."

"Well, who is? I mean, you go far enough back and, if the Bible's right, we're all Jewish. Tower of Babel. Right."

"Hmm, yes." He nodded uncertainly. "Besides all that, most of my caseload is so petty it's hardly worth the effort of my investigating it. That's why I became interested in Max Reles in the first place."

"And you want . . . ? Let's be a bit more specific here, Captain."

"Nothing more than a chance. A chance to prove myself, that's all. A word from the assistant commissioner to the Gestapo in Berlin would surely smooth my transfer. Don't you think so?"

"It might," I admitted. "It might, at that."

We walked through the hotel entrance and made our way to the café, where I ordered us both coffee and cake.

"When I get back to Berlin," I told him, "I'll see what can be done. As a matter of fact, I know someone in the Gestapo myself. He runs his own department in Prinz-Albrecht-Strasse. He might be able to help you. Yes, it's possible he might. Always supposing that you can help me."

These days, that was how everything in Germany worked. For rats like Othman Weinberger, it was probably the only way to get on. And while personally I regarded him as something to be scraped carefully off the sole of my Salamanders, I could hardly blame him for wanting to get out of Würzburg. I'd been there for just twenty-four hours and already I felt as keen to leave the place as the wandering Jew's stray dog.

"But you know," I said, "this case. Together we might yet make something out of it. Something a man might base a career on. You might not need anyone's kind word if this impresses your superiors."

Weinberger smiled wryly and gave the pretty waitress a slow up-and-down as she stooped to serve our coffee and cake. "You think so? I doubt it. No one here seemed very much interested in what I had to tell them about Max Reles."

"I'm not here to pour coffee in my ears, Captain. Let's hear it."

Ignoring his coffee and the excellent cake, Weinberger leaned forward excitedly. "This man is a real gangster," he said. "Just like Al Capone and those other Chicago hoodlums. The FBI—"

"Hold up. I want you to begin at the beginning."

"Well, then, you might know that Würzburg is the capital of the German quarrying business. Our limestone is highly prized by architects all over the country. But there are really only four companies that sell the stuff. One of them is a company called Würzburg Jura Limestone, and it's owned by a prominent local citizen called Roland Rothenberger."

He shrugged, ruefully. "Does that sound any less Jewish than my name? You tell me."

"Get on with it."

"Rothenberger is a friend of my father's. My father's a local doctor and a town councillor. A few months ago, Rothenberger came to see him in his capacity as a councillor and told him that he was being intimidated by a man named Krempel. Gerhard Krempel. He used to be an SA man, but now he's a heavy for Max Reles. Anyway, Rothenberger's story was that someone called Max Reles had offered to buy a share in his company, and that this Krempel character started to get rough when Rothenberger told him he didn't want to sell. So I started to check it out, but I'd hardly finished opening the file when Rothenberger contacted me to say that he wished to withdraw the complaint. He said that Reles had substantially improved his offer and that there had been a simple misunderstanding and that Max Reles was now a shareholder in Würzburg Jura Limestone. That I should forget all about it. That's what he told me.

"But I'm afraid boredom got the better of me, and I thought I'd see what else I could find out about Reles. Right away I discovered he was an American citizen and, on the face of it, an offense had been committed right there. As you probably know, only German-owned companies are allowed to tender for Olympic contracts, and, it transpired, Würzburg Jura Limestone had just outbid the local competition to supply stone for Berlin's new stadium. I also found out that Reles seemed to have important connections here in Germany, so I resolved to see what was known about him in America. Which is why I contacted Liebermann von Sonnenberg."

"What did the FBI tell you?"

"A lot more than I bargained for, to be honest. Enough to persuade me to check him out with the Vienna KRIPO. The picture I've built of Reles is based on two separate sets of information. And what I've managed to work out for myself."

"You have been busy."

"Max Reles is from Brownsville, New York, and he's a Hungarian-German Jew. That would be bad enough, but there's a lot more. His father, Theodor Reles, left Vienna for America at the turn of the century, most likely to escape a murder charge. He was strongly suspected by the Vienna KRIPO of murdering someone—perhaps several people—with an ice pick. It was apparently a secret technique taught to him by a Viennese Jewish doctor by the name of Arnstein. When Theodor settled in America, he married and had two sons: Max and his younger brother, Abraham.

"Now, Max has no convictions, although he was involved in the Prohibition rackets, as well as in loan-sharking and gambling. Since the end of Prohibition in March of last year, he's built connections with the Chicago underworld. Little brother, Abraham, has a conviction for juvenile crime and is similarly involved in organized crime. He's also believed to be one of the most cold-blooded killers in the Brooklyn mob and is reputed to use an ice pick for his murders, like his father. So skilled is he with this weapon that in some cases he leaves no trace."

"How does that work?" I asked. "You stab a man with an ice pick, you figure it leaves more than just a bruise."

Weinberger was grinning. "That's what I thought. Anyway, there was nothing about this technique in the information I had from the FBI. But the Vienna KRIPO still have an old case file on Theodor Reles. You know, the father. Apparently what he used to do was ram the ice pick through the victim's ear, right into his brain; and he was so good at it that many of his victims were thought to have died of a cerebral hemorrhage. Something natural, anyway."

"Jesus," I muttered. "That must be how Reles killed Rubusch."

"What's that?"

I told Weinberger what I knew about the murder of Heinrich Rubusch, and how Würzburg Jura Limestone was now the new owner of the Rubusch Stone Company. "You said Max Reles has built connections with the Chicago underworld," I said. "Such as what?"

"Until recently, Chicago was run by Capone himself. Who also came from Brooklyn. But Capone is now in jail, and the Chicago organization has branched out into other areas, including construction and labor racketeering. The FBI suspects that the Chicago mob was involved in fixing construction contracts for the 1932 Los Angeles Olympics."

"That figures. Max Reles has a close friend on the American Olympic Committee who also owns a Chicago construction company. A fellow named Brundage. He's getting some sort of kickback from our own committee in return for chasing off an American boycott."

"Money?"

"No. He's being drip-fed East Asian art treasures that were part of a collection donated to Berlin's Ethnographical Museum by some old Jew." I nodded appreciatively. "Like I said, you have been busy, Captain. I'm impressed at how much you've been able to find out. Frankly, I think the assistant commissioner is going to be as impressed as I am. With your talents, perhaps you ought to consider a career in the real police. In KRIPO."

"KRIPO?" Weinberger shook his head. "No, thanks," he said. "The Gestapo is the police force of the future. The way I see it, the Gestapo and the SS will have to absorb KRIPO in the long run. No, no, I appreciate your compliment, but from the point of view of my career, I have to stay in the Gestapo. But preferably the Berlin Gestapo, of course."

"Of course."

"Tell me, Herr Gunther, you don't think we're eggs trying to be smarter than the hen, do you? I mean, this Reles may be a Jew and a gangster. But he's got some important friends in Berlin."

"I've already spoken to Frau Rubusch about exhuming her husband's body, which will prove he was murdered. I think I can even lay my hands on the murder weapon. Like most Amis, Reles likes a lot of ice in his liquor. There's a lethal-looking ice pick on the sideboard of his hotel room. And if all that's not enough, then there's his being a Jew, like you said. I'd like to see what all of his important friends in the Party think about that. I don't much like playing that domino, but in the end there might be no other way to nail the bastard. Liebermann von Sonnenberg was appointed by Hermann Goering himself. And possibly we'll have to present all the salient facts to him. And since Goering isn't on any Olympic committee, it's hard to imagine him choosing to ignore corruption among the committee's members, even if some others might."

"You'd better be certain of all your evidence before you do that. What's the saying? The cock that crows too early gets the twisted neck."

"I suppose they teach you that at Gestapo training school. No, I won't do anything until I have all the evidence. I can walk just as well as I can run."

Weinberger nodded. "I'll need to see the widow. To get her written permission to exhume the body. Probably I'll have to involve the Würzburg KRIPO, too. Such as it is. And a magistrate. All of that could take a little time. At least a week. Perhaps longer."

"Heinrich Rubusch has plenty of time, Captain. But he needs to rise up from the dead and start talking if this case is going to get anywhere. It's one thing ignoring a construction racket. It's quite another ignoring the murder of a prominent German citizen. Especially when he's properly Aryan. You're a little folksy for my taste, Weinberger, but we'll make a first-rate policeman out of you yet. Back at the Alex, when I was police, we had a saying of our own. The bone won't come to the dog. It's the dog that goes to the bone."

29

IT WAS THREE HOURS TO FRANKFURT on the passenger train. We stopped at almost every town along the Main valley, and when I wasn't looking out of the window and admiring the scenery, I was writing a letter. I wrote it several different ways. It wasn't the kind of letter I had written before or which made me feel happy, but all the same it needed to be written. And somehow I managed to persuade myself that it was a way to protect myself.

I shouldn't have been thinking of other women, but I was. At Frankfurt, I followed along the platform a woman who was built like a Stradivarius cello, and then felt a bow stroke of disappointment when she climbed up into the ladies' compartment, leaving me in a first-class smoker beside a professional type with a pipe the shape of a tenor saxophone, and an SA leader who favored Zeppelin-sized cigars that smelled more lethal than the locomotive. In the eight hours it took the train to reach Berlin, we generated a lot of smoke—almost as much as the Borsig-built steam R101 itself.

It was raining from a bucket when finally I arrived back in Berlin, and with a hole in the sole of my shoe, I had to wait awhile for a taxi at the rank in front of the station. The rain hit the big glass roof like stair rods and leaked onto the head of the line. The cabdrivers couldn't see it, which meant they always pulled up to exactly the same spot so that the next in line would have to take a shower before he or she could climb inside, like something out of a Fat and Stupid movie. When it was my turn I pulled my coat over my head and ducked into the cab; I was able to wash one whole sleeve of my shirt without a trip to the laundry. But at least it was too early in the winter for snow. Whenever it snows in Berlin, it reminds you that it's nearer to Moscow than Madrid by more than two hundred kilometers.

The shops were closed. There was no booze at home, and I didn't want to go to a bar. I told the driver to take me to the Adlon, remembering that there was half a bottle of Bismarck in my desk at work— the same bottle I'd confiscated from Fritz Muller. I figured I'd use just enough of it to warm myself up and, if Max Reles was out somewhere, to put enough blood and iron in my belly to check out my own typing skills on the Torpedo in his suite.

The hotel was busy. There was a party in the Raphael Room, and undoubtedly the many patrons in the dining room were staring up at the Tiepolo panegyric ceiling, if only to remind themselves of what a blue and cloudless sky actually looks like. Pouches of thick white tobacco smoke gently rolled out of the door of the reading room like a quilt from Freyja's bed in Asgard. A drunk wearing a white tie and tails was holding on to the front desk while he complained loudly to Pieck, the assistant manager, that the phonograph in his suite wasn't working. I could taste his breath from the other side of the entrance hall. But even as I went to lend a hand, the man fell backward, as if he'd been sawn off at the ankles. Luckily for him, he hit a carpet that was even thicker than his head. His head bounced a bit, and then he lay still. It was a near-perfect impersonation of a fight I'd seen on the newsreels, when Mad-cap Maxie Baer laid out Frankie Campbell one night in San Francisco.

Pieck rushed around the desk to help. So did a couple of bellboys, and in the confusion, I managed to lift the key for 114 and drop it into my pocket before kneeling down by the unconscious man. I checked his pulse.

"Thank goodness you're here, Herr Gunther," said Pieck.

"Where's Stahlecker?" I asked. "The guy who's supposed to be filling in for me?"

"There was an incident in the kitchens earlier. Two members of the Brigade were involved in a fight. The rotisseur tried to stab the pastry chef. Herr Stahlecker went to break it up."

The Brigade was what we called the kitchen staff at the Adlon.

"He'll live," I said, letting go of the drunk's neck. "Passed out is all. He smells like the schnapps academy in Oberkirch. That's probably what stopped him from hurting himself when he fell. You could stick a hat pin in this rumrunner, and he wouldn't feel a thing. Here, give me some space here, and I'll take him back to his room and let him sleep it off."

I grabbed the man by the back of his coat collar and dragged him to the elevator.

"Don't you think you should take the service elevator?" protested Pieck. "One of the guests might see you."

"You want to carry him there?"

"Er . . . no. Perhaps not."

A page boy came after me with the guest's room key. In return I handed him the letter I'd written on the train.

"Post that, will you, kid? And not in the hotel. Use the box at the post office around the corner on Dorotheenstrasse." I reached into my pocket and gave him fifty pfennigs. "Here. You'd better take this. It's raining."

I dragged the still-unconscious man into the elevator car and glanced at the number on the key fob. "Three twenty," I told Wolfgang.

"Yes sir," he said, and closed the door.

I bent down, pulled the man forward onto my shoulder, and then lifted him up.

A few minutes later the guest was lying on his bed, and I was wiping the sweat off my face and then helping myself from an open bottle of good Korn that was standing on the floor. It didn't burn, didn't even catch my collar stud. It was the smooth, expensive stuff that you drank to savor while reading a good book or listening to an impromptu by Schubert, not to help you handle an unhappy love affair. But it got the job done all the same. It went down like a clear conscience, or as near to the feeling of a clear conscience as I was going to get after posting that letter.

I picked up the telephone and, disguising my voice, asked one of the hello girls to connect me with suite 114. She let it ring for a while before coming back on the line to tell me what I now knew, that there was no reply. I asked her to put me through to the concierge, and Franz Joseph came on the line.

"Hey, Franz, it's me, Gunther."

"Hey. I heard you were back. I thought you were on holiday."

"I was. But you know, I couldn't keep away. Do you happen to know where Herr Reles is tonight?"

"He's having dinner at Habel. I booked the table myself."

Habel, on Unter den Linden, with its historic wine room and even more historic prices, was one of Berlin's oldest and finest restaurants. Just the kind of place Reles would have chosen.

"Thanks."

I pulled the shirt collar from the neck of the man now sleeping it off on the bed and then, thoughtfully, turned him onto his side. Then I capped his bottle and took it with me, slipping it into my coat pocket on the way out. It was two-thirds full, and I figured the guest owed me that much at least; more than either of us would ever know if he happened to throw up in his sleep.

30

I LET MYSELF INTO SUITE 114 and closed the door behind me before switching on the light. The French window was open, and the room was cold. The net curtains were billowing across the back of the sofa like a couple of comedy ghosts, and the heavy rain had soaked the edge of the expensive carpet. I closed the windows. That wouldn't bother Reles. He'd only expect the maid to have done the same.

Several packages lay open on the floor. Each contained some sort of East Asian objet d'art packed inside a bird's nest of straw. I took a closer look at one. It was a bronze or possibly gold statuette of some Oriental god with twelve arms and four heads. About thirty centimeters high, the figure appeared to be dancing a tango with a rather scantily clad girl who reminded me a lot of Anita Berber. Anita had been the queen of Berlin's nude dancers at the White Mouse Club on Jägerstrasse until the night she'd laid out one of the patrons with an empty champagne bottle. The story was he'd objected to her pissing on his table, which used to be her shtick. I missed the old Berlin.

I stuffed the statuette back into its nest and glanced around the suite. The bedroom beyond the half-open door was in darkness. The bathroom door was closed. I wondered if the tommy gun and the money and the gold coins were still behind the lavatory cistern's tiled panel.

At the same time my eye was caught by the ice bucket next to the drinks tray on the sideboard. Beside the ice bucket was an ice pick.

I picked it up. The thing was about twenty-five centimeters long and as sharp as a bodkin. The heavy steel rectangular handle was embossed with *Citizens Ice 100% Pure* on one side and *Citizens* on the other. It seemed a curious thing to have brought from America until you remembered that it was possibly a favorite murder weapon. Certainly it looked like an effective one. I'd seen less lethal-looking switchblades sticking out of a man's back. But there seemed to be little point in borrowing the ice pick in the hope that someone at the Alex might run some tests on it. Not as long as Max Reles was also using it to break the ice for his drinks.

I put down the ice pick and turned to examine the typewriter. A half-finished letter was still on the platen of the shiny Torpedo portable. I turned the platen knob until the paper was clear of the type guide and the paper fingers. The letter was addressed to Avery Brundage in Chicago and was written in English, but that didn't stop me from seeing that the letter g on the Torpedo was riding one millimeter higher than the other keys.

I had the probable murder weapon. I had the typewriter on which Reles had written false bids for Olympic contracts. I had a copy of the report from the FBI. And a sheet from the Vienna KRIPO. Now all I had to do was check that the machine gun was still where I thought it was. Explaining that would be a tall order even for a man like Max Reles. I looked around for his screwdriver and, not seeing it, began to search the drawers.

"Looking for something in particular?"

It was Dora Bauer. She was standing in the doorway of the bedroom, naked, although she might as easily have covered herself with the object in her hands. It was big enough. A Mauser Bolo is a lot of gun. I wondered how long she would be able to hold it at arm's length before her arms got tired.

"I thought no one was at home," I said. "I certainly didn't expect to see you, Dora dear. And so much of you, too."

"I've been eyeballed before, polyp."

"Whatever gave you that idea? Me, a polyp. Tsk-tsk."

"Don't tell me you're searching the drawers to steal something. Not you. You're not the type."

"Who says I'm not?"

"No." She shook her head. "You got me this job, and you didn't even ask for a cut. What thief would have done that?"

"It proves you owe me something, surely."

"You already collected that debt."

"I did?"

"Sure. A man with a bottle in his pocket lets himself in here and starts raking through the drawers? I could have shot you five minutes ago. And just because I haven't pulled the trigger yet, don't think I won't. Cop or not. From what I already know about you, Gunther, your old colleagues over at the Alex might think I was doing them a favor."

"It's me you're doing a favor, Fräulein. I haven't seen so much of a pretty girl since the Eldorado got closed down. Is this how you normally dress for some shorthand and typing? Or is being naked just the way you end up when Max Reles finishes giving you dictation? Either way, I'm not complaining. Even with a gun in your hand, Dora, you're still a sight for sore eyes."

"I was asleep," she said. "At least I was until the telephone started ringing. I suppose that was you seeing if the coast was clear."

"It's a pity you didn't answer. I could have spared your blushes."

"You can stare at my mouse all you want, polyp, but you won't see me blushing."

"Look. Why don't you put down the gun and then find a dressing gown. After that we can talk. There's a perfectly simple explanation for why I'm here."

"And don't think I don't know what that is, Gunther. We've been expecting you, Max and me. Ever since your little excursion to Würzburg."

"Pretty little town. I didn't like it at first, mind. Did you know they have one of the finest baroque cathedrals in Germany? The local prince-bishops built it, to make up for the fact that the citizens of the town murdered some poor Irish priest back in the year 689. Saint Kilian. Max Reles would fit right in if he ever went there. But then he probably does go, now that he owns a quarry or two, supplying stone to the GOC."

He murdered someone, too, of course. Let's not forget that fact. Using that ice pick on the sideboard."

"You should be on the radio."

"Listen to me, Dora. Right now it's just Max who's staring at the inside of a headsman's basket. Remember Myra Scheidemann? The Black Forest murderess? In case you'd forgotten, we execute women, too, in this great country of ours. Be a shame for you to end up the same way as her. So be sensible and put the gun away. I can help you. The same way I helped you before."

"Shut up." She jerked the long barrel of the Mauser at me and then the bathroom. "In there," she said fiercely.

I did what I was told. I'd seen what a bullet from a Mauser can do to a man. It wasn't the hole it makes going in that gave me pause for thought, but the hole it makes going out. It's the difference between a peanut and an orange.

I opened the bathroom door and switched on the light.

"Take the key out of the door," she said. "And put it back in the lock on this side of the door."

Besides, Dora was an ex-whore. Probably still was a whore. And whores are less particular about shooting people. Especially men. Myra Scheidemann was a whore who had shot three of her clients in the head with a thirty-two while they were having sex in a forest. Sometimes I get the feeling that a lot of whores don't much like men. This one was giving every impression that she didn't mind putting a bullet in me. So I took the key and put it in the lock on the other side of the door, just as she'd told me to do.

"Now close the door."

"And miss the show?"

"Don't make me prove I can handle a gun."

"Perhaps you should try for the Olympic shooting team. I don't think you'd have any problem impressing the selectors, dressed like that. Of course, pinning a medal on your chest might prove to be difficult. Although you could always use an ice pick."

Dora lengthened her arm, took very deliberate aim at my head, and steadied the Mauser.

"All right, all right." I kicked the door shut, angry with myself for not thinking to bring the little automatic I'd taken from Erich Goerz. Hearing the key turn in the lock, I pressed my ear to the door and tried to continue the conversation.

"I thought we were friends, Dora. After all, it was me who got you the job with Max Reles. Remember? It was me who gave you the chance to climb off the sledge."

"By the time you and I met, Gunther, Max was already a client. You just gave me a chance to be here with him legitimately. I told you before. I love being in big hotels like this one."

"I remember. You like the big bathrooms."

"And whoever said I wanted to get off the sledge?"

"You did. And I believed you."

"Then you're a pretty poor judge of character, aren't you? Max thinks you're all over him like fleas, but I think you've just been pinning the tail on the donkey. And got lucky. Max thinks that because you went to Würzburg you must know everything. But I don't think so. How could you?"

"As a matter of interest, how did he find out? That I'd gone to Würzburg."

"Frau Adlon told him. After your trip to Potsdam, he was wondering where you were. And so he asked her. He told her he wanted to give you a reward for finding that Chinese box. Of course, as soon as he knew you were there, he guessed you were on your way to check up on him. With the widow Rubusch or the Gestapo. Maybe both."

"The Gestapo didn't seem particularly interested in Reles and his activities," I said.

"I suppose that's why they asked the FBI for information about Max." Dora laughed. "Yes, I thought that would shut you up. Max got a telegram from his brother in America passing on a tip from someone in the FBI saying that the FBI had received a request for information about him from the Gestapo in Würzburg. You see, Max has friends in the FBI just like he's got a lot of useful friends here. He's clever like that."

"Is that right?"

I glanced around the bathroom. I might have kicked out the window and climbed down to the street but for the fact that the bathroom didn't have a window. I needed the gun behind the panel. I glanced around for the screwdriver and then opened the four bathroom cabinets. "You know, Max is not going to be very happy when he comes back here and finds me in his bathroom," I said. "For one thing, he's not going to be able to use his own toilet."

There wasn't much in the cabinets. Most of the man's toiletries were on the bathroom shelf or on the side of the sink. In one cabinet were a bottle of Elizabeth Arden Blue Grass and some Charbert Grand Prix men's cologne. They looked like a perfect couple. In another I found a bag containing some rather vulgar-looking dildos, a blond wig, some expensive-looking lingerie, and a diamond tiara that was obviously paste. No one leaves a real one in a bathroom cabinet. Not when the hotel has a perfectly good safe. Of a screwdriver, however, there was no sign.

"It gives Max a real problem about what to do with me. I mean, he can hardly kill me here in the Adlon, can he? I'm not the type to sit still and have my ears syringed with an ice pick. And the noise of a gunshot is going to attract some attention and require some explaining. But make no mistake, Dora, he's going to have to kill me. And you'll be an accessory to murder."

Of course, by now I had realized the significance of the wig, and the tiara, and the Blue Grass perfume. I was reluctant to mention this to Dora, as I still hoped she might be persuaded to cooperate with me. But with each passing minute it was becoming clear that I had little choice now but to scare her into cooperation with what I now knew about her.

"Except that you've got no problem with being an accessory to murder, have you, Dora? Because you've already helped out with one murder, haven't you? It was you that Heinrich Rubusch was with the night Max killed him with that ice pick. You were the blond in the tiara, weren't you? Didn't the guy mind when you showed him your mouse? That you weren't a natural blond?"

"He was like any other Fritz when he sees a bit of mouse. All he cared about was that it squeaked when he stroked it."

"Please tell me that Max didn't kill him while you were doing it."

"What's it to you, anyway? He made no noise. There wasn't even any blood. Well, maybe just a bit. Max blotted it up with the guy's pajama jacket. But you couldn't even see a mark. Incredible, really. And, believe me, he didn't feel a thing. Couldn't have. Which is more than I can say. Rubusch wanted a racehorse, not a girl. I had the marks of his hairbrush on my backside for days afterward. If you ask me, the fat pervert had it coming."

"But the door was locked from the inside when we found him. The key was still in the door."

"You opened it, didn't you? I locked it the same way. Lots of hotel whores carry passkeys or key turners. Or know how to get hold of one. Sometimes a client pays you off without a tip. Sometimes they peel some leaves off a bush that's too tempting to leave behind. So you wait outside for a while, and then go back in and help yourself to more money. Some hotel detective you are, Gunther. The other bull. What was his name? The drunk. Muller. He knew the score. It was him that sold me a key turner and a good passkey. And in return, well, you can imagine what he wanted. The first time, anyway. On the night Max killed Rubusch, I bumped into him, and was obliged to pin some notes on his coat."

"Which were some of the same notes you'd been given by Rubusch."

"Of course."

By now I had given up looking for the screwdriver. And I was scrutinizing my change to see if I had a coin thin enough to fit the screw head on the cistern panel. I didn't. I did have a sterling-silver money clip—a wedding present from my late wife—and I spent several minutes using that to try to loosen one of the screws; but I succeeded only in mangling the clip's corner. The way things were looking, very soon I was going to have a chance to apologize to my wife, if not in person, then something vaguely similar.

Dora Bauer had stopped talking. Which was fine. Every time she said something it reminded me of how stupid I'd been. I picked up the tooth glass, washed it out, poured myself a generous measure of Korn, and sat down on the toilet. Things always look a little better over a drink and a cigarette.

You're in a spot, Gunther, I told myself. In a short while, a man is going to come through that door with a gun, and he's going to either shoot you or try to walk you out of the hotel and shoot you somewhere else. Of course, he might try to hit you over the head and then kill you with that ice pick, and take you out of here in a laundry basket. He's been staying here for quite a while. He should know where everything is by now. How things work here.

Or he could just dump your body in the elevator shaft. It might be a while before anyone finds you down there. Or maybe he'll just telephone his friends in Potsdam and have them come and arrest me again. It's not like anyone's going to object. Everyone in Berlin looks the other way whenever someone gets arrested these days. It's nobody's business. No one wants to see anything.

Then again, they can hardly take the risk that I won't say something in front of everyone when they try to sleepwalk me out the front door. Von Helldorf wouldn't like that. Nor would our honored sports leader, von Tschammer und Osten.

I drank some more of the Korn. It didn't make me feel any better. But it did give me an idea. It wasn't much of an idea. Then again, I wasn't much of a detective. That much was already evident.

31

A COUPLE OF HOURS PASSED. So did a couple more drinks. What else was I going to do? I heard the sound of the key in the lock and rose to my feet. The door opened. Instead of Max Reles I found myself face-to-face with Gerhard Krempel, which put a big dent in my idea. Krempel wasn't very bright, and it was hard to see how I was going to talk myself out of anything if it was his cauliflower ears that were doing the listening. He had a thirty-two in one hand and a cushion in the other.

"I see you've been entertaining yourself," he said.

"I need to speak to Max Reles."

"That's too bad, because he's not here."

"I've got a deal for him. He'll want to hear it. I can guarantee that he will."

Krempel smiled bleakly. "So what is it?"

"And spoil the surprise? Let's just say the police are involved."

"Yeah, but which police? The no-account police you used to be, Gunther? Or the ones my boss knows who make problems disappear? You dropped three cards, and now you're trying to raise. Well, I'm calling your bluff. I don't care what you've got to say. Here's what I'm saying. You've got two ways out of this bathroom. Dead, or dead drunk. It's your choice. Both are inconvenient to me, but one choice looks less inconvenient to you. Especially as you've so thoughtfully provided a bottle and, by the look of things, made a head start on what I'm talking about."

"What happens then?"

"That's up to Reles. But there's no way I'm walking you out of this hotel unless you're incapacitated somehow. If you're drunk, you can shoot your mouth off all you like and no one is going to pay a crumb like you much attention. Not even here. In fact, especially here. They don't like drunks at the Adlon. They frighten the ladies. If we see anyone who knows you, then you'll be just another ex-cop who couldn't hold his liquor. The same as that other sot who used to work here. Fritz Muller."

Krempel shrugged.

"Then again, I could shoot you right now, right here, snooper. With a cushion wrapped around this little thirty-two, the noise will pass for a car backfiring. Then I'll push you out the French window. Shouldn't make too much of a splash down there. It's only one floor. By the time anyone notices you in all this rain and in the dark, I'll have you safely folded up in the back of my car. Next stop, the river."

The voice was calm and assured, as if killing me weren't going to give him any sleepless nights. He folded the cushion over the gun, with meaning.

"Better drink up," he said. "I'm done talking here."

I poured a glass and emptied it in one swallow.

Krempel shook his head. "Let's forget we're in the Adlon, shall we? From the bottle, if you don't mind. I don't have all night."

"Care to join me?"

He took a short step forward and hit me hard across the face. It wasn't hard enough to knock me off my feet. Just off my vocal cords.

"Cut the dialogue and drink."

I put the neck of the tall stoneware bottle to my lips and gulped at it like it was water. Some of it tried to come back up, but I gritted my teeth and didn't let it. Krempel didn't look like he had the tolerance to wait for me to puke. I sat down on the edge of the bath, took a deep breath, and drank some more. And then some more. As I lifted the bottle a third time, my hat fell into the empty bath, but it might as easily have been my head. It rolled under the dripping tap and remained on its crown, like a large brown beetle on its back. I reached down to get it, misjudged the depth of the bath, and fell in, but without dropping the schnapps bottle. I think if I had broken it, Krempel would have shot me then and there. I took another swig from the bottle to reassure him there was plenty of alcohol left in it, grabbed my hat, and crushed it back on top of my already swimming head.

Krempel regarded me with no more feeling than if I'd been a dried-up loofah, and sat down on the toilet lid. His eyes were two puffy slits, as if they'd been bitten by a snake. He lit a cigarette, crossed his long legs, and let out a long, tobacco-flavored sigh.

Several minutes passed. They were idle ones for him, but for me they were increasingly hazardous and intoxicated. The booze was strong-arming me into spineless submission.

"Gerhard? How would you like to make a lot of money? And I mean a lot of money. Thousands of marks."

"Thousands, is it?" His body twitched as it expelled a derisive laugh. "And this from you, Gunther. A man with a hole in his shoe who gets the bus home. When you've got the fare."

"You have got that right, my friend." With my backside on the floor of the canyon-deep bath and my Salamanders in the air, I felt like Bobby Leach going over Niagara in a barrel. Every so often my stomach seemed to fall away beneath me. I turned the tap and splashed some cold water onto my sweat-covered face. "But. There is money to be had. My friend. A lot of money. Behind you there's a panel that is screwed on top of the lavatory cistern. Hidden in there is a bag. A bag containing banknotes. In several currencies. A Thompson submachine gun. And enough Swiss gold coins to start a chocolate shop."

"It's a little early for Christmas," said Krempel. He tutted loudly. "And I didn't even leave a boot by the fireplace."

"Last year, mine was full of twigs. But it's there, all right. The money, I mean. I figure Reles must have hidden it there. I mean, a Thompson's not the kind of thing you can leave in the hotel safe. Even here."

"Don't let me stop you drinking," Krempel growled, and, leaning forward on the lavatory seat, he tapped the sole of my shoe—the one with the hole in it—with the barrel of the gun.

I filled my cheeks with the obnoxious liquid, swallowed uncomfortably, and let out a deep, nauseated breath. "I found it. When I searched this suite. A little while ago."

"And you just left it there?"

"I'm a lot of things, Gerhard. But I'm not a thief. You have the advantage of me there. There's a screwdriver old Max keeps in this suite. Somewhere. To remove said panel. I'm sure of it. I was looking for it a bit earlier on. So that I could greet you with it when you showed up with the Mauser in your mitt. Nothing personal, you understand. But a Thompson gets a click of the heels and a salute in any language."

I closed my eyes for a moment, raised the sausagelike bottle in a silent toast, and swallowed some more. When I opened them again, Krempel was examining the screws on the panel with interest.

"There's enough there to buy several companies, or to bribe whoever needs bribing. Yes, there's a lot of coal in that bag. A lot more than he's paying you, Gerhard."

"Shut up, Gunther."

"Can't. I always was a gabby drunk. Last time I got tripped like this was when my wife died. Spanish flu. Have you ever wondered why they call it Spanish flu, Gerhard? It started in Kansas, you know. But the Amis censored that because of the war censorship still in force. And it didn't make the newspapers until it reached Spain, where they didn't have any wartime censorship. Ever had the flu, Gerhard? That's what I feel like now. Like I got a one-man epidemic of the stuff. Jesus, I think I even wet myself."

"You turned the tap, thickhead, remember?"

I yawned. "Did I?"

"Drink up."

"Here's to her. She was a good woman. Too good for me. Do you have a wife?"

He shook his head.

"With the money in that bag you could afford several. And none of them would mind that you're such an ugly bastard. A woman can overlook almost any shortcoming in a man when there's a big bag of money on her dinner table. I'll bet that bitch next door, Dora, doesn't know about the bag, either. Otherwise, she'd have had it for sure. Mercenary little nanny-goat. Mind you, I will say this for her. I've seen her naked, and she's a peach. Of course, you have to remember that every peach has a stone inside it. Dora's got a bigger one than most, too. But she's a peach, all right."

My head felt as heavy as a stone. A giant peach stone. And when my head dropped onto my chest, it seemed to fall such a long way that, for a moment, I thought it had dropped into the leather basket beneath the falling ax. And I cried out, thinking I was dead. Opening my eyes, I took a deep, spasmodic breath and struggled to remain vaguely vertical, but now it was a losing battle.

"All right," said Krempel. "You've had enough. Let's try to get up, shall we?"

He stood up and gathered my coat collars in his pomegranate-sized fists, and hauled me roughly out of the bath. He was a strong man—too strong for me to try anything stupid. But I took a swing at him anyway and missed, before losing my balance and falling onto the bathroom floor, where Krempel kicked me in the ribs for my trouble.

"What about the money?" I asked, hardly feeling the pain. "You're forgetting the money."

"I guess I'll just have to come back for it later." He hauled me onto my feet again and maneuvered me out of the bathroom.

Dora was sitting on the sofa, reading a magazine. She was wearing a fur coat. I wondered if Reles had bought it for her.

"Oh, it's you," I said, raising my hat. "I didn't recognize you with your clothes on. Then again, I expect a lot of people say that to you, sweetheart."

She stood up, slapped my face, and was going to slap it again, only Krempel caught her wrist and twisted it.

"Go and fetch the car," he told her.

"Yes," I said. "Go and fetch the car. And hurry up. I want to fall down and pass out."

Krempel had me propped against the wall like a steamer trunk. I closed my eyes for a moment, and when I opened them again she was gone. He shifted me out of the suite and along to the top of the stairs.

"It's all the same to me how you go down these stairs, Gunther. I can help you down or I can push you down. But if you try anything, I can promise that you'll be holding on to thin air."

"Grateful to you," I heard myself mumble, thickly.

We arrived at the bottom of the stairs, but I don't know how. My legs belonged to Charlie Chaplin. I recognized the Wilhelmstrasse door and thought it was sensible of him to choose this way out of the hotel at that time of night. The Wilhelmstrasse door was always quieter than the one on Unter den Linden. The lobby was smaller, too. But if Krempel had hoped to avoid our meeting anyone I knew, he failed.

Most of the waiters at the Adlon had a mustache or were clean-shaven, and only one, Abd el-Krim, wore a beard. His name wasn't Abd el-Krim. I didn't know his real name, but he was Moroccan, and people called him that because he looked like the rebel leader who had surrendered to the French in 1926 and was now exiled to some shithole of an island. I can't answer for the talents of the rebel, but our Abd el-Krim was an excellent waiter. Being a Mohammedan, he didn't drink and eyed me with a mixture of shock and concern as, with one arm draped around the lintel that was Krempel's shoulders, I lurched toward the exit.

"Herr Gunther?" he said in a voice full of solicitude. "Is everything all right, sir? You don't look well."

Words emptied out of my slack mouth like saliva. Perhaps saliva is all they were. I don't know. Whatever I said didn't make any sense to me, so I doubt that it would have made any sense to Abd el-Krim.

"He's had too much to drink, I'm afraid," Krempel told the waiter. "I'm taking him home before Behlert or either of the Adlons sees him like this."

Abd el-Krim, dressed to go home, nodded gravely. "Yes, that is best, I think. Do you need any assistance, sir?"

"No, thanks. I've a car waiting for us outside. I think I'll manage."

The waiter bowed gravely and opened the door for my kidnapper as he waltzed me outside.

As soon as the cold air and rain hit my lungs, I started to retch into the gutter. The stuff I was retching you could have bottled and sold, as it tasted like pure Korn. A car immediately pulled up in front of me, and the spray from the tires splashed the cuffs of my trousers. My hat fell off again. The car door opened, and Krempel launched me onto the floor with the sole of his shoe. A moment later the car door slammed, and then we were moving—forward, I imagined, but it felt like we were going around and around in circles on a ride at Luna Park. I didn't know where we were going, and I ceased to care very much. I couldn't have felt any worse if I'd been laid out naked in an undertaker's window.

32

THERE WAS A STORM AT SEA. The deck shifted like an accelerating elevator car, and then a wave of cold water hit me full in the face. I shook my head painfully and opened eyes that felt like two scooped-out oyster shells that were still swimming with Tabasco sauce. Another wave of water hit me. Except the water wasn't from a wave, but from a bucket in the hands of Gerhard Krempel. But we were on the deck of a ship, or at least a largish boat. Behind him stood Max Reles, dressed like a rich man playing ship's captain. He wore a blue blazer; white trousers; a white shirt and tie; and a white, soft-peaked cap. Everything around us was white, too, and it took me several moments to appreciate that it was daytime and we were probably surrounded with mist.

Reles's mouth started moving, and white mist came out of that, too. It was cold. Very cold. For a second I thought he was speaking Norwegian. Something cold, anyway. Then it seemed a little closer to home— Danish, perhaps. Only when a third bucket of water, gathered on a rope from over the side of the boat, was flung into my face was I able to grasp that he actually was speaking German.

"Good morning," Reles said. "And welcome back. We were beginning to get a little worried about you, Gunther. You know, I thought you krauts could hold your liquor. But you've been passed out for quite a while. At considerable inconvenience to myself, I might add."

I was sitting on a polished wooden deck, looking up at him. I tried to get up and found my hands were tied on my lap. But worse, given that the boat appeared to be on the water, was that my feet also were tied, to a stack of gray concrete blocks lying beside me on the deck.

I leaned to one side and retched for almost a minute. And I marveled that such a sound could come from my body. It was the sound of a living creature turning itself inside out. While this was going on, Reles walked away, with a look of distaste on his knuckle of a face. When he returned, Dora was beside him. She was wearing her fur coat and a matching fur hat, carrying a glass of water.

She carried it to my lips and helped me to swallow. When the glass was empty I nodded genuine thanks and tried to appreciate my situation. I didn't appreciate it very much. My hat, coat, and jacket were gone, and my head felt as if it had been used for the Mitropa cup final. And the pungent smell of Reles's large cigar was turning my stomach. I was in a tight spot. I had the awful feeling in a whole crowd of awful feelings that Max Reles was planning to give me a practical demonstration of exactly how Erich Goerz had disposed of Isaac Deutsch's dead body. I couldn't have been in a tighter spot if I'd been a starving dog chained to a high-speed railway line.

"Feeling any better?" He sat down on the pile of concrete blocks. "It's a little early for that, you might think. But I'm afraid that the way you are feeling now is likely to be as good as it gets, for the rest of your life. In fact, I can guarantee it."

He relit his cigar and chuckled. Dora leaned on the rail of the boat and looked out into what appeared as a limbo, in which we were floating like lost souls. Standing with his fists on his hips, Krempel looked ready to hit me anytime he was asked.

"You should have listened to Count von Helldorf. I mean, he couldn't have been more explicit. But, no, you had to be Sam fucking Spade and stick your cornet where it wasn't wanted. I just don't get that. Really, I don't. You must have appreciated that there was just too much money involved, and too many important people getting a big fat slice of the Black Forest cherry cake called the Olympic Games for anything to be allowed to spoil that. Certainly anything as easily disposable as you, Gunther."

I closed my eyes for a minute.

"You know, you're not a bad fellow at all. I almost like you. No, really. I even thought of cutting you in and offering you a job. A proper job, not that joke job you have at the Adlon. But there's something about you that makes me think I just couldn't trust you. I think it's that you were once a cop." He shook his head. "No, that can't be right. I've bought plenty of cops in my time. I guess it must be that you were an honest cop. And a good one, from what I hear. I admire integrity. But I've got no use for it right now. I don't think anyone has. Not in Germany. Not this year.

"Really, you wouldn't believe how many fucking pigs there are who want to feed at this trough. Of course, they needed someone like me to show them how it's done. I mean, we—by which I mean the people I represent in the States—we made a lot back in thirty-two with the Los Angeles Olympics. But the Nazis really know how to do business. Brundage couldn't believe it when he first turned up here. It was him who tipped us off in Chicago about all the money that was to be made out here."

"And the East Asian artifacts are some payback for that."

"Right. A few bits and pieces of the kind he collects and appreciates, but which no one here is going to miss. He's also going to pick up a nice contract to build a new German embassy in Washington. Which is the real treasure, if you ask me. You see, with Hitler the sky is the limit. I'm delighted to say that the man has absolutely no idea of economy. If he wants something, he gets it and to hell with the cost. In the beginning the Olympic budget was, what, twenty million marks? Now it's probably four or five times that. And I guess the skim must be fifteen or twenty percent. Can you imagine?

"Of course, it's not always straightforward dealing with Hitler. The man is capricious, you know? You see, I'd already bought a company that makes ready-mixed concrete, and done a deal with the architect, Werner March, only to discover that Hitler doesn't like fucking concrete. In fact, he hates it. He hates anything that's in any way modern. It doesn't matter a damn to him that half of all the new buildings in Europe are made of fucking concrete. That isn't what he wants, and he won't budge.

"When Werner March showed him the plans and specifications for the new stadium, Hitler went nuts. Only limestone would be good enough. And not any goddamn limestone, you understand. It had to be German limestone. So I had to buy a limestone company in a hurry and then make sure my new company—Würzburg Jura Limestone—was awarded the contract. Too much of a hurry, if the truth be told. Given more time, I could have smoothed things over, but. Well, you know all about that part, you sonofabitch. It's left me with a lot of concrete, but you're going to help me to get rid of some of that, Gunther. These three breeze blocks I'm sitting on are going to the bottom of Lake Tegel, and you're going with them."

"Just like Isaac Deutsch," I croaked. "I take it Erich Goerz works for you."

"That's right. He does. He's a good man, Erich. But he lacks experience in this kind of work. So this time I'm doing it myself, to make sure the job gets done properly. We don't want you rising up from the bottom like Deutsch. I always say if you want someone disposed of properly, you'd better do it yourself." He sighed. "These things happen, eh? Even to the best of us."

He puffed the cigar for a moment and then blew out a funnel of smoke that might have come from the funnel above my head. The boat was maybe thirty feet long, and I thought maybe I'd seen it somewhere before.

"I figure it was a mistake to dump that sonofabitch, Isaac, in the canal. Nine meters. Not deep enough. But out here the water is sixteen meters deep. That's not Lake Michigan or the Hudson River, but it'll do. Yes, there's that and the fact that I'm not exactly a stranger to this shit. So relax, you're in good hands. The one remaining question I have for you, Gunther—and it's an important one from your point of view, so I advise you to pay attention—is whether we deep-six you dead or alive. I've seen both, and it's my considered opinion that it's best you go down dead. Drowning's not quick, I don't think. Me, I'd prefer a bullet in the head beforehand."

"I'll try to remember that."

"But don't let me sway you. This is your decision. Only, I need to know what you know, Gunther. Everything. Who you've told about me, and what. Think it over for a minute. I have to take a leak and put a coat on. It's a little chilly out here on the water, don't you think? Dora? Give him another glass of water. It might help to make him talk."

He turned and walked away. Krempel followed, and in the absence of a personal cuspidor, I spat after them.

Dora gave me some more water. I drank it down greedily. "Guess I'll have all the water I can drink in a little while," I said.

"That's not even funny." She wiped my mouth with my tie.

"I'd forgotten how beautiful you are."

"Thanks."

"Nope. You're still not laughing. I guess that wasn't funny, either." She glared at me like I was dermatitis.

"You know, in *Grand Hotel*, Joan Crawford's not supposed to fall for Wallace Beery," I said.

"Max? He's not so bad."

"I'll try to remember that when I reach the bottom of the lake."

"I suppose you think you're like John Barrymore."

"Not with this profile. But I do think I'd like a cigarette, if you have one. You can call it one last request, since I've already seen you naked. At least now I can be sure when you're wearing a wig."

"A regular Curt Valentin, aren't you?"

Under the fur she was wearing a lavender-colored knitted dress that hugged her figure like a coat of emulsion, and over her wrist was a drawstring pouch bag that contained a handsome gold cigarette case and lighter.

"It looks as if Saint Nicholas has been here already," I said as she pushed a cigarette between my cracked lips and lit it. "At least someone thinks you've been a good girl."

"By now anyone would think you'd learned to keep your nose out of other people's business," she said.

"Oh, I've learned that, all right. Perhaps you'd like to tell him that. Maybe a good word from you has a better chance of success than one from me. Better still, perhaps you still have that gun. I'd say that where

Max Reles is concerned, a Mauser has an even better chance than any amount of good words."

She took the cigarette from me, drew in smoke, and then put it back in my mouth with cool fingers that were almost as heavily perfumed as they were ringed. "What makes you think I'd ever betray a man like Max for a dog like you, Gunther?"

"The same thing that makes a man like him attractive to a girl like you. Money. Lots of it. You see, it's my opinion, Dora, that if there was enough money involved, you'd betray the infant Jesus. As it happens, there's even more money than that hidden in Max Reles's bathroom at the Adlon. There's a bag full of money behind a panel that's screwed in front of the lavatory cistern. Thousands of marks, dollars, gold Swiss francs, you name it, angel. All you need is a screwdriver. Reles has one somewhere in his drawers. That's what I was looking for when you and your mouse came and disturbed me."

She leaned toward me. Close enough for me to taste the coffee that was still on her breath. "You'll have to do better than that, polyp, if I'm going to help you."

"No, I don't. You see, angel, I'm not telling you so that you'll help me. I'm telling you so that maybe you'll help yourself and, in the process, you'll have to shoot him. Or maybe he'll shoot you. It certainly won't make any difference to me at the bottom of Lake Tegel."

She stood up abruptly. "You bastard."

"True. But then again, at least this way you can be sure I'm on the level about the money. Because it's there, all right. Enough to start a new life in Paris. To buy a nice apartment in a smart part of London. Hell, there's enough there to buy the whole of Bremerhaven."

She laughed and looked away.

"Don't believe me if you don't want to. It makes no odds to me. But ask yourself this, Dora dear. A guy like Max Reles. And the kind of people he needs to pay off to stay in business. They're not the kind who take a personal check. Graft is a cash racket, Dora. You know it. And a whole sack full of cash is what it takes to keep a racket like this one afloat."

She stayed quiet for a moment, looking preoccupied with something. Probably she was picturing herself walking up Bond Street with a new hat and a thick wad of pound notes underneath her garter. I didn't mind contemplating that picture myself. It was certainly preferable to contemplating my own situation.

Max Reles came up on deck again, followed closely by Krempel. Reles was wearing a thick fur coat and carrying a big Colt .45 automatic attached to a lanyard around his neck, as if he didn't trust himself not to lose it.

"I always say, you can't be too careful with your firearm when you're planning to shoot an unarmed man," I said.

"Those are the only kind I ever shoot." He chuckled. "Do you take me for a fool who would go up against a man with a gun? I'm a businessman, Gunther, not Tom Mix."

He dropped the Colt on the lanyard and put his arm around Dora and pressed her fingers between her legs. The other hand still held his cigar.

Dora let Reles's hand remain where it was as he started to rub her mouse. She looked like she was even trying to enjoy it. But I could see her mind was somewhere else. Underneath the cistern in suite 114, probably.

"The Little Rico kind of businessman," I said. "Sure, I can see that."

"It looks like we have a movie fan, Gerhard. How about *Twenty Thousand Leagues Under the Sea*? Did you see that one? No matter. You can catch the real thing in just a few minutes."

"It's you who's going to get caught, Reles. Not me. You see, I have an insurance policy. It's not Germania Life, but it'll do. And it kicks in the minute I'm dead. You're not the only one with connections, my American friend. I've got connections, and I can guarantee they're not the same ones you've been getting chummy with."

Reles shook his head and pushed Dora away. "It's strange, but no one ever thinks they're going to die. Yet no matter how crowded most cemeteries look, somehow there always seems to be room for one more."

"I don't see any cemetery, Reles. In fact, now that I'm out here on water, you make me glad I never paid up front for my own funeral."

"I really do like you," he said. "You remind me of me."

Reles took the cigarette from my mouth and flicked it over the side. He thumbed the hammer back on the Colt and pointed it at the middle of my face. It was close enough to see down the barrel, to feel the stopping power and smell the gun oil. With a Colt .45 automatic in his hand, Tom Mix could have held up the arrival of talking pictures.

"All right, Gunther. Let's see your cards."

"In my coat pocket there's an envelope. It contains a couple of drafts of a letter addressed to a friend of mine. A fellow named Otto Schuchardt. He works under Assistant Commissioner Volk for the Gestapo, in Prinz-Albrecht-Strasse. You can easily check these names out. When I go missing from the Adlon, another friend of mine at the Alex, a detective commissar, is going to post the final draft of that letter to Schuchardt. And then your meat will be fried in butter."

"And why would the Gestapo be interested in me? An American citizen, like you said."

"A Captain Weinberger showed me what the FBI sent to the Gestapo in Würzburg. It was pretty thin stuff. You're suspected of this. You're suspected of that. Big deal, you say. But about your homicidal brother, Abe, the FBI knows plenty. About him and your father, Theodor. He's an interesting man, too. It seems that he was wanted by the Vienna police when he went to live in America. For murdering people with an ice pick. Of course, it's always possible they framed him. The Austrians are even worse than we are here in Berlin in the way they treat their Jews. But that's what I wanted to tell my friend Otto Schuchardt. You see, he works on what the Gestapo calls the Jew Desk. I think you can imagine the sort of people he's interested in."

Reles turned to Krempel. "Go and fetch his coat," he said. Then he looked at me grimly. "If I find you're lying about this, Gunther"—he pressed the Colt against my kneecap—"I'm going to give you one in each leg before I push you over the side."

"I'm not lying. You know I'm not."

"We'll see, won't we?"

"I wonder how all your smart Nazi friends will react when they find out who and what you are, Reles. Von Helldorf, for instance. You remember what happened when he found out about Erik Hanussen, the clairvoyant? Why, of course you do. After all, this is Hanussen's boat, isn't it?"

I nodded at one of the life preservers attached to the guardrail. On it was painted the name of the boat: *Ursel IV*. It was the boat I'd seen outside von Helldorf's office window in the Potsdam police praesidium. That put a smile on my face.

"You know, it's kind of ironic when you think about it, Reles. That you of all people should be using the *Ursel*. Did von Helldorf sell you this tub, or is it just a loan from an aristocratic friend who's going to feel terribly let down when he discovers the sad truth about you, Max? That you're a Jew. Badly let down, I should say. Betrayed, even. I knew some cops who found Erik Hanussen's body, and they told me he was tortured before he was killed. I even heard tell they did it on this boat. So people wouldn't hear the man screaming. Von Helldorf is an unforgiving man, Max. Unforgiving, and unbalanced. He likes to whip people. Did you know that? Then again, maybe you could be his pet Jew. They say even Goering has one these days."

Krempel returned with my crumpled coat in one hand and in the other the envelope containing drafts of the letter I had asked the page boy at the Adlon to post the previous evening. I watched Max Reles read it with a mixture of keen anticipation and shame.

"You know, it's surprising what a man will find he is capable of doing when it comes right down to it," I said. "I never thought I could write a letter denouncing someone to the Gestapo. To say nothing of basing that denunciation on a man's race. Ordinarily I'd feel pretty disgusted with myself, Max. But in your case it was a real pleasure. I almost hope you do kill me. It'd be worth it just to imagine the look on all their faces. Avery Brundage included."

Reles crushed the letters in an angry-looking fist and threw them over the side.

"That's all right," I said. "I kept a copy."

The Colt .45 was still in his other hand. It looked as big as a four iron.

"You're a clever man, Gunther." He chuckled, but the lack of color in his face told me he wasn't laughing. "You played those cards well, I'll say that for you. However. Even if I spare your life, it still leaves me with a hell of a problem. Yes, sir, a hell of a problem." He puffed the cigar and then threw that over the side, too. "But you know, I think I have the solution. Yes. I really think I know."

"But you, my dear." He turned to look at Dora. She had opened her bag and removed her powder compact and was now checking the perimeters of her lipstick. "You know too much."

Dora dropped the compact. This wasn't a surprise to anyone, as Max Reles was now pointing the Colt not at me but at her.

"Max?" She smiled—nervously, perhaps—thinking for half a moment that he was joking. "What are you talking about? I love you, darling. I'd never betray you, Max. Surely you know that."

"We both know that's not true. And while I think I have a way to guarantee that Gunther here won't actually denounce me to the Gestapo, I don't have a way of ensuring the same thing from you. I wish I could think of some other way. Really, I do. But you are what you are."

"Max!" This time Dora screamed his name. Then she turned and ran, as if there had been someplace else for her to go.

Reles uttered a profound sigh that almost made me feel sorry for him. I could see he regretted having to kill her. But I'd given him no choice. That much was now obvious. He leveled the gun and fired after her. It sounded like a cannon on a pirate ship. The shot took her down like a cheetah tripping a gazelle, and her head seemed to explode with a pinkish thought made entirely of blood and brains.

He fired again, but this time he wasn't aiming the gun at Dora Bauer. Facing me, she was lying in a pool of thick, dark red that was already spreading across the deck, twitching slightly, but probably dead. The second shot hit Gerhard Krempel. It took him by surprise and lifted the crown of his head like the top of a hard-boiled egg. The impact was such that it flipped him over the rail of the boat and into the water.

A strong smell of cordite filled the air and mixed neatly with the acrid scent of my own mortal fear.

"Aw, shit," moaned Reles, staring over the side. "And I was going to weigh them down together. Like something from an opera. One of those fucking German operas that go on forever." He made the gun safe, and dropped it on its lanyard. "I guess I'll have to leave him be. Can't be helped. Dora, on the other hand. Dora?"

He walked fastidiously around the pool of blood and kicked the back of her head softly with the toe of his white shoe, and then kicked it a little harder, as if making quite certain she was dead. Her eyes, still wide with fear, remained motionless, staring at me accusingly, as if she held me entirely responsible for what had happened to her. And she was right, of course. Reles could never have trusted her.

He came over and inspected my ankles and then untied the rope that was attached to the three concrete blocks. Then he tied it tightly around her shapely ankles.

"I don't know why you're looking like that, Gunther. I'm not going to kill you. Of course, that makes it your fault she's dead."

"What makes you think you can afford to let me live?" I asked, trying to contain my very real fear that, in spite of what I'd said by way of a threat, and what he'd said by way of an answer, he was going to kill me anyway.

"You mean, what's to stop you from sending that letter to the Gestapo anyway if you manage to come out of this alive?"

I nodded.

He chuckled his sadistic chuckle and pulled hard on the knot securing Dora's ankles to the concrete blocks. "That's a very good question, Gunther. And I will answer it, just as soon as I've sent this little lady on her last and most important voyage. You can depend on that."

The concrete blocks were attached to the rope like a series of fisherman's weights. One after the other he carried them, grunting loudly, to the side of the boat and then opened a gate in the rail. And then, one after the other, he pushed the blocks over the side with the sole of his shoe. The weight of the blocks turned Dora's body and started to drag her toward the side.

It was probably the sensation of being moved that brought her back to consciousness. First she moaned, then she inhaled loudly, the breasts on her chest lifting up like two tiny lavender-colored circus tents. At the same time she flung out an arm, turned onto her stomach, lifted up what was left of her head, and spoke. To me.

"Gunther. Help me."

Max Reles laughed at the surprise of it and fumbled for his automatic to shoot Dora again before the three weights could drag her through the gate in the rail; but by the time he had worked the slide on the Colt it was too late. Whatever she had tried to say to me was lost in a scream as she realized what was happening. The next second she was dragged over the side of the boat.

I closed my eyes. I could do nothing to help. There was a loud splash, and then another. The screaming mouth filled with water, and then there was a terrible silence.

"Jesus," said Reles, staring down at the water. "Did you see that? I could have sworn the bitch was dead. I mean, you saw me give her a kick to make sure. And I'd have shot her again, to spare her that. If there'd been time. Jesus." He shook his head and let out a nervous breath. "How about that?"

Once more he made the gun safe, and dropped it on the lanyard. From the coat he took out a hip flask and took a large pull on it before offering it to me. "Hair of the dog?"

I shook my head.

"No, I guess not. That's the thing about alcohol poisoning. Be a while before you can even tolerate the smell of schnapps, let alone drink any."

"You bastard."

"Me? It was you that killed her, Gunther. Him, too. Once you'd said what you said, there was no alternative. They had to die. They'd have had me over a barrel with my pants down and fucked me from now until Christmas, and there's nothing I could have done about it." He took another swig of liquor. "You, on the other hand. I know exactly what's to stop you from doing that very same thing. Can you think what it is?"

I sighed. "Honestly? No."

He chuckled, and I wanted to kill him for it. "Then it's lucky I'm here to tell you, asshole. Noreen Charalambides. That's what. She was, is, in love with you." He frowned and shook his head. "Christ only knows why. I mean, you're a loser, Gunther. A liberal in a country full of Nazis. If that doesn't make you a loser, then there's that hole in your fucking shoe. I mean, how could a dame like that fall for a schmuck with a hole in his fucking shoe?

"Just as important, however," he continued, "you are in love with her. No point in denying it. You see, we had a talk, she and I, before she left Berlin to go back to the States. And she told me how you two felt about each other. Which, I have to say, was a disappointment to me. On account of the fact that she and I had a thing ourselves on the boat from New York. Did she tell you that?"

"No."

"It doesn't matter now. All that does matter is that you care enough about Noreen to stop her from being killed. Because here's what's going to happen. As soon as I'm off this boat, I'm going to send a telegram to my kid brother in New York. To be honest, he's my half brother. But blood is blood, right? Kid Twist, they call him, because it's fair to say he's a little bit fucking twisted in the head. Well, there's that and the fact that he used to like twisting the necks of guys he didn't like. Until they broke. That was before he developed his real skill. With an ice pick. Anyway, the fact is, he likes killing people. Me, I do it because I have to. Like just now. But he enjoys his work.

"So what I'm going to tell him. In this telegram I'm going to send. Is this, see? That if anything happens to me while I'm in Germany. Like me getting arrested by the Gestapo. Anything. Then he should track down Mrs. Charalambides and kill her. With a name like that, believe me, she won't be hard to find. He can rape her, too, if he's got half a mind. Which he has. And if he's in the mood. And quite often he is."

He grinned.

"You can think of it as my own denunciation, if you like, except that unlike yours, Gunther, her being Jewish has got nothing to do with anything. Anyway, I'm sure you can grasp the general idea of what I'm

274

talking about. My leaving you alone is guaranteed by the letter you've addressed to the Jew Desk at the Gestapo. And your leaving me alone is similarly guaranteed by the telegram I'm going to send to my kid brother just as soon as I'm back in my suite. We hold each other in check. Just like stalemate in a chess game. Or what the political scientists call a balance of power. Your insurance canceled out by mine. What do you say?"

A sudden wave of nausea hit me. I leaned to the side and retched again.

"I'm going to take that as a yes," said Reles. "Because, let's face it, what other choice do you have? I like to think I can read a man like a newspaper, Gunther. That was easier during Prohibition. The guys I dealt with were black-and-white, and mostly you knew where you were with them just by looking in their eyes. Then, after the repeal of the Volstead Act, my organization had to diversify. Find some new rackets. Gunther, I virtually started labor and union rackets in the States. But a lot of these guys are harder to read. You know, guys in business. It was hard to find out what they fucking wanted because, unlike the guys running booze, they themselves didn't know what that was. Most people don't, and that's their problem.

"You, on the other hand, my friend. You are a little bit of both. You think you're a black-and-white kind of guy. You think you know what you fucking want. But really you're not, and you don't. When I first met you, I thought you were just another dumb ex-copper looking to make a quick bill. I expect there are times when that's even the way you think of yourself. But you're more than that. I expect that's what Noreen saw. Something else. Something complicated. Whatever it was, she wasn't the type to fall for a guy who didn't fall for her in the same way." He shrugged. "With her and me, it was just because she was bored. With you, I think it was the real thing."

Reles spoke calmly, even reasonably, and, listening to him speak, I found it was hard to believe that he had just murdered two people. If I'd felt any better, I might have argued with him, but with the stomach I had and the talking I'd already done, I was more or less exhausted. All I wanted to do was sleep and stay asleep for a very long time. And maybe puke a bit more if and when the need hit me. At least then I would know I was alive.

"As I see it," he said, "there's just one remaining problem."

"I imagine it's not a problem you can fix with that Colt."

"Not directly, no. I mean, you could do it for me, but I bet you're the picky type. Well, you are now. I'd like to meet you in ten years' time to see how picky you are then."

"If you mean I'm picky about murdering people in cold blood, then you're right. Although I could make an exception in your case. At least I could until you've sent that telegram."

"Which is why I'm going to leave you on the boat until I've had time to go to the Palace Hotel in Potsdam and send the message to Abe. That's a nice hotel, by the way. I have a suite there, too, for when I'm in Potsdam." He shook his head. "No, my problem is this. What am I going to do about that Gestapo captain in Würzburg? What was his name? Weinberger?"

I nodded.

"He knows too much about me."

I nodded again.

"Tell me, Gunther. Is he married? Does he have any kids? Anyone he loves who I can threaten if he gets out of line?"

I shook my head. "I can honestly say that the only person he really cares about is himself. To that extent at least he's fairly typical of anyone working for the Gestapo. All Weinberger cares about is his career and getting on, at any price."

Reles nodded and walked around the deck for a moment. "To that extent at least, you said. In what way is he atypical?"

I shook my head and realized I had a blinding headache. The kind that feels likely to leave you blind. "I'm not sure that I understand what you're driving at."

"Is he queer? Does he like little girls? Can he be bribed? What's his Achilles' heel? Does he have one?" He shrugged. "Look, I could have him killed, probably, but it makes waves when a cop gets killed. Like that cop who got killed outside the Excelsior, in the summer. The Berlin polenta made all sorts of heat about that, didn't they?"

"Tell me about it."

"I don't want to have him killed. But everyone's got a weakness. Yours is Noreen Charalambides. Mine is that fucking letter that's in some cop's desk drawer, right? So what's this Captain Weinberger's weakness?"

"Now you come to mention it, there is something."

He snapped his fingers at me. "All right. Let's hear it."

I said nothing.

"Fuck you, Gunther. This isn't about your conscience. This is about Noreen. This is about her opening the door one night and finding my kid brother, Abe, on her doorstep. In truth, he's not as skilled with an ice pick as I am. Few people are, except maybe my old man, and the doctor who taught him. Me, I'm just as happy to use a gun. Gets the job done. But Abe." Max Reles shook his head and smiled. "One time back in Brooklyn, when we were both working the Shapiro brothers—local underworld figures—the kid murdered this guy in a car wash because he didn't clean his car right. He left the wheels dirty. So Abe told me, anyway. Broad daylight, and the kid knocks him out and then stabs him in the fucking ear with an ice pick. Not a mark. The coppers thought the guy had a heart attack. As it happens, the Shapiros? They're dead, too. Me and Abe buried Bill alive in a sandpit last May. That's one of the reasons I came to Berlin in the first place, Gunther. To wait for the heat on that murder to die down a little." He paused. "So. Am I making myself clear? You want that I should tell the kid to bury the bitch alive, like Bill Shapiro?"

I shook my head. "All right," I said. "I'll tell you."

PART TWO

Havana, February 1954

1

WHEN THE WIND BLOWS from the north, the sea smashes into the wall on the Malecón as if it has been unleashed by a besieging army intent on the revolutionary overthrow of Havana. Gallons of water are launched into the air and then rain down upon the broad, oceanfront highway, washing some of the dust from the big American cars heading west, or drenching those pedestrians who are daring or foolish enough to walk along the wall during winter weather.

For a few minutes, I watched the crashing, moonlit waves with real hope. They were near but not quite near enough to reach the windup gramophone belonging to the Cuban youths who had spent most of the night grouped in front of my apartment building, keeping me and probably several others awake with the rumba music that is everywhere on the island. There were times when I found myself longing for the hobnailed, juggernaut rhythms of a German brass band; not to mention the street-cleaning properties of a model twenty-four-stick grenade.

Unable to sleep, I considered going to the Casa Marina, and then rejected the idea, certain that, at this late hour, the particular *chica* I favored would no longer be free. Besides, Yara was asleep in my bed, and while she would never have questioned my leaving the apartment in the small hours of the morning, the ten dollars payable to Doña Marina would probably have been money wasted, since I was no longer equal to the task of making love twice in as many days, let alone in the space of one evening. So I sat down and finished the book I was reading instead.

It was a book in English.

For some time now I'd been learning English, in an effort to persuade an Englishman named Robert Freeman to give me a job. Freeman worked for the British tobacco giant Gallaher, running a subsidiary company called J. Frankau, which had been the UK distributor for all Havana cigars since 1790. I had been cultivating Freeman in the hope that I might talk him into sending me back to Germany—at my own expense, I might add—to see if I couldn't open up the new West German market. A covering letter of introduction and several boxes of samples would, I supposed, be enough to smooth the arrival of Carlos Hausner, an Argentine of German descent, back to Germany and enable me to blend in.

It wasn't that I disliked Cuba. Far from it. I had left Argentina with a hundred thousand American dollars, and I lived very comfortably in Havana. But I yearned for somewhere without biting insects, and where people went to bed at a sensible time of night, and where none of the drinks was made of ice: I was tired of getting a freezing headache every time I went into a bar. Another reason I wanted to return to Germany was that my Argentine passport would not last forever. But once I was safely back in Germany, I could disappear. Again.

Going back to Berlin was out of the question, of course. For one thing, it was now landlocked in the communist-controlled German Democratic Republic; and, for another, the Berlin police were probably looking for me in connection with the murders of two women in Vienna, in 1949. Not that I *had* murdered them. I've done a lot of things in my life of which I'm less than proud, but I haven't ever murdered a woman. Not unless you counted the Soviet woman I'd shot during the long, hot summer of 1941—one of an NKVD death squad who'd just murdered several thousand unarmed prisoners in their cells. I expect the Russians would have counted that as murder, which was another good reason to stay out of Berlin. Hamburg looked like a better bet. Hamburg was in the Federal Republic, and I didn't know anyone in Hamburg. More important, no one there knew me.

Meanwhile, my life was good. I had what most Habaneros wanted: a large apartment on Malecón, a big American car, a woman to provide sex, and a woman to cook my meals. Sometimes it was the same woman who cooked the food and also provided the sex. But my Vedado apartment was only a few tantalizing blocks from the corner of Twenty-fifth Street, and long before Yara became my devoted housekeeper, I'd got into the habit of paying regular visits to Havana's most famous and luxurious *casa de putas*.

I liked Yara, but it wasn't anything more than that. She stayed when she felt like staying, not because I asked her but because she wanted to. I think Yara was a Negress, but it's a little hard to be sure about things like that in Cuba. She was tall and slim and about twenty years younger than I with a face like a much-loved pony. She wasn't a whore, because she didn't take money for it. She only looked like a whore. Most of the women in Havana looked like whores. Most of the whores looked like your little sister. Yara wasn't a whore, because she made a better living as a thief stealing from me. I didn't mind that. It saved me from having to pay her. Besides, she stole only what she thought I could afford to lose, which, as it happened, was a lot less than guilt would have obliged me to pay her. Yara didn't spit and she didn't smoke cigars and she was a devotee of the Santería religion, which, it seemed to me, was a bit like voodoo. I liked that she prayed about me to some African gods. They had to work better than the ones I'd been praying to.

As soon as the rest of Havana was awake, I drove along to the Prado in my Chevrolet Styline. The Styline was probably the commonest car in Cuba and very possibly one of the largest. It took more metal to make a Styline than there was in Bethlehem Steel. I parked in front of the Gran Teatro. It was a neo-Baroque building with so many angels crowded onto its lavish exterior it was clear the architect must have thought being a playwright or an actor was more important than being an apostle. These days, anything is more important than being an apostle. Especially in Cuba.

I had arranged to meet Freeman in the smoking room at the nearby Partagas cigar factory, but I was early, so I went to the Hotel Inglaterra and ordered some breakfast on the terrace. There I encountered the usual cast of Havana characters, minus the prostitutes: it was still a little early for the prostitutes. There were American naval officers on furlough from the warship in the harbor, some matronly tourists, a few Chinese businessmen from the nearby Barrio Chino, a couple of underworld types wearing sharkskin suits and small Stetson hats, and a trio of government officials in pin-striped jackets, with faces as dark as tobacco leaves and even darker glasses. I ate an English breakfast and then crossed the busy, palm-shrouded Parque Central to visit my favorite shop in Havana.

Hobby Center, on the corner of Obispo and Berniz, sold model ships, toy cars, and, most important for my purposes, electric train sets. My own layout was a tabletop three-rail Dublo. It wasn't anything on the scale of the train set I'd once seen in Hermann Goering's house, but it gave me a lot of pleasure. In the shop I collected a new locomotive and tender I'd ordered from England. I got a lot of models from England, but there were several things on my layout I'd made myself in the workshop at home. Yara disliked the workshop almost as much as she feared the train set. To her there was something devilish about it. Nothing to do with the movement of the actual trains. She wasn't entirely primitive. No, it was the fascination a train set held for a grown man that she held to be somehow hypnotic and devilish.

The shop was only a few meters from La Moderna Poesia. This was Havana's largest bookstore, only it looked more like a concrete air-raid shelter. Safely inside, I chose a book of Montaigne's essays in English, not because I had a burning desire to read Montaigne, whom I'd only vaguely heard of, but because I thought it looked improving. And almost anyone at the Casa Marina could have told me that I needed a bit of improving. At the very least, I thought I needed to start wearing my glasses more often. For a moment, I was convinced I was seeing things. There, in the bookshop, was someone I had last seen in another life, twenty years before.

It was Noreen Charalambides.

Except that she wasn't Noreen Charalambides. Not any longer. No more than I was Bernhard Gunther. A long time ago she'd left her husband, Nick, and gone back to being Noreen Eisner, and as the author of more than ten successful novels and several celebrated plays, this was how the reading world now knew her. Under the fawning gaze of some oleaginous American tourist, Noreen was signing a book at the till where I was about to pay for Montaigne, which meant that she and I saw each other simultaneously. But for that I would probably have crept away. I would have crept away because I was living in Cuba under a false name, and the fewer people who knew about that, the better. Another reason was that I was hardly looking my best. I hadn't looked my best since the spring of 1945. Noreen, on the other hand, looked much the same. There were a few flecks of gray in her brown hair and a line or two on her forehead, but she was still a beauty. She wore a nice sapphire brooch and a gold wristwatch. In her hand was a silver fountain pen, and over her arm was an expensive crocodile handbag.

When Noreen saw me she put her hand over her mouth, as if she'd seen a ghost. Maybe she had at that. The older I get, the easier it is to believe that my own past is someone else's life and that I'm just a soul in limbo, or some kind of flying Dutchman figure doomed to sail the seas for all eternity.

I touched the brim of my hat just to check that my head was still working, and said, "Hello." I spoke in English, too, which probably left her even more confused. Thinking she must have forgotten my name, I was on the point of removing my hat and thought better of it. Perhaps after all it was better she didn't remember my name. Not until I'd told her the new one.

"Is it really you?" she whispered.

"Yes." I had a lump in my throat as big as my fist.

"I thought you were probably dead. In fact, I was sure of it. I can't believe it's really you."

"I have the same problem when I get up in the morning and limp toward the bathroom. It always feels like someone must have stolen my real body in the night and replaced it with my father's."

Noreen shook her head. There were tears in her eyes. She opened her handbag and took out a handkerchief that wouldn't have dried the eyes of a mouse. "Perhaps you're the answer to my prayer," she said.

"Then it must have been a Santería prayer," I said. "A prayer to a

Catholic saint who's really just a disguise for some kind of voodoo spirit. Or something worse."

For a moment I held my tongue, wondering what ancient demons, what infernal powers would have claimed Bernie Gunther as one of theirs, and nominated him as the dark, mischievous answer to someone's idle prayer.

I glanced around awkwardly. The fawning American tourist was an overweight lady of around sixty, wearing thin gloves and a summer hat with a veil that made her look like a beekeeper. She was watching Noreen and me carefully, like we were all in a theater. And when she wasn't watching Noreen and me perform our touching little reunion scene, she was glancing at the signature in her book, as if she couldn't quite believe that the author had inscribed it.

"Look," I said, "we can't talk here. The bar on the corner."

"The Floridita?"

"Meet me there in five minutes." Then I looked at the book clerk and said, "I'd like to charge this to my account. The name is Hausner. Carlos Hausner." I spoke in Spanish, but I was sure Noreen understood. She always had been quick to understand what was going on. I shot her a look and nodded. She nodded back, as if to reassure me that my secret was safe. For now.

"Actually, I'm done here," said Noreen. She looked at the tourist and smiled. And the tourist smiled back and thanked Noreen profusely, as if she'd been given not an inscribed book but a signed check for a thousand dollars.

"So why don't I just come with you now?" Noreen said, and threaded her arm through mine. She escorted me to the door of the bookshop. "After all, I wouldn't want you to disappear now that I've found you again."

"Why would I do that?"

"Oh, I can think of any number of reasons," she said. "*Señor Hausner*. I am an author, after all."

We came out of the shop and walked up a gentle slope toward the Floridita Bar.

"I know. I even read one of your books. The one about the Spanish Civil War: *The Worst Turns the Best to the Brave*."

"And what did you think?"

"Honestly?"

"You can give it a try, I suppose, *Carlos*."

"I enjoyed it."

"So it's not just your name that's false."

"No, really, I did."

We were outside the bar. A man jackknifed off the hood of an Oldsmobile and bowed into our path.

"Taxi, *señor?* Taxi?"

I waved the man away and let Noreen go into the bar first.

"I've time for a quick one, and then I have to go. I have an appointment in fifteen minutes. At the cigar factory. It's business. A job, maybe, so I can't break it."

"If that's the way you want it. After all, it's only been half a lifetime."

2

THERE WAS A MAHOGANY BAR the size of a velodrome and, behind it, a dingy-looking mural of an old sailing ship entering the port of Havana. It might have been a slave ship, but another cargo of tourists or American sailors seemed a more likely bet. The Floridita was full of Americans, most of them fresh off the cruise ship parked next to the destroyer in Havana Harbor. Inside the door, a trio of musicians was setting up to play. We found a table, and I quickly ordered some drinks while the waiter could still hear me.

Noreen was busy checking out my shopping. "Montaigne, huh? I'm impressed." She was speaking German now, probably getting ready to ask me some awkward questions without our being overheard and understood.

"Don't be. I haven't read it yet."

"What's this? Hobby Center? Do you have children?"

"No, that's for me." Seeing her smile, I shrugged. "I like train sets. I like the way they just keep on going around and around, like one single, simple, innocent thought in my head. That way I can ignore all the other thoughts that are in there."

"I know. You're like the governess in *The Turn of the Screw*."

"Am I?"

"It's a novel by Henry James."

"I wouldn't know. So. Any kids yourself?"

"I have a daughter. Dinah. She's just finished school."

The waiter arrived and neatly set out the drinks in front of us like a chess grand master castling a king and a rook. When he was gone, Noreen said, "What's the story, Carlos? Are you wanted or something?"

"It's a long story." We toasted each other silently.

"I'll bet."

I glanced at my watch. "Too long to tell now. Another time. What about you? What are you doing in Cuba? Last I heard, you were up before that stupid kangaroo court. The House Committee on Un-American Activities. The HUAC. When was that?"

"May 1952. I was accused of being a communist. And blacklisted by several Hollywood movie studios." She stirred her drink with a cocktail stick. "That's why I'm here. A good friend of mine who lives in Cuba read about the HUAC hearings and invited me to come and live in his house for a while."

"That's a good friend to have."

"He's Ernest Hemingway."

"Now, that's a friend I have heard of."

"As a matter of fact, this is one of his favorite bars."

"Are you and he . . . ?"

"No. Ernest is married. Anyway, he's away right now. In Africa. Killing things. Himself mostly."

"Is he a communist, too?"

"Good grief no. Ernest isn't political at all. It's people that interest him. Not ideologies."

"Wise man."

"Not so you'd notice."

The band started to play, and I groaned. It was the kind of band that made you feel seasick as they swayed one way and then the other. One of the men played a witch doctor's flute, and another tapped a monotonous cowbell that left you feeling sorry for cows. Their sung harmonies were like a freight locomotive's horn. The girl yelled solos and played guitar. I never yet saw a guitar that I didn't want to use to drive a nail into a piece of wood. Or into the head of the idiot strumming it.

"Now I really do have to go," I said.

"What's the matter? Don't you like music?"

"Not since I came to Cuba." I finished my drink and glanced at my watch again. "Look," I said, "my meeting's only going to take an hour or so. Why don't we meet for lunch?"

"I can't. I have to get back. I have people coming to dinner tonight and there are things I have to get for the cook. I'd love you to come if you could."

"All right. I will."

"It's the Finca Vigía in San Francisco de Paula." Noreen opened her bag, took out a notepad, and scribbled down an address and telephone number. "Why don't you come early—say, around five o'clock. Before the rest of my guests arrive. We'll catch up then."

"I'd like that." I took the notepad and wrote out my own address and phone number. "Here," I said. "Just in case you think I'm going to run out on you."

"It's good to see you again, Gunther."

"You too, Noreen."

I went to the door and glanced back at the people in the Floridita Bar. No one was listening to the band or even intending to listen. Not while there was drinking to be done. The barman was making daiquiris like they were on special offer, about a dozen at a time. From everything I'd heard and read about Ernest Hemingway, that was the way he liked drinking them, too.

3

I BOUGHT SOME PETIT ROBUSTOS in the cigar factory shop and took them into the smoking room, where a number of men, including Robert Freeman, inhabited an almost infernal world of swirling smoke and igniting matches and glowing tobacco embers. Every time I went into that room, the smell reminded me of the library at the Adlon Hotel, and for a moment I could almost see poor Louis Adlon standing in front of me with a favorite Upmann in his white gloved fingers.

Freeman was a large, bluff man who looked more South American than British. He spoke good Spanish for an Englishman—about as good as my own—which perhaps was hardly surprising given his family history: his great-grandfather, James Freeman, had started selling Cuban cigars as long ago as 1839. He listened politely to the details of my proposal and then told me of his own plans to expand the family business:

"Until recently I owned a cigar factory in Jamaica. But, like the Jamaicans themselves, the product is inconsistent, so I've sold that and decided to concentrate on selling Cuban cigars in Britain. I have plans to buy a couple of other companies that will give me about twenty percent of the British market. But the German market. I don't know. Is there such a thing? You tell me, old boy."

I told him about Germany's membership in the European Coal and Steel Community and how the country, benefiting from the currency reform of 1948, had seen the fastest growth of any nation in European history. I told him how industrial production had increased by thirty-five percent and how agricultural production had already surpassed prewar levels. It's amazing these days how much real information you can get from a German newspaper.

"The question is not," I said, "*can* you afford to try to gain a share of the West German market, but can you afford *not* to try."

Freeman looked impressed. I was impressed myself. It made a pleasant change to be discussing an export market instead of a pathologist's report.

And yet all I could think about was Noreen Eisner and seeing her again after such a long time. Twenty years! It seemed almost miraculous after all that we had been through—she, driving an ambulance in the Spanish Civil War, and me in Nazi Germany and Soviet Russia. In truth, I had no romantic intentions toward her. Twenty years was too long for any feelings to have survived. Besides, our affair had lasted only a few weeks. But I did hope that she and I might become friends again. I didn't have many friends in Havana, and I was looking forward to sharing a few memories with someone in whose company I might be myself again. My real self, instead of the person I was supposed to be. It was four years since I'd done anything as straightforward as that. And I wondered what a man like Robert Freeman would have said if I'd told him about Bernie Gunther's life. Probably he'd have swallowed his cigar. As it was, we parted amicably with his declaring that we should meet again, just as soon as he had bought the two competing companies, which would give him the rights to sell the brands Montecristo and Ramon Allones.

"Do you know something, Carlos?" he said as we went out of the smoking room. "You're the first German I've spoken to since before the war."

"Argentine-German," I said, correcting him.

"Yes, of course. Not that I've anything against the Germans, you understand. We're all on the same side now, aren't we? Against the communists, and all that. You know, sometimes I wonder what to make of it all. What happened between our two countries. The war, I mean. The Nazis and Hitler. What do you think about it?"

"I try not to think about it at all," I said. "But when I do, I think this: that for a short period of time the German language was a series of very large German words, formed from very small German thinking."

Freeman chuckled and puffed his cigar at the same time. "Quite," he said. "Oh, quite."

"It's the fate of every race to think itself chosen by God," I added. "But it's the fate of only a very few races that they're sufficiently stupid as to try to put that into practice."

In the sales hall I passed a photograph of the British prime minister with a cigar in his mouth, and nodded. "I'll tell you another thing. Hitler didn't drink and he didn't smoke, and he was healthy right up until the day he shot himself."

"Quite," said Freeman. "Oh, quite."

4

FINCA VIGÍA WAS about twelve kilometers southeast of central Havana—a one-story Spanish colonial house set in a twenty-acre estate and boasting a fine view of the bay to the north. I parked next to a lemon Pontiac Chieftain convertible—the one with the chief's head on the hood that glows when the headlights are switched on. There was something vaguely African about the white house and its situation, and as I climbed out of my car and glanced around at all the mango trees and enormous jacarandas, I thought I could almost have been visiting the home of some district high commissioner in Kenya.

This was an impression strongly enhanced by the interior. The house was a museum to Hemingway's love of hunting. Each of the many large, airy rooms, including the master bedroom—but not the bathroom—contained the trophy heads of kudu, water buffalo, and ibex. Anything with horns, in fact. I wouldn't have been surprised to have found the head of the last unicorn in that house. Or maybe a couple of ex-wives. As well as these trophies, there were a great many books, even in the bathroom, and unlike in my own house, most of them looked as if they had been read. The tiled floors were largely uncarpeted, which must have been tough on the feet of the several cats who gave the impression of owning the place. There were very few pictures on the whitewashed walls, just a few bullfighting posters. Furniture had been chosen for comfort rather than elegance. In the living room the sofa and armchairs were covered with a flowery material that struck a discordant, feminine touch in the midst of all that masculine love of death. At the very center of the living room, like the twenty-four-carat diamond that was set into the floor of the entrance hall of Havana's National Capitol Building, and which pinpoints zero for all distance measurements in Cuba, was a drinks table with more bottles than a beer truck.

Noreen poured us a couple of large bourbons, and we carried them out onto a long terrace, where she told me about her life since last I'd seen her. In return I described a version of my own—one that carefully left out my having been in the SS, not to mention my active service with a police battalion in the Ukraine. But I told her about how I'd been a private detective, and a regular cop again, and Erich Gruen and how he and the CIA had managed to frame me as a Nazi war criminal, and how I'd been obliged to seek the help of the Old Comrades to escape Europe and start a new life in Argentina.

"That's how I ended up with a false name and an Argentine passport," I explained, glibly. "I'd probably still be there but for the fact that the Perónists discovered I wasn't really a Nazi at all."

"But why come to Cuba?"

"Oh, I don't know. The same reasons as everyone else, I suppose.

The climate. The cigars. The women. The casinos. I play backgammon in some of the casinos." I sipped the bourbon, enjoying the sweet and sour taste of the famous writer's liquor.

"Ernest came because of the big-game fishing."

I glanced around, looking for a fish, but there weren't any.

"When he's here, he spends most of his time at Cojimar. It's a crummy little fishing village on the crust of a shoreline where he keeps his boat. Ernest loves fishing. But there's a nice bar in Cojimar, and I have the sneaking suspicion he likes the bar more than he likes the boat. Or fishing, for that matter. On the whole, I suspect Ernest likes bars more than just about anything."

"Cojimar. I used to go there a lot until I heard that the militia were using it for target practice. And that sometimes the targets were still breathing."

Noreen nodded. "I've heard that story. And I'm sure it's true. I could believe almost anything about Fulgencio Batista. Just along from that beach he's built a village of exclusive villas behind a wire fence, for all his top generals. I drove past it just the other day. They're all pink. Not the generals—that would be too much to hope for. The villas."

"Pink?"

"Yes. It looks like a holiday camp in a dream described by Samuel Taylor Coleridge."

"He's someone else I haven't read. One of these days I'm going to have to learn how. It's strange. I can buy any amount of books. But I've found it's no substitute for reading them."

Hearing footsteps on the terrace, I turned around and saw a pretty, young woman approaching. I stood up, and trying to wipe some of the wolf-man from my face, I smiled.

"Carlos, this is my daughter, Dinah."

She was taller than her mother, and not just because of the stiletto heels on her feet. She wore a polka-dot halter dress that only just covered her knees and left most of her back and a bit beyond exposed, which made the little net gloves look unnecessary. Over her muscular, sunburned forearm was a mohair handbag that was the shape, size, and color of Karl Marx's best beard. Her own hair was almost blond, but not quite, which suited her better, and all shallow layers and soft waves, and the string of pearls around her slender young neck must have been hung there as tribute from some admiring sea god. Certainly her figure was worth a whole basketful of golden apples. Her mouth was as full as a sail on an oceangoing schooner and lipsticked signal red by a skilled and steady hand that might have been school of Rubens. The eyes were large and blue and twinkling with an intelligence made to look more determined by her square and slightly dimpled chin. There are beautiful girls and there are beautiful girls who know it; Dinah Charalambides was a beautiful girl who knew how to solve a quadratic equation.

"Hey," she said, coolly.

I nodded back, but I'd already lost her attention.

"Can I have the car, Mom?"

"You're not going out?"

"I won't be late."

"I don't like you going out at night," said Noreen. "Suppose you get stopped at an army checkpoint?"

"Do I look like a revolutionary?" asked Dinah.

"Sadly, no."

"Well, then."

"My daughter is nineteen, Carlos," said Noreen. "But she behaves like she's thirty."

"Everything I know, I learned from you, mother dear."

"Where are you going, anyway?"

"The Barracuda Club."

"I wish you wouldn't go there."

"We've been through this before." Dinah sighed. "Look, all my friends are going to be there."

"That's what I'm talking about. Why can't you mix with some friends of your own age?"

"Perhaps I would," Dinah said pointedly, "if we weren't exiled from our home in Los Angeles."

"We're not exiled," insisted Noreen. "I just needed to get away from the States for a while."

"I understand that. Of course I do. But please try to understand what it's like for me. I want to go out and have some fun. Not sit around the dinner table and talk about politics with a lot of boring people." Dinah glanced at me and flashed me a quick, apologetic smile. "Oh, I don't mean you, Señor Gunther. From what Mother's told me, I'm sure you're a very interesting person. But most of Noreen's friends are left-wing writers and lawyers. Intellectuals. And friends of Ernest's who drink too much."

I flinched a bit when she called me Gunther. It meant Noreen had already revealed my secret to her daughter. That irritated me.

Dinah put a cigarette in her mouth and lit it as if it were a firecracker.

"And I do wish you wouldn't smoke," said Noreen.

Dinah rolled her eyes and held out one gloved hand. "Keys."

"On the desk, by the telephone."

Dinah stalked off in a cloud of scent, cigarette smoke, and exasperation, like the ruthless bitch-beauty in one of her mother's gothic-American plays. I hadn't seen any of them onstage, only the movies that had been made of them. These were stories full of unscrupulous mothers, mad fathers, flighty wives, dishonest and sadistic sons, and drunken homosexual husbands—the kind of stories that almost made me glad I didn't have a family myself. I lit a cigar and tried to contain my amusement.

Noreen poured us both another bourbon from a bottle of Old Forester she'd brought from the living room and helped herself to ice from a bucket fashioned from an elephant's foot.

"Little bitch," she said tonelessly. "She has a place at Brown University, and yet she still maintains this fucking fiction that she's obliged to live here in Havana with me. I didn't ask her to come. I haven't written a damn thing since I got here. She sits around and plays records all day. I can't work when someone plays records. Especially the kind of fucking records she listens to. Frank Sinatra and Tommy Dorsey. I ask you. God, I hate those smug bastards. And I can't work at night when she's out, because I'm worried something will happen to her."

A second or two later the Pontiac Chieftain started up and moved off down the drive, with the hood's Indian head scouting out the way forward in the encroaching darkness.

"You don't want her here with you?"

Noreen gave me a narrow-eyed stare over the rim of her glass. "You used to be a little quicker on the uptake, Gunther. What happened? Something hit you on the head during the war?"

"Just the odd bit of shrapnel, now and then. I'd show you the scars, but I'd have to take my wig off."

But she wasn't ready to be amused again. Not yet. She lit a cigarette and flicked the match into the bushes. "If you had a nineteen-year-old daughter, would you want her to live in Havana?"

"That would depend on whether or not she had any good-looking friends."

Noreen grimaced. "It's precisely that kind of remark that made me think she'd be better off in Rhode Island. There are too many bad influences in Havana. Too much easy sex. Too much cheap booze."

"That's why I live here."

"And she's in with the wrong crowd," continued Noreen, ignoring me. "As a matter of fact, that's one of the reasons I asked you here tonight."

"And there I was, naively thinking that you asked me down here for purely sentimental reasons. You can still pack a punch, Noreen."

"I didn't mean it like that."

"No?" I let that one go. I sniffed my drink for a moment, enjoying the combusted aroma. The bourbon smelled like the devil's coffee cup. "Take it from me, angel, there are many worse places to live than Cuba. I know. I've tried living in them. Berlin after the war was no Ivy League dormitory, and neither was Vienna. Especially if you were a girl. Russian soldiers have got pimps and beach-boy gigolos beat for bad influences, Noreen. And that's not anti-communist, right-wing propaganda, sweetheart, that's the truth. And, speaking of that delicate subject, how much did you tell her about me?"

"Not much. Until a few minutes ago I didn't know how much there was to tell. All you said to me this morning—and, by the way, you were speaking not directly to me, but to the book clerk in La Moderna Poesia—was that your name was Carlos Hausner. And why the hell did you pick Carlos as your nom de plume? Carlos is a name for a fat

Mexican peasant in a John Wayne movie. No, I don't see you as a Carlos at all. I expect that's why I used your real name, Bernie—well, it just sort of slipped out when I was telling her about Berlin in 1934."

"That's unfortunate, given how much trouble I went to in order to get a new name. To be quite frank with you, if the authorities found out about me, Noreen, I could be deported back to Germany, which would be awkward, to say the least. Like I told you. There are people—Russian people—who'd probably like to hold a knot under my ear."

She gave me a look that was full of suspicion. "Maybe that's what you deserve."

"Maybe." I put my drink down on a glass table and weighed her remark in my mind for a moment. "Then again, in most cases it's only in books that people get what's coming to them. But if you really think that's what I deserve, then perhaps I'll be running along."

I went into the house and then out again through the front door. She was standing by the railing on the terrace above the steps that led down to my car.

"I'm sorry," she said. "I don't think you deserve it at all, okay? I was just teasing you. Please come back."

I stood there and looked up at her without much pleasure. I was angry and I didn't care that she knew it. And not just about the remark she'd made about me deserving to hang. I was angry with her and with myself that I'd not made it clearer that Bernie Gunther no longer existed, and that Carlos Hausner had taken his place.

"I was so excited to see you again, after all these years—" Her voice seemed to catch on something like a cashmere sweater snagging on a nail. "I'm sorry I let your secret out of the bag. I'll speak to Dinah when she gets home and tell her to keep what I told her in confidence, okay? I'm afraid I didn't think about the possible implications of telling her about you. But you see, she and I have been very close since Nick, her father, died. We always tell each other everything."

Most women have a vulnerability dial. They can turn it up pretty much whenever they want, and it works on men like catnip. Noreen was turning the dial now. First the catch in her voice and then a big, unsteady sigh. It was working, too, and she was operating only at level three or four. There was plenty of what makes the weaker sex seem like the weaker sex still in the tank. A moment later her shoulders dropped and she turned away. "Please," she said. "Please don't go." Level five.

I stood on the step looking at my cigar and then down the long, winding drive that led onto the main road into San Francisco de Paula. Finca Vigía. It meant Lookout Farm, and it was well named, because there was a sort of tower to the left of the main building where someone might sit in a room on the top story and write a book and look out on the world below and think himself a sort of god. That was probably why people became writers in the first place. A cat came along and rubbed its gray body along my shins, as if it too were trying to persuade me to stay. On the other hand, it might just have been looking to get rid of a lot of unwanted cat hair on my best trousers. Another cat was sitting like an erect bedspring beside my car, ready to disrupt my departure if its feline colleague failed to do it first. Finca Vigía. Something told me to look out for myself and leave. That if I stayed I might end up like a character in someone's stupid novel, without any will of my own. That one of them—Noreen or Hemingway—might make me do something I didn't want to do.

"All right." My voice sounded like an animal's in the darkness. Or perhaps an orisha of the forest from the world of Santería.

I threw away the cigar and went back inside. Noreen met me halfway, which was generous, and we embraced fondly. Her body still felt good in my arms and reminded me of everything it was supposed to remind me of. Level six. She still knew how to affect me, that much was certain. She laid her head on my shoulder, but with her face turned away, and let me inhale her beauty for a while. We didn't kiss. That wasn't yet required. Not while we were still on level six. Not while her face was turned away. After a moment or two she broke away and sat down again.

"You said something about Dinah's being in with the wrong crowd," I said. "That it was one of the reasons you asked me here."

"I'm sorry I put it so badly. That's not like me. After all, I'm supposed to be good with words. But I do need your help. With Dinah."

"It's been a long time since I knew anything about nineteen-year-old girls, Noreen. And even then, what I knew was probably hopelessly wrong. Short of spanking her, I don't see what I can do."

"I wonder if that might work," she said.

"I don't think it would help her very much. Of course, there's always the possibility I might enjoy it, which is another reason to pack her off to Rhode Island. But I agree with you. The Barracuda Club is no place for a nineteen-year-old girl. Although there are much worse places in Havana."

"Oh, she's been to them all, I can assure you. The Shanghai Theater. The Cabaret Kursaal. The Hotel Chic. And those are just the matchbooks I've found in her bedroom. It might be even worse than that."

I shook my head. "No, it doesn't get any worse than them. Even in Havana." I fetched my drink off the glass table and poured it safely away in my mouth. "All right, she's wild. If the movies are right, then most kids are these days. But at least they're not beating up Jews. And I still don't see what I can do about it."

Noreen found the Old Forester and refilled my glass. "Well, maybe we can think of something. Together. Like in the old days, remember? In Berlin? If things had worked out differently, we might even have made a difference. If ever I'd written that article, we might even have put a stop to Hitler's Olympiad."

"I'm kind of glad you didn't write it. If you had, I'd probably be dead."

She nodded. "For a while, we made quite an investigative team, Gunther. You were my Galahad. My knight of heaven."

"Sure. I remember your letter. I'd like to tell you I still had it, but the Americans reorganized my filing system when they bombed Berlin. You want my advice about Dinah? I reckon you should fix a lock on her door and put her under a nine o'clock curfew. That used to work back in Vienna. When the Four Powers were in charge of the city. Also, you might think about not lending her the car whenever she asks for it. If it was me wearing those heels she had on, I might think twice about walking nine miles into the center of Havana."

"I'd like to see that."

"Me wearing high heels? Sure, I'm a regular at the Palette Club, although they know me better there as Rita. You know, it's not a bad thing that children should frequently disobey their parents. Especially when you consider the mistakes the parents made. Especially when they're as grown up as Dinah obviously is."

"Perhaps if I gave you all the facts," she said, "you might understand the problem."

"You can try. But I'm not a detective anymore, Noreen."

"But you were, weren't you?" She smiled a cunning smile. "It was me who got you started. As a private detective. Or maybe you need reminding."

"So that's your angle."

She curled her lip with displeasure. "I certainly didn't mean it to be an angle, as you put it. Not in the least. But I'm a mother who's running out of options here."

"I'll send you a check. With interest."

"Oh, stop it, for Pete's sake. I don't want your money. I've got plenty of money. But you might at least shut up for a minute and do me the courtesy of hearing me out before opening fire with both cannons. I figure you owe me that much. That's fair, isn't it?"

"All right. I can't promise to hear anything. But I'll listen."

Noreen shook her head. "You know, Gunther, it beats me how you ever survived the war. I've only just met you again, and already I want to shoot you." She laughed scornfully. "You want to be careful, you know. This house has more guns than the Cuban militia. There are nights when I've sat here drinking with Hem, and he had a shotgun on his lap for taking potshots at the birds in the trees."

"Sounds dangerous for the cats."

"Not just the fucking cats." Still laughing, she shook her head. "People, too."

"My head would look good in your bathroom."

"What a horrid thought. You looking at me every time I took a bath."

"I was thinking of your daughter."

"That's enough." Noreen stood up abruptly. "Damn you, get out," she said. "Get the fuck out of here."

I went into the house again. "Wait," she snapped. "Wait, please."

I waited.

"Why are you such a hard-ass?"

"I guess I'm not used to human society," I said.

"Please, listen. You could help her. You're about the one person who can, I think. More than you know. I really don't know who else to ask."

"Is she in a jam?"

"Not exactly, no. At least, not yet. There's a man, you see, whom she's involved with. Who's much older than her. I'm worried she's going to end up like—like Gloria Grahame in that movie. *The Big Heat*. You know, where that sick bastard throws boiling hot coffee in her face."

"Didn't see it. Last film I saw was *Peter Pan*."

We both turned around as a white Oldsmobile came up the drive. It had a sun visor and whitewall tires and sounded like the motor bus to Santiago.

"Damn," said Noreen. "That's Alfredo."

The white Olds was followed by a two-door red Buick.

"And, it looks like, the rest of my guests."

5

THERE WERE EIGHT OF US FOR DINNER. Dinner was prepared and served by Ramón, Hemingway's Chinese cook, and René, his Negro butler, which only I seemed to find amusing. It certainly wasn't because I had anything against the Chinese or Negroes. But it struck me as ironic that Noreen and her guests were all solemnly prepared to avow their communism while other men did all the work.

There was no denying what Cuba and its people had suffered, first at the hands of the Spanish, then the Americans, and then the Spanish again. But as bad as any of these perhaps had been the Cuban governments of Ramón Grau San Martín and now Fulgencio Batista. Formerly a sergeant in the Cuban army, F.B.—as most of the Europeans and Americans in Cuba called him—wasn't much more than an American puppet. So long as he danced to Washington's tune, American support seemed likely to continue, no matter how brutishly his regime behaved. Yet I couldn't bring myself to believe that a totalitarian system of government in which a single authoritarian party controls the state-owned means of production was, or ever could be, the answer. And I said as much to Noreen's left-leaning guests:

"I think communism's a much greater evil to inflict upon this country than anything that could be conceived and administered by a minor despot like F.B. A small-time thug like him might inflict a few individual tragedies. Perhaps several. But it hardly begins to compare with the rule of genuine tyrants like Stalin and Mao Tse-tung. They've been the manufacturers of national tragedies. I can't speak for all the Iron Curtain countries. But I know Germany pretty well, and you can take it from me that the working classes of the GDR would love to change places with the oppressed peoples of Cuba."

Guillermo Infante was a young student who had just been kicked out of the Havana University School of Journalism. He had also served a short sentence for writing something in a popular opposition magazine called *Bohemia*. This prompted me to point out that there were no opposition magazines in the Soviet Union, and that even the mildest criticism of the government would have earned him a very long sentence in some forgotten corner of Siberia. Montecristo cigar in hand, Infante proceeded to call me a "bourgeois reactionary" and several other phrases beloved of the Ivans and their acolytes that I hadn't heard in a long time. Names that almost made me feel nostalgic for Russia, like some wet character in Chekhov.

I fought in my corner for a while, but when two earnest, unattractive women started to call me an "apologist for fascism," I began to feel beleaguered. It can be fun being insulted by a good-looking woman if you look at it from the point of view that she's bothered to notice you at all. But it's no fun at all to be insulted by her two ugly sisters. Finding not much conversational assistance from Noreen, who had perhaps drunk a little too much to come to my aid, I went to the lavatory, and while I was there, decided to cut my evening's losses and leave.

When I got back to my car, I found one of the other guests already there. He had come to offer an apology of sorts. His name was Alfredo López, and he was a lawyer—one of twenty-two lawyers, it seemed, who had defended the surviving rebels responsible for the attack on the Moncada Barracks in July 1953. Following the inevitable guilty verdict, the judge in the Santiago Palace of Justice had sentenced the rebels to what I considered to be fairly modest terms of imprisonment. Even the leader of the rebels, Fidel Castro Ruz, had been sentenced to just fifteen years. It was true, fifteen years was not exactly a light sentence, but for a man who had led an armed insurrection against a powerful dictator, it compared very well with a short walk to the guillotine at Plötzensee.

López was in his mid-thirties, good-looking in a grinning, swarthy sort of way, with piercing blue eyes, a thin mustache, and a rubber swimming cap of shiny black hair. He wore white linen trousers and a dark blue open-neck guayabera shirt that helped to hide the beginnings of a potbelly. He smoked long cigarillos that were the color and shape of his womanly fingers. He looked like a very large cat that had been handed the cream-colored keys of the Caribbean's largest dairy.

"I am very sorry about that, my friend," he said. "Lola and Carmen shouldn't have been so rude. Putting politics ahead of simple politeness is unforgivable. Especially at the dinner table. If one cannot be civilized over a meal, what hope can there be for proper debate elsewhere?"

"Forget it. I'm thick-skinned enough not to care very much. Besides, I've never been all that interested in politics. Especially not interested in talking about them. It always seems to me that by browbeating others we hope to be able to convince ourselves."

"Yes, there's something in that, I think," he allowed. "But you have to remember that Cubans are a very passionate people. Some of us are already convinced."

"Are you? I wonder."

"Take my word for it. There are many of us who are willing to sacrifice everything for freedom in Cuba. Tyranny is tyranny, no matter what the tyrant's name."

"Perhaps I'll have the chance to remind you of that one day, when your man is in charge of the tyranny."

"Fidel? Oh, he's not at all a bad fellow. Perhaps if you knew a little more about him, you might be a little more sympathetic to our cause."

"I doubt it. Today's freedom fighters are tomorrow's dictators."

"No, really. Castro's very different. He's not out for himself."

"Did he tell you that? Or have you actually seen his bank statement?"

"No, but I've seen this."

López opened the door of his car and fetched a briefcase from which he took a small, pamphlet-sized booklet. He had dozens more in the briefcase. As well as a large automatic pistol. I supposed he kept it handy for the occasions when proper, civilized political debate just wasn't working. He held out the booklet in both his hands, as if it were something precious, like an auctioneer's assistant showing a rare object to a roomful of potential buyers. On the front of the pamphlet was the picture of a rather stout-looking young man, not unlike López himself, with a thin mustache and hooded dark eyes. The man on the pamphlet looked more like a bandleader than the revolutionary I had read about in the newspapers.

"This is a copy of the statement Fidel Castro made at his trial last November," said López.

"The tyranny allowed him the opportunity to speak, then," I said, pointedly. "As I recall, Judge Roland Freisler—Raving Roland, they used to call him—he just screamed abuse at the men who had tried to blow up Hitler. Before sending them to the gallows. Oddly enough, I don't remember any of them writing a pamphlet, either."

López ignored me. "It's called *History Will Absolve Me*. And we've only just finished printing it. So you can have the honor of being one of the first to read it. In the coming months, we're planning to distribute this pamphlet all over the city. Please, *señor*. At least read it, eh? If only because the man who wrote it is currently languishing in the Model Prison of the Isle of Pines."

"Hitler wrote a rather longer book, in Landsberg Prison, in 1928. I didn't read that one, either."

"Don't joke about this, please. Fidel is a friend to the people."

"So am I. Cats and dogs seem to like me, too. But I don't expect them to put me in charge of the government."

"Promise me you'll at least look at it."

"All right," I said, taking it, keen to get rid of him. "If it means that much to you, I'll read it. Just don't ask me questions about it afterward. I'd hate to forget anything that might lose me the chance to gain a share of a collective farm. Or the opportunity to denounce someone for sabotaging the five-year plan."

I climbed back into my car and quickly drove away, hardly satisfied at the way the evening had turned out. At the bottom of the drive, I wound down the window and tossed Castro's stupid pamphlet into the bushes before turning onto the main road north, to San Miguel del Padrón. I had a different plan in mind than the Cuban rebel leader, although it did involve the girls at the Casa Marina: from each according to her abilities, to each according to his needs. That was the sort of Cuban Marxian dialectic with which I was in complete sympathy.

It was just as well that I had thrown away Castro's pamphlet, because in front of the gas station around the next bend in the highway was a military roadblock. An armed militiaman flagged me down and ordered me to step out of the car. With my hands in the air, I meekly stood at the side of the road, while two other soldiers searched me and then my car under the steady gaze of the rest of the platoon and their boyish officer. I didn't even look at him. My eyes were fixed on the two bodies lying facedown on the grass shoulder with most of their brains spilling out from under their hairlines.

FOR A MOMENT it was June 1941, and I was back with my reserve police battalion, the 316th, on the road to Smolensk, at a place called Goloby, in the Ukraine, holstering my pistol. I was the officer in charge of a firing squad that had just executed a security unit of NKVD. This particular unit had recently finished murdering three thousand Ukrainian prisoners in the cells of the NKVD Prison at Lutsk, when our panzer wagons caught up with them. We shot them all. All thirty of them. Over the years I had tried to justify this execution to myself, but without much success. And many were the times when I woke up thinking about those twenty-eight men and two women. The majority of whom just happened to be Jews. Two of them I'd shot myself, delivering the so-called coup de grâce. But there was no grace in it. You could tell yourself it was war. You could even tell yourself that the people of Lutsk had begged us to go after the unit that had murdered their relatives. You could tell yourself that a bullet in the head was a quick, merciful death compared to what these people had meted out to their prisoners—most of them burned to death when the NKVD deliberately set fire to the prison. But it still felt like murder.

AND WHEN I WASN'T LOOKING at the two bodies lying by the side of the road I was watching the police van parked a few meters away, and the several, frightened-looking occupants of its brightly lit interior. Their faces were bruised and bloodied and full of fear. It was like staring into a tank full of lobsters. You had the impression that at any moment one of them might be taken out and killed, like the two on the grass shoulder. Then the officer checked my identity card and asked me several questions in a nasal, cartoonish voice that might have made me smile had the situation seemed less lethal. A few minutes later, I was free to proceed with my journey back to Vedado.

I drove on for about half a kilometer and then stopped at a little pink stone café by the roadside, where I asked the owner if I might use the telephone, thinking to call Finca Vigía and warn Noreen—and, in particular, Alfredo López—about the roadblock. It wasn't that I liked the lawyer so much. I never yet met a lawyer I didn't want to slap. But I didn't think he deserved a bullet in the back of the head—which, almost certainly, was what would happen to him if the militia found him in possession of those pamphlets and a pistol. Nobody deserved that kind of ignominious fate. Not even the NKVD.

The café owner was bald and clean-shaven, with thick lips and a broken nose. The man told me the phone had been out of order for days and blamed it on *pequeños rebeldes* who liked to demonstrate their devotion to the revolution by shooting their *catapultas* at the ceramic conductors on the telephone poles. If I wanted to warn López, it wasn't going to be by telephone.

Experience told me that the militia seldom allowed anyone to drive back through a roadblock. They would assume, rightly, that I intended to warn someone. I would have to find another route back to Finca Vigía—one that took me through the little side streets and avenues of San Francisco de Paula. But it was not an area I knew well, especially in the dark.

"Do you know Finca Vigía—the American writer's house?" I asked the café owner.

"Of course. Everyone knows the house of Ernesto Hemingway."

"How would a man get there who didn't want to drive down the main road, south to Cotorro?" I held up a five-peso note to help him think.

The café owner grinned. "Do you perhaps mean a man who didn't want to drive through the roadblock near the gas station?"

I nodded.

"Keep your money, *señor*. I would not take money from a man who merely wished to avoid our beloved militia." He led me out of the café. "Such a man as yourself would drive north, past the gas station in Diezmero, and turn left onto Varona. Then go across the river in Mantilla. At the junction he would go south, on Managua, and follow the road until he came upon the main highway going west toward Santa María del Rosario. At which point you would cross the main road north again and find Finca Vigía from there."

This series of directions was accompanied by much pointing, and like almost everything in Cuba, we had soon attracted a small crowd of café patrons, small boys, and stray dogs.

"It will take you fifteen minutes, perhaps," said the man. "Assuming you don't end up in the Río Hondo or shot by the militia."

A couple of minutes later I was bouncing through the poorly lit, leafy backstreets of Mantilla and El Calvario like the crew of a stricken Dornier and wearily regretting the consumption of too much bourbon and red wine and probably a brandy or two. I steered the Chevrolet west, south, and then east again. Off the two-lane blacktop the roads weren't much more than dirt tracks, and the Chevy's rear end held its line with less grip than a recently sharpened ice skate. Unnerved by the sight of the two bodies, I was probably driving too fast. Suddenly there was a flock of goats in the road, and I twisted the wheel hard to the left so that the car spun around in a cloud of dust, narrowly missing a tree, and then the fence around a tennis court. Something gave way under the car as I braked and brought the car to a halt. And, thinking I might have a flat or, worse, a broken axle, I flung the door open and leaned out of the car to inspect the damage.

"This is what you get for trying to do someone a favor," I told myself, irritably.

I saw that the car was undamaged and that the front left tire seemed to have broken through several planks of wood that were buried in the ground.

I sat up straight and carefully reversed back onto the road. Then I got out to take another, closer look at what was buried. But because it was dark I couldn't see very clearly, even in the car headlights, and I had to fetch a flashlight from the trunk to shine through the broken planks. Lifting one of the boards, I shone the flashlight through the hole and peered inside what appeared to be a buried crate. The size was difficult to determine, but inside the crate were several smaller wooden boxes. Stenciled on the lid of one of these boxes was MARK 2 FHGS; and on another was BROWNING M19.

I had stumbled onto a hidden weapons cache.

Immediately I switched off the flashlight and then the headlights of the car, and looked around in case anyone had seen me. The tennis court was clay and in a poor state of repair, with some of the white plastic rails missing or broken and the net hanging slackly like an old woman's nylon stocking. Beyond the court was a dilapidated villa with a veranda and a big heavy gate that was badly rusted. Stucco was peeling off the villa's façade, and there were no lights visible anywhere. No one had lived there for some time.

After a while I lifted one of the broken planks and used it like a snowplow to move some dirt back on top of the weapons cache—

enough to conceal it. Then I quickly marked the site with three stones I took from the other side of the road. All this took less than five minutes. It wasn't a place I wanted to linger. Not with militia in the area. They were hardly likely to accept my explanation for how it was I came to be burying a weapons cache at midnight on a lonely road in El Calvario, no more than the people who had buried it there would have believed that I wasn't going to inform the police. I had to get away from there as quickly as possible. So I jumped back in my car and drove off.

I arrived back at Finca Vigía just as Alfredo López was getting back into the white Oldsmobile to drive himself home. I reversed up next to him. Then I wound down my window. López did the same.

"Something wrong?" he asked.

"It could be. If you were a man with a thirty-eight and a briefcase full of rebel pamphlets."

"You know I am."

"López, my friend, you might care to think about getting out of the pamphleteering business for a while. There's a militia roadblock on the main road north, just next to the gas station in Diezmero."

"Thanks for the warning. I guess I'll have to find another route home."

I shook my head. "I drove back here through Mantilla and El Calvario. There was another truckload of them getting ready to deploy down there, as well." I said nothing about the weapons cache I'd found. I thought it was best that I forget all about that. For now.

"It would seem that they're looking to catch some fish tonight," he observed.

"The keep net was full, it's true," I said. "But it looked to me as if they were planning to do a little more than just catch fish. Shoot them in a barrel, perhaps. I saw two on the side of the road. And they looked as dead as a couple of smoked mackerel."

"These were individual tragedies, I suppose," he said. "Of course, a couple of deaths are hardly comparable with the rule of genuine tyrants like Stalin and Mao Tse-tung."

"Think what you like. I didn't come here to make a convert. Just to save your stupid neck."

"Yes, of course, I'm sorry." López pursed his lips for a moment and then bit one of them hard enough to hurt. "They don't usually bother coming as far south of Havana as this."

Noreen came out of the house and down the front steps. A glass was in her hand, and it wasn't empty. She didn't look drunk. She didn't even sound drunk. But since I was probably drunk myself, none of that counted for anything.

"What's the matter?" she asked me. "Change your mind about leaving, did you?" There was a note of sarcasm in her voice.

"That's right," I said. "I came back to see if anyone had an unwanted copy of *The Communist Manifesto*."

"You could have said something when you left," she said stiffly.

"It's a funny thing, but I didn't think anyone would mind."

"So why did you come back?"

"The militia are setting up roadblocks in the area," López explained. "Your friend was kind enough to come back here to warn me of the danger."

"Why would they do that?" she asked him. "There aren't any targets the rebels would want to attack around here. Are there?"

López said nothing.

"What he's trying to say," I said, "is that it depends on what you mean by a target. On the way back here I saw a sign for an electricity-generating station. That's just the kind of target the rebels might pick. After all, there's a lot more to fighting a revolution than assassinating government officials and hiding weapons. Cutting the electricity supply helps to demoralize the population at large. Makes them believe the government is losing control. It's also a lot safer than an attack on an army garrison. Isn't that right, López?"

López was looking bemused. "I don't get it. You're not at all sympathetic to our cause, and yet you took a risk coming back here to warn me. Why?"

"The phone lines are down," I said. "Otherwise I'd have called."

López grinned and shook his head. "No. I still don't get it."

I shrugged. "It's true, I don't like communism. But sometimes it pays to back the underdog. Like Braddock versus Baer in 1935. Besides, I thought it would embarrass you all—me, a bourgeois reactionary and an apologist for fascism, coming back here to pull your Bolshevik nuts out of the fire."

Noreen shook her head and smiled. "With you, that's just bloody-minded enough to be true."

I grinned and bowed slightly in her direction. "I knew you'd see the funny side."

"Bastard."

"You know, it might not be safe for you to go back through the road-block," said López. "They might remember you and put two and two together. Even the militia aren't so stupid that they can't make four."

"Fredo's right," said Noreen. "It's not safe for you to go back into Havana tonight, Gunther. It might be better if you stayed here tonight."

"I wouldn't want to put you to any trouble," I said.

"It's no trouble," she said. "I'll go and tell Ramón to fix you up a bed."

She turned and walked away, humming quietly to herself, scooping up a cat, and placing her empty glass on the terrace as she went.

López watched her behind in retreat for longer than I did. I had time to observe him doing it. He watched her with the eyes of an admirer and possibly the mouth as well: he licked his lips while he was doing it, which made me wonder if their common ground wasn't just political but sexual, too. And, thinking I might prompt him to reveal something of his feelings for her, I said, "Quite a woman, isn't she?"

"Yes," he said, absently. "She is." Smiling, he added, quickly, "A wonderful writer."

"I wasn't looking at her backlist."

López chuckled. "I'm not quite so ready to believe the worst of you. Despite what Noreen said back there."

"Did she say something?" I shrugged. "I wasn't listening when she insulted me."

"What I mean to say is, thank you, my friend. Thank you indeed. Tonight you have undoubtedly saved my life." He fetched the briefcase off the seat of the Oldsmobile. "If I had been caught with this, they would certainly have murdered me."

"Will you be safe driving home?"

"Without this? Yes. I'm a lawyer, after all. A respectable lawyer, too, in spite of what you might think of me. No, really. I have lots of famous and wealthy clients here in Havana. Including Noreen. I drew up her will. And Ernest Hemingway's. It was he who introduced the two of us. If you ever have need of a good lawyer, I would be happy to act for you, *señor*."

"Thanks, I'll bear that in mind."

"Tell me. I'm curious."

"In Cuba? That might not be healthy."

"The pamphlet I gave you. The militia didn't find it?"

"I threw it away in the bushes at the bottom of the drive," I said. "Like I told you before. I'm not interested in local politics."

"I can see Noreen was correct about you, Señor Hausner. You have a great instinct for survival."

"Has she been talking about me again?"

"Only a little. Despite any earlier evidence to the contrary, she has a high opinion of you."

I laughed. "That was maybe true twenty years ago. She wanted something then."

"You underestimate yourself," he said. "Quite considerably."

"It's been a while since anyone said that to me."

He glanced down at the briefcase in his arms. "Perhaps . . . perhaps I could prevail on your kindness and courage one more time."

"You can give it a try."

"Perhaps you would be good enough to bring this briefcase to my office. It's in the Bacardi Building."

"I know it. There's a café there I go to sometimes."

"You like it, too?"

"Coffee's the best in Havana."

"I don't think there's any great risk in your doing this, being a foreigner. But there might be some."

"That's honest, at any rate. All right. I'll do that for you, Señor López."

"Please. Call me Fredo."

"Okay, Fredo."

"Shall we say eleven o'clock, tomorrow morning?"

"If you like."

"You know, it may be that there's something I can do for you."

"You can buy me a cup of coffee. I don't want a will any more than I want a pamphlet."

"But you will come."

"I said I'll be there. And I'll be there."

"Good." López nodded patiently. "Tell me, have you met Noreen's daughter, Dinah?"

I nodded.

"What did you think of her?"

"I'm still thinking."

"Quite a girl, isn't she?" He raised his eyebrows suggestively.

"If you say so. The only thing I know about young women in Havana is that most of them are more efficient Marxists than you and your friends. They know more about the redistribution of wealth than anyone I've ever met. Dinah strikes me as the type of girl who knows just what she wants."

"Dinah wants to be an actress. In Hollywood. In spite of everything that's happened to Noreen with the House Committee on Un-American Activities. The blacklist. The hate mail. I mean, you can see how all that might upset Dinah."

"I got the impression that wasn't what's worrying her."

"There's any number of things to worry about when you have a daughter as headstrong as Dinah, believe me."

"It sounded like just the one thing to me. She mentioned something about Dinah's being in with the wrong crowd. Anything in that?"

"Friend, this is Cuba." López grinned. "We've got wrong crowds like some countries have different religions." He shook his head. "Tomorrow. We'll talk some more. In private."

"Come on. Give. I just saved you from a late night out with the militia."

"The militia's not the only dangerous dog in town."

"Meaning?"

There was a squeal of tires at the bottom of the drive. I looked around as yet another car purred up to the house. I say a car, but the Cadillac with its wraparound windshield was more like something from Mars—a red convertible from the red planet. The sort of car on which the built-in fog lamps might easily have been heat rays for the methodical extermination of earthlings. It was as long as a fire truck and probably as well equipped.

"Meaning, I think you're about to find out," said López.

The Cadillac's big, five-liter engine took a last breath from the four-barrel carburetor and then exhaled loudly through dual exhausts that were built into the bumpers. One of the rakish cut-down doors opened, and out stepped Dinah. She looked great. The drive had stirred her hair a little and made her look more natural than before. Sexier, too, if such a thing was possible. There was a stole over her shoulders that could have been honey-ranch mink, but I wasn't looking anymore. I was too busy noticing the driver stepping out on the other side of the red Eldorado. He was wearing a well-cut, lightweight gray suit with a white shirt and a pair of flashing gem cuff links that matched the car. He stared straight at me with a mixture of amusement and deliberation, as if noting the changes in my face and wondering how I might have come by them. Dinah reached his side after a long pilgrimage around the farthest point of the car and eloquently threaded one arm through his.

"Hello, Gunther," said the man, speaking German.

He had a mustache now, but he still looked like a pit bull in a bucket.

It was Max Reles.

6

SURPRISED TO SEE ME?" He chuckled his familiar chuckle.

"I guess we're both surprised, Max."

"As soon as Dinah told me about you, I started thinking, It couldn't be him. And then she described you, and well. Christ Almighty. Noreen won't like my being here, but I just had to come down to take a look for myself and see if it really was the same fucking pain-in-the-ass guy."

I shrugged. "Who believes in miracles anymore?"

"Jesus, Gunther, I thought you must be dead for sure, what with the Nazis and the Russians and that smart fucking mouth of yours."

"These days I'm a little more close-lipped."

"Only bullshit shoots its mouth off," said Reles. "What's genuine in a man stays silent. Jesus, how long has it been?"

"Must be a thousand years. That's how long Hitler said his Reich would last."

"That long, huh?" Reles shook his head. "What the hell brings you to Cuba?"

"Oh, you know. Getting away from it all." I shrugged. "And by the way, my name is Hausner. Carlos Hausner. At least, that's what it says on my Argentine passport."

"Like that, huh?"

"I like the car. I guess you must be doing all right. What's the ransom for a one-man motorcade like that?"

"Oh, about seven thousand dollars."

"The labor rackets must be good in Cuba."

"I'm out of that shit now. These days I'm in the hotel and entertainment business."

"Seven thousand dollars is a lot of bed and breakfast."

"That's just your copper's nose twitching."

"It does that sometimes. But I don't pay it any mind. These days I'm just a citizen."

Reles grinned. "That covers a lot in Cuba. Especially at this house. There are citizens here who make Joseph Stalin look like Theodore Roosevelt." While he spoke, Reles was looking coldly at Alfredo López, who nodded a farewell at me and then slowly drove away.

"You two know each other?" I asked.

"You could say that."

Dinah interrupted us, speaking in English. "I didn't know you spoke German, Max."

"There's a lot you don't know about me, honey."

"I sure as hell won't tell her anything," I told him, in German. "Not that I'll have to. I expect Noreen has done that already. You must be the bad crowd of people in Havana that she was telling me about. The one Dinah's got herself involved with. I can't say I blame her, Max. If she was my daughter I'd be worried myself."

Reles smiled wryly. "I'm not like that anymore," he said. "I've changed."

"Small world."

Another car came up the drive. It was getting to be like the front door at the National Hotel. Someone was driving Noreen's Pontiac.

"No, really," insisted Reles. "These days I'm a respectable businessman."

The man driving the Pontiac stepped out of the car and silently got into the passenger seat of the car Reles had been driving. Suddenly the Cadillac looked very small. The man's eyes were dark, and his face pale and puffy. He was wearing a loose white suit with big black buttons. His hair was curly and black and gray and plentiful, as if there had been a sale of wire wool at the dollar store on Obispo. He looked sad, perhaps because it was probably several minutes since he'd eaten anything. He looked like he ate a lot. Roadkill probably. He was smoking a cigar the size and shape of an armor-piercing shell, but in his mouth it was like a sty on an eyelid. You looked at him and thought of *Pagliacci* with two tenors in the part of Canio instead of one: a tenor down each trouser leg. He looked about as respectable as a roll of quarters in a boxing glove.

"Respectable, yeah." I eyeballed the big man in the Cadillac. I let Reles see me doing it and said, "I suppose that ogre is really your bookkeeper."

"Waxey? He's a *babke*. A real sweet cake. Besides, I have some very big books."

Dinah sighed and rolled her eyes like a petulant schoolgirl. "Max," she complained, "it's rude to carry on a conversation in German when you know I don't speak the language."

"I can't understand that." Reles spoke in English. "Really I can't, when your mother speaks such excellent German."

Dinah pulled a face. "Who wants to learn German? The Germans murdered ninety percent of the Jews in Europe. Nobody wants to learn German these days." She looked at me and shrugged ruefully. "Sorry, but that's how it is, I guess."

"That's okay. I'm sorry, too. It was my fault. For speaking German to Max, I mean. Not for the other thing. Although obviously I'm sorry for that, as well."

"You krauts are going to be sorry for a long time." Max laughed. "We Jews are going to make sure of that."

"Very sorry. Believe me, I was only obeying orders."

Dinah wasn't listening. She wasn't listening, because it wasn't something she was good at. Although, to be fair, Max had his nose in her ear and then his lips on her cheek, which could have distracted anyone who hadn't had all their shots.

"Forgive me, *honik*," he murmured to her. "But you know it's been twenty years since I saw this *fershtinkiner*." He left off tasting her face for a moment and looked at me again. "Isn't she beautiful?"

"That she is, Max, that she is. What's more, she has her whole life ahead of her, too. Unlike you and me."

Reles bit his lip. I sort of fancied he'd preferred it to have been my neck. Then he smiled and wagged his finger at me. I smiled back, like it was a game of tennis we were playing. I was hitting the ball at him hard. Harder than he was used to, I imagined.

"Still the same awkward bastard," he said, shaking his head. The big face on the front of it had always been square and pugnacious, but now it was tanned and leathery, and there was a scar on his cheek as big as a luggage label. I wondered what Dinah could see in a man like him. "Still the same old Gunther."

"Now, there you and Noreen seem to be in agreement," I said. "You're right, of course. I am an awkward old bastard. And getting worse all the time. Mind you, it's the old part that really pisses down my trouser leg. The fascination I once felt at the contemplation of my own physical excellence is now matched by the horror I find in the evidence of my own advancing middle age. My belly, bowlegs, thinning hair, shortsightedness, and receding gums. By anyone's reckoning, I'm past it. Still there is one consolation, I suppose: I'm not as old as you, Max."

Reles kept on grinning, only this time he had to take a breath to keep on doing it. Then he shook his head and looked at Dinah and said, "Jesus Christ, will you listen to this guy? In front of you he insults me to my face." He let out a laugh of amazement. "Isn't he beautiful? That's what I like about this bum. Nobody has ever talked to me the way this guy talks to me. I love that about him."

"I don't know, Max," she said. "Sometimes you're a very weird kind of guy."

"You should listen to her, Max," I said. "She's not just beautiful. She's very smart, too."

"Enough already," said Reles. "You know, let's you and me talk again. Come and see me tomorrow."

I stared at him politely.

"Come and see me at my hotel." He put his hands together, like he was praying. "Please."

"Where are you staying?"

"The Saratoga in old Havana. Opposite the Capitolio? I own it."

"Right. I get it. The hotel and entertainment business. The Saratoga. Sure, I know it."

"Will you come? For old times' sake."

"You mean our old times, Max?"

"Sure, why not? All that stuff was over and done with twenty years ago. Twenty years. But it feels like a thousand. Just like you said. Come for lunch."

I thought for a moment. I was going to the offices of Alfredo López in the Bacardi Building at eleven, and the Bacardi was just a few blocks from the Saratoga Hotel. Suddenly I was a man with two appointments in one day. Maybe I'd have to buy a diary soon. Maybe I'd have to get my hair and nails done. I was almost feeling relevant again, although in what sense I could ever be relevant, I wasn't quite sure. Not yet, anyway.

I guessed it would take no time at all to return the briefcase with the gun and the pamphlets to Alfredo López. Lunch at the Saratoga sounded all right. Even if it was with Max Reles. The Saratoga was a good hotel. With an excellent restaurant. And lepers can't be choosers in Havana. Especially lepers like me.

"All right," I said. "I'll come around twelve."

7

THE SARATOGA WAS at the south end of the Prado, and just across the street from the Capitolio. It was a fine-looking eight-story white colonial that reminded me of a hotel I'd once seen in Genoa. I went inside. It was just after one o'clock. The girl at the desk in the lobby directed me to the elevators and told me to go up to the eighth floor. I walked into a colonnaded courtyard, which brought to mind a monastery, and waited for the car. In the center of the courtyard was a fountain and the marble figure of a horse by the Cuban sculptress Rita Longa. I knew it was by her because the car took a while and because there was an easel next to the horse with some "useful information" about the artist. The information wasn't particularly useful beyond what I had already worked out for myself, which was that Rita knew nothing about horses and very little about sculpture. And I was more interested in peering through a set of smoked-glass doors that led into the hotel's gaming rooms. With their magnificent chandeliers, tall gilt mirrors, and marble floors, the gaming rooms evoked Belle Époque Paris. Somewhere classier than Havana, anyway. There were no slot machines, only roulette tables, blackjack, craps, poker, baccarat, and punto banco. Clearly no expense had been spared, and perhaps with some justification, the Saratoga's casino described itself—on another easel inside the glass doors—as "the Monte Carlo of the Americas."

Since dollar controls had only just started to be lifted, it seemed less than likely this claim would be put to the test anytime soon by any of the American salesmen and their wives who went gambling in Havana. Myself, I disliked nearly all forms of gambling ever since I had been obliged to drop a small fortune at a casino in Vienna, during the winter of 1947. Luckily the small fortune did not belong to me, but there was something about losing money—even other people's money—that I didn't like. It was one of the reasons that, when I gambled at all, I preferred to play backgammon. It's a game that very few people play, which means you can never lose very much. And, besides, I was good at it.

I rode the car up to the eighth floor and the rooftop pool, which was the only one in Havana.

I say rooftop, but there was another, higher level set back from the pool terrace and, according to my new friend, Alfredo López, this was the exclusive penthouse where Max Reles lived in considerable luxury. The only way up there was to have a special key to the elevator—again, according to López. But glancing around the deserted pool terrace—the weather was too blowy for anyone to be sunbathing—I filled my idle mind with thoughts of how a man with a head for heights might climb up onto that penthouse terrace from the outside. Such a man would have had to clamber out onto the parapet encircling the pool, walk precariously around the corner, and then climb up on some scaffolding being used to repair the hotel's neon sign that adorned the curved corner façade. There were some people who went on a rooftop and enjoyed the view; and there were others, like me, who remembered crime scenes and snipers and, above all, the war on the eastern front. In Minsk, a Red Army marksman had sat on the roof of the city's only hotel for three whole days picking off German army officers before being nailed with an antitank gun. Such a man would have appreciated the rooftop terrace of the Saratoga.

Then again, Max Reles probably had that possibility covered. According to Alfredo López, Reles wasn't the kind of man who took any chances with his personal security. He had too many friends to do something like that. Havana friends, that is. The kind who make enthusiastic understudies of deadly enemies.

"I thought maybe you'd changed your mind," Max said, emerging from a doorway that led along to the elevators. "That you weren't going to show up." His tone was reproachful and a little puzzled, as if he were annoyed that he couldn't work out any good reason why I might have been late for our lunch.

"I'm sorry. I got a little held up. You see, last night I told López about that roadblock on the road north out of San Francisco de Paula."

"What the hell did you do that for?"

"He had a briefcase full of rebel pamphlets, and I don't know why, but I agreed to take them for him and then deliver them back to him this morning. There was a police truck outside the Bacardi Building when I arrived, and I had to wait until it was gone."

"You shouldn't get involved with a man like that," said Reles. "Really, you shouldn't. That shit's dangerous. You want to keep away from the politics on this island."

"You're right, of course. I shouldn't. And I don't know why I said I'd do it. Probably I'd drunk too much. I do a lot of that. There's nothing much else to do in Cuba except drink too much."

"That figures. Everyone at that damn house drinks too much."

"But I said I'd do it, and when I say I'll do something, I generally see it through. I was always kind of stupid like that."

"True." Max Reles grinned. "Very true. Did he say anything about me? López."

"Only that you and he used to be business associates."

"That's almost true. Let me tell you about our pal Fredo. F.B.'s brother-in-law is a man named Roberto Miranda. Miranda owns every one of the *traganiqueles* in Havana. You know, the slot machines. You want some in your place, then you rent them from him. Plus he gets fifty percent of the take. Which, let me tell you, can be a lot in a Havana casino. Anyway, Fredo López used to come and empty the slots for me at the Saratoga. I thought that having a lawyer do it was the best way of preventing any dishonesty. But very early on I discovered that only a quarter of the money was going to Miranda. The rest López was skimming to help feed the families of those men who attacked the Moncada Barracks last year. For a while I turned a blind eye to it. He knew that I was turning a blind eye to it, too. I figured, to hedge my bets with the rebels. But then Miranda figured out that he was being cheated and, wouldn't you know it, he blamed yours truly. Which left me with a choice. Keep the slots, but get rid of López, and risk being made a target by the rebels. Or get rid of the slots and put up with Miranda's displeasure. I chose to get rid of the slots. And as a result of that, once a week I now have to go through my books with F.B. himself on account of the fact that he owns a substantial stake in this place. The whole thing cost me a lot of fucking money and inconvenience. And the way I see it, that bastard Fredo López is a very lucky fuck. Lucky to be alive, that is."

"You're right, Max. You have changed. The old Max Reles would have stuck an ice pick in his ear."

He grinned at the memory of his former self. "Wouldn't I just? Wouldn't I? Things were more straightforward then. I'd have killed him without a second thought." He shrugged. "But this is Cuba, and we try to do things a little differently here. I figured that maybe, when he thought about it, the little prick would realize it. And act like he's just a little grateful. But not a bit of it. He goes behind my back and pours poison in Noreen's ear about me when I'm trying to build some bridges with her because of my relationship with Dinah."

"So you were giving money to Batista *and* the rebels," I said.

"Indirectly," he said. "Frankly, I give them a snowball's chance in hell, but you never know with these bastards."

"But you do give them a chance."

"Before the incident with the slots, I saw something interesting. One day I was looking out of a downstairs window of the hotel, not thinking anything in particular, like you do sometimes, and I saw this young Habañero who was walking along the street outside—just a kid, you know. And as I watched him pass by my Cadillac I saw him kick the fender."

"That cute little ragtop? Where was the ogre?"

"Waxey? He's not nearly quick enough on his toes to have stood half a chance of catching this fucking kid. Anyway, it bothered me. Not the mark on the car. That was nothing really. No, it was something else. I thought about it a lot, see? At first I thought the kid did it to amuse his girlfriend. Then I thought maybe he had something against Cadillacs. Finally it hit me, Bernie. I realized it wasn't fucking Cadillacs he didn't like. It was Americans. Which made me think about this revolution. I mean, like most people, I thought it was all over after last July. After Moncada Barracks, you know? But, seeing that fucking kid kick my car, I thought that maybe it isn't over at all. And maybe they hate Americans as much as they hate Batista. In which case, if they ever get rid of him, they might get rid of us, too."

I was fresh out of insightful incidents of my own, so I stayed silent. Besides, I didn't have a particularly warm opinion of Americans myself. They weren't as bad as the Russians or the French, but then *they* didn't expect to be liked and *they* didn't much care when they weren't. Americans were different: even after they'd dropped a couple of atom bombs on the Japs, they still wanted to be liked. Which struck me as just a little naive. So I stayed silent and, almost like two old friends, together we enjoyed the view from the rooftop for a while. It was a great view. Beneath us were the treetops of Campo de Marte, and to the right, like an enormous wedding cake, was the Capitol Building. Behind that you could see the Partagas cigar factory and the Barrio Chino. I could see as far south as the American warship in the harbor, and west as far as the rooftops of Miramar, but only with my glasses on. The glasses made me look older, of course. Older than Max Reles. Then again, he probably had some glasses of his own somewhere and just didn't want to let me see him wearing them.

He was trying, without success, to light a large cigar in the stiffening rooftop breeze. One of the parasols, which were all closed, blew over, which seemed to irritate him.

"I always say," he said, "that the best way to see Havana is from the rooftop of a good hotel." He gave up with the cigar. "The National has a view, but it's just the fucking sea or the rooftops of Vedado, and in my humble opinion, that view doesn't begin to compare with this one."

"I agree." For the moment I was through needling him. I was just beginning to have my reasons for that.

"Of course, it does get a bit windy up here sometimes, and when I catch up with the sonofabitch who persuaded me to buy all these fucking parasols, I'm going to give him a lesson in what it's like when the wind catches one of these things and carries it over the side." He grinned in a way that made me think he meant every word of it.

"It's a great view," I said.

"Isn't it? You know, I'll bet Hedda Adlon would have given her eyeteeth for a view like this one."

I nodded, hardly wanting to tell him that the Adlon's rooftop had afforded the hotel patrons with one of the best views in Berlin. I'd watched the Reichstag burning from that particular hotel rooftop. And you don't get much better views than that.

"What ever happened to her, anyway?"

"Hedda used to say that a good hotelier always hopes for the best, but expects the worst. The worst is what happened. She and Louis kept the hotel going all through the war. Somehow it always escaped the bombing. Maybe someone in the RAF had stayed there once. But then, during the Battle for Berlin, the Ivans subjected the city to a barrage that destroyed almost everything that hadn't been destroyed by the RAF. The hotel caught fire and was all but destroyed. Hedda and Louis retreated to their country estate near Potsdam and waited. When the Ivans turned up, they looted the house, and mistaking Louis for an escaping German general, they put him in front of a firing squad and shot him. Hedda was raped, many times, like most of the women in Berlin. I don't know what happened to her after that."

"Jesus Christ," said Reles. "What a story. Pity. I liked them both a lot. Jesus, I didn't know."

He sighed and made another attempt to light his cigar, and this time he succeeded. "You know, it's funny you turning up like this, Gunther."

"I told you before, Max. It's Hausner now. Carlos Hausner."

"Hey, don't worry about it. You and me, we don't have to worry about that shit. This island's got more aliases than a filing cabinet in the FBI. If you ever get any problems with the militia about your passport, your visa, anything like that, you come to me. I can fix it."

"All right. Thanks."

"Like I was saying, it's funny you turning up like this. You see, the Adlon's one of the reasons I got into the hotel business here in Havana. I loved that hotel. I wanted to own a classy place like the Adlon here, in old Havana, instead of in Vedado like Lansky and all those other connected guys. I always had the idea that this is the kind of place Hedda would have picked herself, don't you agree?"

"Maybe. Why not? I was just the house peeper, so what do I know? But she used to say that a good hotel is like a car. What it looks like is only half as important as how it drives: how fast it can go and if the brakes work all right and if it's comfortable are what really matters. Everything else is just bullshit."

"She was right, of course," said Reles. "God, I could use some of her old European experience right now. I'm after the same high-end crowd here, you see. The senators and the diplomats. I'm trying to run a quality hotel and an honest casino. The truth is, you hardly need to run a crooked one. The odds always favor the house, and the money floods in. It's as simple as that. Almost. True, in a city like Havana you gotta watch out for the sharks and the grifters. Not to mention the faggots and the female impersonators. Hell, I don't even allow hookers to operate in this place. Not unless they're on the arm of someone important.

I leave that kind of vice to the Cubans. They're a degenerate lot. Those guys would pimp their own grandmothers for five bucks. And, believe me, I should know. I've had more than my fair share of mocha-flavored flesh in this city.

"At the same time," he continued, "you shouldn't ever underestimate these people. They think nothing of putting a bullet in your head if they're connected. Or tossing a grenade in your john if they're into politics. A man in my position needs to get eyes in the back of his head or pretty soon the back of his head will be lying on a floor. Which is where you come in, Gunther."

"Me? I don't see how I can help you, Max."

"Let's have some lunch. And I'll tell you how."

We rode the elevator up to the penthouse, where we were met by Waxey. Seen from up close, his face was like that of a Mexican wrestler—the kind that usually wears a mask. Come to think of it, the rest of him looked like a Mexican wrestler, too. Each of his shoulders resembled the Yucatán peninsula. He didn't say anything. He just frisked me with hands like Esau's black-sheep uncle.

The penthouse was modern and about as comfortable as a spaceship. We sat at a glass table and watched each other's shoes while we ate. Mine were locally sourced and none too clean. My host's shoes were shinier than a brass bell and every bit as loud. To my surprise the food was kosher, or at least Jewish, since the tall, good-looking woman who served it was also black. Then again, maybe she was a convert to Judaism. She was a good cook.

"The older I get, the more I like Jewish cooking," Max explained. "I guess it reminds me of when I was a kid. All the food the other kids had, but never me, because my bitch of a mother ran off with a tailor, and Abe and I never saw her again."

When we got to the coffee, he relit his half-smoked cigar, while I fetched one from his cemetery-sized humidor.

"So let me tell you how you can help me, Gunther. For one thing, you're not Jewish."

I let that one go. A quarter-Jew seemed hardly worth mentioning these days.

"You're not Italian. You're not Cuban. You're not even American, and you don't owe me a damn thing. Hell, Gunther, you don't even like me that much."

I didn't contradict him. We were big boys now. But I didn't underline it, either. Twenty years was a long time to forget a lot, but I had more reason to dislike him than he would ever know or remember.

"All of this makes you independent. Which is a very valuable quality to possess in Havana. Because it means you owe no one allegiance. None of that would matter if you were a *potchka*, but you're not a *potchka*, you're a mensch, and the plain fact of the matter is that I could use a mensch who has grand hotel experience—to say nothing of your years with the Berlin police. Why? To help me keep things straight here, that's why. I want you to take on the role of general manager. In the hotel and in the casino. Someone I can trust. Someone who doesn't give me any shit. Someone who shoots straight from the hip. Who better than you?"

"Look, Max, I'm flattered, don't think I'm not. But I don't need a job right now."

"Don't think of it as a job. This is not a job. There's no nine-to-five with this business. It's an occupation. Every man needs an occupation, right? A place to go every day. Some days you're around more than others. Which is good, because that'll keep the bastards who work for me guessing. Look, I hate to sound like a *noodge*, but you'd be doing me a favor here. A big favor. Which is why I'm prepared to pay you top dollar. How does twenty thousand dollars a year sound? I bet you never made that kind of money at the Adlon. A car. An office. A secretary who crosses her legs a lot and doesn't wear any panties. You name it."

"I don't know, Max. If I did it, I'd have to do it my way. Straight or not at all."

"Didn't you hear me saying that's what I want? There's no other way but straight for a business like this."

"I'm serious. No interference. I report to you and no one else."

"You got it."

"What would I do? Give me an example."

"One of the things I want you to do right away is take charge of the hirings and the firings. There's a pit boss I want you to fire. He's a faggot, and I don't like faggots working in my hotel. Also, I want you to handle all the interviews for any positions in the hotel and casino that come up. You got a nose for these things, Gunther. A cynical bastard like you will want to make certain that we're hiring honest, straight people. That's not always so easy. You can get a lot of smoke blown in your eyes. For instance. I pay top money here. Better than any other hotel in Havana. Which means that most of the girls who want to work here—and it's mainly girls I hire, because that's what the customers want to see—well, they will do anything for a job. And I mean anything. Only that's not always so good for business, see? And it's not always so good for me. I'm only human, and that amount of major fucking temptation is not what I want in my life right now. I'm through with all of that fucking around. You know why? Because I'm going to marry Dinah, that's why."

"Congratulations."

"Thanks."

"Does she know?"

"Of course she knows, you nudnik. The girl's meshugge about me and I feel the same way about her. Yeah, yeah, I know what you're going to say—I'm old enough to be her father. Don't start with the gray hair and false teeth again, like last night, because this is the real thing. I'm going to marry her, and then I'm going to use all my show-business connections to help make that girl a movie star."

"What about Brown?"

"Brown? What's Brown?"

"That's the university Noreen wants her to go to."

Reles grimaced. "That's what Noreen wants for Noreen. Not for Dinah. Dinah wants to be in motion pictures. I already introduced her to Sinatra. George Raft. Nat King Cole. Did Noreen tell you the girl can sing?"

"No."

"With her talent and my connections, Dinah can be pretty much anything she wants."

"Does that include being happy?"

Reles winced. "Including being happy, yeah. God damn it, Gunther, you're a hard fucking bastard. Why is that?"

"I've had a lot of practice. More than you, perhaps. And I guess that's saying something. I'm not going to give you the whole lousy résumé, Max. But by the time the war ended, I'd already seen and done a few things that would have given Jiminy Cricket a heart attack. The conscience I'd started out in with life grew a couple of extra layers, like the skin on my feet. Then I was a houseguest of the Soviets for two years in one of their rest homes for exhausted German POWs. I learned a lot from the Ivans about good hospitality. But only what it isn't. When I escaped I killed two people. That was a pleasure. Like it never was before. And you can take that to mean whatever you want. After that I ran a hotel of my own until my second wife died in a lunatic asylum. I wasn't cut out for that. I might as well have tried running a finishing school in Switzerland for young English ladies. Come to think of it, I wish I had. I could have finished quite a few, forever. Good manners, German courtesy, charm, hospitality—I come up short on all of those, Max. I make hard bastards feel good about themselves. They meet me and then go home and read their Bibles and thank God they're not me. So what makes you think I'm up to this?"

"You really want to know?" He shrugged. "All those years ago. The boat on Lake Tegel? You remember that?"

"How could I forget?"

"I told you then I liked you, Gunther. I told you then that I'd thought of offering you a job, only I had no use for an honest man."

"I remember. The whole evening is still etched on my eyeballs."

"Well, now I have a use for one. It's as simple as that, pal. I need a man of character. Pure and simple."

A person of character, he said. A mensch, he said. I had my doubts. Would a mensch have helped Max Reles to silence Othman Weinberger by handing the American the means to destroy Weinberger's career, and possibly his life, too? After all, it was I who had told Reles about Weinberger's Achilles' heel: that the little Gestapo man from Würzburg was suspected, wrongly, of being a Jew. And it was I who had told Max Reles about Emil Linthe, the forger, and how a man like Linthe might bribe his way in the public records office and give another man like Weinberger a Jewish transfusion just as easily as he'd given me an

Aryan one. In my own defense, I could argue that I'd done all of that to protect Noreen Charalambides from being murdered by Max's brother. But what character was left to a man who'd done something like that? A mensch? No, I was anything but that.

"All right," I said. "I'll take the job."

"You will?" Max Reles sounded surprised. He stared at me for a while with narrowing eyes. "So now I'm curious. What was it persuaded you?"

"Maybe we're more alike than I care to admit. Maybe it was the thought of that brother of yours and what he might do to me with an ice pick if I said no. How is the kid?"

"Dead."

"Sorry."

"Don't be. The kid turned rat on some friends of mine to save his own skin. He sent six guys to the electric chair. Including someone I went to school with. But he was a canary who couldn't fly. Abe was about to finger a boss when he got himself thrown out of a high window of the Half Moon Hotel on Coney Island in November 1941."

"You know who did it?"

"He was in protective custody at the time, so, sure, I know. And one day I'll take my revenge on these guys. Blood is blood, after all, and there never was any permission asked or given. But right now it wouldn't be good for business."

"Sorry I asked."

Reles nodded grimly. "And I'd appreciate it if you never asked me about it again."

"I already forgot the question. Listen, we Germans are good at forgetting all kinds of things. We've spent the last nine years trying to forget there ever was a man called Adolf Hitler. Believe me, if you can forget him, you can forget anything."

Reles grunted.

"One name I do remember," I said. "Avery Brundage. What ever happened to him?"

"Avery? We kind of fell out after he got himself on the America First committee to keep the U.S. out of the war. It made a change from trying to keep Jews out of Chicago country clubs. But that slippery bastard's done all right for himself. He's made millions of dollars. His construction company built a large chunk of Chicago's gold coast: Lake Shore Drive. At one stage he was going to run as a candidate for governor of Illinois until certain people in Chicago told him to stick to sports administration. You might say we're competitors these days. He owns the La Salle Hotel in Chicago. The Cosmopolitan in Denver. The Hollywood Plaza in California. And a large chunk of Nevada." Reles nodded. "Life's been kind to Avery. Recently he got himself elected as president of the International Olympic Committee."

"I suppose you made a fortune in 1936."

"Sure. But so did Avery. After the Olympics were over, he got himself a contract from the Nazis to build the new German embassy in Washington. That was payback from a grateful Führer for heading off an American boycott. He must have made millions. And I didn't see a cent of it." Reles grinned. "But it was all a long time ago. Dinah's the best thing that's happened to me since then. She's a hell of a girl."

"Just like her mother."

"Wants to try everything."

"I guess you must be the one who took her to the Shanghai Theater."

"I wouldn't have done it," said Reles. "Taken her there. But she insisted. And the girl gets what she wants. Dinah's got a hell of a temper."

"And how was the show?"

"How do you think?" He shrugged. "To tell the truth, I don't think it bothered her much. That little girl is game for anything. Right now she wants me to take her to an opium den."

"Opium?"

"You should try it yourself sometime. Opium's great for keeping down the weight."

He slapped his belly with the flat of his hand and, in truth, he did look slimmer than I remembered him in Berlin. "There's a little joint on Cuchillo where you can smoke a few pipes and forget everything. Even Hitler."

"Then perhaps I'll have to try it, after all."

"I'm glad you're on board, Gunther. Tell you what. Come back tomorrow night and I'll introduce you to some of the boys. They'll all be here. Wednesday night's my cards night. You play cards?"

"No. Just backgammon."

"Backgammon? That's dice for queers, isn't it?"

"Not really."

"I'm just kidding you. I had a friend who used to play. You any good?"

"Depends on the dice."

"Come to think of it, García plays backgammon. José Orozco García. The sleazeball who owns the Shanghai. He's always looking for a game." Reles grinned. "Jesus, I'd love it if you could beat that fat bastard. Want me to fix you up to play him? Tomorrow night, maybe? It'll have to be early, because he likes to keep an eye on the theater after eleven. You know, that could work out well. Play him at eight. Come up here around ten forty-five. Meet the boys. Maybe with some extra money in your pocket."

"Sounds good. I can always use a little extra money."

"Speaking of which."

He took me into his office. There was a modern teakwood writing desk with an off-white veneered top and some leather chairs that looked as if they'd come off a sportfishing boat.

He opened a drawer and took out an envelope, which he handed to me. "There's a thousand pesos," he said. "Just to show you my offer is a serious one."

"I always take you seriously, Max," I told him. "Ever since that night on the lake."

On the walls were several big, frameless paintings that were either extremely good representations of vomit or modern abstracts. I couldn't decide. One wall was given over entirely to some dark wood bookshelves that were filled with records and magazines, art objects, and even some books. On the far wall was a big sliding glass door, and through it I could see a smaller, private version of the pool that existed on the floor below. There was a button-backed leather daybed and beside it a tulip table, on which stood a bright red telephone. Reles pointed at the phone.

"See that phone? It's a special line to the Presidential Palace. And it makes just the one call a week. The one I told you about? Every Wednesday, at a quarter to midnight, without fail, I use that phone to call F.B. and take him through the figures. I never knew a guy who was so interested in money as F.B. Sometimes we speak for as long as half an hour. Which is one reason Wednesday night is my card night. I play a few hands with the boys, and then throw them out at exactly eleven-thirty. No broads. I make my phone call and go straight to bed. You work for me, you might as well know you also work for F.B. He owns thirty percent of this hotel. But you can leave that spic to me. For now."

Reles went over to the bookcase, tugged open a drawer, and took out an expensive-looking leather attaché case, which he handed to me.

"I want you to have this, Gunther. To celebrate our new business association."

I brandished the envelope of pesos. "I thought you already gave me something for that."

"Something extra."

I glanced at the combination locks.

"Go ahead," he said. "It's not locked. Incidentally, the combinations are six-six-six on each side. But if you like, you can change it with a little key that's hidden in the carrying handle."

I snapped open the case and saw that it was a handsome backgammon set, custom-made. The checkers were made of ivory and ebony, and the dice and doubling cube had pips made of diamonds.

"I can't take this," I said.

"Sure you can. That set used to belong to a friend of mine called Ben Siegel."

"Ben Siegel, the gangster?"

"Naw. Ben was a gambler and a businessman. Same as me. His girlfriend, Virginia, had that backgammon set especially made for his forty-first birthday, by Asprey of London. Three months later he was dead."

"He was shot, wasn't he?"

"*Mmm-hmm.*"

"Didn't she want it?"

"She gave it to me as a keepsake. And now I'd like you to have it. Let's hope it's luckier for you than it was for him."

"Let's hope."

8

—

FROM THE SARATOGA I DROVE down to Finca Vigía. The Chieftain was exactly where Waxey had parked it, except there was now a cat on the roof. I got out of my car and walked up to the front door and rang the ship's bell hanging on the porch. Another cat was watching me from the bough of a giant ceiba tree. A third on the terrace poked its head through the white railings as if waiting for the firemen to come and get it out. I stroked the cat's head as footsteps came slowly to the door. The door opened, and the slight figure of Hemingway's Negro servant, René, was standing there. He was wearing a white cotton waiter's jacket. Sunlight shining through the house behind him gave him the air of a Santería priest. He said, "Good afternoon, *señor.*"

"Is Señora Eisner at home?"

"Yes, but she is sleeping."

"How about the *señorita?*"

"Miss Dinah. I believe she's in the swimming pool, *señor.*"

"Do you think she'll mind me seeing her?"

"I don't think she minds anyone seeing her," said René.

I didn't pay much attention to that and made my way along the path to the pool, which was surrounded with royal palms, flamboyán trees, and several almond trees as well as flower beds filled with ixora—a hardy red Indian flower better known as jungle flame. It was a nice-looking pool, but even with all that water it was easy to see how any jungle might have caught fire. My own eyeballs felt scorched just looking at it. Dinah was doing a graceful, leisurely backstroke up and down the steaming water. I supposed it was steaming for the same reason my eyeballs were scorched and the jungle was in flames. Her bathing suit was an appropriate-looking leopard print, only at that particular moment it seemed slightly less appropriate, given that she wasn't actually wearing it. The suit lay on the path to the pool alongside my jaw.

She had a beautiful body: long, athletic, shapely. In the water her nude figure was the color of honey. Being German, I wasn't exactly shocked by her nakedness. Naked culture societies had existed in Berlin since before the Great War, and until the Nazis, it had been impossible to visit certain Berlin parks and swimming pools without seeing lots of nudists. Besides, Dinah herself hardly seemed to mind. She even managed to perform a couple of tumble turns that left little to my imagination.

"Come on in," she said. "The water's lovely."

"No, thanks," I said. "Besides, I hardly think your mother would approve."

"Maybe not, but she's drunk. Or at least she's sleeping it off. She was drinking all last night. Noreen always drinks too much after we've had an argument."

"What was it about?"

"What do you think it was about?"

"Max, I suppose."

"Check. So how did you and he get along?"

"We got along just fine, he and I."

Dinah executed another perfect tumble turn. By now I was beginning to know her better than her doctor. I might even have enjoyed the show but for the fact of who she was and why I was there. Turning my back on the pool, I said, "Perhaps I'd better wait in the house."

"Do I embarrass you, Señor Gunther? I'm sorry. I mean Señor Hausner." She stopped swimming, and I heard her climb out of the pool behind me.

"You're nice to look at, but I'm your mother's friend, remember? And there are certain things that men don't do to the daughters of their friends. I imagine she sort of trusts me not to press my nose up against your windowpane."

"That's an interesting way of putting it."

I could hear the water dripping off her naked body. If I had licked her from top to bottom, she wouldn't have sounded any different.

"Why don't you be a good girl and put your bathing suit back on, and then we can talk?"

"All right." A few moments passed. Then she said, "You can relax now."

I turned around and nodded my thanks curtly. She made me feel as awkward as hell, even now that she was wearing her costume again. Avoiding the sight of beautiful young women when they were naked: that was a new thing for me.

"As a matter of fact, I'm glad you're here," she said. "This morning she was kind of suicidal."

"Kind of?"

"Kind of, yeah. What I mean is that she threatened to shoot herself if I didn't promise her that I wouldn't see Max anymore."

"And did you?"

"Did I what?"

"Promise not to see him anymore?"

"No, of course I didn't. I mean that's just emotional blackmail."

"Mmm-hmm. Does she have a gun?"

"Silly question, in this house. There's a gun cupboard in the tower with enough weaponry to start another revolution. But as it happens, she has her own gun. Ernest gave it to her. I guess he thought he could spare her one."

"Think she'd ever do it?"

"I don't know. That's why I mentioned it just now, I suppose. I really don't know. She and Ernest used to talk about suicide. All the time. And she wonders why I want to go out with Max instead of hanging around here."

"When exactly is Hemingway coming back here?"

"July, I think. He'd be back here now, except for the fact that he's in a hospital in Nairobi."

"I guess one of those animals must have fought back."

"No, it was a plane crash. Or a bush fire. Maybe both. I don't know. But he was pretty bad for a while."

"What happens when he does come back? Are he and your mother involved?"

"Christ no. Ernest has a wife, Mary. Although I don't think something like that would stop them. Besides, she's seeing someone, I think. Noreen, I mean. Anyway, she's bought a house in Marianao and we're supposed to move into it sometime in the next month or two."

Dinah found a pack of cigarettes, lit one, and blew smoke down at the ground and away from me. "I'm going to marry him, and there's nothing she or anyone else can do about it."

"Except shoot herself. People have shot themselves for less."

Dinah made a face. It matched the one I might have made when she told me that Noreen was seeing someone.

"And what do you think?" she asked. "About me and Max."

"Would it make the slightest difference if I told you?"

She shook her head. "So what did you and he talk about?"

"He offered me a job."

"Are you going to take it?"

"I don't know. I've said I would. But I'm kind of squeamish about working for a gangster."

"Is that what you think he is?"

"I told you. It doesn't matter what I think. And all he offered me was a job, angel. Not a proposal of marriage. If I don't like working for him, I can quit, and he won't lose any sleep over it. But somehow I have the romantic idea that he feels differently about you. Any man would."

"You're not making a pass at me, are you?"

"If I was going to do that, I'd be in the swimming pool."

"Max is going to help me become a movie actress."

"So I heard. Is that why you're going to marry him?"

"As a matter of fact, it isn't." She colored a little, and her voice became more petulant. "It just so happens that we love each other."

It was my turn to pull a face.

"What's the matter, Gunther? Weren't you ever in love with someone?"

"Oh, sure. Your mother, for instance. But that was twenty years ago. In those days I could still tell someone I was in love with her and mean it with every fiber of my being. These days they're just words. A man gets to my age and it's not about love. He can persuade himself it's love. But it's not that at all. It's always about something else."

"You think he just wants to marry me for sex, is that it?"

"No. It's more complicated than that. It's about wanting to feel young again. That's why a lot of older men marry younger women. Because they think youth is infectious. And it isn't, of course. Old age, on the other hand, now, that is infectious. I mean, I can more or less guarantee that, in time, you'll catch it, too." I shrugged. "But like I keep telling you, angel, it doesn't matter what I think. I'm just some slob who used to be in love with your mother."

"That's not such an exclusive club."

"I don't doubt it. Your mother's a beautiful woman. Everything you got, you got from her, I guess." I nodded. "What you were saying. About her being suicidal. I'll look in on her before I go."

I quickly went away from her and back to the house before I said anything nasty. Which was what I felt like saying.

At the rear of the house, the French doors were open and just an antelope was on guard, so I went inside and took a squint in Noreen's bedroom. She was sleeping, naked on the top sheet, and I stood there looking for all of a minute. Two naked women in one afternoon. It was like going to the Casa Marina except for the fact that now I realized I was in love with Noreen again. Or maybe they were the same feelings I'd always had and, perhaps, I'd just forgotten where I'd buried them. I don't know, but in spite of what I'd told Dinah, there were plenty of feelings I could have tossed Noreen's way if she'd been awake. And probably I'd have meant a few of them, too.

Her thighs yawned open, and courtesy obliged me to look away, which was when I noticed the gun on the bookshelves next to some photographs and a jar containing a frog preserved in formaldehyde. It looked like any old frog. But it wasn't just any old gun. It might have been designed and produced by a Belgian who had given the revolver his name, but the Nagant had been the standard-issue sidearm for all Russian officers in the Red Army and NKVD. It was an odd, heavy weapon to have found in that house. I picked it up, curious to find myself reacquainted with it. This one had an embossed red star on the handle, which seemed to put its origins beyond any doubt.

"That's her gun," said Dinah.

I looked around as she came into the bedroom and drew the sheet across her mother. "Not exactly a ladies' gun," I said.

"You're telling me."

Then she went into the bathroom.

"I'll leave my number on the desk by the telephone," I called after her. "You can give me a ring if you really think she's serious about harming herself. It doesn't matter what time."

I buttoned my jacket and walked out of the bedroom. Momentarily I caught sight of Dinah sitting on the lavatory and, hearing the sound of her peeing, I hurried on through to the study.

"I don't think she meant it," said Dinah. "She says a lot of things she doesn't mean."

"We all do."

There was a three-drawer wooden desk covered with carved animals and different-sized shotgun cartridges and rifle bullets that someone had stood on their ends like so many lethal lipsticks. I found a piece of paper and a pen and scribbled out my telephone number in large writing so that it wouldn't be missed. Unlike me. And then I left.

I drove home and spent the rest of the day and half the night in my little workshop. While I worked I thought about Noreen and Max Reles and Dinah. Nobody called me on the phone. But there was nothing unusual about that.

9

H AVANA'S CHINESE QUARTER—the Barrio Chino—was the largest in Latin America, and since it was Chinese New Year the streets off Zanja and Cuchillo were decorated with paper lanterns and given over to open-air markets and lion-dance troupes. At the intersection of Amistad and Dragones was a gateway as big as the Forbidden City. Later that evening, it would be the center of a tremendous fireworks barrage, which was the climax of the celebrations.

Yara loved any kind of noisy parade, and this was the reason why, unusually, I had chosen to take her out for the afternoon. The streets of Chinatown were full of laundries, noodle houses, dried-goods shops, herbalists, acupuncturists, sex clubs, opium dens, and brothels. But above all, the streets were full of people. Chinese people, mostly. So many that you wondered where they had been hiding themselves.

I bought Yara some small gifts—fruit and candies—which delighted her. In return she insisted on buying me a cup of macerated medicinal liquor at a traditional medicine market, which, she assured me, would make me very virile; and it was only after drinking it that I found out that it contained wolfberry, iguana, and ginseng. It was the iguana ingredient I objected to, and for several minutes after drinking this horrible beverage I was convinced I had been poisoned. So much so that I was firmly of the opinion that I must be hallucinating when, right on the edge of Chinatown, on the corner of Manrique and Simón Bolívar,

I came across a shop I had never seen before. Not even in Buenos Aires, where the existence of such a business might, perhaps, more easily have been explained. It was a shop selling Nazi memorabilia.

After a moment or two I realized Yara had seen the shop, too, and, leaving her on the street, I went inside, as curious to know what kind of person might sell this kind of stuff as I was about who might buy it.

Inside the shop were glass cases containing Luger pistols, Walther P-38s, Iron Crosses, Nazi Party armbands, Gestapo identity tokens, and SS daggers. Several copies of *Der Stürmer* newspapers were laid out in cellophane, like freshly laundered shirts. A mannequin was wearing the dress uniform of an SS captain, which somehow seemed only appropriate. Behind a counter and between two Nazi banners stood a young-ish man with a black beard who couldn't have looked less German. He was tall and thin and cadaverous, like someone from a painting by El Greco.

"Looking for something in particular?" he asked me.

"An Iron Cross, perhaps," I told him. I asked to see an Iron Cross not because I was interested in it but because I was interested in him.

He opened one the glass cases and laid the medal on the counter as if it had been a ladies' diamond brooch, or a handsome watch.

I looked at it for a while, turning it over in my fingers.

"What do you think of it?" he asked.

"It's a fake," I said. "And not a very good fake. And another thing: the cross belt on the SS captain's uniform is over the wrong shoulder. A fake is one thing. But an elementary mistake like that is something else."

"You know about this stuff?"

"I thought it was illegal in Cuba," I answered, hardly answering at all.

"The law forbids only the promotion of Nazi ideology," he said. "Selling historic mementos is permitted."

"Who buys this stuff?"

"Americans, mostly. A lot of sailors. Then there are also tourists who saw military service in Europe and want to obtain the souvenir they never managed to get when they were over there. Mostly it's SS stuff they want. I guess there's a certain gruesome fascination with the SS, for obvious reasons. I could sell any amount of SS stuff. For example, SS daggers are very popular as paper knives. Of course, collecting this sort of memorabilia doesn't mean you sympathize with Nazism, or condone what happened. It happened, and it's a part of history, and I don't see anything wrong with being interested in that, to the extent of owning something that's an almost living part of that history. How could I see anything wrong with it? I mean, I'm Polish. My name's Szymon Woytak."

He held out his hand, and I took it limply and without much enthusiasm for him or his peculiar trade. Through the shop window I could see a troupe of Chinese dancers. They'd removed their lion heads and paused for a cigarette, as if hardly aware of the evil spirits that dwelled within, otherwise they might have come through the door. Woytak picked up the Iron Cross I had asked to see. "How can you tell it's a fake?" he asked, examining it closely.

"Simple. The fakes are made from one piece of metal. The originals were made of at least three pieces and soldered together. Another way to tell is to get a magnet and see if the cross really is made of iron. Fakes are made from a cheap alloy."

"How do you know that?"

"How do I know?" I grinned at him. "I had one of these iron baubles myself once, in the Great War," I said. "But you know, all of it's fake. All of this. Everything in here." I waved my hand at the shop. "And the creed that made all of these ridiculous objects? That, too, was just a cheap alloy meant to fool people. A stupid fake that shouldn't have tricked anyone, except for the fact that people wanted to believe in it. Everyone knew it was a lie. Of course they did. But they wanted, desperately, to believe that it wasn't. And they forgot to remember that just because Adolf Hitler liked kissing little children it didn't mean he wasn't a big, bad wolf. He was that, and much, much worse. That's history for you, Señor Woytak. Real German history, not this—this ridiculous souvenir shop."

I took Yara home and spent the rest of the day in my workshop feeling a little depressed. But it wasn't because of anything I had seen in

Szymon Woytak's shop. That was just Havana. You could always buy anything in Havana, provided you had the money to pay for it. Anything and everything. It was something else getting me down. Something closer to home. Or at least the home of Ernest Hemingway.

Noreen's daughter, Dinah.

I wanted to like her, but found I couldn't. Not by a long way. Dinah struck me as willful and spoiled. The willfulness was okay. She'd probably grow out of it. Most people did. But she was going to need a pair of hard slaps to stop her from being such a spoiled brat. It was too bad that Nick and Noreen Charalambides had divorced when Dinah was still a child. Probably her young life had lacked a father's discipline. Maybe that was the real reason Dinah was planning to marry a man more than twice her age. Lots of girls married father substitutes. Or maybe she was simply trying to get even with her mother for leaving her father. Lots of girls did that, too. Maybe it was both of these things. Or maybe I didn't know what I was talking about, never having raised a child myself.

It was fortunate that I was in the workshop. "Maybe" is not a word you use in there. When you're operating a lathe to cut a length of metal, "exactly" is a better word. I had the patience for metalworking. That was easy. Being a parent looked much more difficult.

Later on I had a bath and put on a good suit. Before I went out I bowed my head for a few moments in front of the Santería shrine Yara had built in her room. It was really just a doll's house covered with white lace and candles. But on each floor of the doll's house were little animals, crucifixes, nuts, shells, and black-faced figurines in white dresses. There were also several pictures of the Virgin Mary and one picture of a woman with a knife through her tongue. Yara told me this was to stop gossip about her and me, but I hadn't a clue about what any of the other stuff meant. With the possible exception of the Virgin Mary. I don't know why I bowed my head to her shrine. I could say that I wanted to believe in something, but in my heart of hearts, I knew Yara's souvenir shop was just another stupid lie. Just like Nazism.

On my way to the door I picked up Ben Siegel's backgammon set, and then Yara took me by the shoulders and looked into my eyes as if searching for some effect that her peculiar shrine had worked in my soul. Always supposing I had such a thing as that. And, finding something, she took a step back and crossed herself several times.

"You look like the Lord Eleggua," she said. "He is the owner of the crossroads. And who guards the home against all dangers. He is always justified in all that he does. And it is he who knows what nobody else knows and who always acts according to his perfect judgment." She took off the necklace she was wearing and tucked this into the breast pocket of my jacket. "For good luck in your game," she said.

"Thank you," I said. "But it is only a game."

"Not this time," she said. "Not for you. Not for you, master."

10

I PARKED MY CAR ON ZULUETA, in sight of the local police station, and walked back to the Saratoga, where there were already plenty of taxis and cars, including a couple of the black Cadillac Seventy-fives, which were beloved to all senior government officials.

I walked through the hotel and into the monastery courtyard, where a series of lights was turning the water in the fountain into several pastel shades of color and left the marble horse looking somewhat bemused— as if it hardly dared to take a drink of the exotic-looking water for fear that it might be poisoned. It was, I reflected, a perfect metaphor for the experience of being in a Havana casino.

A doorman dressed like a wealthy French impressionist opened the door for me, and I entered the casino. It was early, but the place was busy, like a bus station during rush hour, only with chandeliers, and noisy with the clack of chips and dice, the tap-running-into-a-steel-sink sound of metal balls rolling around wooden roulette wheels, the squeals of winners, the groans of losers, the clink of glasses, and always the clear, unexcited, declarative voices of the croupiers jostling the bets and calling the cards and the numbers.

I glanced around and noticed that some local celebrities were already in the place: Desi Arnaz the musician, Celia Cruz the singer, George Raft the movie actor, and Major Esteban Ventura—one of the most feared police officials in Havana. Gamblers in white tuxedoes drifted about, shuffling plaques and prevaricating about where their luck might lie that night: on the roulette wheel or at the craps table. Glamorous women with high hairdos and plunging necklines patrolled the edges of the room like cheetahs trying to identify the weakest men to hunt and bring down. One stalked toward me, but I flicked her off with a toss of my head.

I spotted what looked like the casino manager. I figured he was the one with the folded arms and the tennis umpire's eyes; also, he wasn't smoking or holding chips. Like most Habañeros, he wore a schoolboy's doodle of a mustache and more grease on his head than a Cuban hamburger. He caught my eye and then my nod, unfolded his arms, and walked my way.

"Can I help you, *señor*?"

"My name is Carlos Hausner," I said. "I have a meeting upstairs with Señor Reles just before eleven tonight. But before then I'm supposed to meet Señor García, to play backgammon."

Some of the grease off the manager's hair must have been on his fingertips, because he started to wring his hands like Pontius Pilate. "Señor García is already here," he said, leading the way. "Señor Reles asked me to find you both a quiet corner in our lounge. Between the *salon privé* and the main gaming room. I shall endeavor to make sure you are not disturbed."

We went over to a spot next to a palm tree. García was seated on a fancy French dining chair facing the room. There was a gilt, marble-topped table in front of him on which a backgammon set had already been laid out. Behind him, on the canary-yellow wall, was a Fragonard-style mural of a naked odalisque lying with her hand on the lap of a rather bored-looking man wearing a red turban. Considering where her hand was, you'd have thought he might have looked more interested. García's ownership of the Shanghai made it seem like an entirely appropriate spot to have chosen for our game.

The Shanghai on Zanja was Havana's most obscene and, as a result, most notorious and popular burlesque house. Even with 750 seats, there was always a long line of excited men outside the place—mostly juvenile American sailors—waiting to pay $1.25 to get in and see a show that made anything I had seen in Weimar Berlin look tame. Tame and, by comparison, rather tasteful, too. There was nothing in the least bit tasteful about the show at the Shanghai. Mostly this was thanks to the presence on the bill of a tall mulatto called Superman whose erect member was as big as a cattle prod and which he used to rather similar effect. The climax of the show involved the mulatto outraging a succession of innocent-looking blondes to the vociferous encouragement of Uncle Sam. It wasn't a place to take a liberal-minded satyr, let alone a nineteen-year-old girl.

García stood up politely, but I disliked him on sight in the same way I would have disliked a pimp or, for that matter, a gorilla in a tuxedo, which is what he looked like. He moved with the economy of a robot, his thick arms held stiffly at his sides until, equally stiffly, one of them came my way, extending a hand the size and color of a falconer's glove. The bald head, with its enormous ears and thick lips, might have been looted from some Egyptian archaeological site—if not the Valley of the Kings, then perhaps the gully of the slimy-looking satraps. I felt the strength in his hand before he took it away and slipped it into the pocket of his tuxedo. The hand came out with a bundle of money, which he tossed onto the table beside the board.

"A cash game would be best, don't you agree?" he said.

"Sure," I said, and laid the envelope of money Reles had given me earlier beside García's. "But we can settle up at the end of the evening, surely. Or do you want to do it at the end of every game?"

"At the end of the evening is fine," he said.

"In which case," I said, pocketing my envelope, "there's no real need for this, now that we both know the other is carrying a substantial amount of cash."

He nodded and took back the bundle of money. "I have to leave for a while at around eleven," he said. "I have to be back to supervise the door at the Shanghai for the eleven-thirty show."

"And what about the nine-thirty show?" I asked. "Or does that just run itself?"

"You know my theater?"

He made it sound like the Abbey Theatre in Dublin. The voice was what I expected: too many cigars and not enough exercise. A wallowing hippo's voice. Muddy and full of yellowing teeth and gas. Dangerous, too, probably.

"I know it," I said.

"But I can always come back afterward," he said. "To give you a chance to win back your money."

"And I can always extend you the same courtesy."

"To answer your earlier question." The thick lips stretched like a cheap, pink garter. "The eleven-thirty show is always the more difficult one to handle. People have had more to drink by that time of the evening. And sometimes there's trouble if they can't get in. The police station on Zanja is conveniently close, but it's not unknown that they need a cash incentive to put in an appearance."

"Money talks."

"It does in this city."

I glanced down at the backgammon board if only to avoid looking at his ugly face and inhaling the even uglier stink of his breath. From almost a meter away I could smell it. To my surprise, I found myself staring at a backgammon set of a design that was remarkable in its obscenity. The points on the board, black or white and shaped like spearheads on any ordinary set, were here each shaped like erect phalluses. Between phalluses, or perhaps draped over them like artists' models, were naked figures of girls. The checkers were painted to look like the bare behinds of black and white women, while the two cups from which each player would throw his dice were the shape of a female breast. These slotted together to form a chest that would have been the envy of any Oktoberfest waitress. Only the four dice and the doubling cube met the eye with any kind of decorum.

"You like my set?" he asked, chuckling like a foul-smelling mud bath.

"I like mine better," I said. "But my set is locked, and I can't remember the combination. So if it amuses you to play with this one, that's fine by me. I'm quite broad-minded."

"Have to be if you live in Havana, right? Play on pips or just the cube?"

"I'm feeling lazy. All that math. Let's stick to the cube. Shall we say ten pesos a game?"

I lit a cigar and settled into my chair. As the game progressed, I forgot about the board's pornographic design and my opponent's breath. We were more or less even until García threw two more doubles in a row and, turning the four to an eight, pushed the doubling cube my way. I hesitated. His two doubles in a row were enough to make me cautious to accept the new stake. I'd never been the kind of percentage player who could look at the positions of all the checkers on the board and calculate the difference in pips between myself and the other player. I preferred to base my game on the look of things and my remembering the run of the dice. Deciding I had to be due a double soon to make up for his three, I picked up the cube and immediately threw a double five, which at that particular moment was exactly what I needed, and left both of us bearing off, neck and neck.

We were each down to the last few checkers in our home boards—twelve in his and ten in mine—when he offered me the cube again. The math was on my side, so long as he didn't throw a fourth double, and since this seemed improbable, I took it. Any other decision would have demonstrated a lack of what the Cubans called *cojones* and would certainly have had a disastrous effect on the rest of the evening's play. The stake was now 160 pesos.

He threw a double four, which now left him even with me and likely to win the game unless I threw a double myself. His eyes hardly flickered as once again I threw a one and a two when I needed it least and managed to bring off only one checker. He threw a six and a five, bearing off two. I threw a five and a three, bearing off two. Then he threw another double and took off four more—his two against my five. Not even a double could save me now.

García didn't smile. He just picked up his cup and emptied the dice, with no more feeling than if it had been the first throw of the game. Meaningless. Everything still to play for. Except that the first game was now over, and I had lost.

He bore off his last two checkers and slipped the big paw into the pocket of his tuxedo again. This time it came out with a little black leather notebook and a silver mechanical pencil, with which he wrote the number 160 onto the first page.

It was eight-thirty. Twenty minutes had passed. An expensive twenty minutes. García might have been a pornographer and a pig, but there wasn't much wrong with his luck or his ability to play the game. I realized this was going to be harder than I'd thought.

11

I HAD STARTED PLAYING BACKGAMMON IN URUGUAY. In the café of the Hotel Alhambra in Montevideo, I had been taught to play by a former champion. But Uruguay was expensive—much more expensive than Cuba— which was the main reason I had come to the island. Usually I played with a couple of secondhand booksellers in a café on Havana's Plaza de Armas, and only for a few centavos. I liked backgammon. I liked the neatness of it—the arrangement of checkers on points and the tidying of them all away that was required to finish the game. The neatness and order of it always struck me as very German. I also liked the mixture of skill and luck; more luck than was needed for bridge and more skill than was needed for a game like blackjack. Above all I liked the idea of taking risks against the celestial bank, of competing against fate itself. I liked the feeling of cosmic justice that could be invoked with every roll of the dice. In a sense my whole life had been lived like that. Against the grain.

It wasn't García I was playing—he was merely the ugly face of Chance—it was life itself.

So I relit my cigar, rolled it around in my mouth, and waved a waiter toward me. "I'll have a small carafe of peach schnapps, chilled, but no ice," I told the man. I didn't ask if García wanted a drink. I hardly cared. All I cared about now was beating him.

"Isn't that a woman's drink?" he asked.

"I hardly think so," I said. "It's eighty proof. But you may believe what you like." I picked up my dice cup.

"And for you, *señor*?" The waiter was still there.

"A lime daiquiri."

We continued with the game. García lost the next game on pips, and the one after that when he declined my double. And gradually he became a little more reckless, hitting blots when he should have left them alone and then accepting doubles when he should have refused. He began to lose heavily, and by ten-fifteen I was up by more than a thousand pesos and feeling quite pleased with myself.

There was still no trace of emotion on the argument in favor of Darwinism my opponent called his face, but I knew he was rattled by the way he was throwing his dice. In backgammon, it's customary to throw your dice in your home board, and both dice have to come to rest there, completely flat. But several times during the last game, García's hand had got a little overexcited, and his dice had crossed the bar or not landed flat. In each case the rules required him to throw again, and on one occasion this meant he had missed out on a useful double.

There was another reason I knew I had rattled him. He suggested that we should increase our ten-peso game stake. When a man does that, you can be certain he thinks he's already lost too much and is keen to win it back and as quickly as possible. But this is to ignore the central principle of backgammon, which is that it's the dice that dictate how you play the game, not the cube or the money.

I sat back and sipped my schnapps. "How much were you thinking of?"

"Let's say a hundred pesos a game."

"All right. But on one condition. That we also play the beaver rule."

He grinned, almost as if he had wanted to suggest it himself.

"Agreed." He picked up the cup, and although it wasn't his turn to throw first, he rolled a six.

I rolled a one. García won the throw and simultaneously made his bar point. He pushed himself close to the table, as if eager to win back his money. A little sheen of sweat appeared on his elephantine head, and, seeing it, I doubled immediately. García took the double and tried to double back until I reminded him that I hadn't yet taken my turn. I rolled a double four, which took both of my runners past his bar point for the moment, rendering it redundant.

García winced a little at this but doubled all the same and then threw a two and a one, which disappointed him. I had the doubling cube now and, sensing I had the psychological advantage, turned the cube and said, "Beaver," effectively doubling the cube without the requirement of his consent. I then paused and offered him a double on top of my beaver. He bit his lip at this and, already facing a potential loss of eight hundred pesos—on top of what he had already lost—he ought to have declined my double. Instead he accepted. Now I rolled a double six, which left me able to make my bar point and the ten point. The game had already turned my way, with a stake of sixteen hundred pesos.

His throwing became more agitated. First he cocked his dice. Then he threw a double four, which might have dug him out of the hole he was in but for the fact that one of the fours was in his outer board and therefore could not count. Angrily he snatched up both dice, dropped them into the cup, and threw them again, with considerably less success: a two and a three. Things deteriorated rapidly for him after that, and it wasn't long before he was locked out of my home board, with two checkers sitting on the bar.

I started to bear off, with him still locked out. Now there was a real danger that he might not get any of his checkers back to his own home board before I finished bearing off. This was called a "gammon" and would have cost him double the stake on the cube.

García was throwing like a madman now, and there was no sign of his earlier sangfroid. With each roll of the dice he remained locked out. The game was lost, with nothing left to play for but the possibility of saving the gammon. Finally he was back on the board and racing for home, with me left with only six checkers to bear off. But low throws continued to dog his progress. A few seconds later, the game and gammon were mine.

"That's gammon," I said quietly. "That makes double what's on the cube. I make that thirty-two hundred pesos. Plus the eleven hundred forty you already owe me, and that makes—"

"I can add," he said brusquely. "There's nothing wrong with my math."

I resisted the temptation to point out that it was his skill at backgammon that was at fault, not his math.

García looked at his watch. And so did I. It was ten-forty.

"I have to leave," he said, closing the board abruptly.

"Are you coming back?" I asked. "After you've been to your club?"

"I don't know."

"Well, I'll be here for a while. To give you a chance to win it back."

But we both knew he wouldn't be returning. He counted out forty-three hundred-peso notes from a fifty-note bundle and handed them over.

I nodded and said, "Plus ten percent for the house, that's two hundred each." I riffled my fingers at his remaining cash. "I'll pay for the drinks myself."

Sullenly he thumbed another couple of bills at me. Then he closed the catches on top of the ugly backgammon set, tucked it under his arm, and quickly walked away, shouldering his way through the other gamblers like a character in a horror movie.

I pocketed my winnings and went to find the casino manager again. He looked as if he'd hardly moved since I'd last spoken to him.

"Is the game over?" he asked.

"For the moment. Señor García has to visit his club. And I have a meeting upstairs with Señor Reles. After that we may resume. I said I'd wait here to give him a chance to win back his money. So we'll see."

"I'll keep the table free," said the manager.

"Thank you. And perhaps you'd be kind enough to let Señor Reles know that I'm on my way up to see him now."

"Yes, of course."

I handed him four hundred pesos. "Ten percent of the table stakes. I believe that's normal."

The manager shook his head. "That won't be necessary. Thank you for beating him. For a long time now I've been hoping that someone could humiliate that pig. And from the look of things, you must have beat him good."

I nodded.

"Perhaps, after you have finished your meeting with Señor Reles, you could come to my office. I should like to buy you a drink to celebrate your victory."

12

STILL CARRYING BEN SIEGEL'S BACKGAMMON SET, I caught the elevator car up to the eighth floor and the hotel pool terrace, where I found Waxey and another elevator car already waiting for me. Max's bodyguard was a little friendlier this time, but not so as you'd have noticed unless you were a lip-reader. For a big man he had a very quiet voice, and it was only later on I discovered that Waxey's vocal cords had been damaged as a result of being shot in the throat. "Sorry," he whispered. "But I gotta frisk you before you go upstairs."

I put down the case and lifted my arms and looked past him while he went about his job. In the distance, the Barrio Chino was lit up like a Christmas tree.

"What's in the case?" he asked.

"Ben Siegel's backgammon set. It was a gift from Max. Only he didn't tell me the correct combination for the locks. He said it was six-six-six. Which would seem appropriate if it was. Only it's not."

Waxey nodded and stood back. He was wearing loose black slacks and a gray guayabera that matched the color of his hair. When his jacket was off I could see his bare arms, and I got a better idea of his probable strength. His forearms were like bowling pins. The loose shirt was probably supposed to conceal the holstered weapon on the back of his hip, except that the hem had got caught under the polished-wood grip of a .38 Colt Detective Special—probably the finest snubbie ever made.

He reached down into his trouser pocket and took out a key on a silver chain, stuck it into the elevator panel, and turned it. He didn't have to press any other button. The car went straight up. The doors opened again. "They're on the terrace," Waxey said.

I smelled them first. The powerful scent of a small forest fire: several large Havana cigars. Then I heard them: loud American voices, raucous male laughter, relentless profanity, the odd Yiddish and Italian word or phrase, more raucous laughter. I came past the detritus of a card game in the living room: a big table covered with chips and empty glasses. Now that the card game was over, they were all out on the little pool terrace: men in sharp suits with blunt faces, but maybe not so tough anymore. Some of them wore glasses and sports coats with neat handkerchiefs in their breast pockets. All of them looked exactly like what they claimed to be: businessmen, hoteliers, club owners, restaurateurs. And perhaps only a policeman or FBI agent would have recognized these men for what they really were—all of them with reputations earned on the streets of Chicago, Boston, Miami, and New York during the Volstead years. The minute I walked onto that terrace, I knew I was among the big beasts of Havana's underworld—the high-profile Mafia bosses Senator Estes Kefauver was so keen to talk to. I'd watched some of the Senate committee testimonies on the newsreels. The hearings had made household names out of a lot of the bosses, including the little man with the big nose and neat, dark hair. He was wearing a brown sports coat with an open shirt. It was Meyer Lansky.

"Oh, here he is," said Reles. His voice was a little louder than usual, but he was a model of sartorial rectitude. He wore gray flannel trousers, neat brown shoes with Oxford toe caps, a blue button-down shirt, a blue silk cravat, and a cashmere navy blue blazer. He looked like the membership secretary of the Havana Yacht Club.

"Gentlemen," he said, "this is the guy I was telling you about. This is Bernie Gunther. This is the guy who's going to be my new general manager."

Like always, I flinched at the sound of my own name, put down the attaché case, and took Max's hand.

"Relax, will you?" he said. "There's not one of us here that doesn't have as much fucking history as you do, Bernie. Maybe more. Nearly all of the guys here have seen the inside of a prison cell at one time or another. Including myself." He chuckled the old Max Reles chuckle. "You didn't know that, did you?"

I shook my head.

"Like I say, we all of us got plenty of fucking history. Bernie, say hello to Meyer Lansky; his brother, Jake; Moe Dalitz; Norman Rothman; Morris Kleinman; and Eddie Levinson. I bet you didn't know there were so many heebs on this island. Naturally, we're the brains of the outfit. For everything else we got wops and micks. So say hello to Santo Trafficante, Vincent Alo, Tom McGinty, Sam Tucker, the Cellini brothers, and Wilbur Clark."

"Hello," I said.

Havana's underworld stared back at me with modest enthusiasm.

"It must have been some card game," I observed.

"Waxey, get Bernie a drink. What are you drinking, Bernie?"

"A beer's fine."

"Some of us play gin, some of us play poker," said Max. "Some of us don't know a game of cards from a sorting office in a post office, but the important thing is that we meet and we talk, in the spirit of healthy competition. Like Jesus and the fucking disciples. You ever read Adam Smith's *Wealth of Nations*, Bernie?"

"Can't say that I have."

"Smith talks about something he calls the 'invisible hand.' He said that in a free market, an individual pursuing his self-interest tends to promote the good of his community as a whole through a principle that he called 'the invisible hand.'" He shrugged. "What we do. That's all it is. An invisible hand. And we've been doing it for years."

"That we have," growled Lansky.

Reles chuckled. "Meyer thinks he's the clever one, on account of how he reads a lot." He wagged his finger at Lansky. "But I read, too, Meyer. I read, too."

"Reading. It's a Jew thing," said Alo. He was a tall man with a long, sharp nose that might have made me think he was one of the Jews; but he was one of the Italians.

"And they wonder why the Jews do well," said a man with an easy grin and a nose like a speed bag. This man was Moe Dalitz.

"I read two books in my life," said one of the micks. "Hoyle on gambling, and the Cadillac handbook."

Waxey returned with my beer. It was cold and dark, like his eyes.

"F.B.'s thinking of resurrecting his old rural education program," said Lansky. "Sounds like some of you guys should try to get in on it. You could use a bit of education."

"Is that the same one he ran in thirty-six?" said his brother, Jake.

Meyer Lansky nodded. "Only he's worried that some of the kids he's teaching to read, that they're going to be tomorrow's rebels. Like this last lot that's now doing a stretch on the Isle of Pines."

"He's right to worry," said Alo. "They get weaned on communism, some of these bastards."

"Then again," said Lansky, "when the economy of this country takes off, really takes off, then we're going to need educated people to work in our hotels. To be tomorrow's croupiers. You gotta be smart to be a croupier. Math smart. You read much, Bernie?"

"More and more," I admitted. "And for me it's like the French Foreign Legion. I do it to forget. Myself, I think."

Max Reles was looking at his wristwatch. "Talking of books, it's time I threw you guys out. I got my call with F.B. To go through the books."

"How does that work?" asked someone. "On the telephone."

Reles shrugged. "I read out the numbers, and he writes them down. We both know that one day he's gonna check, so why the fuck would I cheat him?"

Lansky nodded. "That is definitely *verboten*."

We moved off the terrace toward the elevators. As I stepped into one of the cars, Reles took my arm and said, "Start work tomorrow. Come around ten and I'll show you around."

"All right."

I went back down to the casino. I felt a certain amount of awe at the company I was keeping these days. I felt like I'd just been up to the Berghof for an audience with Hitler and the other Nazi leaders.

13

WHEN I RETURNED TO THE SARATOGA the following morning at ten o'clock, as arranged, a very different scene presented itself. There were police everywhere—outside the main entrance of the hotel and in the lobby. When I asked the receptionist to announce my arrival to Max Reles, she told me that no one was being allowed up to the penthouse except the hotel owners and the police.

"What's happened?" I asked.

"I don't know," said the receptionist. "They won't tell us anything. But there's a rumor that one of the hotel guests has been murdered by the rebels."

I turned and walked back to the front door and met the diminutive figure of Meyer Lansky.

"You leaving?" he asked. "Why?"

"They won't let me upstairs," I said.

"Come with me."

I followed Lansky to the elevator car, where a policeman was about to prevent our using it, until his officer recognized the gangster and saluted. Inside the car, Lansky produced a key from his pocket—one like Waxey's—and used it to take us up to the penthouse. I noticed that his hand was shaking.

"What's happened?" I asked.

Lansky shook his head.

The elevator doors parted to reveal yet more police, and in the living room we found a captain of militia, Waxey, Jake Lansky, and Moe Dalitz.

"Is it true?" Meyer Lansky asked his brother.

Jake Lansky was a little taller and more coarse-featured than his brother. He had thick, bottle-glass spectacles and eyebrows like a pair of mating badgers. He wore a cream-colored suit, a white shirt and a bow tie. His face had laugh lines, only he wasn't using them right now. He nodded gravely. "It's true."

"Where?"

"In his office."

I followed the two Lanskys into the office of Max Reles. A uniformed police captain brought up the rear.

Someone had been redecorating the walls. They looked as if Jackson Pollock had come in and actively expressed himself with a ceiling brush and a large pot of red paint. Only it wasn't red paint that was splashed all over the office; it was blood, and lots of it. Max Reles was going to need a new chinchilla rug, too, except that it wasn't going to be he who would go to a store to buy a replacement. He was never going to buy anything again—not even a funeral casket, which was what he now needed most. He lay on the floor, still in what seemed to be the same clothes he'd been in the night before, but the blue shirt now had some dark brown spots. He was staring at the cork-tiled ceiling with only one eye. The other eye appeared to be missing. From the look of him, two shots had hit him in the head, but there was a strong case for thinking that at least two or three more had ended up in his back and chest. It seemed like a real gangster-style murder, in that the gunman had done a very thorough job of making sure he was dead. And yet, apart from the police captain who had followed us into the office—more out of curiosity than anything else, it seemed—there were no police in there, no one taking photographs of the body, no one with a measuring tape, nothing of what might normally have been expected. Well, this was Cuba, after all, I told myself, where everything took just that little bit longer to get done, including, perhaps, the dispatching of forensic scientists to the scene of a homicide. Max Reles was already dead, so where was the hurry?

Waxey appeared behind us in the doorway of his dead master's office. There were tears in his eyes, and in his encyclopedia-sized hand, a white handkerchief that looked as if it might have been tugged off one of the double beds. He sniffed for a moment and then blew his nose loudly, sounding like a passenger ship making port.

Meyer Lansky looked at him with irritation. "So where the hell were you when he got his brains blown out?" he said. "Where were you, Waxey?"

"I was right here," whispered Waxey. "Like I always am. I thought the boss had gone to bed. After his phone call to F.B. He always had an early night after that. Regular as clockwork. First thing I knew about it was when I came in here at seven o'clock this morning and found him like this. Dead."

He added the word "dead" as if there had been some doubt about that fact.

"He wasn't shot with a BB gun, Waxey," said Lansky. "Didn't you hear nothing?"

Waxey shook his head, miserably. "Nothing. Like I said."

The police captain finished lighting a little cigarillo and said, "It's possible Señor Reles was shot during last night's fireworks," he said. "For Chinese New Year? That would certainly have covered up the sound of any gunshots."

He was a smallish, handsome, clean-shaven man. His neat olive-green uniform seemed to complement the light brown color of his smooth face. He spoke English with only a trace of a Spanish accent. And all the time he was speaking he leaned casually on the doorjamb, as if doing nothing more pressing than offering a halfhearted solution for fixing a broken-down car. Almost as if he didn't really care who had murdered Max Reles. And perhaps he didn't. Even in Batista's militia there were plenty of people who didn't much care for the presence of American gangsters in Cuba.

"The fireworks started at midnight," continued the captain. "They lasted approximately thirty minutes." He moved through the open sliding glass door and out onto the terrace. "My guess is that during the noise, which was considerable, the assassin shot Señor Reles from out here on the terrace."

We followed the captain outside.

"Possibly he climbed up from the eighth floor using the scaffolding erected around the hotel sign."

Meyer Lansky glanced over the wall. "That's a hell of a climb," he murmured. "What do you think, Jake?"

Jake Lansky nodded. "The captain is right. The killer had to come up here. Either that or he had a key, in which case he would have to have gotten past Waxey. Which doesn't seem likely."

"Not likely," said his brother. "But all the same, it is possible."

Waxey shook his head. "No fucking way," he said. Suddenly his normally whispering voice sounded angry.

"Maybe you were asleep," said the police captain.

Waxey looked very indignant at this suggestion, which was enough to have Jake Lansky stand between him and the police captain and try to defuse a situation that threatened to get ugly. Anything involving Waxey would have threatened that much.

With one hand placed firmly on Waxey's chest, Jake Lansky said, "I should introduce you, Meyer. This is Captain Sánchez. He's from the police station around the corner on Zulueta. Captain Sánchez, this is my brother, Meyer. And this"—he looked at me—"this is . . ." He hesitated for a moment, as though trying to remember not my real name—I could see that he knew what that was—but my false one.

"Carlos Hausner," I said.

Captain Sánchez nodded and then addressed all of his remarks to Meyer Lansky. "I spoke to His Excellency the president just a few minutes ago," he said. "First of all, he wishes me to express his sympathies to you, Señor Lansky. For the terrible loss of your friend. He also wishes me to reassure you that the Havana police will do everything in its power to catch the perpetrator of this heinous crime."

"Thank you," said Lansky.

"His Excellency tells me he spoke with Señor Reles on the telephone last night, as was his custom every Wednesday evening. The call commenced at exactly eleven forty-five p.m. and terminated at eleven fifty-five. Which would also seem to suggest that the time of death was during the fireworks, between twelve and twelve-thirty. In fact, I am convinced of it. Let me show you why."

He held out a mangled-looking bullet in the palm of his hand.

"This is a bullet that I dug out of the wall in the study. It looks like a thirty-eight-caliber round. A thirty-eight would be a lot of gun to keep quiet at any time. But during the fireworks, six shots might easily be fired without anyone hearing."

Meyer Lansky looked at me. "What do you think of that idea?" he asked.

"Me?"

"Yeah, you. Max said you used to be a cop. Kind of cop were you anyway?"

"The honest kind."

"Fuck that. I mean what was your area of investigation?"

"Homicide."

"So what do you think of what the captain says?"

I shrugged. "I think we've been jumping over one guess after another. I think it might be an idea to let a doctor examine the body and see if we can pin down the time of death. Maybe that will tie in with the fireworks, I don't know. But that would make sense, I think." I glanced over the floor of the terrace. "I don't see any shell casings, so either the killer used an automatic and picked them up in the dark, which seems unlikely, or the gun was a revolver. Either way, it would seem best to find the murder weapon as a matter of priority."

Lansky looked at Captain Sánchez.

"We already looked for it," said the captain.

"Looked?" I said. "Looked where?"

"The terrace. The penthouse. The eighth floor."

"Maybe he threw it into that park," I said, indicating the Campo de Marte. "A gun might land there in the dark and nobody would notice."

"Then again, maybe he took it with him," said the captain.

"Maybe. On the other hand, Major Ventura was in the casino last night, which meant there were plenty of police in and around the hotel. I can't see that anyone who had just shot someone dead would risk running into a cop with a gun that had just been fired six or seven times. Especially if this was a professional killer. Frankly, it looks professional. It takes a cool head to fire that many shots and hit the target several times and expect to get away with it. An amateur would probably have panicked and missed more. Maybe even dropped the gun here. My guess is that he just dumped the gun somewhere on his way out of the hotel. In my experience, all sorts of stuff can get smuggled in and out of a hotel as big as this. Waiters walk around with covered trays. Porters carry bags. Maybe the killer just dropped the gun in a laundry basket."

Captain Sánchez called one of his men and ordered a search to be made of the Campo de Marte and the hotel laundry baskets.

I went back into the office and, tiptoeing around the bloodstains, stared down at Max Reles. There was something covered with a handkerchief: something bloody that had leaked through the cotton. "What's that?" I asked the captain when he had finished giving orders to his men.

"His eyeball. It must have popped out when one of the bullets exited the victim's head."

I nodded. "Then that's a hell of a thirty-eight. You might expect that with a forty-five, but not a thirty-eight. May I see the bullet you found, Captain?"

Sánchez handed over the bullet.

I looked at it and nodded. "No, I think you're right, it does look like a thirty-eight. But something must have given this bullet an extra velocity."

"Such as?"

"I have no idea."

"You were a detective, *señor?*"

"It was a very long time ago. And I didn't mean to suggest that you don't know your job, Captain. I'm sure that you have your own way of handling an investigation. But Mr. Lansky here asked me what I thought, and I told him."

Captain Sánchez sucked the little cigarillo and then dropped it on the floor of the crime scene. He said, "You said Major Ventura was in the casino last night. Does that mean you were here also?"

"Yes. I played backgammon in the casino last night until around ten forty-five, when I came up here to join Señor Reles and his guests for a drink. Mr. Lansky and his brother were among those other guests. And the gentleman in the living room. Mr. Dalitz. Waxey, too. I stayed until about eleven-thirty, when we all left, so that Reles could prepare for his phone call with the president. I'd arranged for my backgammon opponent—Señor García, who owns the Shanghai Theater—to return to the casino and continue our game. Well, I waited, but he didn't come back. Meanwhile I had a drink with Señor Núñez, the casino manager. Then I went home."

"At what time was that?"

"Just after twelve-thirty. I remember the time because I'm sure the fireworks ended a few minutes before I got in my car."

"I see." The captain lit another cigarillo and allowed some of the smoke to escape from between his extremely white teeth. "So it could have been you who killed Señor Reles, could it not?"

"It could have been, yes. It could have been me who led the attack on the Moncada Barracks, too. But it wasn't. Max Reles had just given me an extremely well paid job. A job I no longer have. So my motive for killing him looks less than convincing."

"That's quite correct, Captain," said Meyer Lansky. "Max had made Señor Hausner here his general manager."

Captain Sánchez nodded, as if accepting Lansky's corroboration of my story; but he wasn't quite finished with me, and now I was cursing myself for being rash enough to have answered Lansky's earlier question to me concerning the murder of Max Reles.

"How long did you know the deceased?" asked the captain.

"We first met in Berlin, about twenty years ago. Until a couple of nights ago, I hadn't seen him since then."

"And straightaway he offers you a job? He must have thought very highly of you, Señor Hausner."

"He had his reasons, I suppose."

"Perhaps you were holding something over his head. Something from the past."

"You mean like blackmail, Captain?"

"I most certainly do mean that, yes."

"That might have been true twenty years ago. As a matter of fact, we both had something on each other. But it certainly wasn't enough to give me any power over the man. Not anymore."

"And him. Did he hold any power over you?"

"Sure. You could put it that way, why not? He offered me money to work for him. That's about the most powerful thing there is on this island that I know of."

The captain pushed his peaked cap onto the back of his head and scratched his forehead. "But I'm still puzzled. Why? Why did he offer you this job?"

"Like I said, he had his reasons. But if you want me to speculate, Captain, I suppose he liked it that I kept my mouth shut for twenty years. That I kept my word to him. That I wasn't afraid to tell him to go and fuck himself."

"And maybe you were not afraid to kill him, either."

I smiled and shook my head.

"No, hear me out," said the captain. "Max Reles has lived in Havana for many years. He is a law-abiding, taxpaying, upstanding citizen. He's a friend of the president. Then one day he meets you, someone he hasn't seen for twenty years. Two or three days later, he's murdered. That's quite a coincidence, isn't it?"

"When you put it like that, I wonder why the hell you don't arrest me. It would certainly save you the time and trouble of conducting a proper murder investigation with forensic evidence and witnesses who saw me do the shooting. The usual stuff. Run me down to the station, why don't you? Maybe you can strong-arm a confession out of me before you finish your shift. I can't imagine it would be the first time you've done something like that."

"You mustn't believe everything you read in *Bohemia, señor*."

"No?"

"Do you really think we torture suspects?"

"Mostly I don't give the matter any thought at all, Captain. But maybe I'll go and visit some prisoners on the Isle of Pines and see what they have to say about it and then get back to you. It'll make a change from picking my feet at home."

But Sánchez wasn't listening. He was looking at the revolver one of his men was presenting to him on a towel, like a crown of laurel or wild olive. I heard the man say that the gun had been found in a laundry basket on the eighth floor. There was a red star on the handle. And it certainly looked like the murder weapon. For one thing, it was wearing a silencer.

"It looks like Señor Hausner was right, wouldn't you say, Captain?" said Meyer Lansky.

Sánchez and the cop turned and went into the living room.

"And not a moment too soon," I told Lansky. "That stupid cop liked me for it."

"Didn't he just? Me, I liked you for the way you spoke to him. It reminded me of me. I suppose that was the murder weapon."

"I'd bet the hard way on it. That's a seven-shot Nagant. My guess is they'll dig seven out of Max's body and the walls."

"A Nagant? I've never heard of it."

"Designed by a Belgian. But the red star on the handle means that one's Russian made," I said.

"Russian, huh? Are you telling me Max was killed by communists?"

"No, Mr. Lansky, I was telling you about the gun. Soviet murder squads used that type of gun to murder Polish officers in 1940. They shot them in the back of the head and then buried the bodies in the Katyń Forest and later blamed the Germans for it. There were plenty of guns like that in Europe at the end of the war. But oddly, not that many on this side of the Atlantic. Especially not with a Bramit silencer. That alone makes this killing look professional. You see, sir, even with a silencer, all pistols will still make a noise. Maybe enough noise to alert Waxey. But a Nagant's the only kind of pistol you can silence completely. You see, there's no gap between the cylinder and the barrel. It's what they call a 'closed firing system,' which means you can suppress whatever noise comes out of the barrel one hundred percent—provided, that is, you have a Bramit silencer. Frankly, it's the perfect weapon for a clandestine killing. The Nagant would also account for the higher velocity of the thirty-eight-caliber bullet, too. Enough to knock out an eyeball that got in the way. So what I'm saying is this. Whoever shot Max Reles didn't need to do it during last night's fireworks. They could have shot him at any time between midnight and when Waxey found the body this morning, and nobody would have heard a damn thing. Oh, and by the way, this isn't exactly the kind of gun you can buy in your local gun store. Least of all with a silencer. These days the Ivans prefer the much lighter Tokarev TT. That's an automatic, in case you didn't know."

"I didn't know," agreed Lansky. "But as it happens I'm not as ignorant about the Russians as you might think, Gunther. My family was from Grodno, on the Russian–Polish border. Me and my brother, Jake, we left when we were kids. To get away from the Russians. Jake here knew one of those Polish officers who got themselves killed. People today talk about German anti-Semitism, but for my family, the Russians were just as bad. Maybe worse."

Jake Lansky nodded. "I think so," he said. "And so did Pop."

"So how come you know so much about this stuff?"

"During the war, I was in German military intelligence," I said. "And for a short while afterward I was in a Soviet POW camp. If I'm cagey about my name, it's because I killed a couple of Ivans while making my escape from a train bound for a uranium mine in the Urals. I doubt I'd have come back from there. Very few German POWs have ever come back from the Soviet Union. They ever catch up with me, I'm soap on a rope, Mr. Lansky."

"I figured it was something like that." Lansky shook his head and glanced down at the dead body. "Someone should cover him up."

"I wouldn't do that, Mr. Lansky," I said. "Not yet. It's just possible that Captain Sánchez will get wise to the proper procedures here."

"Don't you worry none about him," said Lansky. "He gives you any trouble, I'll call his boss and have him lay off. Maybe I'll do that anyway. Come on. Let's get out of this room. I can't bear to be here any longer. Max was like a second brother to me. I knew him since I was fifteen years old in Brownsville. He was the smartest kid I ever knew. With the proper education Max could have been anything he wanted. Maybe even the president of the United States."

We went into the living room. Sánchez was there with Waxey and Dalitz. The gun was lying in a plastic bag, on the table where Max and I had eaten lunch less than forty hours before.

"So what happens now?" asked Waxey.

"We bury him," said Meyer Lansky. "Like a good Jew. That's what Max would have wanted. When the cops have finished with the body, we got three days to make the arrangements and everything."

"Leave it to me," said Jake. "It'd be an honor."

"Someone ought to tell that girl of his," said Dalitz.

"Dinah," whispered Waxey. "Her name is Dinah. They were going to get married. With a rabbi and the whole broken wineglass, everything. She's Jewish, too, you know."

"I didn't know that," said Dalitz.

"She'll be all right," said Meyer Lansky. "Someone ought to tell her, sure, but she'll be all right. The young always are. Nineteen years old, she's got her whole life ahead of her. God rest Max's soul, I thought she was too young for him, but what do I know? You can't blame a guy for wanting a little piece of happiness. For a guy like Max, Dinah was as good as it gets. But you're right, Moe, someone ought to tell her."

"Tell me what? Has something happened? Where's Max? Why are the police here?"

It was Dinah.

"Well, isn't anyone going to say anything? Is Max all right? Is he sick? God damn it, what the hell is happening here?"

Then she saw the gun on the table. I suppose she must have guessed the rest, because she started to scream, loudly. It was a sound that could have raised the dead.

But not this time.

14

WAXEY DROVE DINAH BACK to Finca Vigía in the red Cadillac Eldorado. Under the circumstances, perhaps it ought to have been me who took her home. I might have been able to offer Noreen some support in dealing with her daughter's grief. But Waxey was eager to get out from under Meyer Lansky's shrewd, searching eye, as if he felt the Jewish gangster suspected him of some involvement in the murder of Max Reles. Besides, it was much more likely that I'd only have been in the way. I wasn't much of a shoulder to cry on. Not anymore. Not since the war, when so many German women had, of necessity, learned to cry by themselves.

Grief: I no longer had the patience for it. What did it matter if you grieved for people when they died? It certainly couldn't bring them back. And they weren't even particularly grateful for your grief. The living always get over the dead. That's what the dead never realize. If ever the dead did come back, they'd only have been sore that somehow you managed to get over their dying at all.

It was about four o'clock in the afternoon when I felt equal to the task of driving down to the Hemingway house to offer my sympathies. Despite the fact that Max's death had done me out of a salary worth twenty-thousand dollars a year, I wasn't sorry he was dead. But for Dinah's sake I was willing to pretend.

The Pontiac wasn't there, just a white Oldsmobile with a sun visor I seemed to recognize.

Ramón admitted me to the house, and I found Dinah in her room. She was seated in an armchair, smoking a cigarette, watched closely by a glum-looking water buffalo. The buffalo reminded me of myself, and it was perhaps easy to see why he was looking glum: Dinah's suitcase was open on her bed. It was packed neatly with her clothes, as if she were preparing to leave the country. On a table by the arm of her chair were a drink and a hardwood ashtray. Her eyes were red, but she seemed to be all cried out.

"I came to see how you are," I said.

"As you can see," she said, calmly.

"Going somewhere?"

"So you *were* a detective."

I smiled. "That's what Max used to say. When he wanted to needle me."

"And did it?"

"At the time, yes, it did. But there's not much that gets to me now. I'm rather more impervious these days."

"Well, that's a lot more than Max can say."

I let that one go.

"What would you say if I told you that my mother killed him?" she said.

"I'd say that it might be best to keep a wild thought like that to yourself. Not all of Max's friends are as forgetful as me."

"But I saw the gun," she said. "The murder weapon. In the penthouse at the Saratoga. It was my mother's gun. The one Ernest gave her."

"It's a common enough gun," I said. "I saw plenty of guns like that during the war."

"Her gun is missing," said Dinah. "I already looked for it."

I was shaking my head. "Do you remember the other day? When you said you thought she was suicidal? I took the gun away just in case she decided to use it on herself. I should have mentioned it at the time. I'm sorry."

"You're lying," she said.

She was right, but I wasn't about to admit it. "No, I'm not," I said.

"The gun is missing, and so is she."

"I'm sure there's a perfectly simple explanation for why she's not here."

"Which is that she murdered him. She did it. Or Alfredo López. That's his car out there. Neither of them liked Max. One time Noreen as good as told me that she wanted to kill him. To stop me from marrying him."

"Just how much do you really know about your late boyfriend?"

"I know he wasn't exactly a saint, if that's what you mean. He never professed to be." She flushed. "What are you driving at?"

"Just this: Max was a very long way from being a saint. You won't like this, but you're going to hear it anyway. Max Reles was a gangster. During Prohibition he was a ruthless bootlegger. Max's brother, Abe, was a hit man for the mob before someone tossed him out of a hotel window."

"I'm not listening to this."

Dinah shook her head and stood up, but I pushed her back down onto the chair again.

"Yes, you are," I said. "You're listening to it because somehow you've never heard it before. Or if you did, then maybe you just buried your head in the sand like some stupid ostrich. You're going to listen to it because it's the truth. Every damned word. Max Reles was into every dirty racket that there is. More recently he was part of an organized crime syndicate started in the 1930s by Charlie Luciano and Meyer Lansky. He stayed in business because he didn't mind murdering his rivals."

"Shut up," she said. "It's not true."

"He told me himself that he and his brother murdered two men, the Shapiro brothers, in 1933. One of them he buried alive. After Prohibition ended, he went into labor racketeering. Some of it was in Berlin, which was where I first met him. While he was there, he murdered a German businessman called Rubusch who refused to be intimidated by him. I myself witnessed him murder two other people. One of them was a prostitute, Dora, with whom he had been conducting a relationship.

He shot her in the head and dumped her body in a lake. She was still breathing when she hit the water."

"Get out," she snapped. "Get out of here."

"And maybe your mother already told you about the man he murdered on a passenger ship between New York and Hamburg."

"I didn't believe her, and I don't believe you now."

"Sure you do. You believe all of it. Because you're not stupid, Dinah. You've always known what kind of a man he was. Maybe you liked that. Maybe it gave you a cheap little thrill to be near someone like that. It can happen like that sometimes. There's a fascination all of us feel for the kind of people who inhabit the shadows. Maybe that's it, I don't know, and I really don't care. But if you didn't know Max Reles was a gangster, then you certainly suspected as much. Strongly suspected, because of the company he kept. Meyer and Jake Lansky. Santo Trafficante. Norman Rothman. Vincent Alo. Every one a gangster. With Lansky the most notorious gangster of them all. Just four years ago Lansky was facing a congressional committee investigating organized crime in the United States. So was Max. That's why they came to Cuba.

"I know of six people that Max has murdered, but I'm certain there are plenty more. People who crossed him. People who owed him money. People who were just inconveniently in his way. He'd have killed me, too, but I had something on him. Something he couldn't afford to let be known. Max was shot. But his own weapon of choice was an ice pick, with which he stabbed people in the ear. That's the kind of man he was, Dinah. A rotten, murdering gangster. One of many rotten, murdering gangsters who run the hotels and casinos here in Havana, any one of whom probably had his own very good reasons for wanting Max Reles out of the way.

"So keep your stupid mouth shut about your mother. I'm telling you now that she had nothing to do with it. You keep your mouth shut, or she'll wind up dead on account of you. You, too, if you happen to get in the way. You don't tell anyone what you told me. Got that?"

Dinah nodded, sullenly.

I pointed at the glass by her arm. "You drinking that?"

She looked at it and then shook her head. "No. I don't even like whiskey."

I reached forward and picked it up. "Do you mind?"

"Go ahead."

I poured the contents into my mouth and sucked on them for a while before letting the whiskey drip down my throat. "I talk too much," I said. "But this certainly helps."

She shook her head. "All right. You're right. I did suspect what he was like. But I was afraid to leave him. Afraid of what he might do. In the beginning it was just a bit of fun. I was bored here. Max introduced me to people I'd only ever read about. Frank Sinatra. Nat King Cole. Can you imagine it?" She nodded. "You're right. And what you said. I had it coming."

"We all make mistakes. God knows, I've made a few myself." There was a pack of cigarettes on top of her clothes in the suitcase. I picked them up. "Do you mind? I've given up. But I could use a smoke."

"Help yourself."

I lit it quickly and sent some smoke down my hatch to go after the whiskey.

"Where will you go?"

"The States. To Rhode Island and Brown University, like my mother wanted. I suppose."

"What about the singing?"

"I suppose Max told you that, did he?"

"As a matter of fact, he did. He seemed to think very highly of your talents."

Dinah smiled sadly. "I can't sing," she said. "Although Max seemed to think I could. I don't know why. I suppose he thought the best of me in all respects, including that one. But I can't sing, and I can't act. For a while it was fun pretending that any of that might be possible. But in my heart of hearts I knew it was all pie in the sky."

A car came up the drive. I looked out of the open window and saw the Pontiac pull up next to the Oldsmobile. The doors opened, and a man and a woman got out. They weren't dressed for the beach, but that was where they had been, all right, and you didn't need to be a detective to know it. With Alfredo López, the sand was mostly on his knees and on his elbows; with Noreen it was almost everywhere else. They didn't see me. They were too busy grinning at each other and dusting themselves off as they sauntered up the steps to the front door. Her smile faltered a little as she caught sight of me in the window. Perhaps she blushed. Maybe.

I went into the hall and met them as they came through the front door. By now the grins on their faces had turned to guilt, but it had nothing to do with the death of Max Reles. Of that much I was certain.

"Bernie," she said awkwardly. "What a lovely surprise."

"If you say so."

Noreen went to the drinks trolley and began fixing herself a large one. López was smoking a cigarette and looking sheepish while pretending to read a magazine from a rack as big as a newspaper kiosk.

"What brings you down here?" she asked.

So far she had done a great job of not meeting my eye. Not that I was trying to put it in her way, exactly. But both of us knew that I knew what she and López had been doing. You could actually smell it on them. Like fried food. I decided to offer a swift explanation and then make myself scarce.

"I came to see if Dinah was all right," I said.

"Why shouldn't she be all right? Has something happened?" Noreen was looking at me, her embarrassment now temporarily overcome by concern for her daughter. "Where is she? Is Dinah all right?"

"She's fine," I said. "But Max Reles isn't looking his best right now, on account of how someone pumped seven bullets into him late last night. As a matter of fact, he's dead."

Noreen stopped making her drink for a moment. "I see," she said. "Poor Max." Then she pulled a face. "Listen to me. What a damn hypocrite I am. As if I'm actually sorry he's dead. And it's not like I'm in the least bit surprised, given who and what he was." She shook her head. "I'm sorry to sound callous. How's Dinah taken it? Oh, Lord—she wasn't there, was she, when he . . . ?"

"No, she wasn't," I said. "Dinah's just fine. Already getting over it, wouldn't you know?"

"Do the police have any idea who killed Max?" asked López.

"Now, that's a question, isn't it?" I said. "I formed the impression that this is one crime the police are hoping will solve itself. Either that or someone else will solve it for them."

López nodded. "Yes, you're probably right, of course. The Havana militia can hardly start asking too many questions without the risk of upsetting the whole rotten apple cart. In case it turns out that one of Havana's other gangsters should prove to be responsible for Max's murder. There's never been a gangland murder in Cuba. Not of a boss, anyway. The last thing I imagine Batista needs is a gangland war on his doorstep." He smiled. "Yes, I think I'm pleased to say that the politics of this thing look fiendishly complicated."

As it turned out, things were a lot more complicated than that.

15

I GOT BACK AROUND SEVEN and ate the cold dinner that Yara had left for me on a covered plate. While I ate I looked through the evening newspaper. There was a nice picture of the president's wife, Marta, opening a new school in Boyeros; and something about the forthcoming visit to Havana of the U.S. senator from Florida, George Smathers. But Max Reles didn't get a mention, not even in the obituaries column. After dinner I fixed myself a drink. There wasn't much to that. I just poured some vodka from the refrigerator into a clean glass and drank it. I was settling down to take the place of Montaigne's dead friend. It seemed a pretty good definition of a reader. Then the telephone rang, which reminded me that there are times when a dead friend is your best friend.

But it wasn't a friend. It was Meyer Lansky, and he sounded annoyed.

"Gunther?"

"Yes."

"Where the hell have you been? I've been ringing all afternoon."

"I went to see Max's girl, Dinah."

"Oh. How is she?"

"Like you said. She'll be all right."

"Listen, Gunther, I want to talk to you, only not on the telephone. I don't like telephones. Never have liked them. This number you're on: 7-8075. That's a Vedado number, right?"

"Yes. I live on Malecón."

"Then we're practically neighbors. I'm in a suite at the National Hotel. Could you come here at nine?"

I turned over a few polite rebuffs in my mind, but none of them sounded polite enough for a gangster like Meyer Lansky. So I said, "Sure. Why not? I could use a stroll along the seafront."

"Do me a favor, will you?"

"I thought that's what I was doing."

"On your way over here, get me a couple of packs of Parliament, will you? The hotel's run out."

I walked west, along Malecón, bought Lansky's smokes, and went into Havana's largest hotel. This was more like a cathedral than Havana's cathedral on Empedrado. The lobby was easily bigger than San Cristóbal's nave, with a fine painted wooden ceiling that would have been the envy of many a medieval *palacio*. It smelled a lot better than the cathedral, too, since the hotel lobby was swarming with well-washed or even scented human traffic, although, to my tutored eye, the hotel itself looked badly understaffed, with long lines of guests in front of the reception desk, the cashier, and the concierge, like so many people queuing for tickets in a railway station. Somewhere, someone was playing a tinny piano that brought to mind a dance class in a girls' ballet school.

Four long-case clocks were arranged along the length of the lobby. They were not synchronized, and they struck the hour consecutively, one after the other, as if time itself was an elastic concept in Havana. Near the elevator doors was a wall adorned with a full-length picture of the president and his wife, both dressed in white—she in a two-piece tailored suit, and he in a tropical-weight military uniform. They looked like a cut-rate version of the Peróns.

I rode the elevator to the top of the building. In contrast with the railway-station atmosphere of the lobby, the executive floor was sepulchrally quiet. Very possibly it was even quieter than that, since most sepulchers don't have carpets that run to ten dollars a square meter. The doors to the executive suites were all louvered, which may have been meant to help the free flow of air or cigar smoke. The whole floor smelled like a tobacco grower's humidor.

Lansky's suite was the only one with its own doorman. He was a tall man, wearing square sleeves and with a chest like a housekeeping cart. He turned to face me as I walked as silently as Hiawatha along the corridor, and I let him pat me down as if he were looking for his matches in my pockets. He didn't find them. Then he opened the door, admitting me to a suite the size of an empty billiard hall. The atmosphere was every bit as hushed. But instead of another Jew with an overactive pituitary gland, I was met by a petite, green-eyed redhead in her forties who looked and sounded like a New York hairdresser. She smiled pleasantly, told me her name was Teddy, and that she was Meyer Lansky's wife, and ushered me through a living room and a set of sliding windows onto a wraparound balcony.

Lansky was seated on a wicker chair, staring out into darkness over the sea, like Canute.

"You can't see it," he said. "The sea. But you can sure smell it. And you can hear it. Listen. Listen to that sound." He held up his forefinger as if drawing my attention to the song of a nightingale on Berkeley Square.

I listened, carefully. In my unreliable ears it sounded very much like the sea.

"The way the sea draws back and off the beach and then begins again. Everything in this lousy world changes, but not that sound. For thousands of years that sound has always been exactly the same. That's a sound I never get tired of." He sighed. "And there are times when I get very tired of almost everything. Do you ever get like that, Gunther? Do you ever get tired?"

"Tired? Mr. Lansky, there are times when I get so tired of things that I think maybe I must be dead. If it wasn't for the fact that I'm sleeping all right, life might be almost intolerable."

I gave him his cigarettes. He started to get out his wallet until I stopped him. "Keep it," I told him. "I like the idea of you owing me money. It feels safer than the other way round."

Lansky smiled. "Drink?"

"No, thanks. I like to keep a clear head when I'm talking business with Lucifer."

"Is that what I am?"

I shrugged. "It takes one to know one." I watched him light one of the cigarettes and added, "I mean, that is why I'm here, isn't it? Business? I can't imagine you want to reminisce about what a great guy Max was."

Lansky gave me a narrow look.

"Before he died, Max told me all about you. Or at least as much as he knew. Gunther, I'll come straight to the point. There were three reasons Max wanted you to work for him. You're an ex-cop, you know hotels, and you're not affiliated with any of the families who've got business here in Havana. I've got two of those reasons and one of my own that make me think you're the man to find out who killed Max. Hear me out, please. The one thing we can't have here in Havana is a gang war. It's bad enough we've got the rebels. More trouble we don't need. We can't rely on the cops to investigate this thing properly. You must have gathered that yourself from your conversation with Captain Sánchez this morning. Actually, he's not a bad cop at all. But I liked the way you spoke to him. And it strikes me that you're not someone who's easily intimidated. Not by cops. Not by me. Not by my associates.

"Anyway, I spoke to some of the other gentlemen you met last night, and we're all of us of the opinion that we don't want you managing the

Saratoga, like you agreed with Max. Instead, we want you to investigate Max's murder. Captain Sánchez will give you any assistance you require, but you can have carte blanche, so to speak. All we want is to avoid any possible dispute among ourselves. You do this, Gunther, you investigate this murder, and I'll owe you more than the price of two packs of cigarettes. For one thing, I'll pay you what Max was going to pay you. And for another, I'll be your friend. You think about that before you say no. I can be a good friend to people who've done me a service. Anyway, my associates and myself, we're all agreed. You can go anywhere. You can speak to anyone. The bosses. The soldiers. Wherever the evidence takes you. Sánchez won't interfere. You say jump, he'll ask how high."

"It's been a long time since I investigated a murder, Mr. Lansky."

"I don't doubt it."

"I'm not as diplomatic as I used to be, either. Dag Hammarskjöld, I am not. And just suppose I do find out who killed Max. What then? Have you considered that?"

"You let me worry about that, Gunther. Just make sure you speak to everyone. And that everyone can give you an alibi. Norman Rothman and Lefty Clark at the Sans Souci. Santo Trafficante at the Tropicana. My own people, the Cellini brothers at the Montmartre. Joe Stassi, Tom McGinty, Charlie White, Joe Rivers, Eddie Levinson, Moe Dalitz, Sam Tucker, Vincent Alo. Not forgetting the Cubans, of course: Amedeo Barletta and Amleto Battisti at the Hotel Sevilla. Relax. I'll supply you with a list to work from. A list of suspects, if you like. With my name at the top."

"That could take a while."

"Naturally. You'll want to be thorough. And just so as everyone knows it's fair, you shouldn't leave anyone out. Justice being seen to be done, so to speak." He tossed the cigarette over the balcony. "You'll do it, then?"

I nodded. I still hadn't thought of any rebuffs that were polite enough to give the little man, especially after he'd offered to be my friend. Plus, there was a flip side to that.

"You can start right away."

"That would probably be best."

"What will you do first?"

I shrugged. "Go back to the Saratoga. Find out if anyone saw anything. Review the crime scene. Speak to Waxey, I guess."

"You'll have to find him first," said Lansky. "Waxey's gone missing. He drove the broad to her house this morning, and no one's seen him since." He shrugged. "Maybe he'll turn up at the funeral."

"When's that?"

"Day after tomorrow. At the Jewish cemetery in Guanabacoa."

"I know it."

My route back home from the National took me right past the Casa Marina again. And this time I went in.

16

—————

THE FOLLOWING MORNING WAS BRIGHT but windy, and half the winter sea was crashing down on the Malecón, like a deluge sent by a God saddened at the wickedness of mankind. I woke early, thinking that I would have liked to sleep longer and probably would have done so, except for the fact that the phone was ringing. Suddenly everyone in Havana seemed to want to speak to me.

It was Captain Sánchez.

"How's the great detective this morning?"

He sounded like he didn't much like the idea of my playing the sleuth for Lansky. I wasn't too happy about it myself.

"Still in bed," I said. "I had a late night."

"Interviewing suspects?"

I thought of the girls at the Casa Marina and the way Doña Marina, who also ran a chain of lingerie stores across Havana, liked it when you asked her girls lots of questions before deciding which one to take up to the third floor. "You could say that."

"Think you're going to find the killer today?"

"Probably not today," I said. "Wrong kind of weather for it."

"You're right," said Sánchez. "It's a day for finding bodies, not the people who killed them. Suddenly we've got corpses all over Havana. There's one in the harbor at the petrochemical works in Regla."

"Am I an undertaker? Why tell me?"

"Because he was driving a car when he went into the water. Not just any car, mind you. This is a big red Cadillac Eldorado. A convertible."

I closed my eyes for a second. Then I said, "Waxey."

"We wouldn't have found him at all but for the fact that a fishing boat dragging its anchor snagged the car's bumper and pulled it up to the surface. I'm just on my way over to Regla now. I was thinking that maybe you'd like to come along."

"Why not? It's been a while since I went fishing."

"Be outside your apartment building in fifteen minutes. We'll drive over there together. On the way maybe I can pick up a few tips from you on how to be a detective."

"It wouldn't be the first time I've done that."

"I was joking," he said stiffly.

"Then you're off to a great start, Captain. You'll need a sense of humor if you're going to be a good detective. That's my first tip."

Twenty minutes later we were driving south, east, and then north around the harbor, into Regla. It was a small industrial town that was easily identified from a distance by the plumes of smoke emanating from the petrochemical plant, although historically it was better known as a center of Santería and as the place where Havana's *corridas* had been fought until Spain lost control of the island.

Sánchez drove the large black police sedan like a fighting bull, charging red lights, braking at the last moment, or turning suddenly and without warning to the left or the right. By the time we skidded to a halt at the end of a long pier, I was ready to stick a sword in his muscular neck.

A small group of policemen and dockworkers had gathered to view the arrival of a barge and the drowned car it had taken from the fishing boat's anchor and then hoisted on top of a large heap of coal. The car itself looked like a fantastic variety of sport fish, a red marlin—if there was such a thing—or a gigantic species of crustacean.

I followed Sánchez down a series of stone steps made slippery from the recent high tide, and as one of the men on the barge grabbed hold of a mooring ring, we jumped onto the moving deck.

The barge captain came forward and spoke to Sánchez, but I didn't understand his very broad Cuban accent, which was not uncommon whenever I moved outside Havana. He was a bad-tempered sort with an expensive-looking cigar, which was the cleanest and most respectable thing about him. The rest of the crew stood around chewing gum and awaiting an order. Finally one came, and a crewman jumped down onto the coal mountain and drew a tarpaulin over it so that Sánchez and I might climb up to the car without becoming as dirty as he was. Sánchez and I clambered down onto the tarpaulin and picked our way up the shifting slope of coal to look over the car. The white hood—which was up—was dirty but largely intact. The front bumper where the fishing boat had hooked it was badly out of shape. The interior was more like an aquarium. But somehow the red Cadillac still managed to look like the handsomest car in Havana.

The crewman, still mindful of Sánchez's well-pressed uniform, had gone ahead of us to open the driver door on the captain's say-so. When the word came and the door opened, water flooded out of the car, soaking the crewman's legs and amusing his chattering colleagues.

The driver of the car slowly leaned out like a man falling asleep in the bath. For a moment I thought the steering wheel would check his exit, but the barge wallowed in the choppy, undulating sea, then came up again, tipping the dead man onto the tarpaulin like a dirty dishcloth. It was Waxey, all right, and while he looked like a drowned man, it wasn't the sea that had killed him. Nor was it loud music, although his ears, or what was left of them, were encrusted with what resembled dark red coral.

"Pity," said Sánchez.

"I didn't really know him," I said.

"The car, I mean," said Sánchez. "The Cadillac Eldorado is just about my favorite car in the world." He shook his head in admiration. "Beautiful. I like the red. Red's nice. But me, I think I'd have had a black one, with whitewall tires and a white hood. Black has much more class, I think."

"Red seems to be the color of the moment," I said.

"You mean his ears?"

"I wasn't talking about his manicure."

"A bullet in each ear, it looks like. That's a message, right?"

"Like it was Cable and Wireless, Captain."

"He heard something he wasn't supposed to hear."

"Flip the coin again. He didn't hear something he was supposed to hear."

"You mean like someone shooting his employer seven times in the adjoining room?"

I nodded.

"Think he was involved in the shooting?" he asked.

"Go ahead and ask him."

"I guess we'll never know for sure." Sánchez took off his peaked cap and scratched his head. "Too bad," he said.

"The car again?"

"That I couldn't have interviewed him first."

17

JEWS HAD BEEN ARRIVING IN CUBA since the time of Columbus. Many who had been forbidden entry to the United States of America more recently than that had been given sanctuary by the Cubans, who, with reference to the Jews' most common country of origin, called them *polacos*. Judging from the number of graves in the Jewish cemetery in Guanabacoa, there were a lot more *polacos* in Cuba than might have been thought. The cemetery was on the road to Santa Fé, behind an impressive gated entrance. It wasn't exactly the Mount of Olives, but the graves, all white marble, were set on a pleasant hill overlooking a mango plantation. There was even a small monument to the Jewish victims of the Second World War in which, it was said, several bars of soap had been buried as a symbolic reminder of their supposed fate.

I might have told anyone who was interested that while it was now widely believed that Nazi scientists had made soap from the corpses of murdered Jews, this had never actually happened. The practice of calling Jews "soap" had simply been a very unpleasant joke among members of the SS, and merely another way of dehumanizing—and sometimes threatening—their most numerous victims. Since human hair from concentration camp inmates had commonly been used on an industrial scale, describing Jews as "felt"—felt for clothes, roofing materials, carpeting, and in the German car industry—might have been a more accurate epithet.

But this wasn't what people arriving for Max Reles's funeral wanted to hear about.

Myself, I was little surprised when I was offered a yarmulke outside the gate of Guanabacoa. Not that I didn't expect to cover my head at a Jewish funeral. I was already wearing a hat. What surprised me about being offered a yarmulke was the person handing them out. This was Szymon Woytak, the cadaverous Pole who owned the Nazi memorabilia store on Manrique. He was wearing a yarmulke himself, and I took this and his presence at the funeral to be a strong clue that he was also a Jew.

"Who's minding the store?" I asked him.

He shrugged. "I always close the shop for a couple of hours when I'm helping out my brother. He's the rabbi reading kaddish for your friend Max Reles."

"And who are you? The program seller?"

"I'm the cantor. I sing the Psalms and whatever else the deceased's family requests."

"How about the Horst Wessel song?"

Woytak smiled patiently and handed the person behind me a yarmulke. "Look," he said, "everyone has to make a living, right?"

There was no family. Not unless you counted Havana's Jewish mob. The chief mourners seemed to be the Lansky brothers; Meyer's wife, Teddy; Moe Dalitz; Norman Rothman; Eddie Levinson; Morris Kleinman; and Sam Tucker. But there were plenty of Gentiles other than myself present: Santo Trafficante, Vincent Alo, Tom McGinty, and the Cellini brothers, to name just a few. What was interesting to me—and might have been of interest to the racial theorists of the Third Reich, such as Alfred Rosenberg—was how Jewish everyone looked when he was wearing a yarmulke.

Also present were several government officials and policemen, including Captain Sánchez. Batista did not attend the funeral of his former partner for fear of being assassinated. Or so Sánchez told me afterward.

Noreen and Dinah didn't come, either. Not that I had expected them to come. Noreen didn't come, for the simple reason that she had feared and detested Max Reles in equal measure. Dinah didn't come, because she had already returned to the United States. Since this was exactly what Noreen had always wanted her daughter to do, I imagined she was now feeling too happy to come to a funeral. For all I knew, she had gone to the beach with López again. Which wasn't any of my business. Or so I kept telling myself.

As the pallbearers carried the casket, haltingly, to the graveside, Captain Sánchez appeared at my elbow. We still weren't friends, but I was beginning to like him.

"What's the German opera where the murderer gets fingered by the victim?" he asked.

"*Götterdämmerung,*" I said. "*The Twilight of the Gods.*"

"Maybe we'll get lucky. Maybe Reles will point him out to us."

"I wonder how that would play out in court."

"This is Cuba, my friend," said Sánchez. "In this country, people still believe in Baron Samedi." He lowered his voice. "And talking of the voodoo master of death, we have our own creature of the invisible world here with us today. He who escorts souls from the land of the living to the graveyard. Not to mention two of his most sinister avatars. The man in the beige uniform who looks like a younger General Franco? That's Colonel Antonio Blanco Rico, head of the Cuban military intelligence service. Take my word for it, *señor*, that man has made more souls disappear in Cuba than any voodoo spirit. The man to his left is Colonel Mariano Faget, of the militia. During the war Faget was in charge of a counterespionage unit that successfully targeted several Nazi agents who were reporting on the movements of Cuban and American to German submarines."

"What happened to them?"

"They were shot by firing squad."

"Interesting. And the third man?"

"That's Faget's CIA liaison officer, Lieutenant José Castaño Quevedo. A very nasty piece of work."

"And why are they here, exactly?"

"To pay their respects. It's certain that from time to time the president would ask your friend Max to pay off these men by making sure they won in his casino. Actually, most of the time they don't even have to take the trouble to gamble. They just go into the *salon privé* at the Saratoga, or for that matter any of the other casinos, collect several handfuls of chips, and cash them in. Of course, Señor Reles knew exactly how to look after men such as these. And it is certain they will have taken his death very personally. So they too are very interested in the progress of your inquiry."

"They are?"

"For sure. You may not know it, but it's not just Meyer Lansky you're working for, it's them, too."

"That's a comforting thought."

"You should be especially careful of Lieutenant Quevedo. He is very ambitious, and that's a bad thing to be if you're a policeman here in Cuba."

"Aren't you ambitious, Captain Sánchez?"

"I intend to be. But not right now. I will be ambitious after the election in October. Until I see who wins, I will be very happy to achieve very little in my career. Incidentally, the lieutenant has asked me to spy on you."

"That seems rather presumptuous, you being a captain."

"In Cuba, one's rank is not an indicator of one's importance. For example, the head of the National Police is General Canizares, but everyone knows that the power lies with Blanco Rico and with Colonel Piedra, the head of our Bureau of Investigation. Similarly, before he was president, Batista was the most powerful man in Cuba. Now that he is, he isn't, if you follow me. These days, all power lies with the army and the police. Which is why Batista always thinks he is a target for assassination. In a sense, that is his job. To draw attention away from others. Sometimes it is best to appear to be what you are not. Wouldn't you agree?"

"Captain. That has been the story of my life."

18

A COUPLE OF DAYS LATER I was at the Tropicana watching the show while I waited to speak to the Cellini brothers. Bare flesh was the order of the day for the performers, and lots of it. They tried to make it seem more glamorous by wearing some thoughtfully placed sequins and triangles, but the result was much the same: it was bacon with cheese on top, however you cooked it. Most of the chorus boys looked as if they'd have been a lot happier wearing a cocktail dress. Most of the chorus girls didn't look happy at all. All of them smiled, but the smiles on their rigid little faces had been molded on, back at the doll factory. Meanwhile they danced with all the joie de vivre of kids who knew that one fluffed pirouette or ill-timed lift would earn them a one-way ticket back to Matanzas or whatever crummy peasant town they came from.

On Truffin Avenue in the Havana suburb of Marianao, the Tropicana occupied the lushly landscaped gardens of a mansion—now demolished—formerly owned by the U.S. ambassador to Cuba. The mansion had been replaced by a building of striking modernity with five reinforced concrete semicircular vaults connecting a series of glass ceilings, which created the illusion of a semi-feral show staged under the stars and the trees. Next to this amphitheater, which seemed like something out of a pornographic science-fiction movie, was a smaller glass ceiling that housed a casino. And here there was even a *salon privé* with an armor-plated door, behind which government officials could gamble without fear of assassination.

I wasn't interested in any of that any more than I was interested in the show, or listening to the band. Mostly I just watched the ash on the end of my cigar or the faces of the suckers at the other tables: women with bare shoulders and too much makeup, and men with Vaselined hair, clip-on ties, and Cricketeer suits. A couple of times the showgirls came parading around the tables just so that you could get a closer look at their costumes and wonder how something so small could keep a girl decent. My eyes were still brimful of wonder when, to my surprise, I saw Noreen Eisner coming through the club in my direction. And, sidestepping a girl who was all breasts and feathers, she sat down opposite me.

Noreen was probably the one woman at the Tropicana who wasn't displaying either some cleavage or the whole toy shop. She wore a two-piece lavender-colored suit with tailored pockets, high shoes, and a couple of strings of pearls. The band was too loud for her to say anything or for me to hear it, and until the number finished, we just sat looking at each other dumbly and tapping our fingers impatiently on the table. It gave me plenty of time to wonder what was so urgent that she had driven all the way from Finca Vigía. I certainly didn't think her being there was a coincidence. I supposed she had gone to my apartment first, and Yara had told her where I was. Maybe Yara would have let off some steam about how I hadn't allowed her to come with me to the Tropicana, which meant that Noreen's arrival wouldn't have helped persuade her that my visit to the nightclub was for the strictly business reasons I had claimed. There probably would be some kind of scene when I got home.

I hoped Noreen was there to tell me what I wanted to hear. Certainly she looked grave enough. And sober, too. Which made a change. She was carrying a navy blue beaded evening bag with a petit-point floral chintz decoration. Opening the silver metal clasp, she took out a pack of Old Gold and lit one with a pearl gray lacquer cigarette lighter with little rhinestones on it, the only thing about her that was at all in keeping with the Tropicana.

Like most bands in Havana, this one took a while longer than was tolerable. I didn't own a gun in Cuba, but if I had, I might have enjoyed using a set of maracas or a conga drum for a little target practice— really, any Latin American instrument, as long as it was actually in use at the time. Finally I could stand it no longer. I stood up and, taking Noreen's hand, led her out.

In the foyer, she said, "This is where you spend your spare time, is it?" Out of habit she spoke German to me. "So much for Montaigne."

"As a matter of fact, he already wrote an essay about this place and the custom of wearing clothes. Or not wearing them. If we were born with the need for wearing petticoats and trousers, nature, he says, would no doubt have equipped us with a thicker skin to withstand the rigors of the seasons. On the whole, I think he's pretty good. Gets it right most of the time. About the only thing that man doesn't explain is why you came all the way over here to see me. I've got my own ideas about that."

"Let's take a walk in the garden," she said, quietly.

We went outside. The Tropicana's garden was a jungle paradise of royal palms and towering mamoncillo trees. According to Caribbean wisdom, girls learn the art of kissing by eating the sweet flesh of the mamoncillo fruit. Somehow I had the feeling that kissing me was the last thing on Noreen's mind.

In the center of the sweeping driveway was a large marble fountain that had once graced the entrance of the National Hotel. The fountain was a round basin surrounded by eight life-sized naked nymphs. It was rumored that the Tropicana's owners had paid thirty thousand pesos for the fountain, but it reminded me of one of those Berlin culture schools once run by Adolf Koch at Lake Motzen for overweight German matrons who liked to throw medicine balls at each other in the nude. And, in spite of what Montaigne has to say about the matter, it made me glad that mankind had invented the needle and thread.

"So," I said, "what did you want to tell me?"

"This isn't easy for me to say."

"You're a writer. You'll think of something."

She puffed silently on her cigarette, considered this idea for a moment, and then shrugged, as if she'd thought of a way, after all. Her voice was soft. In the moonlight she looked as lovely as ever. Seeing her, I was filled with a dull ache of longing, as if the scent of the mamoncillo's greenish-white flowers contained some sort of magical juice that made fools like me fall in love with queens like her.

"Dinah's gone back to the States," she said, still not quite coming to the point. "But you knew about that, didn't you?"

I nodded. "Is this about Dinah?"

"I'm worried about her, Bernie."

I shook my head. "She's left the island. She's going to Brown. I don't see what you could possibly have to worry about. I mean, isn't that what you wanted?"

"Oh, sure. No, it's the way she suddenly changed her mind. About everything."

"Max Reles was murdered. I think that might have had something to do with her decision."

"Those gangsters he associated with. You know some of them, don't you?"

"Yes."

"Do they have any idea who killed Max yet?"

"None at all."

"Good." She threw away her cigarette and quickly lit another. "You'll probably think me crazy. But you see, it crossed my mind that, perhaps, Dinah might have had something to do with his murder."

"What makes you say that?"

"For one thing, my gun—the one Ernest gave me—it's gone. It was a Russian revolver. I had it lying around the house somewhere, and now I can't find it. Fredo—Alfredo López? My lawyer friend has a friend in the police who told him that Reles had been shot with a Russian revolver. It sort of made me wonder. If Dinah could have done it."

I was shaking my head. I hardly liked to tell her that Dinah had suspected that her own mother might be the murderer.

"There's all that, and there's the fact that she seemed to get over it so quickly. Like she wasn't in love with him at all. I mean, didn't it make any of those Mafia guys suspicious that she wasn't at the funeral? Like she didn't care?"

"I think people thought she was probably too upset to go."

"That's my point, Bernie. She wasn't. And this is why I'm worried. If the Mafia comes around to the opinion that she did have something to do with Max's murder, then maybe they'll do something about it. Maybe they'll send someone after her."

"I don't think it works like that, Noreen. Right now all they're really concerned about is the possibility that Max Reles was killed by one of their own. You see, if it turns out that one of the other hotel and casino owners was behind the killing, then there could be a gang war. That would be very bad for business. Which is the last thing they want. Besides, it's me they've asked to help find out who killed Max."

"The mob has asked you to investigate Max's murder?"

"In my capacity as a former homicide detective."

Noreen shook her head. "Why you?"

"I guess they think I can be objective, independent. More objective than the Cuban militia. Dinah's nineteen years old, Noreen. She strikes me as a lot of things. As a selfish little bitch, for one. But she's not a murderer. Besides, it takes a certain kind of person to climb over a wall eight floors up and shoot a man seven times in cold blood. Wouldn't you say?"

Noreen nodded and stared off into the distance. She dropped her second cigarette on the ground, half smoked, and then lit a third. Something was still troubling her.

"So, you can rest assured I'm not about to lay the blame at Dinah's door."

"Thanks. I appreciate it. She is a bitch, you're right. But she's mine and I'd do absolutely anything to keep her safe."

"I know that." I flicked my cigar at the fountain. It hit one of the nymphs on her bare behind and fell into the water. "Is that really what you wanted to tell me?"

"Yes," she said. She thought for a moment. "But it wasn't everything, you're right, damn you." She bit her knuckle. "I don't know why

I ever try to deceive you. There are times when I think you know me better than I know myself."

"It's always a possibility."

She threw the third cigarette away, opened her bag, took out a little matching handkerchief, and blew her nose with it. "The other day," she said. "When you were at the house. And you saw Fredo and me coming back from the beach at Playa Mayor. I suppose you must have guessed that he and I have been seeing each other. That we've become, well, intimate."

"I try not to do too much guessing these days. Especially concerning things I know absolutely nothing about."

"Fredo likes you, Bernie. He was very grateful to you. The night of the pamphlets."

"Oh, I know. He told me himself."

"You saved his life. I didn't really appreciate it at the time. Or thank you properly. What you did was very courageous." She closed her eyes for a moment. "I didn't come to see you about Dinah. Oh, perhaps I just wanted to hear you reassure me that she couldn't have done it, but I'd have known. A mother knows that kind of thing. She couldn't have hid that from me."

"So what did you come to see me about?"

"It's Fredo. He's been arrested by the SIM—the secret police—and accused of helping the former minister of education in the Prío government, Aureliano Sánchez Arango, to enter the country illegally."

"And did he?"

"No, of course not. When he was arrested, however, he was with someone who is in the AAA. That's the Association of Friends of Aureliano. It's one of the leading opposition groups in Cuba. But Fredo's loyalty is to Castro and the rebels on the Isle of Pines."

"Well, I'm sure when he explains that, they'll be happy to send him home."

Noreen didn't share the joke. "This isn't funny," she said. "They could still torture him in the hope that he'll tell them where Aureliano is hiding. That would be doubly unfortunate, because of course he doesn't know anything."

"I agree. But I really don't see what I can do."

"You saved his life once, Bernie. Maybe you can do it again."

"So López can have you instead of me?"

"Is that what you want, Bernie?"

"What do you think?" I shrugged. "Why not? Under the circumstances that's not so very strange. Or have you forgotten?"

"Bernie, it was twenty years ago. I'm not the same woman I used to be. Surely you can see that."

"Life will do that to you sometimes."

"Can you do *anything* for him?"

"What makes you think that's even a possibility?"

"Because you know Captain Sánchez. People say that you and he are friends."

"What people?" I shook my head, exasperated. "Look, even if he was my friend—and I am not at all sure about that—Sánchez is militia. And you said yourself that López has been arrested by the SIM. That means it's nothing to do with the militia."

"The man who arrested Fredo was at the funeral of Max Reles," said Noreen. "Lieutenant Quevedo. Perhaps, if you asked him, Captain Sánchez would speak to Lieutenant Quevedo. He could intercede."

"And say what?"

"I don't know. But you might think of something."

"Noreen, it's a hopeless case."

"Aren't they the ones you used to be good at?"

I shook my head and turned away.

"You remember that letter I wrote to you, when I left Berlin?"

"Not really. It was a very long time ago, like you said."

"Yes, you do. I called you my knight of heaven."

"That's the plot of *Tannhäuser*, Noreen. Not me."

"I asked you always to seek the truth and to go to the aid of the people who needed your help. Because it's the right thing to do, and in spite of the fact that it's dangerous. I'm asking that now."

"You've no right to ask it. Can't be done. I've changed too, in case you hadn't noticed."

"I don't think so."

"More than you could ever know. Knight of heaven, you say?" I laughed. "More like knight of hell. During the war, I got drafted into the SS, because I was a policeman. Did I tell you that? My armor's very dirty, Noreen. You don't know how dirty."

"You did what you had to do, I expect. But inside, I think you're probably the same man you always were."

"Tell me this: Why should I look out for López? I've got enough on my plate. I can't help him, and that's the truth, so why should I even bother to try?"

"Because that's what life is about." Noreen took my hand and searched my face—for what, I don't know. "That's what life is about, isn't it? Looking for the truth. Going to the aid of the people we don't think we can help, but trying all the same."

I felt myself flush with anger.

"You've got me confused with some kind of saint, Noreen. The kind who's okay with being martyred as long as his halo's straight in the photograph. If I'm going to throw myself to the lions, I want it to mean a lot more than just being remembered in some milkmaid's prayers on a Sunday morning. I never was a man for a useless gesture. That's how I stayed alive this long, angel. Only there's more to it than that. You talk about the truth like it means something. But when you throw the truth in my face, it's just a couple of handfuls of sand. It's not the truth at all. Not the truth I want to hear, anyway. Not from you. So let's not fool ourselves, eh? I won't play the sucker for you, Noreen. Not until you're prepared to stop treating me like one."

Noreen did an impersonation of a tropical fish that was all popping eyes and open mouth, and then shook her head. "I'm sure I don't have the least idea of what you're talking about." Then she laughed an off-key laugh in my face and, before I could say another word, turned on her heel and walked quickly toward the parking lot.

I went back inside the Tropicana.

The Cellinis didn't give me much. Giving wasn't exactly their strong suit. Nor was answering questions. Old habits die hard, I suppose. They kept on telling me how sorry they were about the death of a great guy like Max and how keen they were to cooperate with Lansky's investigation and, at the same time, not having the first clue about anything I asked them. If they had been asked Capone's Christian name, they would probably have shrugged and said they didn't know it. Probably even denied he had one.

It was late when I got home, and Captain Sánchez was waiting for me. He'd helped himself to a drink and a cigar and was reading a book in my favorite armchair.

"It seems I'm popular with all kinds of people these days," I said. "People just drop in, like this is some kind of club."

"Don't be like that," said Sánchez. "We're friends, you and I. Besides, the lady let me in. Yara, isn't it?"

I glanced around the apartment for her, but it was plain that she'd already gone.

He shrugged apologetically. "I think I scared her off."

"I expect you're used to that, Captain."

"I should be at home myself, but you know what they say. Crime doesn't keep office hours."

"Is that what they say?"

"Another body has been found. A man called Irving Goldstein. At an apartment in Vedado."

"I never heard of him."

"He was an employee of the Hotel Saratoga. A pit boss in the casino."

"I see."

"I was hoping you might accompany me to the apartment. You being a famous detective. Not to mention his employer. In a manner of speaking."

"Sure. Why not? I was only planning to go to bed and sleep for twelve hours."

"Excellent."

"Give me a minute to change, will you?"

"I will wait for you downstairs, *señor*."

19

THE NEXT MORNING I was awakened by the telephone.

It was Robert Freeman. He'd telephoned to offer me a six-month contract to open up the West German Havana cigar market for J. Frankau.

"However, I don't think that Hamburg's the right place to base yourself, Carlos," he told me. "It's my opinion that Bonn would be better. There's the fact that it's the West German capital, of course. Both houses of parliament are situated there, not to mention all the government institutions and foreign embassies. Which is the kind of well-heeled market we're looking for, after all. Then there's the fact that it's in the British zone of occupation. We're a British company, so that should make things easier for us, too. Plus, Bonn is only twenty miles from Cologne, one of the largest cities in Germany."

All I knew about Bonn was that it was the birthplace of Beethoven, and before the war that it had been the home of Konrad Adenauer, the first chancellor of the Federal Republic of Germany. When Berlin ceased being the capital of anything except the cold war, and West Germany needed a new capital, Adenauer had, very conveniently for himself, chosen the quiet little town where he had lived quietly throughout the years of the Third Reich. As it happened, I'd been to Bonn. Just once. By mistake. But before 1949 few people had ever heard of Bonn, let alone known where it was, and even today it was jokingly known as "the federal village." Bonn was small, Bonn was insignificant, and Bonn was above all things a backwater, and I wondered why I hadn't considered living there before. For a man like me, intent on living a life of complete anonymity, it seemed perfect.

Quickly I told Freeman that Bonn was fine by me and that I would begin to make travel arrangements to go there as soon as possible. And Freeman told me he would go about drawing up my all-important business credentials.

I was going home. After almost five years of exile, I was going back to Germany. With money in my pocket. I could hardly believe my luck.

There was that, and the events of the previous evening, at an apartment in Vedado.

As soon as I was washed and dressed, I drove to the National and went up to that big, spacious suite on the executive floor to inform the Lansky brothers that I had "solved" the Reles case. Not that you could ever have really called it a case. Public-relations exercise might have been a more accurate way of describing my investigation, provided your idea of a public was all of the mobbed-up casinos and hotels in Havana.

"You mean you've got a name?" Meyer's voice had the deep-fried, rich tone of an Indian chief in a western. Jeff Chandler, maybe. The little man had the same sort of inscrutable face, too. Certainly the nose was exactly the same.

As before, we sat on the balcony with the same ocean view, except that now I could see the ocean as well as hear and smell it. I was going to miss the grating roar of that ocean.

Meyer wore a pair of gray gabardine trousers, a matching cardigan, a plain white sports shirt, and thick-framed sunglasses that made him look more like an accountant than a gangster. Jake was similarly informal. He wore a loose terry-cloth shirt and a bookmaker's little straw Stetson with a hatband that was as tight and narrow as his mouth. And hovering in the background was the tall, angular figure of Vincent Alo, whom I now knew better as Jimmy Blue Eyes. Alo wore gray flannels, a white mohair cardigan with a wide collar, and a patterned silk cravat. The cardigan was bulky, but not enough to hide the spare rib he was wearing under his arm. He looked like anyone's idea of an Italian playboy as long as the play was a Roman revenge tragedy written by Seneca for the amusement of the Emperor Nero.

We were drinking coffee from little cups, Italian style, pinkies out.

"I've got a name," I told them.

"Let's hear it."

"Irving Goldstein."

"The guy who killed himself?"

Goldstein had been a pit boss at the Saratoga, occupying a high chair over the craps table. Originally from Miami, he had trained as a croupier in several illegal gambling houses in Tampa before his arrival in Havana in April 1953. This followed the deportation from Cuba of thirteen American-born card dealers who were employees of the Saratoga, the Sans Souci, the Montmartre, and Tropicana casinos.

"With the help of Captain Sánchez I searched his apartment in Vedado last night. And we found this."

I handed Lansky a technical drawing and let him stare at it awhile.

"Goldstein had become involved with a man who was a female impersonator at the Palette Club. It's my information that before he died, Max had found out about it and, not at all comfortable with Goldstein's homosexuality, he subsequently told him to look for a job at another casino. The Saratoga casino manager, Núñez, confirmed that the two men argued about something not long before Max died. It's my belief that this is what they argued about. And that Goldstein murdered Max in revenge for his dismissal. So he probably had the motive. He almost certainly had the opportunity: Núñez told me that Goldstein went on his break at around two a.m. on the night of the murder. And that he was away from the craps tables for about thirty minutes."

"And your proof is . . . this?" Lansky brandished the sheet of paper I had given him. "I'm looking at it and I still don't know what the hell it is. Jake?" Lansky handed the paper to his brother, who stared at it uncomprehendingly, as if it were the blueprint of a new missile-guidance system.

"That's a very accurate and precise drawing for a Bramit silencer," I said. "A custom-made sound suppressor for the Nagant revolver. Like I said before, because of the Nagant's closed firing system—"

"What does that mean?" asked Jake. "'Closed firing system.' All I know about guns is how to shoot them. And even then they make me nervous."

"Especially, then," said Meyer. He shook his head. "I don't like guns."

"What does it mean? Just this. The Nagant has a mechanism which, as the hammer is cocked, first turns the cylinder and then moves it forward, closing the gap between the cylinder and the barrel that exists with every other model of revolver. With this gap sealed, the velocity is increased; more important, it makes the Nagant the only weapon you can effectively silence. During the war, Goldstein was in the army and afterward he was stationed in Germany. I imagine he must have swapped revolvers with a Red Army soldier. A lot of men did."

"And you think this *faygele* made the silencer himself? Is that what you're saying?"

"He was a homosexual, Mr. Lansky," I said. "That doesn't mean he couldn't handle precision metalworking tools."

"Got that right," muttered Alo.

I shook my head. "The drawing was hidden in his bureau. And to be honest, I don't think I'm going to find any better proof than that."

Meyer Lansky nodded. He fetched a pack of Parliaments off the coffee table and lit one with a silver table lighter. "What do you think, Jake?"

Jake pulled a face. "Bernie's right. Proof is always hard to come by in these situations, but that drawing sure looks like the next best thing. As you yourself know only too well, Meyer, the Feds have made a case with a lot less. Besides, if this guy Goldstein did whack Max, then it's one of ours and there's no debt to settle with anyone else. He's a Jew. From the Saratoga. It keeps everything neat and tidy, just the way we wanted. Frankly, I don't see how we could have ended up with a better result. Business can proceed without any interruptions."

"Nothing is more important," said Meyer Lansky.

"How'd he kill himself, anyway?" asked Vincent Alo.

"He opened his veins in a hot tub," I said. "Roman style."

"I guess that makes a change from doggy style," said Alo.

Meyer Lansky winced. It was plain he didn't much like that kind of joke. "Yes, but why?" he asked. "Why kill himself? With all due respect to you, Bernie, he'd got away with the murder, hadn't he? More or less. So why do himself in? His secret was safe."

I shrugged. "I spoke to some people at the Palette Club. The whole point of the club is that some of the girls are real and some are cut-jobs. The club's shtick is that you can't tell the difference. It seems that in the beginning Irving Goldstein might have had the same problem. That the girl he thought he fell in love with was in fact a man. When he discovered the truth, he tried to live with it, which is when Max found out about it. Some of the people at the Palette think that the shame finally got to him. I think that maybe he planned to kill himself, but before he did, he decided to get even with Max."

"Who knows what's in the mind of a guy like that?" said Alo. "Confused, or what?"

Meyer Lansky nodded. "All right. I'll buy it. You've done a good job, Gunther. A nice quick result with no one offended. I couldn't have ordered it better if I was in La Zaragozana."

This was the name of a famous restaurant in Old Havana.

"Jimmy? Get this man his money. He earned it."

Vincent Alo said, "Sure, Meyer," and went out of the suite.

"You know, Gunther," said Lansky, "next year, things are really going to take off for us here in Havana. We got this sweet new law coming. The Hotel Law. All new hotels are going to be granted tax-exempt status, which means there's going to be more money to be made on this island than anyone ever dreamed of. I'm planning a new casino hotel myself, which is going to be the biggest in the world, outside of Las Vegas. The Riviera. And I could use a man like you in a place like that. Until then, I'd like you to come over to the Montmartre and work for me there. You can do the same thing you were going to do at the Saratoga."

"I'll certainly give it some thought, Mr. Lansky."

"Vincent's going to run the Saratoga now."

Vincent Alo had returned to the balcony. He was holding out a gambler's chip bag for high rollers. He smiled, but his blue eyes remained without emotion. It was easy to see how he'd earned his nickname, Jimmy Blue Eyes. His eyes were as blue as the sea on the other side of the Malecón, and just as cold.

"That doesn't look like twenty thousand dollars," I said.

"Looks can be deceptive," said Alo. He loosened the neck of the drawstring bag and took out a purple thousand-dollar plaque. "There are nineteen more like this one in the bag. You take this to the cash desk at the Montmartre, and they'll give you your money. Simple as that, my kraut friend."

The neoclassical Montmartre on P Street and Twenty-third was just a short walk from the National. Formerly a dog track, it occupied a whole block and was the only casino in Havana open twenty-four hours a day. It wasn't even lunchtime, and the Montmartre was already doing a brisk business. At that early hour, most of the gamblers were Chinese. But they usually are, at any hour of the day. And they couldn't have looked less interested in the evening's big *Midnight in Paris* stage show being announced on the casino's public-address system.

For me, on the other hand, Europe already seemed a little nearer and more attractive as I walked away from the cash window with forty pictures of President William McKinley. And the only reason I hadn't turned Lansky's offer of a full-time job down flat was that I hardly wanted to tell him I was leaving the country. That might have made him suspicious. Instead I was hoping to deposit my money with the rest of what I'd saved in the Royal Bank of Canada and then, armed with my new credentials, leave Cuba as soon as possible.

I felt a spring in my step as I went back through the gates of the National Hotel to get the car I was planning to give Yara as my leaving-her present. I hadn't felt quite so optimistic about my prospects since being reunited with my late wife Kirsten in Vienna, during September of 1947. So optimistic that I felt I might even go see Captain Sánchez and discover if there wasn't something I could do for Noreen Eisner and Alfredo López after all.

At the end of the day, optimism is nothing more than a naive and ill-informed hope.

20

THE CAPITOLIO WAS BUILT in the style of the United States Capitol in Washington, D.C., by the dictator Machado, but it was too big for an island the size of Cuba. It would have been too big for an island the size of Australia. Inside the rotunda was a seventeen-meter-high statue of Jupiter, which looked a lot like an Academy Award, and certainly most of the tourists who visited the Capitolio seemed to think it was a good picture. Now that I was planning to leave Cuba I was thinking I might have to take a few photographs of my own. So that I could remind myself of what I was missing when I was living in Bonn and going to bed at nine o'clock at night. What else is there to do in Bonn at nine o'clock at night? If Beethoven had lived in Havana—especially if he'd lived around the corner from the Casa Marina—it's almost certain he'd have been lucky to write just one string quartet, let alone sixteen of them. But you could live all your life in Bonn and not even notice that you were deaf.

The police station on Zulueta was a few minutes' walk from the Capitolio, but I didn't mind the walk. Only a few months before, outside the police station in Vedado, a Havana University professor had been killed by a car bomb when rebels had mistaken his 1952 black Hudson for an identical model driven by the deputy head of the Cuban Bureau of Investigations. Ever since, I had been careful never to leave my Chevrolet Styleline outside a police station.

The station itself was an old colonial building with a peeling white stucco facade and louvered green shutters on the windows. A Cuban flag hung limply over the square portico like a brightly decorated beach towel that had fallen from one of the upper-floor windows. On the outside, the drains didn't smell so good. On the inside, you barely noticed it as long as you didn't breathe in.

Sánchez was on the second floor, in an office overlooking a small park. There was a flag on a pole in the corner, and on the wall, a picture of Batista facing a cabinet full of rifles in case the parade-ground patriotism of the flag and the picture didn't pay off. There was a small, cheap wooden desk and a lot of space around it if you had a tapeworm. The walls and ceiling were dust-bowl beige, and the brown linoleum on the warped floor resembled the shell of a dead tortoise. An expensive rosewood humidor that belonged on a presidential sideboard sat on the desk like a Fabergé egg in a plastic picnic set.

"You know, it was quite a stroke of luck, me finding that drawing," said Sánchez.

"There's an element of luck in most police work."

"Not to mention your murderer being dead already."

"Any objections?"

"How could there be? You solve the case and at the same time you take the loose ends and make a bow. Now, that's what I call detective work. Yes indeed, I can see why Lansky thought you were the man for the case. A real Nero Wolfe."

"You say all that like you think I chalked him up for it, like a tailor."

"Now you're being cruel. I've never been to a tailor in my life. Not on my salary. I own a nice linen guayabera, and that's about it. For anything more formal I usually wear my best uniform."

"Is that the one without the bloodstains?"

"Now you're confusing me with Lieutenant Quevedo."

"I'm glad you mentioned him, Captain."

Sánchez shook his head. "Such a thing is not possible. No one with ears is ever glad to hear the name of Lieutenant Quevedo."

"Where might I find him?"

"You do not find Lieutenant Quevedo. Not if you had any sense. He finds you."

"Surely he can't be that elusive. I saw him at the funeral, remember?"

"It's his natural habitat."

"A tall man. Buzz-cut hair, with a sort of clean-cut face, for a Cuban. What I mean is, there was something vaguely American about his face."

"It's as well we only see the faces of men and not their hearts, don't you think?"

"Anyway, you said that I was working not just for Lansky, but also for Quevedo. And so—"

"Did I say that? Perhaps. How shall we describe someone like Meyer Lansky? The man is as slippery as chopped pineapple. But Quevedo is something else. We have a saying here in the militia: 'God made us, and we wonder at it, but more especially in the case of Lieutenant Quevedo.' Mentioning him to you as I did at the funeral, I intended only to make you aware of him as I would perhaps draw your attention to a venomous snake. So that you could avoid him."

"Your warning is noted."

"I'm relieved to hear it."

"But I'd still like to speak to him."

"About what, I wonder." He shrugged and, ignoring the expensive humidor, lit a cigarette.

"That's my business."

"In point of fact, no, it's not." Sánchez smiled. "Certainly it is the business of Señor López. Perhaps in the circumstances it is also the business of Señora Eisner. But your business, Señor Hausner? No, I don't think so."

"Now it's you who looks like chopped pineapple, Captain."

"Perhaps that's only to be expected. You see, I graduated from law school in September 1950. Two of my contemporaries at university were Fidel Castro Ruz and Alfredo López. Unlike Fidel, Alfredo and I were politically illiterate. In those days the university was closely tied to the government of Grau San Martín, and I was convinced that I might help to effect democratic change in our police force by becoming a policeman myself. Of course, Fidel thought differently. But after Batista's coup in March 1952, I decided I was probably wasting my time and resolved to be less strenuous in my defense of the regime and its institutions. I would try to be a good policeman only and not an instrument of dictatorship. Does that make sense, *señor*?"

"Strangely enough, it does. To me, anyway."

"Of course, this isn't as easy as it might sound."

"I know that, too."

"I have had to make compromises with myself on more than one occasion. I have even thought of leaving the militia. But it was Alfredo who persuaded me that perhaps I might do more good by remaining a policeman."

I nodded.

"It was I," he continued, "who informed Noreen Eisner that Alfredo had been arrested and by whom. She asked me what was to be done, and I told her I could think of nothing. But, as I'm sure you know, she is not a woman who gives up easily, and, aware that you and she were old friends, I suggested that she ask you to help her."

"Me? Why on earth would you say that?"

"The suggestion was not entirely serious. I was exasperated with her, it's true. I must confess I was also exasperated with you. Exasperated and, yes, a little jealous of you, too."

"Jealous? Of me? Why on earth should you be jealous of me?"

Captain Sánchez shifted on his chair and smiled sheepishly.

"A number of reasons," he said. "The way you solved this case. The faith that Meyer Lansky seems to have in your abilities. The nice apartment on Malecón. Your car. Your money. Let's not forget that. Yes, I freely admit it, I was jealous of you. But I am not so very jealous that I would let you do this thing that you are thinking of. Because I must also freely admit that I like you, Hausner. And I couldn't in all conscience allow you to put your head into the lion's mouth." He shook his head. "I told her I was not serious about this suggestion, but evidently she did not believe me and spoke to you herself."

"Maybe I've put my head in a lion's mouth before," I said.

"Maybe. But this isn't the same lion. All lions are different."

"We're friends, right?"

"Yes. I think so. But Fidel used to say you shouldn't trust someone merely because he is a friend. It's good advice. You should remember that."

I nodded. "Oh, sure. And believe me, I know. Looking out for number one is usually what I do best. I'm an expert in survival. But from time to time I get this stupid urge to do a good turn for someone. Someone like your friend Alfredo López. It's been a while since I did anything as selfless as something like that."

"I see. At least I begin to think I do. You think that by helping him you'll be helping her. Is that it?"

"Something like that. Perhaps."

"And what do you think you can tell a man like Quevedo that might persuade him to release López?"

"That's between me and him and what I rather quaintly used to call my conscience."

Sánchez sighed. "I did not take you for a romantic. But that is what you are, I think."

"You forgot the word 'fool,' didn't you? But it's more what the French call 'existential' than that. After all these years I still haven't quite admitted my own insignificance. I still believe what I do makes a difference. Absurd, isn't it?"

"I've known Alfredo López since 1945," said Sánchez. "He's a decent enough fellow. But I fail to see how Noreen Eisner prefers him to a man like you."

"Maybe that's what I want to prove to her."

"Anything is possible, I suppose."

"I don't know. Maybe he is a better man than me."

"No, just a younger one."

21

THE SIM BUILDING in the center of Marianao looked like something out of *Beau Geste*—a white, two-story, comic-book fort wherein you might have discovered a company of dead legionnaires propped up along the blue castellated rooftop. It was a strange building to find in an area otherwise given over to schools and hospitals and comfortable-looking bungalows.

I parked a few streets away and walked along to the entrance, where a dog was lying on the grass shoulder. Dogs sleeping on the streets of Havana were neater and tidier about the way they did this than any dogs I had seen before, as if they were keen not to get in anyone's way. Some were so neat and tidy about how they slept on the street that they looked dead. But you stroked any of them at your peril. Cuba was the very well-deserved home of the expression "Let sleeping dogs lie." It was good advice for everyone and everything. If only I had taken it.

Inside the heavy wooden door, I gave my name to an equally sleepy-looking soldier and, having delivered my request to see Lieutenant Quevedo, I waited in front of another portrait of F.B., the one with him wearing the uniform with the lampshade epaulettes and a cat-that-had-all-the-cream smile. Knowing what I now knew about his share of casino money, I thought he probably had a lot to smile about.

When I had tired of being inspired by the self-satisfied face of the Cuban president, I went to a big window and stared out at a parade ground, where several armored cars were parked. Looking at them, I found it hard to see how Castro and his rebels had ever thought they stood a chance against the Cuban army.

Finally I was greeted by a tall man in a beige uniform, with gleaming leather, buttons, teeth, and sunglasses. He looked dressed up for a portrait of his own.

"Señor Hausner? I'm Lieutenant Quevedo. Would you come this way, please?"

I followed him upstairs, and while we walked, Lieutenant Quevedo talked. He had an easy way about him and seemed different from the picture Captain Sánchez had painted of the man. We came along a corridor that looked as if it could be a *Life* magazine pictorial biography of the little president: F.B. in sergeant's uniform; F.B. with President Grau; F.B. wearing a trench coat and accompanied by a trio of Afro-Cuban bodyguards; F.B. and several of his top generals; F.B. wearing a hilariously outsized officer's cap, making a speech; F.B. sitting in a car with Franklin D. Roosevelt; F.B. gracing the cover of *Time* magazine; F.B. with Harry Truman; and, finally, F.B. with Dwight D. Eisenhower. As if the armored cars weren't enough for the rebels to deal with, there were the Americans, too. Not to mention three American presidents.

"We call this our wall of heroes," Quevedo said, jokingly. "As you can see, we have only the one hero. Some people call him a dictator. But if he is, then he's a very popular one, it seems to me."

I halted momentarily in front of the *Time* magazine cover. I had a copy of the same magazine somewhere in my apartment. There was a critical remark about Batista on my copy that was absent from this one, but I couldn't remember what it was.

"You're wondering where the title went, perhaps," observed Quevedo. "And what it said?"

"Was I?"

"Of course you were." Quevedo smiled benignly. "It said, 'Cuba's Batista: He Got Past Democracy's Sentries.' Which is something of an exaggeration. For example, in Cuba there are no restrictions on freedom of speech or freedom of the press or freedom of religion. The Congress can override any legislation or refuse to pass what he wants passed.

There aren't any generals in his cabinet. Is this really what dictatorship means? Can one really compare our president to a Stalin? Or a Hitler? I don't think so."

I didn't reply. What he said reminded me of something I myself had said at Noreen's dinner party; and yet, in Quevedo's mouth, it sounded somehow less than convincing. He opened the door to an enormous office. There was a big mahogany desk; a radio with a vase on top; another, smaller desk with a typewriter on it; and a television set that was switched on but had the sound turned down. A baseball game was in progress; and on the walls were pictures not of Batista but ballplayers such as Antonio Castaño and Guillermo "Willie" Miranda. There wasn't much on the desk: a pack of Trend, a tape-recording machine, a couple of highball glasses with American flags embossed on their outsides, a magazine with a picture of mambo dance star Ana Gloria Varona on the cover.

Quevedo waved me to a seat in front of the desk and, folding his arms, sat on the edge and looked down at me as if I were some kind of student who had brought him a problem.

"Naturally I know who you are," he said. "And I believe I'm right in thinking that the unfortunate murder of Señor Reles has now been satisfactorily explained."

"Yes, that's right."

"And are you here on Señor Lansky's account, or on your own?"

"My own. I know you're a busy man, Lieutenant, so I'll come straight to the point. You have a prisoner named Alfredo López here. Is that correct?"

"Yes."

"I was hoping I might persuade you to let him go. His friends assure me that he has had nothing to do with Arango."

"And your interest in López is what, exactly?"

"He's a lawyer, as you know. As a lawyer, he did me a good service, that's all. I was hoping to be able to return the favor."

"Very commendable. Even lawyers need representation."

"You were talking about democracy and freedom of speech. I feel much the same way as you, Lieutenant. So I'm just here to help prevent

411

a miscarriage of justice. I'm certainly not a supporter of Dr. Castro and his rebels."

Quevedo nodded. "Castro is a natural criminal. Some of the newspapers compare him to Robin Hood, but I myself don't see it. The man is quite ruthless and dangerous, like all communists. Probably he has been a communist since 1948, when he was still a student. But in his heart he's worse than a communist. He's a communist and a natural autocrat. He's a Stalinist."

"I'm sure I agree with you, Lieutenant. I certainly have no desire to see this country collapse into communism. I despise all communists."

"I'm pleased to hear it."

"As I said, I'm hoping to do López a good turn, is all. It just happens that I might be able to do you a good turn too."

"A quid pro quo, so to speak."

"Maybe."

Quevedo grinned. "Well, now I'm intrigued." He collected the pack of Trend off the desk and lit one of the little cigars. It seemed almost unpatriotic to smoke such a diminutive cigar. "Please, do go on."

"According to what I read in the newspapers, the Moncada Barracks rebels were poorly armed. Shotguns, a few M1 rifles, a Thompson, a bolt-action Springfield."

"That's quite correct. Most of our efforts are directed toward preventing ex-President Prío from getting arms to the rebels. So far we've been very successful. In the last couple of years we've seized over one million dollars' worth of arms."

"What if I was to tell you the location of an arms cache that contains everything from grenades to a belt-fed machine gun?"

"I should say that it was your duty as a guest in my country to tell me where those arms can be found." He sucked on the little cigar for a moment. "Then I should also say that I could certainly arrange for your friend to be freed immediately once the arms cache is found. But might I inquire how it is you come to know about these weapons?"

"A while ago I was driving my car in El Calvario. It was late, the road was dark, I'd probably had a little too much to drink, and I was certainly driving too fast. I lost control of my car and skidded off the road.

At first I thought I had a flat or a broken axle, and I got out to take a look with a flashlight. In fact, my tires had churned up a lot of dirt and broken through some wooden planks that were covering up something buried underneath. I lifted one plank, shone the flashlight inside, and saw a box of Mark 2 FHGs and a Browning M19. Probably there was a whole lot more, only I didn't figure it was safe to stay there for very long. So I covered the boards with earth again and marked the spot with some stones so that I could find it. Anyway, last night I went to check, and the stones hadn't been moved, which leads me to suppose that the cache is still there."

"Why didn't you report this at the time?"

"I certainly intended to, Lieutenant. But by the time I got back home I decided that if I told the authorities, someone might get the idea that there was a lot more to tell than I've told you, and I lost my nerve."

Quevedo shrugged. "There doesn't seem to be much that's wrong with your nerves now."

"Don't be too sure of that. Inside, my stomach is turning over like a washing machine. But as I told you, I owe López a favor."

"He's a lucky man to have a friend like you."

"That's for him to say."

"True."

"Well? Do we have a trade?"

"You'll take us to where this arms cache is hidden?"

I nodded.

"Then, yes. We have a trade. But how shall we do this?" He stood up and walked around his office thoughtfully. "Let's see now. I know. We'll take López with us, and if the weapons are where you say they are, then you can take him with you. As simple as that. Do you agree?"

"Yes."

"All right. I'll need a little time to organize everything. Why don't you wait in here and watch the television while I go and set things up? Do you like baseball?"

"Not particularly. I can't relate to it. In real life there are no third chances."

Quevedo shook his head. "It's a cop's game. Believe me, I've thought about it. You see, when you hit something with a club, it changes every-thing." Then he went out.

I picked up the magazine on the desk and got a little better acquainted with Ana Gloria Varona. She was a little bombshell type with a back-side for cracking walnuts, and a large chest that was crying out for a child-sized sweater. When I had finished admiring her I tried to watch the baseball. But I figured it was one of those curious sports in which the history is obviously more important than the game. After a while I closed my eyes, which usually takes some doing in a police station.

Quevedo came back about twenty minutes later, alone and carrying a briefcase. He raised his eyebrows and looked at me expectantly. "Shall we go?"

I followed him downstairs.

Alfredo López was standing between two soldiers in the entrance hall, but only just. He was filthy and unshaven and had two black eyes, except that wasn't the worst of it. Both his hands were freshly ban-daged, which made the manacles on his wrists look pointless. Seeing me, he tried to smile, only the effort was probably too much for him and he almost fainted. The two soldiers grabbed him by the elbows and held him up like the accused at some sort of show trial.

I wanted to ask Quevedo about his hands and then changed my mind, anxious not to say or do anything that might prevent me from achieving what I had set out to do. But I had little doubt that López had been tortured.

Quevedo was still being pleasant. "Do you have a car?"

"It's a gray Chevrolet Styline," I said. "I'm parked just down the street. I'll drive back here, and then you can follow me."

Quevedo looked pleased. "Excellent. To El Calvario, you say?"

I nodded.

"Havana traffic being what it is, if we are separated, we shall meet at the local post office."

"Very well."

"One more thing." The smile turned wintry. "If this is some kind of trap. If this has been an elaborate hoax to lure me out into the open and have me assassinated—"

"It's not a trap," I said.

"Then the first person to be shot will be our friend here." He tapped the holster on his belt with meaning. "In any event, I shall shoot you both if the weapons cache is not where you say it is."

"The weapons are there, all right," I said. "And you're not going to be assassinated, Lieutenant. People like you and me are never assassinated. We're murdered, pure and simple. It's the Batistas and Trumans and King Abdullahs of this world who get themselves assassinated. So take it easy. Relax. Because this is your lucky day. You're about to do something that'll make you a captain. So maybe you should ride that luck and buy a lottery ticket or a number on the *bolita*. If it comes to that, maybe we should both buy a number."

It was probably just as well that I didn't.

22

WITH ONE EYE on my rearview mirror and the army car tailing me, I drove east through the new tunnel underneath the Almendares River and then south through Santa Catalina and Vibora. Along the central divider of the boulevard, city gardeners were trimming trees into the shape of bells, only none of them was going off in my head. I was still telling myself that I could get away with making a deal with the devil. I'd done it before, after all, and with many worse devils than Lieutenant Quevedo. Heydrich, for one. Goering, for another. They didn't come any more devilish than them. But no matter how smart you think you are, there's always something unexpected that you have to be prepared for. I thought I was prepared for anything. Except the one thing that happened.

It got a little warmer. Warmer than on the north coast. And most of the houses here were owned by people with money. You could tell they were people with money because they were also people with big gates on their big houses. You could tell how much money a man had by the height of the white walls and the amount of iron on his black gates. A set of imposing gates was an advertisement for a ready supply of wealth for confiscation and redistribution. If the communists ever reached Havana, they wouldn't have to look hard for the best people to steal money from. You didn't have to be clever to be a communist. Not when the rich made it as easy as this.

When I reached Mantilla, I turned south on Managua, which was a poorer, more down-at-heel district, and followed the road until I came upon the main highway going west toward Santa María del Rosario. You could tell the neighborhood was poorer and more down-at-heel because children and goats wandered freely by the side of the road, and men were carrying machetes with which to work in the surrounding plantations.

When I saw the disused tennis court, and the dilapidated villa with the rusted gate, I held the steering wheel tight and rode the bump as I turned the Chevrolet off the road and through the trees. As I hit the brakes, the car bucked like a rodeo bull and made more dust than an exodus from Egypt. I switched off the engine and sat there doing nothing, my hands clasped behind my head, just in case the lieutenant was the nervous type. I hardly wanted to get shot reaching for my pocket humidor.

The army car pulled up behind me, and the two soldiers got out, followed by Quevedo. López stayed put in the rear seat. He wasn't going anywhere. Except maybe the hospital. I leaned out of my window and, closing my eyes, pushed my face into the sun for a moment and listened to the engine block cool. When I opened them again the two soldiers had fetched shovels from the trunk of the car and were awaiting instructions. I pointed in front of us.

"See those three white rocks?" I said. "Dig in the center."

I closed my eyes again momentarily, but this time I was praying that everything was going to work out the way I had hoped.

Quevedo came toward the Chevrolet. He was carrying his briefcase. He opened the front passenger door and slid in beside me. Then he wound down the window, but it wasn't enough to spare me the smell of his pungent cologne. For a moment, we sat watching the two soldiers shoveling dirt, not saying anything at all.

"Mind if I turn on the radio?" I said, reaching for the knob.

"I think you'll find I have more than enough conversation to keep your attention," he said ominously. He took off his cap and rubbed his buzz-cut head. It sounded like someone polishing a shoe. Then he grinned, and there was humor in his grin, but I didn't like the look of it. "Did I tell you I trained with the CIA, in Miami?"

We both knew that it wasn't really a question. Few of his questions were. Most of the time they were meant to be unsettling, or he already knew the answers.

"Yes, I was there for six months, last summer. Have you ever been to Miami? It's probably the least interesting place you could ever hope to see. It's like Havana without a soul. Anyway, that's neither here nor there. And now that I'm back here, one of my functions is to liaise with the Agency's chief of station here in Havana. As you can probably imagine, U.S. foreign policy is driven by a fear of communism. A justifiable fear, I might add, given the political loyalties of López and his friends on the Isle of Pines. So the Agency is planning to help us set up a new anti-communist intelligence bureau next year."

"Just what the island needs," I said. "More secret police. Tell me, how will the new anti-communist intelligence bureau differ from the current one?"

"Good question. Well, we'll have more money from the Americans, of course. Lots more money. That's always a good start. The new bureau will also be trained, equipped, and tasked directly by the CIA to identify and repress only communist activities; as opposed to the SIM, which exists to eliminate all forms of political opposition."

"This is the democracy you were talking about, right?"

"No, you're quite wrong to be sarcastic about this," insisted

Quevedo. "The new bureau will be commanded directly by the greatest democracy in the world. So that ought to count for something, surely. And, of course, it goes without saying that international communism isn't exactly known for its own toleration of opposition. To some extent you have to fight like with like. I'd have thought you of all people would understand and appreciate that, Señor Hausner."

"Lieutenant, I meant what I said when I told you I have no desire to see this country turn red. But that's all I meant. My name is not Senator Joseph McCarthy, it's Carlos Hausner."

Quevedo's smile widened. I imagine he could have done a pretty good imitation of a snake at a children's party, if ever any children had been allowed near a man like Quevedo.

"Yes, let's talk about that, shall we? Your name, I mean. It isn't Carlos Hausner, any more than you are or ever were a citizen of Argentina, is it?"

I started to speak, but he closed his eyes as if he wouldn't hear of being contradicted, and patted the briefcase on his lap. "No, really. I know quite a bit about you. It's all in here. I have a copy of the CIA's file on you, Gunther. You see, it's not just Cuba where there's a new spirit of cooperation with the United States. It's Argentina, too. The CIA is just as keen to prevent the growth of communism in that country as it is here in Cuba. Because the Argentines have their own rebels, just as we do. Why, only last year the communists exploded two bombs in the main square of Buenos Aires, killing seven people. But I'm getting ahead of myself here.

"When Meyer Lansky told me about your background in German intelligence, fighting Russian communism during the war, I must confess I was fascinated and decided to find out more. Selfishly I wondered if we might be able to make use of you in our own war on communism. So I contacted the Agency chief and asked him to check with his opposite number in Buenos Aires, to see what they could tell us about you. And they told us a great deal. It appears that your real name is Bernhard Gunther and that you were born in Berlin. There you were first a policeman, then something in the SS, and finally something in German military intelligence—the Abwehr. The CIA checked you out with the Central Registry of War Criminals and Security Suspects—CROWCASS—and also the Berlin Document Center. And while there's no record of your being wanted for any war crimes, it does seem that there's a warrant out on you from the police in Vienna. For the murders of those two unfortunate women."

There seemed little point in denying what he'd said, even though I hadn't murdered anyone in Vienna. But I thought I might explain it away to his political satisfaction.

"After the war," I said, "and because of my experience fighting the Russians, I was recruited by American counterintelligence: first by the 970th CIC in Germany, and then the 430th in Austria. As I'm sure you're aware, the CIC was the forerunner of the CIA. Anyway, I was instrumental in uncovering a traitor in their organization. A man named John Belinsky, who turned out to have been working for the Russian MVD. This would have been in September 1947. The two women were much later on. That was in 1949. One of them I killed because she was the wife of a notorious war criminal. The other was a Russian agent. The Americans will probably deny it now, of course, but they were the ones who got me out of Austria. On the ratline they provided for escaping Nazis. They provided me with a Red Cross passport in the name of Carlos Hausner and got me on the boat to Argentina, where, for a while, I worked for the secret police. The SIDE. At least I did until the job I was on turned into an embarrassment for the government, and I became persona non grata. They fixed me up with an Argie passport and some visas, which is how I fetched up here. Since then I've been trying to keep out of trouble's way."

"There's no doubt about it, you've had an interesting life."

I nodded. "Confucius used to think so," I said.

"What's that?"

"Nothing. I've been living here quietly since 1950. But recently I bumped into an old acquaintance, Max Reles, who, knowing my background with the Berlin Criminal Police, offered me a job. I was going to take it, too, until he got himself killed. By now Lansky knew something of my background as well, and when Max got himself killed, he asked me to look over the shoulder of the local militia. Well, you don't say no to Meyer Lansky. Not in this town. And now here we are. But I really don't see how I can help *you*, Lieutenant Quevedo."

There was a shout from one of the soldiers digging in front of us. The man threw down his shovel, knelt down for a moment, peered into the ground, straightened, and then gave us a sign that he had found what they were looking for.

I pointed at them. "I mean, beyond the help I've already given you with this arms cache."

"For which I am very grateful, as soon I'll prove to your satisfaction, Señor Gunther. I may call you that, may I not? It is your name, after all. No, I want something else. Something quite different. Don't get me wrong. This is good. This is very good. But I want something more enduring. Let me explain: it's my understanding that Lansky has offered you a job working for him. No, that's not quite the truth. It's rather more than an understanding. As a matter of fact, it was my idea—that he offer you a job."

"Thanks."

"Don't mention it. I imagine he'll pay well. Lansky is a generous man. For him, this is simply good business. You get what you pay for. He's a gambler, of course. And like most intelligent gamblers he dislikes uncertainty. If he can't have certainty, he'll do the next best thing and hedge his bet. Which is where you come in. You see, my employers would like to know if and when he tries to hedge his bet on Batista by offering the reds financial support."

"You want me to spy on him, is that it?"

"Exactly so. How difficult can this be for a man such as yourself? Lansky is a Jew, after all. Spying on a Jew should be second nature to a Nazi."

There seemed to be no point in arguing with that. "And in return?"

"In return, we agree not to deport you to Austria to face those murder charges. You also get to keep whatever Lansky pays you."

"You know, I had been planning a short trip home to Germany. To take care of some family business."

"I regret that will no longer be possible. After all, if you left, what guarantee could we have that you would ever return? And we would have lost this excellent chance to spy on Lansky. Incidentally, for your sake it might be best if you didn't report our conversation to your new employer. With this man, people whose loyalties are in any way questionable have a dreadful habit of disappearing. Señor Waxman, for example. Almost certainly Lansky had this man killed. It would be no different for you, I think. He is the kind of man for whom the saying 'Better safe than sorry' is a way of life. And who can blame him for being so cautious? After all, he has millions invested in Havana. And it's certain he won't allow anything to get in the way of that. Not you. Not me. Not even the president himself. All he wants to do is keep on making money, and it makes little or no difference to him and his friends if he does it under one regime or another."

"This is fantasy," I insisted. "Surely Lansky's not going to help the communists."

"Why not?" Quevedo shrugged. "Now you're just being stupid, Gunther. And you're not a stupid man. Look here, it might interest you to know that, according to the CIA, in the last American presidential election Lansky gave a substantial donation to both the Republicans, who won, and the Democrats, who lost. That way, whoever won would be sure to be grateful to him. That's what I'm getting. Do you see? You can't put a price on political influence. Lansky knows this only too well. As I say, it's just good business. I'd do the same in his shoes. Besides, I already know that Max Reles secretly paid money to the families of some of the Moncada rebels. How do I know this? López volunteered the information."

I looked back at the other car. López was asleep in the backseat. Then again, maybe he wasn't asleep at all. The sun was shining directly on his unshaven face. He looked like a dead Christ.

"Volunteered. You think I believe that?"

"Eventually, I could not stop him from telling me things. You see, I had already pulled out every one of his fingernails."

"You bastard."

"Come now. That's my job. And perhaps, a long time ago, it was yours, too. In the SS. Who can say? Not you, I'll bet. I'm sure that with a bit more digging we could find some dirty secrets of your own, my Nazi friend. But that's of no interest to me. What I should like to know now is if Reles gave this money with the knowledge of Lansky. And I should very much like to know if ever he does the same thing himself."

"You're crazy," I said. "Castro got fifteen years. The revolution's a toothless lion with him behind bars. And if it comes to that, so am I."

"You're wrong on both counts. About Castro, that is. He has plenty of friends. Powerful friends. In the police. In our judicial system. Even in government. You doubt me, I can tell. But did you know that the army officer who captured Castro after the Moncada Barracks attack also saved his life? That the court which tried him in Santiago allowed the man to make a two-hour speech in his own defense? That Ramón Hermida, our present minister of justice, made sure that instead of keeping Castro separate from all the other prisoners, as was the army's recommendation, they were all sent to the Isle of Pines, where they've been allowed books and writing materials? And Hermida is not the only one in government who is a friend to this criminal. There are already those in the senate and the house of representatives who speak of amnesty. Tellaheche. Rodríguez. Agüero. Amnesty, I ask you. In almost any other country, such a man as this would have been shot. And deservedly so. I tell you this quite frankly, my friend. That I will be surprised if Dr. Castro serves more than five years in jail. Yes, he's a lucky man. But you need more than good fortune to be as lucky as him. You need friends. And this leopard does not change his spots. The day Castro is released from prison is the day that the revolution begins in earnest. But I for one hope to prevent this from ever happening."

He lit a little cigar. "What? Nothing to say? I thought you would need more persuasion. I thought you would need documentary evidence that I know your real identity. But now I can see I needn't have bothered bringing the briefcase."

"I know who I am, Lieutenant. I don't need anyone to prove it. Not even you."

"Cheer up. It's not like you'll be spying for nothing. And there are worse places to be than Havana. Especially for a man as comfortably off as you. But you're mine now. Is that quite clear? Lansky will think you are his, but you'll report to me, once a week. We'll arrange to meet somewhere nice and quiet. The Casa Marina, perhaps. You like it there, I believe. We can choose a room where we won't be disturbed, and everyone will think that we are spending time with some obliging little whore. Yes. You'll jump when I tell you to jump, and squeak when I tell you to squeak. And maybe when you're old and gray—that is to say, older and grayer than you are now—I'll let you crawl back under your stone like the nasty little Nazi you are. But listen. You cross me just once, and I promise that you'll be on the first plane back to Vienna with a rope under your ear. Which is very probably what you deserve."

I took all of that without a word. He had me cold. Like I was a billfish hanging by my tail over the pier at Barlovento's having my photograph taken. And not just any billfish. A billfish that had been heading home when it got itself hauled out of the gulf on a rod and reel. I hadn't even managed to put up much of a fight. But I wanted to. More than that. I badly wanted to kill Quevedo now, even assassinate him— yes, I was more than happy to give him an opera-sized death. Just as long as I could pull the trigger on that smug bastard and his smug-bastard smile.

I glanced across at the army car and saw that López had recovered a little and was staring straight back at me. Probably wondering what kind of a lousy deal I had made to save his lousy skin. Or maybe it was Quevedo he was looking at. Possibly López was hoping he might get a chance to pull a trigger on the lieutenant himself. Just as soon as he had grown some new fingernails. He had more right to do it than I did, too. My hatred of the young lieutenant was only getting started. López had a good head start on me in that respect.

López closed his eyes again and laid his head on the seat. The two soldiers were pulling a box out of a hole in the ground. It was time to leave. If we were allowed. Quevedo was just the type to break a deal just because he could. And there would be nothing that I could do about it, either. I had always known that was a possibility, and had figured it was worth the risk. After all, it wasn't my weapons cache. But I hadn't figured on Quevedo turning me into his pet informer. Already I hated myself. More than I already hated myself.

I bit my lip for a moment, and then said, "All right. I kept my end of the deal. This deal. The arms cache for López. So how about it? Are you going to let him go, like you agreed? I'll be your dirty little spy, Quevedo, but only if you keep your end of this. D'you hear? You keep your word or you can send me back to Vienna and be damned."

"That was a brave speech," he said. "I admire you for it. No, really I do. One day in the future when you're feeling a little less emotional about this, you can tell me all about being a policeman in Hitler's Germany. I'm sure I'd be fascinated to find out more and understand what it must have been like. I've always been interested in history. Who knows? Maybe we'll discover that we have something in common."

He raised a forefinger as if he'd only just thought of something.

"One thing I really don't understand: why you ever wanted to stick your neck out for a man like Alfredo López."

"Believe me, I'm asking myself the same question."

Quevedo smiled a smile of disbelief. "I don't buy that. Not for a moment. When we were driving over here from Marianao just now, I asked him about you. And he told me that before today he'd only met you three times in his life. Twice at the home of Ernest Hemingway. And once at his office. And he said it was you who did him a good turn, not the other way around. Before today, that is. That you got him out of a tight spot once before. He didn't say what that was. And frankly, I've already asked him so many questions I didn't feel like pursuing the matter. Besides, he has no more fingernails to lose." He shook his head. "So. Why? Why help him again?"

"Not that it's any of your damn business, but López gave me a reason to believe in myself again."

"What reason?"

"Nothing you would understand. I hardly understand it myself. But it was enough to make me want to carry on in the hope that my life might mean something."

"I must have misjudged him. I took him for a deluded fool. But you make him sound like some kind of saint."

"Every man finds his redemption where and when he can. One day, perhaps, when you're where I am now, you'll remember that."

23

———

I DROVE ALFREDO LÓPEZ BACK TO FINCA VIGÍA. He was in bad shape, but I didn't know where the nearest hospital was, and neither did he.

"I owe you my life, Gunther," he said. "And a great deal of thanks."

"Forget it. You don't owe me anything. But please don't ask me why. I'm through explaining myself for one day. That bastard Quevedo has an annoying habit of asking questions you'd rather not answer."

López smiled. "Don't I know it?"

"Of course. I'm sorry. It was nothing compared to what you must have been through."

"I could use a cigarette."

I kept a pack of Luckies in the glove box. At the junction of the road north into San Francisco de Paula I pulled up and put one in his mouth.

"Here," I said, finding a match and lighting it.

He puffed for a moment and nodded his thanks.

"Let me do that for you." I fetched the cigarette from his lips. "Just don't expect me to come into the bathroom with you."

I put the cigarette back in his mouth and drove on.

We reached the house. There had been a strong wind the previous night, and some of the ceiba tree's leaves and branches were strewn across the steps in front of the house. A tall Negro was picking them up and putting them in a wheelbarrow, but he might just as easily have been putting them on the ground, as if someone had ordered the man to honor López's return with a carpet of palms. Either way, he was making slow work of it. Like he'd just got two numbers on the *bolita*.

"Who's that?" asked López.

"The gardener," I said. I pulled up next to the Pontiac and switched off the engine.

"Yes, of course. For a moment—" He grunted. "The previous gardener committed suicide, you know. Drowned himself in the well."

"I guess that explains why no one here seems to drink water very much."

"Noreen thinks there's a ghost."

"No, that would be me." I looked at him and frowned. "Can you make it up the steps?"

"I might need a bit of help."

"You should be in a hospital."

"That's what I kept on telling Quevedo. But by then he'd stopped listening to me. That was after he gave me the free manicure."

I got out of the car and slammed the door. Around there, that was like ringing the doorbell. I went around to the passenger's side and opened the door for him. He was going to need a lot of that in the coming days, and I was already imagining myself driving away again, leaving her to it. I'd done enough. If he wanted to scratch the back of his head, Noreen could do it.

She came out of the front door as López stepped out of the car and swayed like a drunk who still had room for more. Gingerly he held on to the window pillar for a moment with the inside of his wrists and then put his spine into a smile for Noreen as she hurried down the steps. His lips parted, and the cigarette he was still smoking fell onto his shirtfront. I grabbed the cigarette, like the shirt actually mattered. It was a sure thing he wouldn't be wearing it to the office again. Lots of blood on sweat-stained white cotton was hardly fashionable that year.

"Fredo," she said, anxiously. "Are you all right? My God, what has happened to your hands?"

"The cops were expecting Horowitz at their annual fund-raiser," I said.

López smiled, but Noreen wasn't amused.

"I don't see what there is to joke about, Bernie," she said. "Really I don't."

"You had to be there, I guess. Look, when you've finished getting stiff with me, your legal friend here deserves to be in a hospital. I'd have driven him to one myself, but Fredo insisted we drive here first and convince you that he's all right. I guess he rates you a higher priority than playing the piano again. That's quite understandable, of course. I feel much the same way."

Noreen wasn't listening to most of that. She retuned her wavelength the moment I said "hospital." She said, "There's one in Cotorro. I'll take him there myself."

"Hop in and I'll drive you."

"No, you've done enough. Was it very difficult? Getting him out of police custody."

"A little more difficult than putting a request in the suggestion box. And it was the army that had him, not the police."

"Look, why don't you wait in the house? Make yourself at home. Fix yourself a drink. Ask Ramón to make you something to eat if you want. I won't be long."

"I really ought to be running along. After the events of this morning, I feel a pressing need to renew all my insurance policies."

"Bernie, please. I want to thank you properly. And speak to you about something."

"All right. I can put up with that."

I watched her drive him away and then went inside and flirted with the drinks trolley, but I was in no mood to play hard-to-get with Hemingway's bourbon, and swallowed a glass of Old Forester in less time than it took to pour. With another large one waiting in my hand, I took a tour of the house and tried to ignore the obvious comparison between my own situation and that of a trophy on Hemingway's wall. I'd been bagged by Lieutenant Quevedo just as surely as if I'd been shot with an express rifle. And Germany now looked about as far away to me as the snows of Kilimanjaro or the green hills of Africa.

One of the rooms was full of packing cases and suitcases, and for one stomach-churning moment I thought she might be leaving Cuba until I realized that Noreen was probably getting ready to move into her new house in Marianao.

After a while, and another drink, I walked outside and climbed the four-story tower. It wasn't difficult. A half-covered staircase on the outside went right up to the top. There was a bath on the first floor and some cats playing cards on the second. The third floor was where all the rifles were kept, in locked glass cabinets, and the way I was feeling it was probably just as well I hadn't brought any keys. The uppermost story was furnished with a small desk and a large library full of military books. I stayed there for a long while. I didn't much care for Hemingway's taste in literature, but there was no arguing with the view. Max Reles would have liked it a lot. From each of the windows the view was all you could see. For miles around. Right up until the moment that the light began to fade. And then some.

When just a ribbon of orange was left over the trees, I heard a car and saw the Pontiac's headlights and the little chieftain's head coming back up the drive. When Noreen got out of the car she was alone. By the time I had descended the tower, she was in the house and fixing herself a drink with a bottle of Cinzano vermouth and some tonic water. Hearing my footsteps, she said, "Freshen your glass?"

"I'll help myself," I said, coming over to the little table. She turned away as I came alongside her. I heard a little peal of ice cubes as she upended the tall glass and swallowed the frozen contents.

"They're keeping him in for observation," she said.

"Good idea."

"Those fucking bastards pulled out all his fingernails."

Without López around to see the funny side of that, I was through making jokes about it. I hardly wanted Noreen getting sharp with me again. I'd had enough of that for one day. I just wanted to sit down in an armchair and have her stroke my head, if only to remind me that it was still on my shoulders and not hanging on anyone's wall.

"I know. They told me."

"The army?"

"It certainly wasn't the Red Cross that did it."

She was wearing navy blue slacks and a matching bouclé cardigan. The slacks weren't particularly slack in the only place it counted, and the cardigan seemed to be short a couple of little plaited leather buttons on the lower slopes of her bosom. Her hand sported a sapphire that was the bigger sister of the two in her earlobes. The shoes were dark brown leather, as were the belt around her waist and the handbag she had tossed onto an armchair. Noreen had always been good at matching things. It was only me that seemed to clash with the rest of her. She looked awkward and ill at ease.

"Thanks," she said. "For what you did."

"I didn't do it for you."

"No. And I think I can understand why. But thank you anyway. I'm sure it's the most courageous thing I've heard of since I came to Cuba."

"Don't tell me that. I feel bad enough already."

She shook her head. "Why? I don't understand you at all."

"Because it makes me sound like what I'm not. In spite of what you once thought, angel, I was never cut out to be a hero. If I was anything like the person you think I am, I wouldn't have lasted half as long as I have. I'd be dead in some Ukrainian field, or forgotten forever in some stinking Russian prison camp. Not to mention what happened before all that, in those comparatively innocent times when people thought the Nazis were the last word in true evil. You tell yourself you can put aside your principles and make a pact with the devil just to keep out of trouble and remain alive. But you do it often enough, and it gets so that you've forgotten what those principles were. I used to think I could stand apart from it all. That I could somehow inhabit a nasty, rotten world and not become like that myself. But I found out that you can't. Not if you want to see another year. Well, I'm still alive. I'm still alive because, if the truth be told, I'm just as bad as the rest of them. I'm alive because other people are dead, and some of them were killed by me. That's not courage. That's just this." I pointed at the antelope head on the wall. "He understands what I'm talking about even if you don't. The law of the jungle. Kill or be killed."

Noreen shook her head. "Nonsense," she said. "You're talking nonsense. That was war. It *was* kill or be killed. That's what war is. And it was ten years ago. Lots of men feel the way you do about what they did in the war. You're being much too hard on yourself." She took hold of me and put her head on my chest. "I won't let you say those things about yourself, Bernie. You're a good man. I know it."

She looked up at me, wanting me to kiss her. I stood there, letting her hold me tight. I didn't pull away or push her off. I didn't kiss her, either. Although I badly wanted to. Instead I grinned at her, tauntingly.

"What about Fredo?"

"Let's not talk about him right now. I've been stupid, Bernie. I can see that now. I should have been honest with you from the beginning. You're not really a killer." She hesitated. Her eyes were filling with tears. "Are you?"

"I love you, Noreen. Even after all these years. I didn't know it myself until quite recently. I love you, but I can't lie to you. A man who really wanted to have you would do that, I think. Lie to you, I mean. He'd say anything to get you back at all costs. I'm certain of it. Well, I can't do it. There has to be someone in this world you can tell the truth to."

I took hold of her elbows and looked her squarely in the eye.

"I've read your books, angel. I know what kind of a person you are. It's all there, between the covers, hidden under the surface like an iceberg. You're a decent person, Noreen. Well, I'm not. I'm a killer. And I'm not just talking about the war. As a matter of fact, I killed someone only last week, and it certainly wasn't a case of kill or be killed. I killed a man because he had it coming and because I was afraid of what he might do. But mostly I killed him because I wanted to kill him.

"It wasn't Dinah who killed Max Reles, angel. It wasn't even any of his Mafia friends in the casino, either. It was me. I killed him. I shot Max Reles."

24

A S YOU KNOW, Reles had offered me a job at the Saratoga, and I'd accepted it, but only with the intention of finding an opportunity to kill him. How to do this looked more difficult. Max was heavily protected. He lived in a penthouse at the Saratoga that could only be accessed by a key-operated elevator. And the elevator doors in the penthouse were watched closely by Max's bodyguard, Waxey, who searched everyone going into the penthouse.

"But I had the idea how I might do it almost as soon as I saw the type of revolver that your friend Hemingway had given you. The Nagant. I came across that type of pistol a lot during the war. It was the standard-issue sidearm for all Russian army and police officers, and with one important modification—a Bramit silencer—it was the execution weapon of choice for the Russian special services. Between January 1942 and February 1944 I worked for the Wehrmacht War Crimes Bureau investigating both Allied and German atrocities. One of the crimes we investigated was the Katyń Forest massacre. This would have been in April 1943, after an Army Group intelligence staff officer had found a mass grave containing the bodies of four thousand Poles some twenty kilometers west of Smolensk. All of the men were officers of the Polish army and had been executed with a single shot in the back of the head by NKVD death squads. And all using the same type of revolver: the Nagant.

"The Russians were devious and methodical in the way they had gone about things. The way they are about everything. Sorry, but that's just the truth. It would have been impossible to execute four thousand men unless certain precautions were first taken to conceal the sound of these executions from those who were yet to die. Otherwise they'd have rioted and overrun their captors. So the murders themselves took place at night, in windowless cells that had been sound-insulated with several mattresses, and using silenced Nagant revolvers. One of these silencers came into my possession during the investigation, and I was able to study its design and to test a silenced weapon on a firing range. Which meant that as soon as I saw your revolver I knew that I could manufacture a Bramit silencer in my metal shop at home.

"My next problem was this: How was I going to get into the penthouse carrying the revolver? It so happened that Max had given me a gift—a custom-made backgammon set in an attaché case that contained all the checkers and the dice and the dice cups. But there was also room for a revolver and its newly made silencer. And I thought there was little chance of Waxey searching it, especially as the case had combination locks.

"Max had told me that he used to play cards once a week with some of the Havana underworld. He also told me that the game always ended at eleven-thirty, exactly fifteen minutes before he retired to his office and took a phone call from the president, who owns a piece of the Saratoga. He asked me to come along, and when I went, I took with me the attaché case containing the silenced revolver, and placed it on his pool terrace. When I left the penthouse with everyone else at eleven-thirty, I went back down to the casino and waited a few minutes. It was Chinese New Year, the night when they set off a lot of fireworks at the Barrio Chino. It's pretty deafening, of course. Especially on the rooftop of the Saratoga.

"Anyway, because of the fireworks I figured Reles would finish his call with the president early. And as soon as I had let the casino manager see me back in the casino after going up to the penthouse for the first time, I returned to the eighth floor. Which was as far as I could go, of course, without an elevator key.

"But on the corner of the building they're repairing the Saratoga's neon sign, which meant that there was some scaffolding on which someone might climb up from the eighth floor to the penthouse terrace. Someone with a head for heights. Or someone who was determined to kill Max Reles at almost any cost. It was quite a climb, I can tell you. And I needed both hands to do it. I certainly couldn't have managed that climb with the revolver in my hand, or tucked into my belt. That was why I needed to leave the weapon on Max's terrace.

"Max was still on the phone when I got up there again. I could hear him talking to Batista, going through the figures with him. It seems that the president takes his thirty percent stake in the Saratoga very seriously. I opened the case, took out the revolver, screwed on the silencer, and quietly approached the open window. Maybe I had a few second thoughts at that moment. And then I remembered 1934 and how he'd shot two people in cold blood right in front of me, when we were aboard a boat on Lake Tegel. You were already on your way back to the States when it happened, but he threatened to have his brother, Abe, kill you when you arrived back in New York unless I cooperated with him. I knew I was safe. More or less. I already had evidence of his corruption that would have put him away. But I had no means of stopping his brother from killing you. After that, we kind of held each other in check, at least until the Olympics were over and he went back to the States. But like I said earlier: he had it coming. And as soon as he put the phone down I fired. Actually, that's not quite accurate. He saw me just before I pulled the trigger the first time. I think he even smiled.

"I shot him seven times. I went to the edge of the little terrace and tossed the revolver into a basket of towels by the swimming pool on the eighth floor. Then I climbed down. I covered the revolver with some more towels and went into a bathroom to clean myself up. By the time the firecrackers started I was already in the elevator, going back down to the casino. The plain fact of the matter is that I'd forgotten about the fireworks when I made the silencer, otherwise I might not have bothered. But as it happened, it enabled me to use the fireworks after the fact, as a different kind of cover.

"Well, the next day I went back to the Saratoga, like everything was normal in my life. There was no way around that. I had to act normally, or suspicion would have fallen on me. As it was, Captain Sánchez marked my card for the murder right from the very beginning. He might have made it stick, too, until I managed to convince Lansky that the murder might not have taken place under cover of the noise from the fireworks—as everyone seemed to think it had. And the police were helpful there. They hadn't even bothered to search for the murder weapon. I flexed my Adlon Hotel detective muscles and suggested a search of the laundry baskets. Not long afterward, they found the gun.

"As soon as those mobsters saw the silencer on the revolver, they began to think it might be a professional killing—something to do with their business in Havana and probably nothing to do with something that started twenty years ago. Better still, I was able to suggest that the silencer meant that the murder could have happened at any time, not necessarily during the fireworks, as the captain had suggested. Effectively that discredited his theory about my being the killer and left me looking like Nero Wolfe. Anyway, that was Gunther in the clear, I thought, only I'd been too convincing for my own good. Meyer Lansky appreciated the way I'd bested the cop; and since Max had already told him something about my background as a Berlin homicide detective, Lansky decided that, in the interest of avoiding a Mafia war in Havana, I was now the man best qualified to handle the investigation of Max Reles's death.

"For a moment or two I was horrified. And then I began to see the possibility of putting myself completely in the clear for it. All I needed was somewhere safe to lay the blame that wouldn't result in anyone else getting killed. I had no idea that they would kill Waxey, Max's bodyguard, as a sort of insurance policy, just in case he really did have something to do with it. So you could say I killed him, too. That was unfortunate. Anyway, by a stroke of good luck for me, although not for him, one of the pit bosses at the Saratoga, a fellow named Irving Goldstein, was involved with a female impersonator at the Palette Club; and when I found out that he'd killed himself because Max had been on the brink of firing him for being a pansy, well, he seemed made to order to take the blame. So the night before last I went to search his apartment with Captain Sánchez, and I planted the technical drawing I'd made of the Bramit silencer and made sure that Sánchez found it.

"Later on I showed the drawing to Lansky and told him it was prima facie evidence that it had probably been Goldstein who murdered Max Reles. And Lansky agreed. He agreed because he wanted to agree, because any other result would have been bad for business. More importantly, it left me in the clear. So. There it is. You can relax. It certainly wasn't your daughter that killed him. It was me."

"I don't know how I could ever have suspected her," said Noreen. "What kind of mother am I?"

"Don't even think about it." I smiled wryly. "As a matter of fact, when she saw the murder weapon at the penthouse, she recognized it straightaway and later on she told me she thought it might have been you who killed Max. It was all I could do to convince her that the gun was a common one in Cuba. Even though it isn't. That's the first Russian weapon I've ever seen in Cuba. Of course, I could have told her the truth, but when she announced that she was going back to America, I couldn't see the point. I mean, if I'd told her that, I might have had to tell her everything else. I mean, that's what you wanted, isn't it? Her to leave Havana, and go to college?"

"And that's why you killed him," she said.

I nodded. "You were quite right. You couldn't let her stay with a man like that. He was going to take her somewhere they could smoke opium, and God only knows what else. I killed him because of what she might have become if she'd actually married him."

"And because of what Fredo told you when you went to his office in the Bacardi Building."

"He told you about that?"

"On the way to the hospital. That's why you helped him, isn't it? Because he told you that Dinah is your daughter."

"I was waiting to hear you say it, Noreen. And now you have, I guess I can mention it. Is it true?"

"It's a little late to be asking that, isn't it? In view of what happened to Max."

"I could say much the same thing to you, Noreen. Is it true?"

"Yes. It's true. I'm sorry. I should have told you, but that would have meant telling Dinah that Nick wasn't her father; and until he died, she'd always had a much better relationship with him than with me. It felt like I'd have been taking that away from Dinah at a time when I most needed to exercise some influence over her, do you see? If I'd told her, I don't know what the result might have been. When it happened—I mean, in 1935, when she was born—I thought about writing to you. Several times. But each time I thought about it, I saw how good Nick was with her, and I simply couldn't do it. He always thought Dinah was his daughter. But a woman always knows these things. As the months and then the years went by, it seemed less and less relevant. Eventually the war came, and that appeared to end for good any idea of telling you that you had a daughter. I wouldn't have known where to write. When I saw you again, in the bookstore, I couldn't believe it. And naturally I thought about telling you that same evening. But you made a rather tasteless remark that left me thinking you might be another of Havana's bad influences. You seemed so hard-bitten and cynical I hardly recognized you."

"I know the feeling. These days I hardly recognize myself. Or even worse, I recognize my own father. I look in the mirror and see him staring back at me with amused contempt for my own previous failure to understand that I am and always would be exactly like him. If not him exactly. But you were quite right not to tell her I'm her father. Max Reles wasn't the only man Dinah couldn't be around. It's me, too. I know that. And I don't intend to try and see her and establish some kind of relationship with her. It's rather late in the day for that, I think. So you can rest assured on that count. It's enough for me to know that I have a daughter and to have met her. All thanks to Alfredo López."

"As I said, I didn't know he'd told you until we went to the hospital just now. Lawyers aren't supposed to tell strangers about their clients' affairs, are they?"

"After I pulled his nuts out of the fire with those pamphlets, he figured he owed me and that I was the kind of father who might be able to help her somehow. That's what he told me, anyhow."

"He was right. I'm glad he did." She hugged me closer. "And you did help her. I'd have killed Max myself if I'd been able."

"We all do what we can do."

"And this is why you went to SIM headquarters and persuaded them to let Fredo go. Because you thought you wanted to pay Fredo back."

"What he said. It gave me some kind of hope that my life hasn't entirely been wasted."

"But how? How did you persuade them to let him go?"

"A while ago I stumbled across a weapons cache on the road to Santa María del Rosario. I traded it for his life."

"Nothing else?"

"What else could there be?"

"I don't know how to begin to thank you," she said.

"You go back to writing books, and I'll go back to playing backgammon and smoking cigars. From the look of things, you're getting ready to move into that new house of yours. I hear Hemingway will soon be back here again."

"Yes, he'll be here in June. Hem's lucky to be alive after what happened. He was seriously injured in two consecutive plane crashes. He then got himself badly burned in a bushfire. By rights, the man should be dead. Some American newspapers even published his obituary."

"So he's risen from the dead. It's not all of us who can say as much."

Later on, I went out to my car, and in the shifting dark I thought I saw the figure of the dead gardener, standing beside the well where he'd drowned. Maybe the house was haunted, after all. And if the house wasn't haunted, I know I was, and probably always would be. Some of us die in a day. For some, like me, it takes much longer than that. Years, perhaps. We all die, like Adam, it's true, only it's not every man that's made alive again, like Ernest Hemingway. If the dead rise not, then what happens to a man's spirit? And if they do, with what body shall we live again? I didn't have the answers. Nobody did. Perhaps, if the dead could rise and be incorruptible, and I could be changed forever in the blinking of an eye, then dying might just be worth the trouble of getting killed, or killing myself.

Back in Havana, I went to the Casa Marina and spent the night with a couple of willing girls. They didn't make me feel any less alone. All they did was help me to pass the time. What little of it we have.